Published by Curious Fox, an imprint of Capstone Global
Library Limited, 264 Banbury Road, Oxford, OX2 7DY –
Registered company number: 6695582

www.curious-fox.com

Originally published in the United States as separate stories,
copyright © Stone Arch Books 2015
This edition copyright © Curious Fox 2017

The author's moral rights are hereby asserted.

Image Credits: Shutterstock: Chris Tefme, Click Bestsellers,
frankie's, kasha_malasha, Miloje, sattva78,
valeryKIT, Wendy Yang

ISBN 978 1 782 02691 4
20 19 18 17 16
10 9 8 7 6 5 4 3 2 1

A CIP catalogue for this book is available from
the British Library.

Printed and bound by CPI Group (UK) Ltd, Croydon, CR0 4YY

TWICETOLD TALES

FAIRY TALES FOR THE REAL WORLD

OLIVIA SNOWE

Curious Fox
a capstone company-publishers for children

CONTENTS

You know the story.
You've heard it before.
Everyone has.
Now, read it again.
A new twist. A new gasp.
The story is told again.

TWICETOLD.

Cassie Cloak held her red raincoat closed at the neck. Thunder clapped and the rain fell hard in big, swollen drops. The corners and kerbs vanished under deepening puddles as piles of snow – still sitting where they'd been pushed aside during winter – melted, joining the torrents of rain. Before long, Forestville was half flooded.

Cassie jumped from bit of pavement to bit of kerb, avoiding the deeper puddles. Still, the water sloshed up and into her rubber boots, soaking her favourite rainbow socks. By the time she reached Maurice's Deli, she could hardly keep her footing.

The bell rang as she pushed through the heavy glass door. She shook off as much rain as possible and dragged her feet along the long black mat towards the counter.

Maurice himself stood behind the high counter, his hands folded on the glass, with his red and white paper hat just a little crooked on his bald head.

"Hello, little Cassie," he said. He always called her that: "little Cassie". She used to like that nickname. She wasn't little anymore, though. She'd turn thirteen next month. She was out here – in the rain, right in the centre of Forestville

– all by herself. Do little girls turn thirteen and go to the middle of a city all by themselves? No.

"Hi," Cassie said. "Um, I'm picking up the order for my grandma."

Maurice frowned at the girl and shook his head. "Yes, little Cassie," he said. "I know this. You've been in here to pick up your grandma's Sunday dinner order for as long as I can remember."

Even when she'd make the trip with her mum, Cassie had always been there to pick up the meal. The meal was always the same. It came in a box, holding two plastic shopping bags. In each plastic bag, there'd be two paper bags. And the paper bags would be filled to bursting with soups and noodle casseroles and sandwiches and pickles.

Every once in a while, Grandma would add some treat to the order: a couple of slices of honey cake or a big square of halvah.

"It's heavy today," Maurice said with a wink. He came around the counter in that uneven shuffle he had, like one of his knees refused to bend.

"It smells delicious," Cassie told him. "I can't wait."

With both arms, Cassie took the cardboard box. The wonderful smells wafted up into her face and the steam fogged her glasses. "Thanks," she said.

"I'll get the door for you," Maurice said. He shuffled past her and she heard the chime of the bell over the door.

She thanked him again and stepped back out into the rain. Once outside, she had to adjust her bags. Maurice had tied the plastic bags tight, but Cassie didn't think they'd hold for long. The cardboard box would probably disintegrate before she made it to her grandma's block of flats. Instead of walking on, she hurried under the awning of the office next door. There, she leaned against the big plate window to wait for the rain to slow down, even a little bit.

* * *

Caleb Woolf didn't care. The rain poured over him in sheets. It collected in his matted hair – too long and ragged, like it had been shorn with a pair of a lawn shears – and ran down the back of his neck and the bridge of his nose.

He grinned. He always grinned. His teeth were too big and too white, and even most of his friends thought he might lunge for them and take a bite.

With his back to the basket, Caleb dribbled the ball in front of him, using his legs and back as a shield, protecting it from his defender. It was a game of two-on-two half-court basketball.

"Hit me!" called out Caleb's teammate, Finn Transom.

But Caleb wouldn't pass. The score was ten up, and the next two-point basket would win the game. He wasn't about to hand off that glory to anyone. He'd get those two points himself.

"Come on, Woolf," said Andrew Hunter, the defender. Caleb could feel Andrew's big hand on his back. "Make a move."

Caleb's smile widened. He jerked his head one way, then stepped the other. He dribbled far out in front of him, where Andrew had no chance to steal. Then Caleb pulled up, stopping suddenly. Andrew slipped on the wet cement, and Caleb lifted the basketball and shot.

Two points. Caleb clapped once. "Nice try, boys," he said, grinning at Andrew and Andrew's teammate, Otto Blank.

Caleb's teammate – who'd scored a couple of baskets himself – rolled his eyes and checked his phone for the time. "I better get home," he said. "I'm late for supper."

"Yeah, me too," said Andrew. "Not to mention I'm soaked to the bone. My mum's going to skin me alive for staying out in this hurricane."

Caleb cackled. "Hurricane?" he said. "It's a spring shower." He turned to Otto. "How about you, Otto?" He fired the basketball at him. Otto caught it before it collided with his face – but only just. "Quick game of one-on-one?" Caleb asked. "Come on. I'll give you a five-point lead to start."

"Can't," Otto said. "Homework. Supper." He tossed the ball back to Caleb, who caught it, dribbled it twice, and shot a perfect three-pointer.

"Swish!" he said.

The other three boys gathered their bags and jackets and headed off.

"Honestly," Caleb called after them through the driving rain. "I've never met three bigger babies and mummy's boys." He watched them, calling out insults and taunts, until they turned the corner and disappeared. He was alone in Forestville Park now, the only one brave or foolish enough to stand in the downpour.

Caleb sat on the metal bench on the edge of the basketball court and took a long swig from his bottle of water. Soon it was empty and his stomach roared.

"Man, I'm hungry," he said. He could have gone home for supper, but with his older brother home from college and his mum's boyfriend over...

"I'd rather sit in the rain and starve," he muttered to himself. Then he happened to look up. He happened to glance towards the corner of the street as a bolt of lightning struck the metal rod at the top of Forestville Tower, blanketing the city with an eerie, pale-blue light, just for that instant.

He happened to spot Cassie Cloak, huddled out of sight under an awning, and clutching a big, heavy-looking box.

A heavy-looking box of food.

* * *

Cassie had been staring out into the rain, letting the sound of the heavy drops and the thunder wash over her. She let it take her mind into the fairy tales of her childhood. She remembered Mr Jenkins's Year 1 class.

It was a rainy afternoon like this one – when it got as dark at one in the afternoon as it ought to get at one in the morning. Mr Jenkins turned off all but one light in the classroom, and Cassie and the rest of the class sat cross-legged around his chair, eager for a story.

He told them about the Frog Prince, and about Snow White and her dwarfs, and about Red Riding Hood. She'd been Cassie's favourite, of course, because Cassie's raincoat was red. She always bought red raincoats, ever since then.

Before long it must have been six. The sound of Maurice's shop door slamming shook her from her daydreaming.

"I'm closing up, little Cassie," said the old deli man. "Hadn't you better hurry along? You shouldn't dally around here when all the shops are closed. It's not safe."

"I will, Maurice," Cassie replied. She peeked out from under the awning, up at the dark and heavy sky. "Just waiting for this rain to let up a little."

Maurice jogged through the rain, holding his jacket over his head. When he got to Cassie, he stooped and smiled at her, and he wiped the rain from his face. "I can give you a ride," he said. "Grandma's over at the Tall Pines Apartments, right?"

Cassie nodded. "Yes," she said. "But I'm fine. I'm sure this won't last."

Maurice frowned at her. "Are you sure?" he said. "It's no bother."

Under the dim street lamps, with the rainwater still on his beaklike nose and dripping from his big hairy ears, Maurice didn't look like himself. In some ways he did – he was obviously Maurice – but it was like Cassie was seeing him for the first time.

She took a step back and tried to smile. "No, really," she said. "I'm fine. Have a good night."

So the old man shrugged, and when he did his mouth twisted a little. Lightning cracked behind him, casting flickering, harsh shadows across his bent face. To Cassie, he was a monster. A troll. A hungry demon.

"Suit yourself," Maurice said. "Say hello to Grandma Helen for me." Then he finally retreated to his van and climbed in.

★ ★ ★

Caleb leaned against a cold, black post inside the bus shelter at the corner of Rose Avenue and High Street.

He held his basketball with a limp hand against his hip and drummed on its surface with his fingertips.

He was hidden in shadows.

From where he stood, he watched the old man from the deli climb into his van. He watched the van roar to life and slowly roll off. The old man tooted the horn twice, saying goodbye to the girl he'd left behind.

Cassie waved awkwardly at the van as it drove off. Both of her arms were still wrapped around the box of food.

Caleb could almost smell it. No, he really could smell it. He could smell chicken soup. He could smell corned beef. It made his mouth water, and he smiled and licked his lips.

He stared at the slicked streets of Forestville. The streetlights reflected in the puddles. They splattered and spit with the rainfall. Then they went still.

He shook and looked up. There was Cassie Cloak. Slowly, she stepped out from under the awning. The rain had stopped, and she started to walk.

Caleb stayed close to the buildings on his side of Rose Avenue. As he walked, he started to dribble. The sound of his basketball striking the pavement echoed through the canyon of buildings.

He watched Cassie, too, as he walked. As he strutted along the pavement, he took long strides – one long stride for each of her three little steps. They reached the corner of Sharp Street at the same time.

Caleb knew where the girl was headed. He'd heard Maurice say the name: Tall Pines, the building right on the edge of the city, and on the edge of the woods beyond. It wasn't far.

* * *

Cassie tried so hard not to look. She knew he was there. That sound – his basketball thumping against the cement over and over, echoing through the air. It seemed louder to Cassie than the thunder had.

But that was impossible.

It was just that in the eerie quiet right after the storm, the *boom boom boom* made her whole body quiver. *Don't be afraid,* she told herself. *He's just a boy. He's been playing ball, and now he's walking home.*

She tried so hard not to look. But she couldn't help it. She stole a glance.

He's tall, she thought. *He's tall and he's watching me.* He'd been staring right at her. When she looked – just for an instant – he was staring right at her. His big eyes shone in the dark, stormy evening like a fox's behind the rubbish bins. And he grinned. The moment she stole a look, he grinned at her. His teeth were as big and bright as the moon on a clear night. Then the *boom boom boom* stopped. Cassie stopped too; the light ahead said DON'T WALK.

And the boy called out to her.

"Hey," he called, and she looked again.

He was crossing. He was jogging across the street towards her. He didn't care about the puddles and the rain-water splattering up his legs, soaking his basketball shoes, soaking his socks.

She could have run. She could have at least kept walking. There was no traffic at this hour on a Sunday. Why did she stop? Why did she stand there, watching him?

"You're Cassie Cloak, right?" he said as he got closer.

She didn't say anything. She might have nodded.

He reached her and stopped. He cradled his basketball under one arm and smiled down at her. He stood tall and straight. He was lean and strong. He was good-looking, too, Cassie thought. *He's also a little mean-looking*, she decided.

"I go to Perrault Secondary School too," the boy said. "I'm in Year 9."

"Oh," Cassie said. She checked the light. WALK.

"Come on," he said, and he patted her shoulder. She flinched, but she followed as he started across the street. She knew him now, she realized, from school. She'd seen him and his big Year 9 friends. They were rough kids. They galloped and shouted in the halls. They mucked around in front of the school before boarding their buses for home. The drivers had to practically shove and drag them onto the buses most days.

Cassie would climb right on, though. She'd take her seat near the middle. She'd pull out a book and open it on her lap, and then she'd stare out the window, watching the Year 9 boys as her mind wandered.

"That sure smells good," the boy said.

Cassie didn't ask his name. She didn't know if she should. Or maybe that wasn't true. Maybe she knew she should, but she didn't know how to do it.

"It's dinner for me and my grandma," she said instead.

"I know," Caleb said. "I heard you talking to the old man from the deli."

"Oh," she said, but the very idea – of this boy standing near enough to hear, listening to her conversation with Maurice – sent a chill wiggling up her back and across her shoulder. She shook.

"Hey, you cold?" the boy asked.

She shook her head quickly.

"Me either," Caleb said. "I'm hungry, though. Boy, that smells good." When they reached the other corner, he started dribbling again. The ball sent a spray of water up from the pavement. When it bounced in a big puddle, a wave splashed up and fell onto Cassie's shoes.

"Do you mind?" she snapped.

She didn't mean to snap. She hardly meant to say anything. But that's how it came out.

The boy shot her an angry look. His smile dropped away for a moment, then came back twice as big. He grabbed his basketball with both hands, jumped ahead a couple of steps, and slammed the ball down, right into the biggest puddle on the block.

Cassie shrieked.

* * *

Caleb laughed.

He caught the basketball as it bounced back towards him, and then he bent over, slapped his thigh, and laughed.

"You should see your face!" he said. He pointed at Cassie and laughed some more.

She was drenched head to toe, and the box in her arms was splattered and stained, dark here and there from the wet.

"What's the matter with you?!" Cassie shrieked. She stomped her foot, splashing in the same puddle again.

"Whoa, watch it!" Caleb said through more laughter.

Cassie grunted and shoved past him. "Just leave me alone, you hyena!" she snapped.

Caleb chuckled one more time and stopped laughing. "Hey, don't freak out. I was just kidding around," he said. "I didn't mean to make you mad."

Cassie didn't reply. She just stomped on, farther along Rose Avenue, as the rain started again, this time just a drizzle.

"Wait up!" Caleb called after her. He started heading in her direction. He didn't hurry, though. He just loped along a few metres behind her, dribbling his basketball in a high, exaggerated bounce.

"Why should I wait?" Cassie snapped without even turning around. "I don't even know you!"

"Sure you do," he said through a smile. "We go to school together."

"I'm not in a single one of your classes," she said.

"You know what I mean," Caleb said. He watched her ahead of him, her bright red raincoat squeaking and swishing back and forth as she walked.

Cassie wasn't taking short strides anymore. She was stomping and hurrying along the avenue. Still, as tall as he was, he didn't have to try too hard to keep up.

"It's very nice of you to visit your grandma," he said, trying to work out what to say. He really hadn't meant to make her mad. "Is she ill or something?"

Cassie stomped her foot and stopped. Caleb stopped too, still behind her.

"Yes!" she said. "She is, actually!" It was the maddest she'd been so far. Obviously Caleb had asked the wrong question.

"Sorry," he said, kind of meekly. "Is it serious?"

She shrugged. Her raincoat squeaked. She pulled up the big red hood. Caleb took that as a yes.

"Hey!" he said in the brightest voice he could manage. "You should get her some flowers."

She shrugged again.

"Honest," Caleb said. "The shop on the next corner is open late. They probably have bouquets."

Cassie looked at him over her shoulder. He nodded, and she smiled.

"Good idea," she said. "Thanks."

"Sure," said Caleb. He took a long, deep breath through his nose. The smell of chicken soup and warm sandwiches filled his soul. His stomach growled and roared.

"I better get home," he said. "Bye, Cassie."

As the boy turned and started off along Oak Street, Cassie called out, "I don't know your name."

He turned, and the light from a street lamp shone down from behind him.

"My name is Woolf," he said. "Caleb Woolf."

"Bye, Caleb Woolf," Cassie said. The rain started falling harder.

"Bye, Cassie Cloak," he said as he started off again. "See you soon."

* * *

The shop on the corner was still open. Just inside the front door, on a tiered wooden display, were buckets of flower bouquets, all premade and wrapped in thick cellophane.

Cassie stood in front of them, letting her gaze fall from one to the next and the next. There were too many, in every colour and every size, and she couldn't decide.

Her phone rang in her pocket. Quickly, she put down the heavy box of food and dug into her jeans pocket.

"Hi, Mum," she said.

"Cassie!" her mum said. Her voice was too loud, like it usually was on the phone. Cassie could tell she was anxious, too. "I just got off the phone with your grandma. We're both worried sick!"

"I'm fine," Cassie said. Maurice's troll face flashed across her mind. An instant later, she remembered Caleb Woolf's toothy grin. Her breath caught in her chest.

"Why aren't you there yet?" her mum pleaded. "You should have been there ages ago!"

"It's raining!" Cassie squealed back at her mum. "I had to wait for it to stop. Also I decided to pick up some flowers."

The phone was quiet a moment.

"Hello?" Cassie said, squinting at the phone.

"Hi," her mum said. "Okay, sweetie. We just worry about you. Now hurry along and get to your grandma's flat so we know you're safe."

"I will," Cassie said. Her eyes settled on a simple bouquet of small yellow flowers. "You'll pick me up at eight thirty, right?"

"Right-o," her mum said. Cassie could hear that she was smiling now. She hung up, bought the flowers and laid them on top of her box of food. It was only another couple of blocks to Tall Pines.

* * *

Caleb stood at the far corner, hidden in shadow, and watched Cassie Cloak step into the late-night shop. He counted to five to make sure she wasn't coming right back out. Then, with his basketball tucked under his arm, he sprinted back up Oak Street.

At the avenue, he didn't stop. He turned hard to the right and ran as fast as he could straight to Tall Pines.

The storm had fully passed Forestville. Up ahead, low

over the woods beyond the city, Caleb could see the flat bottoms of dark, heavy clouds. Thunder clapped. Lightning crashed across the sky, threatening to connect with the treetops.

At the building's front door, Caleb stopped. He tossed his basketball behind the shrubs that flanked the main entrance. He didn't think anyone would want him to bring it inside, and behind the bushes it would be hidden well enough.

Caleb pushed through the front door. He tried the second door, but found it locked.

A phone hung on the wall beside the door. Next to the phone was a list of names. Caleb ran his finger down the list. "Abramson … Bennet … Breslin … ah!" he said, grinning. "Here it is: Cloak. Number 516."

He grabbed the phone and dialled the number. It rang several times. He nearly gave up. But finally a woman answered. Her voice was deep and husky, like she was very tired. Her accent, too, betrayed her age. It was just like the old man's at the deli.

"You're late," she said.

Caleb didn't speak. He held his breath, hoping the old lady wouldn't press for a response.

A moment passed. The woman sighed. "Just a second," she said, as if she were out of breath.

Caleb quickly set down the phone. A few seconds later, there came a loud and irritating buzz. The second door unlocked. He slipped in, letting the door close behind him. He hurried to the lift and soon was on his way to the fifth floor.

The corridor smelled of lemon-scented cleaner. The lights – long and white – flickered as he passed under them. He heard televisions and laughter coming through the door as he passed Flat 507.

He passed Flat 511. There were children screaming and running, thumping into walls. "Quiet down!" their mother shouted, and everything went silent.

At 516, Caleb found the door open, just a little. Cassie's grandmother must have opened it for her after buzzing the downstairs door. Caleb just strolled in. He let the door close and lock behind him.

The flat was mostly dark. A light shone in the kitchen and down the little front hall. Caleb could smell flowers and tea.

"I've set the table," Cassie's grandma called from the other room. "And please, dear, take a moment to hang up your raincoat in the bathroom. I don't want you dripping water all over my flat."

Caleb pulled off his hoodie and tossed it into the bathroom as he walked past. His basketball shoes squeaked and squished on the parquet floor.

"Your shoes, too!" Grandma called out. Then she muttered under her breath, "Fool child."

Caleb smiled. He stepped into the light of the kitchen, grinning as big and bright as all outdoors.

Grandma dropped her teacup. It shattered as it hit the ceramic tile floor.

* * *

Grandma buzzed her in without a word. She usually said "Hello", or "You're late" or "Come on up, Cassandra!"

But this night, the door buzzed an instant after Cassie called 516. The intercom phone went quiet immediately after.

"She must be really annoyed," Cassie said to herself.

The lift bumped and shook its way up to the fifth floor. She pulled out her phone to check the time: nearly an hour late. And as usual, no service in Grandma's building.

"Must be made of lead blocks or something," Cassie muttered. She walked down the corridor on the fifth floor, looking at the bars on her phone display. She'd have one, then none, then one again.

The door to 516 stood just a little open, as always. "Knock, knock," she called into the dark flat. "Grandma?" She pushed the door open all the way with her foot.

She could smell Grandma's jasmine tea. She could also smell a bouquet of flowers. *Oh well,* Cassie thought, thinking about the bouquet she'd picked out. *Can never have too many flowers, I guess.*

"Grandma?" she called.

She set down the box of food and pulled off her red raincoat. It wasn't so wet anymore, so she hung it up next to the door. She left her shoes on the mat and carried the box to the kitchen.

"Where are you?" she said, setting the food on the table. It was set for the two of them, and the kitchen light was on and flickering, like always. The bouquet of flowers in the centre of the table was bright yellow.

She must be in the bathroom, Cassie decided, and she began unloading the big box from Maurice's. "I got extra soup," she called. Some noise came from the bathroom, but no response. "I thought it might make you feel a little better."

In the bathroom, behind the closed door, something fell and shattered.

"Grandma?" Cassie said. She stepped slowly down the dark back hall towards the bathroom. The light from inside shone under the door, sending shadows of hanging family photos in long, angular shapes up the hall walls and onto the ceiling.

A chill struck Cassie's shoulders and she shook. "Grandma?" she said. "Are you okay?"

No answer. She reached very slowly for the doorknob. "I'm coming in," she said. The moment her hand was on the knob, the door burst open, knocking her onto her back.

Her head struck the parquet floor hard – too hard. The last thing she saw was a vaguely familiar face with a big, white smile. As she drifted out of consciousness, the face became a wolf's face, baring its fangs in a wicked grin, the look of hunger about to be sated.

* * *

Caleb dropped to one knee beside the girl.

"Oh, no," he said to himself. "I didn't mean to knock her down."

Cassie's belly was moving, Caleb noticed. He could even see her pulse on her throat. "She'll be okay," he said to himself.

He looked back into the open bathroom. Cassie's grandma lay on her belly on the floor with her hands and feet tied and tape placed over her mouth.

"Sorry," Caleb said. "She'll wake up in a minute, I think." Then he jumped to his feet and ran for the kitchen. The box was empty, its contents placed out on the table.

There was soup – two big containers of it. There was a small cake in a paper box. There were two foil packages – sandwiches, probably. There was a plastic box, too, filled with cubes of something chocolatey.

Caleb grabbed the sandwiches and the chocolate. Then he ran for the front door, made sure it was locked behind him and ran all the way down the stairs.

He sat on a bench beside the basketball court. In seconds one sandwich was gone, down his hungry gullet. He peeled the foil off the second. This one was turkey and cheese, drowning in mayo. He smiled his toothy grin at it and licked his lips. He could still taste the mustard and corned beef from the first sandwich on the edge of his mouth.

That's when it struck him that he'd left his hoodie in Flat 516.

* * *

Cassie woke up with a headache and blurry vision. She stumbled to her feet, holding the wall for support. She knocked a framed photo from the wall, and its glass shattered on the parquet floor.

She hurried to the bathroom.

"Cassie," Grandma said when the girl had removed the tape on her mouth. "I thought it was you at the door. That's why I let the person in."

"I know, Grandma," Cassie said. "Who was he?" She hadn't even got a look at him – not that she could remember. All she could see when she tried to recall his face was the hungry face of a sinister wolf.

"I don't know," Grandma said. She shook her head and sat up, rubbing her wrists where they'd been tied. He'd used the laces from his trainers. They were wet and tight, and they left red welts on her skin.

"Oh, Grandma," Cassie said. "Are you okay?"

Grandma nodded. "Aside from the rash on my wrists, that is," she said. Cassie helped her to stand. "And it seems he took our supper, I'm afraid."

Cassie staggered to the kitchen. "Not all of it," she said.

Grandma put a hand on her back and picked up the old phone from the kitchen wall. "Never mind," she said. "I'm not hungry anyway. But I'm going to call the doctor for that head of yours. Could be a concussion."

"Oh, Grandma," said Cassie. "I'm fine." Her vision was back to normal. "I'll just take a couple of aspirin."

She started for the bathroom, but Grandma grabbed her wrist and put her in a chair at the kitchen table.

"Nonsense," said her grandma as she punched the

buttons on her phone. "Doctor Hunter is right here in the building. He'll be happy to come up."

* * *

Caleb was so tired, and so full of soup and meat and ... whatever that chocolate stuff was. It was nutty and smooth and rich. He wanted more of it. But he couldn't think about that now. He had to get his hoodie back – somehow.

With any luck, the girl was still passed out on the hall floor. If she was, Grandma would still be helpless too.

He ran. He wasn't moving so fast now, though. His gut was heavy with food and his muscles ached from a long day of playing basketball, not to mention tricking Cassie and her grandma. That had taken a lot of running.

The storm was past now. The night sky was clear, and the full moon shone over Forestville. It reflected in the wet streets and the puddles at the corners.

Caleb's shoes – now without their laces – slipped up and down his heels as he jogged through the city streets. He thought about abandoning them completely. He could stay on the grass the whole way to Tall Pines.

But no. His mum would kill him if he showed up tonight without his trainers. They hadn't been cheap, after all, and he'd only convinced her to buy them for him after weeks of pleading. She'd probably make him quit the basketball team at school rather than buy him a new pair.

It was bad enough he'd need new laces. How would he explain that, anyway? *Idiot*, he thought as he ran. *All for a couple of sandwiches. What was I thinking?*

But it was too late to change his mind now. He had to get that hoodie back. He was pretty sure Cassie hadn't seen him before she'd collapsed, and her grandma – well, she wouldn't recognize him anyway. He'd just have to make sure she never saw him again.

How hard could that be?

* * *

"That'll be a nasty bump," Dr Hunter said. "Keep the ice on it for at least twenty minutes, okay?"

Cassie nodded and pressed the towel, wrapped around a bag of frozen peas, against her head a little more firmly.

"Thanks for coming up," Grandma said.

The doctor shrugged. "It's no trouble," he said. Then he added, more quietly, "Keep a close eye on your grand-daughter, though. These head injuries can really sneak up on a person."

"I will," Grandma assured him. She smiled at Cassie. Cassie rolled her eyes.

"Now, then," the doctor said, and he pulled his phone from his pocket. "Let's see about getting a police officer down here."

Grandma sat down and nodded gravely. "So sad," she said. "What is this neighbourhood coming to?"

"Yes, is this the police station?" the doctor said into his phone as he stepped out of the kitchen.

Grandma put a hand on Cassie's knee. "How's your head, sweetie?" she said.

"It hurts," Cassie said. "A little."

"You'd better call your mum," Grandma said. With a groan, she stood. Then, to Cassie's surprise, she pulled three bowls from the cupboard.

"What are you doing?" Cassie said, looking up from her phone's keypad.

"No sense in letting this soup go to waste," Grandma said. "I expect Dr Hunter will join us for a bowl, too."

Cassie managed a smile as her mum answered the phone at home.

"Hi, Mum," she said. She took a deep breath. "First of all, I'm fine."

* * *

Caleb had no breath. He squatted just outside the shrubbery that lined the Tall Pines Apartments' grounds. Sweat ran down his face. His arms were wet. His shoes were soaking, and his feet were blistered. The night air was chilly, though, and he shivered as he caught his breath.

A police car, with its blue and red lights spinning and flashing, sat right in front of Cassie's grandmother's block of flats.

"I'm too late," he muttered. He rubbed his hands together and breathed warm air onto them. "No way I can get back in there now, not with the police here."

He took a deep breath and scanned the area. No one was around.

"Tomorrow," he said to himself. Then he scurried away, into the darkness. When he was around the corner, he stood up and took off running for home.

* * *

The police officer had a lot of questions for Cassie and her grandma. What did the boy look like? They couldn't say. It was so dark. All Cassie could remember was a grinning wolf. Did he have a weapon? They didn't know. Everything happened so fast. Grandma didn't put up a fight, after all, and Cassie was knocked out by the parquet floor. What was he wearing? Cassie shrugged. Grandma said she thought she remembered a black sweater. Maybe a sweatshirt.

The police officer had a look around the flat. He reminded Grandma to make sure she knew who was downstairs before she buzzed anyone into the building. Finally, just as Cassie's mum arrived to pick her up, the police officer left.

"I don't feel great leaving you alone tonight, Mum," Cassie's mother said. "Come and stay with us."

"Nonsense," Grandma said. "I'll be fine."

Cassie's mum gave Grandma a long look. Finally she sighed. "I know you're a stubborn woman," she said, standing up from her seat at the kitchen table. "I'll just go to the bathroom and Cassie and I will be out of your hair."

Grandma put a hand over Cassie's hand. "I'm sorry, dear," she said quietly.

"For what?" Cassie asked.

"For letting that maniac in here," she said. "This whole mess was my fault."

"I just wish I'd got here on time," Cassie said. "If I had, this never would have happened."

Mum came into the kitchen. "Is this yours, Cassie?" she

said. She was holding up a black hooded sweatshirt. It was sopping wet.

"No," Cassie said. She looked at Grandma, then quickly back at the sweatshirt. "It's his, isn't it?"

"His?" Mum repeated.

Cassie's body went cold. She jumped out of her chair and grabbed the hoodie. "It's the maniac who knocked me out," she said. She spun to face Grandma and added, "And I know who he is."

* * *

Cassie planned every minute of it. It wasn't raining, but she wore her red raincoat.

She stalked the halls of Perrault Secondary School with her hood up, casting a shadow over her face. Her mind raced with sinister plans of revenge and justice. The school was mostly empty that early in the morning. She'd got there early, quite on purpose, so she could be ready for Caleb when he reached his locker.

At 7.30, the corridors began to fill as the buses arrived outside the school. Cassie stood in the stairwell closest to Caleb's locker, and she watched and waited.

By 7.45, most pupils were already in their first lesson. The first bell would ring any minute. Still, Cassie stood. Cassie watched and waited.

Finally, with only seconds until the first bell, Caleb appeared. He ran down the hall with his backpack slung over one shoulder. When he reached his locker, he hurried to open it and dropped the bag at his feet.

Cassie stepped quietly out of the shadows and stood behind the boy.

When he stood up and turned around, he jumped. "Ah!" he said. "You– you scared me. What are you doing?"

"Doing?" Cassie said, smiling. She pulled off her hood. "I'm not doing anything."

"Okay," Caleb said. He tried to shove past her, but Cassie stepped to the side to block him. "I have to get to first period," Caleb said.

"I know," Cassie said. "I just want to apologize for yesterday."

"What?" Caleb said.

"I should have offered to share that big supper my grandma and I had," Cassie said. "That was very rude of me."

"Oh," Caleb said, looking at his feet. Cassie noticed the laces were missing from his trainers. A burst of anger flooded her chest: he'd used them to tie up Grandma.

"I want to make it up to you," Cassie said. "Will you come to my grandma's flat for supper?"

"Really?" Caleb said. He shuffled in place a little. "Tonight?"

Cassie nodded.

"Oh, I don't know," Caleb said. "Um, I'll think about it, okay?"

Cassie smiled. "Of course," she said. "I'll get whatever you want from Maurice's, too. It's on me and my grandma!"

She made a point of looking at his feet and asked,

"What happened to your trainers?"

"Nothing," Caleb said. He slipped away and started down the corridor. "I have to go," he called as he ran to his first class.

Cassie stood there, grinning, even as the first bell rang. She was late, but she didn't care. The plan would work.

* * *

Caleb couldn't concentrate on his lessons. All he could think about was Cassie Cloak. Her face flashed through his mind whenever he blinked. When his maths teacher, Dr Maple, asked him to come up to the board to find x, Caleb stumbled out of his desk.

At the front of the room, his mind reeled. The dry-erase marker in his hand felt like it weighed a tonne. His hands sweated. He dropped the marker twice before making a single mark on the board.

He scribbled mindlessly. He was not a maths genius, but mostly his mind was elsewhere. As he frantically added numbers and symbols and xs and ys to the board, he thought about Cassie, in that sinister red coat of hers. He thought about his hoodie, balled up on the floor of Grandma's flat. He remembered the taste of those sandwiches in his mouth.

He'd nearly forgotten where he was and what he was doing by the time he lowered the marker from the board. He stood back and looked at what he'd done.

The class laughed behind him. Dr Maple cleared his throat and said, "Shush."

On the board was a series of large, wild numbers and letters. Total gibberish. At the bottom, Caleb had written "x = Cassie Cloak."

* * *

Cassie couldn't concentrate on her lessons. It didn't matter much. She was far ahead in English class. In maths, they had dozens of problems to solve independently. And as for French, Cassie was fairly sure she spoke the language better than her teacher.

All she could think about was Caleb Woolf.

The night before, after her mum found that black hoodie, and after Cassie identified it as belonging to Caleb, Cassie and Grandma agreed to turn the hoodie over to the police straight away.

Then, the moment Mum left the kitchen, they'd got to scheming.

"Let's not go to the police," Cassie said. She narrowed her eyes at the light fixture hanging over the kitchen table.

"No, let's not," Grandma said.

"We'll take care of this ourselves," Cassie said. She thought about Caleb's grinning face. Of course it was him! Why hadn't she realized it sooner? Who else grinned like a wolf – a hungry, conniving wolf?

"Definitely," Grandma said. "Do you have a plan?"

Cassie did. And now it was in motion.

After French, Cassie pulled up her hood and entered the crowded corridor of Perrault Secondary School. No one seemed to notice her – they usually didn't. But Cassie knew one person would recognize the red coat. She moved slowly through the halls towards the canteen.

Caleb was tall – taller than most of the Year 9 boys. She saw his face, near the canteen doors, and he saw her. Cassie could tell. His eyes went wide. His grin – that toothy grin he always wore – was gone.

He hurried into the canteen. Cassie slid through the crowd and followed him. She slipped past the back of the queue. She ignored people saying, "Hey!" and "No pushing in!" She stopped behind Caleb.

"Hi," she said.

He didn't look at her. Cassie thought he couldn't look at her.

"Did you decide?" she said. "About dinner." Before he could answer, she added, "Is that a new sweatshirt?"

It was a bright green one, and it looked a bit big.

"What?" Caleb said, like he had just remembered where he was. "No … it's– it's my brother's."

"It's too big for you," Cassie said.

"What do you want?" Caleb snapped.

Snapped like a wolf, Cassie thought.

She smiled at him just as pleasantly as she could.

"Fine, I'll come," Caleb said. "I'll come to dinner at your grandma's flat."

"Great!" said Cassie. She hopped a little. She didn't even have to fake it. She was thrilled he'd be coming to dinner. Ecstatic.

Caleb moved forward in the queue. Cassie followed.

"Leave me alone!" Caleb snarled.

"Don't you want to know what time?" Cassie asked. Her smile was tight and thin.

Caleb grunted.

"Seven o'clock," Cassie said.

"Fine," said Caleb under his breath.

Cassie's heart raced. She took deep breaths. It took all of her willpower not to run out of the school that very instant, right to Grandma's – clear across Forestville – to start getting ready for dinner.

* * *

The girl finally walked away. Caleb's heart pounded in his chest behind the borrowed green sweatshirt of his brother's. Suddenly it struck him. He left the queue. He dodged between people and trays and tables and bins. He spotted the red hood. He grabbed her by the arm. She spun to face him – her mouth open, her brow raging.

"Where?" he said without breath.

"What?" Cassie said.

"Where does she live?" he said. "Where does your grandma live?"

"Oh!" Cassie said. "Don't you remember?"

Remember? he thought. *Oh no. She knows. She really knows.*

He tried to laugh. "Like I've had dinner with your grandma before?" he said. He grinned. His biggest, toothiest grin. He forced it onto his face.

Cassie smiled. "Silly," she said. "We talked about it yesterday, remember? Tall Pine Apartments."

"Oh yeah!" Caleb said.

His heart slowed down a little. She didn't know. He was safe. "I remember now. See you later."

Cassie smiled at him. Then she turned and left the canteen.

* * *

"So much to do," Cassie said as she hurried through the city streets. "So much to do and not a lot of time."

She'd left school early. No one would care. No one would even notice. Mum already knew Cassie wasn't going home after school. "I want to check on Grandma," Cassie had told her over breakfast that morning.

Mum had looked at her adoringly. "That's very sweet," she said. "I don't know if I like the idea of you being in the middle of the city on your own, though. I mean, after what happened and everything."

"I'll be back before dark," Cassie said. She kept a serious look on her face. Inside, she was grinning.

She wasn't feeling very helpless, truth be told. That morning, she'd felt like a predator herself.

The centre of Forestville was crowded at three o'clock on a Monday. The streets were full of shoppers and office workers. The shops were open. The restaurants were open. It was a sunny afternoon, and some people were having a late lunch.

Maurice leaned on the door of his deli. He smiled as Cassie walked by.

"Hello, little Cassie," he said.

Cassie waved, but she didn't stop. Her part of the plan was to get Caleb to Grandma's flat at seven. The trap was up to Grandma, and Cassie was dying to see what she'd come up with.

* * *

Caleb tried to take his mind off it. At the court that afternoon, he snapped at his friends and growled and grunted so much that eventually they'd given up on him.

"You're in a foul mood today," said Andrew, the last of his friends to leave the court. He rocketed the basketball at Caleb. Caleb caught it.

"Whatever," said Caleb. "So go home."

"I plan to," Andrew said. "Later." And he walked off.

Caleb was alone, which was how he wanted it anyway. A lone wolf.

It was only four o'clock. Three hours till he was supposed to be at Cassie's grandma's place. *I should just skip it,* he thought. He shouldered the ball at the top of the three-point line and took a shot.

Air ball.

He watched the ball roll on the grass towards the playground, where a few younger kids were playing while their mums looked on from nearby benches. *I'll just skip it,* he thought again. *This is stupid. What is that weird Cassie girl going to do if I just don't show up at her grandma's house? Nothing.*

He walked slowly to collect his ball. He found the basketball up against the big sand pit on the edge of the playground and scooped it up. *But my hoodie*, he thought. *I have to get it back. If no one's seen it yet...*

He tucked the ball under one arm as he walked back to the court. *They must have seen it*, he realized. *Then this is a trap. And if I go, I'll be walking right into it.*

I'm not going to go. No way. His stomach growled.

He reached the foul line and stared up at the orange rim of the basket. If it wasn't for the hoodie, he'd go. Just for the food.

But she wouldn't recognize it, he thought. *No way. It's just a black hoodie. I'm not the only one who has one. Probably everyone in the whole world has a black hoodie.*

He took a shot. The ball slammed into the rim and bounced off. He watched it fly off the court and clear into the street. It bounced across and rolled into the gutter.

* * *

"Are you sure about this?" Cassie asked. She sat at the kitchen table while Grandma slid a huge roast into the oven.

"Quite sure, yes," Grandma said. She stirred the big pot of simmering chicken soup on the hob.

"We're not going to actually feed him, are we?" Cassie asked.

"Of course not," said Grandma. "But the boy isn't stupid, even if he is a dirty little dog."

"Grandma!" Cassie said.

"He is," Grandma insisted. "And he'll be having second thoughts about coming here tonight." She turned from the hob and put her fists on her hips. The wooden spoon she wielded jutted out from her side like a dagger. "Really, Cassie," she said. "I wish you hadn't mentioned his sweat-shirt."

Cassie shrugged. "I couldn't help it," she said. "You should have seen him. Squirming and afraid."

"I know," Grandma said. "But he must realize we found the hoodie now. He'll suspect we're setting him up."

"Maybe so," Cassie said.

"The point is," Grandma went on, "we need every possible thing to seem right. To seem normal."

"I know," Cassie said.

"We need that boy to smell this food from clear across Forestville," Grandma said as she put down the spoon and went to the window. She threw it open and waved her towel in front of the window. "Fly, scents of supper! Fly!"

Cassie giggled. She could just imagine Caleb on the basketball court with his friends. He'd smell the roast and the soup. It would be so distracting that he'd miss a foul shot. His nose would tickle, and he'd practically float the whole way here, lured by the delicious aroma of Grandma's cooking.

* * *

The sun just peeked over the top of Forestville's tallest building. Caleb sat on his basketball, watching the sunset, trying to ignore the rumbling in his stomach.

He could go home and face his obnoxious older brother and doting mother. He could stay here on the basketball court until his brother came to find him, sent out by their mum, both of them angry and red-faced.

Or he could go to Tall Pines. He could pretend he's never been inside before. He could sit down with Cassie and her grandma and hope they're not up to something.

"I'll think about it," he said to himself. He stood up, cradled his ball under one arm, and started walking towards Tall Pines. "I'll think about it while I walk."

And think about it he did. He couldn't think about anything else, in fact, because clear across Forestville, he was sure he could smell his supper.

"Impossible," he muttered. He was probably smelling the deli, or the steakhouse on Park Boulevard, or even the fast-food chicken place behind the stadium. But his supper, all the way across town, coming from a little flat on the fifth floor? "Impossible."

But it wasn't impossible. Caleb could have walked the whole way with his eyes closed. The smell grew stronger, and it carried him along the streets and avenues of Forestville.

By the time he reached Tall Pines, it was as if he floated on a stream of fragrant air – a roast chicken, soup, an apple pie, a heaped bowl of mashed potatoes, rich gravy. His eyes were half closed. His mouth hung open in a grin. His tongue nearly rolled from his mouth. He reached up and poked at the numbers 5, 1 and 6.

"It's me," he said, breathless. "It's Caleb. Cassie invited me–"

The door buzzed. "Come right up," said Grandma. "Come right up, dearie." As the phone clicked off, he thought she might be laughing.

* * *

"Where's the sweatshirt?" Cassie said. She hurried around the little flat, switching off this light, switching on that one, then reversing it.

"Don't worry, dear," Grandma said. She sat at the kitchen table, nibbling halvah. "I washed it and folded it and set it down on the table near the door."

"He'll see it?" Cassie said.

"He will if you stop messing with the lights," Grandma said with a wink.

Cassie took a deep breath. "How can you be so calm?" she said. "I'm a bundle of nerves."

"I see that," said Grandma. "But I'm old hat with this stuff. Back in the old country – well, let's say we had our share of wolves."

Cassie smirked and dropped into the chair next to Grandma. She let her head fall onto the old woman's shoulder. Grandma pulled her close in a one-armed hug.

"Then we're all set?" Cassie said.

Grandma nodded slowly. "The trap is set and ready to spring," Grandma said. "Now we'd better get ourselves in position."

"Or we'll become our own prey," Cassie said.

"And I for one am not quite ready to see your grandpa again," Grandma said.

With that, they both stood up. Grandma closed the kitchen window, and then they left the flat, leaving the door open, just the tiniest bit, for the company.

* * *

The ride up the lift seemed to last forever.

Though he'd been enjoying and luxuriating in the sumptuous odours of supper for the whole walk across Forestville, here in the lift, the smell was gone.

Caleb's brain fought with itself. *I miss that smell,* he thought first. *Get a hold of yourself,* he thought next. *This is a trap. The old woman and that snivelling little girl of hers are tricking you.*

Nonsense, he thought. *They're feeding you. Remember those smells? Oh, that roast chicken. And the mashed potatoes and gravy. You can almost taste it, the meat falling off the bone. The steaming, simmering soup, full of vegetables and dumplings. So rich...*

Snap out of it! he thought. *Snap out of it!*

And the lift pinged. The doors opened, and the lift filled with the scents of supper. He closed his eyes and smiled, letting the delicious smells rush over him. His mind was clear once again. Nothing in the world would keep him out of Flat 516 now.

Caleb nearly staggered down the corridor, past the screaming mothers and wild children, towards the slightly open door of Flat 516.

"Cassie?" he said as he got close. He thumped the door twice with his fist. "It's me."

The door swung open as he knocked, and he went in.

"Should I close it?" he asked, though he still didn't see anyone inside, and no one had responded to his greetings from the doorway.

And it didn't matter, because when he'd taken a few steps into the flat, the door closed behind him. He spun, surprised, and spotted the sweatshirt, folded and clean and sitting on a small table. He picked it up.

"Uh-oh," he said quietly to himself as he dropped the hoodie.

"Is anyone here?" he called out. He moved slowly along the dark hall. A light shone into the hall from the kitchen, and Caleb could practically see the scents of his supper slithering along the walls and floor like snakes made of steam.

He rounded the corner and stepped into the light of the kitchen. His eyes fell first on the banquet arranged on the table.

It was everything he knew it would be: a huge roast chicken surrounded by vegetables; a heaped bowl of mashed potatoes beside a ceramic gravy boat, sending delicious steam through the kitchen; a covered tureen, with its ladle beside it and with drippings of soup running down one side; and a beautiful pie, with a crisscross pattern across its top. From the smell he could tell it was apple pie.

Caleb nearly fell upon the food, hungry like a wolf as he was, but something else caught his eye. In fact, it seemed to catch all his senses at once, and he felt himself snap awake. He realized he was suddenly alert, aware of where he was, how far he'd walked. The kitchen had no air in it, he realized, and the windows were all closed and covered with steam. He couldn't catch his breath.

But that's not what startled him so. That's not what sent a cold shiver up his sweating back.

The oven door stood open. All the burners were on. But the hob and the oven gave no heat. All they gave was the hiss of gas entering the little flat, filling it up.

Caleb, forgetting the feast, turned and ran for the door. He pulled and pounded, but it wouldn't open. He ran for the living room and struggled with the window, then with the door to the balcony. Both were sealed shut.

"Help!" he shouted, pounding on the big glass panes. But help didn't come. Caleb ran for the bedroom, hoping a window in there might work, even a crack – even the tiniest bit of fresh air might save him.

He collapsed in the hall, dropped to the parquet floor like a heap of rags, and everything went black.

* * *

Cassie rode in the back of the ambulance with the boy. Grandma sat in front. Cassie sat right next to Caleb, stroking his limp hand, feigning tears. Once in a while, she would sniff loudly.

"You okay?" the paramedic asked her. "He's going to be fine."

Cassie sniffed and nodded. "I hope you're right," she said. "He's my best friend."

The paramedic patted her shoulder. "It's a good thing you got there when you did," he said. "I just can't understand why he didn't open a window or get out of the flat. He really could have died."

Cassie peeked out from under her red hood. "It's all my fault," she said. "I should have got there sooner. This is all my fault." She pretended to cry again.

"Now don't say that," said the paramedic. "It was an accident."

Cassie sniffed again, but she didn't respond. The ambulance sped through Forestville. The siren was on, and cars were pulling over to let them rush by.

"That's right, darling," Grandma called from the passenger seat in front. "Don't blame yourself, dear Cassie. It's really my fault. There's no one to blame but me. You know that. I forget things, now that I'm getting old. I feel terrible."

The paramedic caught Cassie's eye and smiled.

She smiled back, and the paramedic didn't notice anything sinister about it.

* * *

Caleb woke up under spotless white sheets in a spotless white room. His vision was blurry, and for an instant he thought for sure he was dead and waking up in heaven.

But then there was beeping like an old computer quite near his head. Something tugged at his arm when he moved. Something pressed against his nose.

His vision cleared, and he saw tubes and wires running from here and there, to his arm and his face and his chest, and to machines and plastic bags hanging on his right and left on either side of the bed.

The bed. Next to the bed, something red. A red shape.

Cassie, with her hood.

She smiled at him. Caleb felt her hand on his.

"Where am I?" Caleb said. His voice was cracked and dry.

"Oh, Caleb," said Cassie. Her voice sounded so strange. "I'm so glad you're okay."

His mind reeled. He remembered the feast – had he eaten? His memory was so fuzzy.

"It was all our fault!" Cassie said. She sounded like she'd been crying. She dropped her head and rolled it back and forth on his hand. "We're so sorry."

"He's going to be fine," said a woman's voice nearby. Caleb found the doctor standing at the foot of his bed.

She smiled at him. "You'll be out of here really soon, Caleb," the doctor said. "Don't worry." On the way out, she dropped his file in a slot by the door.

Cassie leaned in closer. "I'm so glad you're okay," she said. Behind her, the blue curtain that encircled Caleb's bed ruffled and shook on its hooks.

"I don't get it," Caleb said.

He could remember more clearly now. He hadn't eaten. There'd been no one else there. The door had closed behind him. The windows were locked. The oven was on.

It was–

"A trap," he said. "You trapped me."

Cassie's mouth fell open and her eyes grew wide. "What?" she said. "Why would I trap you?"

"I found my hoodie, by the door," Caleb said. "You knew it was me."

"Why, whatever are you talking about?" Cassie said, her hand on her chest.

"Stop," Caleb said. He sat up, just the tiniest bit. The cables and tubes and wires prevented him from sitting up straight. "I know you trapped me. You were getting revenge."

"Revenge?" Cassie said. "Revenge for what, Caleb?"

She smiled, just a tiny bit, and Caleb was sure he was right.

He nodded and snarled. "Revenge because you and your crazy grandma knew it was me," he said. "You knew it was me who tied her up and knocked you down and stole your food."

Cassie jumped to her feet and looked shocked. "It was?" she said.

Caleb crossed his arms. Cassie grinned down at him, her teeth white and shining.

That smile made Caleb shiver.

The curtain flew back. There was Grandma, and a man was with her.

"That's enough, dear," Grandma said. She was smiling too. "You've had your fun."

Cassie shrugged, pulled up her red hood and walked out. Her raincoat squeaked as she went. Grandma followed her.

The man, though, with his loose brown tie and wrinkled blue dress shirt, stayed right there. "I suppose you know who I am," the man said.

Caleb nodded. "Yes, officer," he said.

"They knew it was you, all right," the policeman said, sitting down in the empty chair. "They knew it was you the whole time."

Caleb stared at the ceiling.

"The only thing I don't get," the officer said, "is why you went back."

Caleb remembered the smells of that supper, pulling him from the park and clear across Forestville. "Me either," he said. "Me either."

I've been sitting here for like an hour. My beautiful and insane stepmother told me to come. She sent Hunter, the old valet, to fetch me. I'd just finished supper, and though I adore good old Hunter, I was trying to enjoy a little sunshine on the rooftop patio before heading out for an evening with my friends.

Our apartment is the top three floors of a high-rise building close to Central Park in Manhattan, New York. It's not too shabby, as my dad likes to say.

"Lady Eira," Hunter said as he stepped onto the veranda. That's me. I mean, not the Lady part. He's just silly like that. I'm just Eira. It means "snow" in Welsh.

"Her Majesty" – he meant my stepmum, queen in her own mind – "requires the honour of your company in her personal study directly," Hunter said.

"Directly" I learned rather quickly after my dad married the "queen" means "right now". So I got up from my towel and chaise, pulled a sundress on over my bathing suit, and followed Hunter inside. "Directly," I should explain, only applies to me. My stepmum can take her sweet time. I've had an hour to stare blankly around the queen's study.

Funny thing about the study: it's really my mum's studio. Or it was, until she died.

Then my dad remarried.

Immediately after my dad said "I do", the queen paraded in here with an entourage of contractors, decorators and curators. She tore out all of my mum's photography supplies, took down all her photos and remade the room as an office fit for a queen – albeit one with awful taste.

I was four then. I'm sixteen now.

I remember my real mum, but hardly at all. I remember her smile, which was as big a smile as you can imagine, and it gleamed white between ruby-red lips. Her skin was like ivory, and her hair like ebony, but in all other respects she was nothing like a piano.

She looked just like me, and I have pictures to prove it.

My stepmum looks like us, too. She's pale as death, though, not as ivory or snow or a lonely cloud. And her lips are red like fresh blood, not a ruby. And her hair is black like a haunted dungeon or the deep darkness of a wolf's den, not like a summer midnight or wet ink.

We don't get along, my stepmother and I. This wouldn't be too big a deal – it's a large apartment – but most of the time, she's my only parental unit. Dad travels for business almost non-stop. I suppose apartments like this don't come cheap.

My friend Giselle claims the queen is jealous of the princess, like we're living in some old fairy tale and I'm too beautiful to have around. It's crazy. Giselle also claims the queen is a witch – which is not as crazy as it sounds.

A couple of years ago, one of the staff spoke sharply to my stepmother. Apparently the staff person – it was Lucy, from the laundry service – hadn't done a perfect job removing a "pomegranate juice" stain from a white handkerchief.

It was on my stepmum's favourite hanky, too, and I don't for a moment believe the stain was pomegranate juice, but that's not the point.

Stepmum summoned Lucy and scolded her. Lucy, though, didn't put up with it. After all, she'd washed clothes for my mother for years, and my mother never spoke to anyone unkindly.

"The stain won't come out," Lucy said. I imagine she set her jaw and clasped her hands. "I'm not a magician."

"Then you're sacked," said the queen. She no doubt waved her away. "Out of my sight."

"How dare you!" Lucy said, and we're all very proud of her to this day.

But the queen shook with rage, and she shouted, "Out of my sight or I'll snap your neck!" in her loudest, most terrifying voice. Lucy was brave, certainly, but not made of steel. She fled the office and fled the building. She never came back.

But the queen wasn't satisfied. For the next twelve months, the workers in the laundry service – every last one of them – suffered grave injuries, weird diseases and financial ruin. When Abraham, the laundry staff chief, broke both of his legs in a freak dryer accident and was told he'd never walk again, perhaps the queen was satisfied. That was the last of the laundry incidents.

Giselle and most of the staff claims it was witchcraft, and that Stepmother is the witch. I don't believe a word of it. I think my stepmum is a lot of things, but a witch? I'm sitting in her office guest chair, looking at a horrible sculpture, a painting that looks like the work of a three-year-old, and a view of Central Park through the grandest windows on the west side. There's not a raven, spellbook or bubbling cauldron in sight.

"There you are, Eira," she says as she appears in her office and strides across the hugely expensive rug, as if I might have been somewhere else and she'd been searching absolutely everywhere. "I have an errand for you."

She sits at her desk and her face flashes – in an instant she is the picture of pleasant. Sometimes she seems so kind and beautiful and nice.

"You're well?" she asks, her smile as sincere as you please, the colours of her teeth and lips like bone and blood.

I shrug. "I'm fine."

"Grand," she says, and the moment is passed. Her smile is gone. "So. An errand. Hunter will escort you."

She is scribbling on a pad – she keeps these pads all over the house. They're square and seem made of pressed paper pulp and gold flecks, and they probably are. She tears the sheet from the pad and reaches across her desk – just a bit, so I still have to get up and reach most of the way to grab the paper.

It's just got an address on it – not one I recognize. It might even be in the suburbs.

"What's the errand?" I ask, but the queen is already on her feet, which means – house rules – I have to stand too.

She ushers me out of the room. "Hunter will explain everything," says my stepmum. "Please do hurry. I want Hunter back as soon as possible."

"Okay," I say to the door as it closes in my face.

* * *

Hunter is standing there in the hall. "This way, Lady Eira, come on," he says, and he's smiling. But his voice sounds a bit off. Just something weird about it. I can't put my finger on what it is. I don't know.

I follow him towards the lift. "Is everything all right, Hunter?" I ask.

He glances quickly over his shoulder at me and flashes another fake smile.

"Fine, fine," he says, as brightly as ever. "You know I always get nervous running important errands for Her Highness."

I pretend to chuckle, but Hunter's nerves are shakier than normal. Something's up.

On family outings with my dad and the queen, we keep to ourselves. We often put the opaque window up between us and the driver's seat, even. But when it's just me and Hunter, we like to keep things informal.

"So," I say, leaning forward in the back seat. "Where are we going?"

"Is your seatbelt on?" Hunter says. He's dodging the question.

I lean back and clip in. "It's cool," I say. "Secrets are cool."

But it's not cool for long. The limo slips onto the West Side Highway, and now we're zooming along Manhattan Island to its end at the Bronx.

"Seriously, Hunter," I say, calling over the roar of the traffic and the engine and sounds of the city. "Where are we going? Why am I on this errand?"

He doesn't even flinch, so maybe he can't hear me, but I'm beginning to get weirded out. When he pulls off the motorway and crawls through the streets of the Bronx – unfamiliar streets; crowded streets; dirty streets – I try the door handle.

Locked.

"Hunter!" I snap.

This time he flinches. "I'm sorry, Eira," he says, hardly loud enough to hear. The limo slips from the wide main avenue and down a narrow side street.

Cars are double-parked. The locals congregate in doorways. They lean on the hoods of their old, rusting cars and their new, flamboyant SUVs. At least three different songs boom from apartment windows and car stereos.

"It's not much farther," Hunter says. After a beat, he adds, "You're going to be okay."

The limo lurches as he turns slowly off the street, up a bumpy driveway, and into an alley barely wide enough for the car.

"What is this?" I say. I finally stop tugging at the door handle. "Hunter, tell me what's going on."

But he doesn't answer. He just opens his door and climbs out of the car. A moment later, mine opens, and Hunter offers his hand. It's like instead of stopping in some smelly, desolate alley deep in the Bronx, we have just pulled up to the Waldorf for one of Dad's big charity dinners.

But I'm not wearing a gown, and Hunter's not wearing his driving suit. I'm in a sundress over my bathing suit. I don't even have my handbag. I don't even have my phone.

"I'm not getting out," I say, and I slide across the huge seat and cross my arms.

"Please, Eira," Hunter says. "I have to be quick or her ladyship will begin to check on us."

"Then take me home," I say. "I'll explain everything to her."

Hunter leans in, with both his gloved hands on the seat. "It's impossible," he says, shaking his head.

"What is impossible, Hunter?" I ask.

"Eira," he says, his eyes red and tired, his voice rough and worn. "Dear. She wants me to kill you. She wants me to strangle you and leave you here in this alley."

My face goes cold and my whole body gets tingly and itchy. In an instant, my eyes are full of tears, and then Hunter's are too. He crawls into the backseat and reaches for me, so I swing my knees up, throw my back against the door, and kick up my foot, right into his nose.

He screams and pulls back his head, and it crashes into the roof of the car. The blood starts from his nose in a drip at first, and then flows freely. Hunter sits back and cups his hands over his nose, swearing up a storm.

"I'm not going to kill you, Eira!" he shouts, as if to be heard over the flow of his blood and the sobbing from my chest.

"Then let me go now," I say, barely a whisper.

"I was going to," Hunter says, leaning his head back. He looks at me sideways over the tips of his bloody fingers. "The door's unlocked behind you."

I check, and it is. I shove it. The door swings open and bangs into a rubbish bin.

"Careful," he says. "You'll scratch the paint."

So I slam it again, and then again, and then one more time. "Tell her she won't get away with this."

He shakes his head. "I'm going to tell her you're dead, beautiful," Hunter says. "Or I'll be dead."

I climb out backwards and look at Hunter a moment. Then I look up the alley towards the crowded side street – a foreign country. "What should I do?"

Hunter reaches one bloody hand into his trouser pocket and pulls out an envelope. He reaches it out to me. "It's not a lot," he says. "A few of us pitched in."

I open the envelope. It's stuffed with cash. There's a decent stack of it, but not enough to stay alive in the Bronx all by myself for long.

"I can't," I say, reaching it out to him. "Besides, I can't walk around this neighbourhood with that much cash. It's not safe. It'd be a liability."

"You're probably right," Hunter says, shaking his head with a big sigh. "Whatever, Eira. Just get out of here. Find a way out of town, even. Head to the trains. Go to Jersey. Get lost."

He reaches across and gives me a little shove. Then he pulls the door closed. I hear the locks fall into place. I can't see him through the black-tinted windows, but he must have climbed into the front seat, because a moment later the limo roars to life and the tyres squeal as he pulls away, leaving me pressed against a rubbish bin with nowhere to go.

* * *

The action on the street has doubled with the setting of the sun. I do my best to pass unnoticed, but that isn't happening.

"Hey, beautiful," someone shouts from a doorway or an idling sports car.

"You lost, baby?" shouts someone else. I feel the crowd find me. I feel it swell. I feel them move towards me.

I put my head down and walk faster. I slip between men and boys, and I hear the women call out. They say things like, "Leave her alone," and "What's she doing here?"

Then I run, and they laugh at me, but I don't care. I run until I reach the big avenue at the corner. Then I turn and run some more, till the rain starts. I duck into a bus shelter and almost smile when the inviting glow of a for-hire taxi appeared on the nearly empty road.

"Taxi!" I shout, throwing out my arm, waving it around.

The taxi pulls up, and I have to jump back to avoid being splashed by its wake. I climb in quickly.

"Hi," I say, offering my biggest, brightest smile. The driver doesn't even notice. "So, I have to get to Central Park West, but I don't have any money."

Now he notices. He gives me the old withering glance in the rearview.

"But where I'm going, there's loads of money," I add quickly, "and someone will be able to pay you. And tip you really well."

"Out," he says. "Wait for the bus."

"I don't have money for the bus," I say.

"Exactly," the driver says. "Out."

I lean forward, so my forehead is right against the thick plastic divider between us. "Listen," I say, in my kindest and gentlest begging voice. "I really need help. I know it's a lot to take on faith, but I promise to make it worth your while. You can charge whatever you like."

He gives me a long look in the mirror, his mouth twisted in disbelief, and for an instant – for a wonderful, soul-quenching moment – I think I have him. But it's gone. He pulls away his gaze. "Out."

"You're a bad, bad man," I say, but I climb out, because I don't want to kick anyone else in the face if it comes to an altercation in the backseat. The cabbie speeds away, and this time I'm not quick enough to avoid the spray. The hem of my sundress, already smelling of rubbish bins, is now speckled with muddy water.

I wish I'd accepted Hunter's cash. All I can do now is find a doorway, somewhere hidden and dry, and cry the night away. But when I look up from my disgusting and mangled dress, I see three figures – the only other people on the avenue – walking towards me.

Casually – because there's no reason to overreact, or make it look like I'm overreacting, anyway – I turn and walk slowly the other way. But immediately, I spot another three people coming from that way.

I'm stuck on this block. I can't run across the street. That would make me look like a victim right away. So I don't see how I can avoid these people.

I take a deep breath. They're not criminals. They're just people, probably walking home. And in the rain, too, just like me. If anything, they'll feel some empathy towards me, like I should for them.

There's an alcove in the middle of the block. I spot it and head there at once, my head down, my legs moving quickly in long strides. The rain coats my face now, plastering my hair to my forehead and ears and the back of my neck, but I don't care. I can just make out the faces of the men coming towards me from the far corner.

They're close, and they're smiling – not pleasantly.

I'm into the alcove, and the moment I'm out of sight, I start to run. It cuts clear through the block, sheltered above, like a pedestrian tunnel through the belly of a building. My feet ring on the giant marble tiles. It's slippery, but I can't slow down. Behind me, the men are running too.

I'm halfway through. The tunnel is lit with dim, square fixtures above me, a gross yellow colour. The rhythm of my feet as I run matches the rhythm of the light flashing in my eyes. At the far end, one light is out, and the last light flickers and cracks randomly. One instant the far end is pitch dark, and the next it flashes brightly, like lightning cracking across the sky at night.

I'm only paces away when the light flashes out and the alcove goes dark. Behind me, all six men are following. I glance over my shoulder, and there they are.

But they're not hurrying. I'm nearly through the alcove, and they're not hurrying. As I turn my head again and the light flashes on, I know why.

A seventh figure waits for me at the alcove's exit.

I skid to a stop, my hands up, fingers splayed, nails out, ready to claw, but he just grabs my wrists and says, "Boo."

"Let me go!" I snap at him, kicking at his legs as he dodges and laughs.

"Easy, girl," he says through his sniggers. The rest of the gang comes up behind me, but they don't touch me. Finally the seventh lets go of my wrist and I slap his face.

He makes an "ooh" face and rubs his cheek. "Wow," he says. "That was uncalled for."

He must be crazy. Uncalled for? I'm surrounded by seven men! Okay, a couple of them are pretty young, I realize now, in the flickering yellow light at the end of the tunnel. One is probably not even twelve. One is right around my age.

The one who had my wrist seems to be the oldest, around Hunter's age, probably almost sixty, and he's got a stubby and stinky cigar clenched between his big teeth, like Spider-Man's boss at the newspaper.

"What do you weirdoes want, anyway?" I say, wondering if I'm better off without Hunter's cash or whether it would suffice to pay these thugs off.

"We don't want nothin'," says another of the guys from behind me. I can't see which of them is talking. But as he finishes talking, his words get higher and squished together, and then – BOOM – he sneezes. "Ain't that right, boys?"

The others mutter in agreement.

"My boys and I just want to be sure you're all right," says the first one – the old one with the stinky cigar. "Do we look like violent people to you?"

I turn, in the middle of this circle of strange men, and really look at them all. They wear nice clothes, well past the expiration date. Their trousers are stained and frayed. Their suit jackets are mismatched and ill-fitted. Their shirts are missing buttons and have collars the colour of urine.

I find the oldest one's face again. "I don't know," I say. "I've never known a violent person."

"Never?" he says.

I nearly take it back. An image of my stepmother, with that insincere grin splashed across her face like a scar, appears in my mind. But what business is it of his?

So I say, "Never," and I cross my arms in front of myself. He pulls the cigar from his mouth.

"You're all right, then?" he asks.

"Peachy," I say.

"Then you live near here," he adds.

"Of course," I say.

And he shrugs. "If the girl don't want help," he says to his boys, "the girl don't get help. Let's head home."

The circle evaporates. Six men follow their elder from the tunnel, into the drizzle of the night. But one, as he steps out of the alcove, pauses and looks back at me. He's one of the younger ones, about my age.

"You sure?" he says as his friends or brothers or family walk off. "Because, listen. I grew up on these streets, and I can spot an outsider, like finding a glittering coin in a heap of compost. You ain't a local."

I narrow my eyes at him, trying to look tough, like I belong, but in the back of my mind I know he can see my bathing suit through my sundress. And I know as well as he does that no one wanders the Bronx alone in a bathing suit under a sundress.

"You're also really pretty," he says. "I don't like the idea of you bein' on your own out here. Not at night, especially."

He's pretty too, somewhere under the grime of the streets and the yellowing of his clothes, so I pull my eyes away and look at my feet.

My shoes are wet. My feet are covered with the same grime he's wearing all over. But I say nothing.

"All right," he finally says – a vocal shrug. "I'll let you be." With that, he's jogging after the others.

When I'm alone in the flickering light at the mouth of the tunnel, unharmed and feeling like a fool, I call out, "Wait!" I start running, taking my best guess where they headed. "I do need help. Please wait!"

I only run for a short time before I find them – all seven, waiting in front of a 24-hour pharmacy. The youngest one comes out of the pack. He's small for his age, looks like, and barely half my height, but he holds out a bright-yellow rain coat, just bought. The tags are still on it.

"I bought it for you," he says.

I take it and pull it on and offer a very quiet and embarrassed thank you. The pretty one offers a soft grin, and the cigar smoker claps me on the shoulder and says, "Come on. We've got a safe place to wait out this rain and let you dry off."

The seven lead me down side streets, through alleys and holes in fences, and up five flights of crumbling steps in an old, red-brick building next to some overgrown train tracks.

"It's safe enough," says the pretty one. "I promise."

Ahead of us, the oldest pulls a key ring from his belt and unlocks no fewer than ten bolts. Then he swings open the heavy-looking metal door.

Inside is a big, empty room. When I say big, I mean almost the size of our palace on the park. But this place doesn't have any of the comforts I'm used to at home. A few chairs sit randomly here and there, along with a pair of folding tables, set next to each other as if for family meals at Thanksgiving.

Along the length of the place, there are square, thick columns holding up the industrial ceiling. One wall is floor-to-ceiling windows, stained or painted green and black. In a handful of the windows, old-fashioned fans spin.

I follow the others inside and pull off my raincoat.

"Make yourself at home," says the oldest. "Then we'll do introductions and see what we can do for you."

He falls against a pile of pillows against the wall nearby. The others join him in a lazy slouch. I wonder if they're thinking I'll do the same as I pull a chair across the floor for myself. I place it near their lounging pile and sit.

"So," says the smoker as he pulls a half-smoked cigar from his pocket. "Who are you? What's your story?"

I wait a moment and cross my legs at the knees. "You first," I say, looking the oldest right in the eye.

He shrugs and smiles. "Fair enough," he says. "Seems to me you've had a pretty rough day. First of all, I'm Smoky."

Obviously.

He looks over the pile of boys and men, finally pointing at the youngest. "That's Sprite."

I smile at the boy, and he blushes and grins and looks away.

"He's bashful," said the oldest, "but he'll rob you blind."

Sprite takes a pebble from his coat pocket and throws it at the oldest. The others laugh.

"Next is Snick." The pretty one, with beautiful, tired eyes and a mop of hair that's probably never been washed. "He made sure we helped you out tonight."

I nod at Snick, and he nods back. Smoky runs through the rest of the group: Bright-Eyes, Stupid, Grumper and Sneeze. I get a handshake, a dramatic bow, a grunt and a booming achoo.

"And I'm Eira Blanc," I say.

The moment the words leave my lips, Smoky's eyebrows go up and Grumper sighs and grunts.

"What?" I say. "Do you know me?"

Smoky nods as Grumper gets up from his cushion, gives the brick wall a solid kick, and waddles off, deep into the empty warehouse.

"I don't get it," I say.

"Neither do I," says Snick, getting to his feet. "What's goin' on?"

"This," says Smoky, pointing at me with his cigar, "is the daughter – excuse me, stepdaughter – of none other than the Witch of the West Side."

A gasp. A hand on a mouth. A "whoa".

"The Witch of the–" I start to say. "Wait a minute. You've heard of my stepmum?"

They have, obviously, and they've got stories. From the youngest to the oldest, they start in with them, all talking at once, all on their feet or their knees, leaning towards me with excitement and wonder.

"Please," I say, my hands up, "not all at once." But over the noise of their own voices, no one's listening to me.

"Quiet!" comes a bellow from across the floor. It echoes through the cavernous space like a thunderclap.

And it works. All the voices stop, and we wait for Grumper to waddle back to our corner. When he does, he says in a voice so deep that it shakes my insides, "This is no time for stories. It's no time for shivering in fear, either. This girl is in trouble if she is who she says she is, and if we've helped her tonight, then we're in trouble too."

No one speaks. They look at me, and I look at my hands. Finally I mutter, "It's not as bad as that, is it?"

But it is – we all know it, and I know it especially, because if it were up to Stepmum, I'd be lying dead in an alley less than a mile from here, with the marks of Hunter's gloves around my throat.

"There's one story you need to hear," I say, and I tell them what's happened tonight so far.

* * *

"Let me get this straight," says Stupid. He's the tallest of the group, and the skinniest. He's got the same moppy hair as Snick, but none of his good looks. "You don't have the cash your driver gave you?"

"No," I say.

"You didn't accept it?" he says, leaning forward.

I shake my head.

"I do not understand people," Stupid says. "I never will."

"The money would have been helpful," Smoky says, "but it's not the point." He stands in front of my chair and puts a hand on my shoulder. "You can stay here, long as you need to. Till it's safe for you to leave."

"Oh, no!" I say. "I don't need anything like that. I need to get back to the apartment. I need to make sure Hunter is okay. I need to make sure my father is okay!"

Smoky shakes his head, eyes closed and very calm. "You're crazy," he says. "If the Witch of the West Side wants you dead, she'll kill you. The minute you show up at that apartment–" And he drags his finger across his throat like a blade. "Dead."

I lean back and swallow hard.

"Listen, Eira," says Snick. I didn't notice him move, but he's on one knee next to my chair. He takes my hand. "The boys and Smoky – we know how to get around this town. All five boroughs. And we can keep an eye on your friends on the west side."

"But you're stayin' put," Smoky adds. He looks down at Snick and adds, "You and Bright-Eyes, set up a place for our guest to sleep."

"Can do," says Snick. He motions towards Bright-Eyes, who grins – he always grins – and seems to float up from the cushions. The two walk across the room.

"But," I say as I get up from my chair, "I can't pay you."

"You'll help out around here," says Smoky. He takes my hand and leads me across the giant room. "You know the last time we had a home-cooked meal, or even swept the joint?"

"Most days we just have ketchup sandwiches on white bread," moans Grumper, sighing his grumpiest sigh.

"Delicious!" says Stupid.

I don't mention I've never cooked anything more than toast. Before long, Snick and Bright-Eyes have set up a bed, barriers and privacy screens.

"Thank you," I say.

Smoky leads me to my new bedroom, such as it is. He stays there with me till I sit down on the edge of the bed – it's really just a wood platform and an old straw mattress. It doesn't look comfortable. But I'm so tired, I know I'll be asleep quick. "We'll get you some clothes tomorrow," Smoky adds as he leaves. "Good night."

"Good night!" the others call out.

I pull off my sundress and curl up under a pair of musty and threadbare blankets. As I drift off to sleep, I can hear them talking – talking about me – on the other side of the barriers.

"The poor girl," says one – it's Smoky, I think.

"Is she going to be okay?" says Sprite in his pipsqueaky little voice.

"She's gotta be," says Snick, and a couple of them laugh.

"Ugh," says a rough and deep voice that has to be Grumper. "He's in love with her."

"She's beautiful," says Snick. "Skin like snow. Lips like rubies. And hair like the black keys on a piano."

Ebony, he means. The last thing I have before I fall asleep is a memory of Mum saying just the same thing.

* * *

I'm the first awake. It's not even dawn; I can just make out a tiny piece of the Manhattan lights through a scratch in the paint on the window. The others are asleep in their corner of pillows, so I decide I better get started in my new position as homemaker.

I find an old T-shirt and a pair of shorts in a corner. They fit well enough. First things first: those windows. Without sunlight in here, we'll all go mad or get rickets or something.

With a quick look around, I spot a flat blade. It's easy to find things when everything is out in the open and there's not much to begin with.

Trying not to imagine why the boys need a blade at all, I get to scraping.

* * *

I've nearly finished the eighth window when Sprite comes up behind and tugs on my T-shirt.

"Whatcha doin'?" he says.

"Letting in some sunlight," I say with a smile as I stoop beside him. "It's so gloomy in here, don't you think?"

He doesn't seem to have an opinion on the matter.

Instead he says, "Smoky ain't gonna be happy about this."

Right on cue, Smoky sits up. I swear, a second ago he was fast asleep, snoring like a bear. But the instant Sprite said the old man's name, he sat up like a shot, jumped to his feet and stormed across the wood-plank floor.

"Girly!" he snaps from half his mouth. How did he grab a cigar already? "What in the name of all that is good and holy are you doin'?!"

I've made him mad, it seems. "I thought I'd let some light in here," I say. My mouth twists and I add, "A woman's touch, right?"

He considers me, chewing on his unlit cigar, and calms down a bit. "The thing of it is," he says, dropping a beefy arm around my shoulders, "the boys and I, we like a little privacy."

"I see."

"Quite a lot of privacy, actually," he says.

I nod.

"In our particular line of work," he goes on, walking me away from the window and gingerly prying the flat blade from my callused fingers, "a fair amount of secrecy is necessary."

"Line of work?" I say. The others are awake now, sitting up groggily on the pillows. Only Snick stays asleep, rolling onto his belly and snoring on.

Bright-Eyes hurries over, his eyes wide and tired, his mouth in a giant luminescent grin. "We're capital assessors and reinvestors."

"Well…" says Smoky.

"We're liberators," says Sneeze. He sniffles and coughs. "Of funds and financials."

"I don't know…" says Smoky.

"We're Robin Hood!" Sprite says, and Smoky chuckles.

Snick sits up and leans back on his arms. "We're thieves," he says. "We're good-for-nothing, scum-of-the-earth crooks, liars, robbers and cheats."

Smoky shrugs. "Not to put too fine a point on it," he says.

"Oh," I say. I look at my feet. There they are, dirty as they were last night, and this morning my fingers – covered in dry flecks of paint, red with calluses and little nicks and cuts – make a matching set.

"You're disappointed," says Smoky, and I nearly protest, but he cuts me off. "But we never hurt no one."

Sprite shakes his head vigorously.

"Not a fly," says Bright-Eyes through his smile.

Snick walks up and takes my hand from Smoky. "But we work hard at what we do," he says, "and we do it well. So we know this city and its people."

"Especially the nasty ones," says Grumper from the end of the room, where he's examining my handiwork on the windows. "We'll need thick curtains. Pronto."

"Which is why," Snick goes on, holding my eyes in his, "you'll stay here, while we do our work and see what the witch is up to this morning." He lets go of my hands and grabs his rucksack on his way to the door.

Smoky claps me on the back as the rest of the crew gets the gear together. "The old dame might not even know you're still alive," he says with a wink.

"But it's a long shot," adds Grumper. He shoulders a bag that looks heavy and heads for the door.

I bend over so Sprite can give me a hug around the neck. "Don't open the door for anyone," he whispers at my ear. "Same rule as when I was little."

"You're not little anymore?" I ask him, and he shakes his head, his eyes squinty and twisted like I'd asked the dumbest question ever.

Then they're gone, so I find a broom. It looks like it's probably been here longer than the seven thieves, like maybe back in the day, this building was actually a house for storing wares.

I get to work. Just call me Cinderella.

* * *

I'm not very good at this. That's the first problem. I've never actually held a broom before, and maybe it's because this one is shockingly old, but the straw bundled at the end, which is supposed to be helping me gather dust and detritus into nice tidy piles, is itself falling out of the broom and becoming more mess to clean up.

The second problem is the seven thieves. There doesn't seem to be any rhyme or reason to how they live, and when I sweep up a pile of twigs, rubber bands, three little stones, and a sock, I don't know if I've made a pile of rubbish or of their most prized possessions.

After a solid three hours of sweeping, I've created five piles, one of which, I think, must be rubbish. That's when someone bellows outside.

"Yoo-hoo!"

From the newly cleaned windows I can see her down there, wrapped in a grey shawl, with a black and white scarf tied around her white hair.

"Please, pretty child," she calls up at me, rubbing her

hands together as if she's freezing in the cold, though it's summer. She's covered in rags, but she seems really kind. The sort of old woman that you'd expect to see in some old film, but not in real life.

She's waving at me. "Please," she says. "I'm very hungry."

"I'm sorry," I call down. "I have nothing to give you!" It's probably true, unless there's a kitchen hidden around here somewhere.

"Then at least let me come in to warm up," she says.

Is she kidding? But she's on the verge of tears, judging from the strain in her voice. What choice do I have?

"Come up," I shout down. "I'll let you in."

I hurry across the floor and open all ten bolts, then pull open the door. It is heavy, and when it's open all the way, I gasp.

"Good morning," says the woman.

"H-how did you get up here so fast?" I ask. "It's five flights."

"Was it?" she says, hobbling past me into the apartment. "I hardly noticed."

She pulls off her headscarf and shoves it into her shawl somewhere. "Now," she says, holding my arm for support, and at the same time leading me deeper into the big empty room. "Let's see what these lads have in the kitchen."

"Wait, what?" I say, trying to stop her. But she's strong, so much stronger than she looks. "Do you know these guys?"

She giggles, kind of. It sounds like a dry leaf bouncing along a pavement, plus the bells of an old-fashioned ice cream cart and just as chilly. "My beautiful child," she croaks, "everyone knows 'these guys'."

She takes me across the huge space, right up to the far wall, and stops.

"Um," I say. "The end. Can't walk any further."

But she lets go of my arm, puts a hand on the wall, and presto! A door appears.

She pushes it open, and there it is: the kitchen.

"Whoa," I say as she totters inside.

"Come, come," she says. "Don't stand there ogling. Time to start cooking lunch."

There's a tall stool in this magical kitchen as tall as the old woman herself, but she manages to climb it and perch there. From its top, she directs me around the kitchen. I go from the magical fridge to the magical hob, and from the magical cutting board to the magical sink. Soon I've chopped onions and carrots and potatoes and celery and so many herbs that I lose count.

"All of it, into the pot," she instructs, always smiling, always pleasant, and I obey.

Before long, the biggest shining pot in the kitchen is full almost to the rim, bubbling and steaming, filling the cavernous apartment with the most amazing smells.

"There is only one more ingredient," she says. She's got a bag on her lap. I didn't notice it when she came in, but it's some kind of lumpy old woman's handbag. She's digging through it. "Ah! Here it is." She pulls out a tiny yellow enve-lope and holds it out to me.

"What is it?" I ask, and I open the little top and bring it to my nose. It smells heavenly.

"Don't inhale too much, beautiful," she says. "On its own, it's far too strong."

It is strong, but so delicious smelling. I find it difficult to pull the envelope from my face. "Dump it in?" I ask.

She nods, so I do. The soup seems to bubble a little more as the powder sinks in, as if it, too, is relishing the flavour of the spice.

"Now, we wait," she says, and she drops from the stool and takes my arm. "Let's get some cleaning done around here, yes?"

* * *

This old woman is wonderful. She's fixed the broom and produced another from a hidden cupboard. She's taught me to mop, and she's helped me scrape the windows. I can't believe the thieves have a friend like this woman. Why is their place so messy all the time?

"I'll have to ask them about it," I mumble aloud.

"Ask them what, my pretty dear?" asks the woman.

"Oh, I was just wondering," I say. "Why do the seven thieves live like slobs when they have a friend like you, per-fectly willing to help out around here?"

She clucks her tongue – it sounds oddly familiar. "Oh, you doll," she says. "Men like that don't want an old hag like me hanging about. They prefer a pretty young thing."

Like me.

I know she means it as a compliment, but it reminds me of the back-handed comments Queen Stepmum would offer, when she caught me checking my hair in the mirror by the front door as I put on my coat before school, or while I lay out on the deck under the summer sun, trying to darken my snow-white skin and failing to tan at all.

Giselle says Stepmum is jealous. She always says Stepmum is jealous. But my stepmother is a grown woman. She's married and she has riches unimaginable to 99 per cent of the world. Why would she be jealous of a sixteen-year-old girl? It's insane.

Then again, she did try to kill me, like, yesterday.

I stare at my hand as I work on a stubborn bit of scuff. My hand is ragged and red, and the rag it's pushing across the floor is dirty. "Oh," I say, a bit meek – meeker than I like, to be honest.

I snap out of it when the old woman claps, like a mosquito came too close: it's sudden and sharp. But it wasn't a bug; it was a notion.

"Do you smell it?" she says, leaning her mop against the nearest steel column.

I sniff the air, and then shrug. "The chilli, my dear," she says, lifting me by the armpit. She's stronger than she looks. "It's ready."

I sniff the air again, and yes – there it is!

It's delightful, too. Rich and spicy and intoxicating. I'm almost light-headed as she pulls me towards the kitchen

– the kitchen revealed behind the magical door. *The magical door*, I think somewhere in my muddled mind. *The magical kitchen. The magical broom cupboard, too.*

"Come, come," she says, because I'm stumbling over my own feet. I'm drowsy. I'm floating. The smell of the chilli and the sound of her voice make me dizzy.

"I'm coming," I say. "It smells ... it smells very good."

"Yes," she says. The *s* at the end of the word is like a leaking tyre or a stream of sand. It makes me sleepy.

"Oh, I'm so tired," I say.

"You've been working hard, dear," she says. We've reached the kitchen now and she deposits me on a chair. "You're just hungry. I'll get you a bowl."

The bowl is in front of me already, and the spoon is in my hand.

"It's not too hot," she says, right at my ear, and it tickles a little when she whispers, "Taste it."

It's delicious. It's spicy and sweet and rich and fresh. It's like every flavour of the city in one spoonful – all its people and all its history and all its warm summer nights and frigid winter mornings. The bowl is empty now.

"It's wonderful," I tell her. "I'd like some more."

"When you wake, beautiful child," she says, because, of course, I'm in bed now, and the kind old woman pulls the covers up to my chin. "When you wake, you will have more."

"Yes," I say, a little smile forming on my face. I close my eyes. The old woman runs her hand gently over my head, pushing my hair back from my forehead. It's nice.

"You're such a pretty girl," she says, and her voice is smoother now – still tiring, still gentle, but without the roughness of a long life. And it's familiar.

"Your lips," she says, "are so red, the colour of blood. And your hair " – her hand pauses on top of my head – "as black as ebony."

I want to open my eyes. I cannot.

"But your skin," she says, and she runs the backs of her fingers over my cheek, "is the most lovely of all."

I know her voice now. This is no old woman. I want to grab her wrist and snap it, but my hands won't move.

"So white and soft and clear," she says, "like snow."

Why can't I open my eyes?

"Beautiful Eira," she says in her true voice – my step-mother's voice. "Your mother must have been very beautiful indeed."

She stands; I feel her weight leave the bed beside me. "Sleep well, princess," she says. "Sleep forever."

* * *

They're back. The seven of them stand around my bed. Still, I can't move. I can't open my eyes. It's lucky I can breathe, I suppose. I wonder if Bright-Eyes is grinning. Sprite is crying, sounds like.

"It was the witch," says Grumper. "She was here. I can still smell her in this place. It's like sulphur."

"And…" says Sneeze, and his voice goes high and nasal, "cayenne pepper. Achoo!"

"I knew the girl would be trouble," Grumper grumbles.

"Enough of that," says Smoky. "No point standin' around goin' over what the problem is. We all know what the problem is. The point now is to solve it."

"Should we take her to the hospital?" one of them asks.

Someone else laughs. "No. How would we explain her being here? We have to work out something else."

"I'll kill her," says a voice, thick and quiet. "That'll end any curse: kill the witch."

"Don't be a fool, Snick," says Smoky. "Even if you could get close enough to her, she'd snap you in two like a dry old twig. You'll stay here with Sprite, keep an eye on Eira. Clear?"

"Fine," says Snick, but I can tell that he's not happy about it. "What's your plan, then?"

Smoky is chomping on his cigar. It's lit today, and the smell, though strong and awful, is comforting somehow. I can't see them. I can't reach out for Snick's hand. But I can smell Smoky's cigar, and that's something.

"We'll go into Manhattan," Smoky says through his teeth. "Tonight. Right now. And we'll get inside her house."

No! I want to shout. *You must not do that. She'll kill you all!*

But I can't. With all my strength, I will my arms to move to grab Smoky. I urge my mouth to open, my eyes to widen. But I have no strength, and I have no will, and I lie there like a useless lump.

"She'll kill you," says Snick. He sits on the edge of the bed – or I think it's him. It's hard to say for certain.

"We won't confront her," says Smoky, and he sits beside Snick. Maybe he puts that meaty arm around his shoulder. I wonder if they're father and son. They don't look it, at least, not genetically. "We'll snoop around, like we do. We'll take what we can, anything relevant."

Grumper laughs. "We won't find a flashing sign that says 'Spell books in here'," he says.

Smoky chuckles. "We'll find something," he says, and I can hear the smile in his voice. I can also hear it fade when he adds, "We have to."

The bed shifts as Smoky gets up. Their footsteps ring and stomp and drag across the huge floor. The door opens and closes, the slam ringing through the giant apartment. And the five are gone, and Sprite sniffles at my bedside.

"We won't let you go, Eira," whispers Snick. He puts a hand on mine. "I promise."

* * *

Snick won't sit down. He just walks back and forth and around my bed, now and then kneeling briefly to press his forehead against the back of my hand. *I'm not dead*, I want to scream at him. I can't, of course. I can't do anything at all.

Now and then, I drift off to sleep somehow. Sleep is better than wakefulness today, because when I sleep, I can see and I can move. I can jump up from the bed and throw my arms around Snick.

I don't know why, but since I've been lying here I've wanted nothing more than a kiss – a kiss from Snick.

Right on the mouth.

* * *

Sprite's asleep now. I can hear his snoring from the corner. If I could move, I'd have to twist my neck half-way around to see him, but I can picture him, with his knees pulled up and his head down on his knees, his arms wrapped around, so he's a little snoring ball.

Snick is worn out too. He's pulled a second chair right up to my bed, and he's holding my hand. I can feel the warmth and the pressure, but I can't wrap my fingers around his. I can't twist our fingers together.

"Oh, Eira. I don't know if you can hear me, sweet-heart," he says, his voice rough and tired. "But we're going to help you. I promise. My brothers will be back soon, and they'll know how to fix this."

I have no idea how long they've been gone. Without movement, without sight, with only dreams and a thief boy's hand to keep me company, time hardly exists. It could have been an hour; it's probably been a day and a night.

"You're so beautiful," he says, and his voice is now gentle and even joyful.

"I know, I know," he says, as if I've responded. Did my lips move? I wanted to smile. "I hardly know you. In fact, I don't actually know you at all." He's up and pacing again. My hand feels cold and heavy.

"It's probably just magic," he says, and I'm afraid his heavy steps across the cement floor will wake Sprite, and then Snick won't keep talking to me.

Sprite only snores on, though, even as Snick's voice gets nasty and he says, "You probably picked it up, hanging around in that witch's palace."

What? I think. *How dare he?*

"How else could you explain it?" he says, and he drops back into the chair. "Why else would I fall in love with some rich girl from the west side? Why else would I even care?" His voice is soft again.

Love? He's right; it must be magic.

"Every time I take your hand," he says, "I expect it to be cold."

The thought chills me, but his hands are warm, and soon I'm warmed right through.

"Your stepmother is very clever," he says, whispering, "and very powerful. But she's evil. Right down to the centre of her heart, she's evil. We might just be a pack of common thieves, but we have good hearts, you know?"

He stands, still holding my hand. "Oh, I don't even know what I'm saying," he says. "You probably can't hear me anyway."

Oh, but I can!

"If you can hear me..." he says. Then his voice is right next to my ear. I can feel the warmth of his breath on my neck. "Forgive me for this."

His lips press against mine gently, and it's like I'm coming up from the bottom of a crystal-clear lake. My body fills up with breath and life. The tingle of the kiss spreads across my face and down my neck and all over my body. My eyes open — I can open my eyes! I can lift my arms, and I can wrap them around Snick's body.

"Whoa!" he says, and he jumps up from the bed.

I laugh and smile up at him. "Hello."

* * *

We're sitting there on the bed, his hand in mine, and his cheeks as red as delicious apples when the rest of the boys slam through the door. They're all shouting:

"We're back!" they bellow.

"We know!" they holler.

"It is magic!" they roar.

"We know what to do!" they scream.

Their footsteps thunder along the cement floor of the apartment. Smoky's voice rises above the rest like a steamship foghorn. "A kiss!" he shouts. "She must be kissed by the one she loves—"

And he stops short, and they screech to a halt as they come around the side of the blind and into my funny little bedroom.

"Ah," says Smoky, shuffling like the others, looking at his feet.

He pulls a cigar from his vest pocket. The cigar is half smoked and tattered at its tip. He sticks it between his teeth, while Snick's face gets somehow redder.

"Kissed her, then?" says Grumper as he lifts his chin and looks down his nose at me and Snick.

It breaks the ice, and the rest of them can laugh. I drop my head onto Snick's shoulder and giggle along with them.

"That's that dealt with," Grumper says. "But there's still a witch to deal with."

"Do we have to?" I say, looking from eager thief to eager thief. "I'm okay now. She won't come after me again."

Smoky sits on my other side on the bed as Grumper gives Sprite a hard shove to wake him up.

"The witch tried to poison you, Eira," Smoky says. "We'll not let her get away with that, will we?"

I check Snick. He shakes his head at me and squeezes my hand a little tighter.

"You can say no," he whispers, though in the dead-quiet warehouse, he might as well have shouted.

"Smoky's right," I say, getting to my feet. "And I know who might help us."

* * *

I've been gone less than three days, but my apartment building on the west side feels like a foreign country to me now.

At the entrance to the underground car park is a woman walking her three purebred Pomeranians. She's head-to-toe in boutique fashions, with one lead in one hand and two in the other, and chatting away on her hands-free mobile phone, laughing and cackling.

I slip in through the pedestrian entrance. No key required – it's a keypad entry. Just then, a classic Jaguar coupé zips up the ramp. The engine sings and roars like a real Jaguar as it squeals around the tight little bends of the car park and out into the nighttime Manhattan streets.

There's no echo tonight as I cross the huge cement car park. My feet are bare and silent, free of the clip-clopping heels I'd usually have on. Hunter doesn't know I'm there until I'm right behind him.

"Eira!" he shouts, rather by accident, I think. When I laugh at his reaction, he shushes me and pulls me out of the light and into a dark corner behind the family limo. "What are you doing here?"

"I live here," I say, mostly as a joke. But it's true – I think.

He grabs my wrist – a little too hard – and growls at me. "I told you never to come back here," he says. "She'll tear my head off if she finds out I've been talking to you."

I tug my hand away and he lets me go. His shoulders droop as he goes on. "She has a way of finding things out."

"If that's so," I say, "then she must know that you let me go in that alley instead of wringing my neck."

His eyes go wide and then close in despair. Through a frown, he says, "She was looking at me in an especially strange way over her soup spoon as she ate this evening."

"Then she'll have your head no matter what," I say. "Unless you help me stop her."

He looks at me sideways, his eyes narrowed. "What exactly did you have in mind, princess?"

"First tell me," I say. "Will you help?"

I've never seen Hunter look so horrible and grey. His back slumps even more and his eyes close as if he's expecting the blade of a guillotine.

"Remember how it used to be?" I prod. "Before the witch lived with us. You were so committed to my parents – to my real mother."

He opens his eyes and they soften. "You look more like her every day." He even smiles just the tiniest bit and I know he's with us.

"Okay," I call into the darkness of the car park. "You can come out!"

The seven thieves emerge from the darkness – Sprite from beneath a nearby SUV, Smoky from behind a hefty column – and stand in their motley circle around us. I find Snick's hand and pull him into the circle.

"This is Snick," I tell Hunter. "He's in love with me."

"Aw, Eira," Snick says, and his face goes red. I'm finding it fun to make him blush already.

"I don't blame him," says Hunter, his eyes still on me. "Ach," he goes on, slapping himself on the forehead, "how could I have been so weak? How could I have let that witch control me for so long?"

"It's not your fault," Smoky says. "She's a powerful witch. It'd take a very strong man to stand up to her."

Hunter throws back his shoulders – it's like he's throwing off a heavy, musty blanket he's had over his head since Mum died – and looks me right in the eyes. "Then that's what I'll have to be."

* * *

The thieves and I crouch between cars, huddled together like wolf pups during a storm, anxious for their first hunt.

From where I'm kneeling, with Smoky on one side and Snick on the other, his hand on my shoulder, heavy and present, I can see Hunter lean across the roof of the limo. He's rubbing a stubborn spot with a soft cloth. He knows the smallest things send Her Highness into a fit of rage.

And finally she appears. One of the building's doormen appears first, of course. It's Antoine, and he's wearing the garage doorman jacket, which is black with red stripes instead of red with gold. It's all pomp and circumstance around here.

Antoine steps through the door and holds it open, standing far back with his eyes on his feet. That's his most professional pose. If it were me coming through the door and if I didn't quickly say "Don't get up!" as I hurried past, he'd be smiling. We might even high five.

Then Her Majesty steps through. She wears her finest coat. I wonder where she thinks she's going. It's down to her ankles and billows out in a ring of white fur trim, which runs all the way up the coat and around the collar. I've seen it before; she can pull up a hood of the same fine red fabric and white fur trim. You might think a coat like that would remind you of Santa Claus, but you'd be wrong. There is nothing joyful about it.

"Already nearly nine," she says as she strides up to the limo. "You'll have to make up the time on the road."

"Yes, ma'am," says Hunter. He pulls open the passenger door and, as she takes his hand and climbs in, catches my eye – only for an instant. I smile and flash a thumbs up.

Hunter closes the witch's door and gets into the driver's seat. They're off.

As the car slides up the ramp at Hunter's predictably safe pace, Smoky gets to his feet and groans. With his hands on his lower back, he stretches and says, "We'd better hurry. I don't think your valet, good a man as he is, stands a chance without a little support from us."

I grab Snick's hand as I stand up. "Then let's run."

* * *

The police station isn't far, and thanks to typical Manhattan cross-town traffic, Hunter and Stepmum have only been there a few minutes when the thieves and I barrel into the waiting area.

Even before the arrival of seven thieves and a sixteen-year-old girl in a tattered sundress and with dirty bare feet, the police station's lobby area is a madhouse.

Four uniformed cops, New York's finest, stand around, all staring. They've taken off their caps in respect, and they look at Stepmum and smile and babble. A couple of detectives, in their dress shirts with wet armpits and loosened ties, lean on the high counter and flutter their eyes. Hunter, the poor good-hearted man, has removed his cap as well. He wrings it in his hands like a wet rag and nods and bows in apology.

And in the middle of it all? Of course, it's Stepmum. Her glorious red coat is open, revealing a shimmering white cocktail dress subtly speckled with diamond dust. Her arms are up and open, and her soul seems to absorb the adoration of the men who surround her. That is a lie, though. Really the men absorb her magic – it comes from her like a foul poison scented with perfume.

"Stop this!" I shout at once. I shove through two cops and a pair of cuffed criminals. They don't notice me, but I don't mind. I stand face-to-face with Stepmum, or as near as I can. In her mile-high heels, and with my bare feet, the top of my head hardly reaches her chin.

"Stop what, my dearest daughter?" she says, her mouth wide and smiling. "I've had the strangest evening."

Hunter sees me and it's like a light flicks on in his brain. He tugs at his hat, struggles to make it smooth and slaps it onto his head. "I've been trying, Eira," he says. "I really have, I swear."

Smoky is beside him now and holding his arm. "You've done fine, man," he says. Then he faces the witch. "It's over, my lady," he says. "If you please, lower your arms and remove your spell from these good people."

"Why is he being so polite?" I whisper to Snick.

"You should always be polite to witches," he replies. "Everyone knows that."

I shrug, since I didn't know that, but these thieves seem to know the city and its secrets much better than I do.

Polite or not, the witch laughs at Smoky. "Take that cigar out of your mouth, you filthy mongrel," she says. I guess the politeness rule doesn't work both ways.

Smoky nods pleasantly and removes the cigar from his teeth. "As you wish," he says. I wonder for a moment if he, too, is falling under the spell. "But if you please, end this spell and surrender for your crime."

Stepmum leans over and laughs in his face – right in his face! With her mouth only centimetres from his nose. Still, he smiles and nods.

"Not you too," says one of the detectives behind the counter. He has a thick and dark moustache that nearly hides the magical-lovesick smile on his lips. "Her driver made the most absurd accusations. He claimed this lovely woman was a murderer."

"She is!" I scream over the laughter of adoring policemen. "She poisoned me!" The room fills with laughter.

Hunter catches my eye, and his are wet.

"Please, listen," I call over the roar of laughter. Though my thieves are safe from the witch's spell of adoration, the policemen and other criminals in the lobby are nearly doubled over. They think it's the funniest thing ever, that their new object of love and desire could ever harm another.

"Aren't there any female police officers in this precinct?" Snick says to me.

Hunter is still watching me. His eyes are still wet, but he throws back his shoulders. He sees my mother in my face, and it gives him strength. He seems to grow half a foot – he's as tall as the witch now, although he seemed bent and beaten seconds ago.

I push through the crowd and take his hand. "Help me."

He nods and he calls out. "It's all true." The laughter surges, but he goes on. "This woman poisoned her own stepdaughter."

I nod at him, urge him on, despite the thundering jeers of the policemen. Around us, the thieves clamp their hands over mouths, struggling to stifle the laughter.

"Her stepdaughter?" one of the detectives says through gasps for air and huge guffaws. "Isn't that her stepdaughter, right next to you?"

He pats a handcuffed thug on the shoulder. "She look poisoned to you?" he says. For a split second, the laughter stops. Then it erupts with more hysterical violence.

Hunter – his eyes still on mine, and still red and filling with tears – shakes his head and slumps his shoulders. He stares at his feet. He can't go on, and I realize now why.

I take my stepmother by the wrists and pull her arms down to her sides. The men stop their laughter. A couple even growl a little, their stares on me now, like attack dogs snarling at a burglar.

"She tried to kill me," I say, my gaze fixed on the witch. She looks right back, and though her stare is usually enough to subdue me – enough even to burn an ant on the pavement, like a ray of sunshine through a magnifying glass – tonight, it only gives me strength. "She murdered my mother."

There are gasps. Snick puts a hand on my arm. Smoky replaces his cigar and chews it and closes his eyes like a mourner.

"It's true, isn't it, Hunter?" I say. He nods, like I knew he would. He looks beaten and sad, but I don't blame him. I'm not even sure he believed it himself, although deep down,

I think he and I always knew the truth. Her spell kept us from seeing it.

"You've done it, Eira," says Hunter. "Her magic is fading."

He's right. Around us, police officers rub their eyes and stretch and yawn, like they've just woken up. The witch's smile is drooping and weak. We've beaten her, I think. It took seven thieves – seven wonderful boys and men I hardly know – and a valet whose love for me and my mum was not enough on its own. It also took my own love for my mum and the tears that now run down my cheeks.

* * *

I'm back in the office. This time, though, I'm not waiting for my stepmother. I'm practically holding my breath, watching my father pace across the huge red rug that sits in the centre of the room. And I'm watching from her side of the big desk, too, in her big chair. I'm also secretly hoping that once my dad has had some time to come to grips with what's happened, he'll let me redecorate in here and make it just like it was before the witch came along.

"I can hardly believe what you've told me," he says. He looks from me to Hunter, seated in the guest chair.

Then Dad lets his eyes slowly pass over the seven thieves, lined up against the long bookcase, all of them with their hats and caps off and grinning as pleasantly and honestly as they know how. Smoky doesn't even have his cigar.

"But I know I must," Dad says with a tired sigh. He leans on the desk beside me and pushes my hair back from my forehead. "I was in my hotel room in Tokyo, and I just … felt it." He stares out the window behind me at the setting sun. "It was as if someone pulled a blindfold off me, or flicked on the light…"

"Or pulled a blanket off your head," says Hunter.

"Or showed you the truth in your heart," I say, and I take my father's hand.

"Yes," he says. "All those things."

I stand and put my arms around him. "She's gone now," I say. "The witch is gone, and we can start to make things right."

We hold each other till someone coughs. I open my eyes and see Smoky, a shy smile on his face.

"Forgive me," he says. "We've taken up too much of your time, and we'll leave now and let you handle your family business in private."

"Ah," Dad says. He sits me back down and in two long strides stands in front of Smoky. "A band of thieves," he says. "How very … Robin Hoodish."

Sprite says, "Ha!" and points. "See? See?" he says.

Smoky chuckles and shushes the boy. "We're not nearly as noble as we seem," he says.

"Think you've got a huge bag of money coming to you?" Dad says as he crosses his arms across his huge chest. "A handsome reward?"

Smoky reaches into his coat pocket for a cigar stub. "It's nothing like that," he says. He looks down the line of thieves at Snick and winks. Dad sees it and steps down the line to look down his nose at Snick.

"Oh, no," I mutter. "Dad, please, let him be."

"So?" Dad says in his deepest, most intimidating voice. He may not have the witch's magic – I refuse to call her Stepmother any longer – but he can be just as persuasive. "What is it you want? A reward? Maybe a job – a good position with my firm?"

"N–no sir," Snick says. He squeezes his hat in his hands and his face reddens. It's tough not to jump from my seat and take his hand to pull him away from Dad.

But I've forgotten. He's so kind and shy, but he's also a boy who grew up in the Bronx, living day to day with a band of thieves. Of course he can handle one man – even a man like Dad.

"What I'd really like," Snick says, "is your permission to date Eira."

Dad's eyes go wide and he gasps and stutters a moment, and now he's blushing. Everyone in the room – except Snick and my dad, of course – burst out laughing at the sight of Dad speechless and red-faced. Even Dad has to smile and that's not something he's fond of doing.

He looks over his shoulder at me. "What about it, princess?" he says. "Do you want to date a thief from the Bronx?"

"More than anything," I say. I feel my face get hot as I smile back at him and then at Snick.

"All right, then," says Dad, looking Snick right in the face and putting out his hand to shake. Snick takes it, though it's twice as big as his. "And maybe we'll see about getting you that job, too. I can't have my daughter dating a criminal."

Snick says, "Thanks!"

Dad looks over the other thief faces. "And that goes for the rest of you, too," he says. "If you'll have the jobs."

The thieves say their thank yous, and Dad takes them around to meet the rest of the staff. Snick hangs back. "I can hardly believe my luck," he says as he moves towards me.

I swivel the big desk chair to face the window. The sun has nearly set now, and I can see Snick's reflection in the plate glass.

He comes up behind my chair and puts his hands on my shoulders and leans down. I close my eyes and feel him press his lips against the top of my head. I feel his breath as he whispers, "The fairest girl in the city."

Jessamine Wood knelt on the cold tile floor of her flat's tiny bathroom. Her feet stuck out of the doorway into the hall.

"Oh, no," she said quietly.

Then she said it louder. Her moans of agony and dread echoed off the bathroom walls and floated out to the rest of the flat.

Her husband, Bodhi, called from the kitchen. "I can take the night off. They'll never miss me!"

Jessamine tried to reply, but she felt too sick. She heard his footsteps approaching on the creaky wood floor. "Don't come in here!" she said. "Please. Also, you can't stay home today. We can't afford for you to miss work."

Bodhi sighed, but he didn't argue. Jessamine hadn't been able to work in weeks. Without Bodhi's two jobs, they'd be out in the street.

Thinking about money made her sick again. She felt her husband's hand on her back, and, after wiping her mouth with the back of her hand, snarled at him, "I said don't come in here."

"Sorry," Bodhi said. He handed her a glass of cold

water. "I wanted to say good night. I'd better get going if I'm going."

Jessamine took the glass with a quiet thank you and sipped slowly. "What time will you be home tonight?" she said. As the cold water rushed through her empty system, she felt a series of tiny kicks in her belly.

"I'm on till three," Bodhi said. "Franklin can't take his shift. His grandmother is dying."

"Again?" Jessamine said. She put down the glass and put out her hands so her husband could help her to her feet. Her head swam a bit as she stood. It always did.

"For the sixth time this year," Bodhi said. He kissed his wife on the forehead. "Get some sleep."

She almost laughed. She couldn't remember the last time she'd got more than an hour of shut-eye at a stretch.

Instead of trying to sleep in their stuffy flat with no air-conditioning, Jessamine grabbed an empty paper bag from under the kitchen sink, slipped on her flip-flops and followed her husband out into the night.

It was a fifteen-minute walk to the cinema. She didn't care what they were showing. She'd enjoy the air-conditioning, see as many films as she could till the last one ended around two and then she'd head home.

She'd done this before, nearly every time her husband had to cover the late shift.

Tonight the cinema was showing an old animated film she'd seen a hundred times. Still, it reminded her of her childhood. She stayed and watched the six o'clock showing, the nine o'clock showing, and the midnight showing. She cried the hardest the last time, even though she'd already seen it twice that night.

When the midnight showing was over, Jessamine was hungry.

The Woods lived in a busy area. Even at this hour, several businesses' doors stood open, letting their air-conditioning waft out to the street. Some of those open doors also released the scents of delicious-smelling food.

There was the doughnut shop at the corner of Grimm Street. There was Mario's All-Night Pizza on Andersen Avenue. There was the noodle shop on Collodi Street, close to Jessamine's flat. Some nights, even inside with the windows closed, all she could smell was fish sauce and onions.

But tonight, none of it smelled delicious. It was all she could do to hold her breath as she passed these places. She reached her block of flats, still gasping with hunger, but unable to think of a single thing she wanted to eat.

Standing in front of her building, digging through her huge handbag for her keys, Jessamine caught a whiff of something. It was something familiar but exciting. It was strange and new but earthy and everlasting.

Dandelions. Their little yellow heads had closed for the night, but their greens, shaped like lion's teeth, grew like … well, like weeds all over the building's front lawn.

Jessamine's heart pounded. For the first time since she'd been pregnant, she knew what she wanted. She wanted dandelion leaves.

Before she knew what she was doing, Jessamine dropped her bag, fell to her knees on the front lawn and grabbed handfuls of leaves. She put them in her mouth and chewed. They were peppery and fresh, sunny and cool.

She pulled up handfuls of dandelions as she went across the lawn, shoving them into her handbag till it was almost bursting. Then she headed home.

Shaking with anticipation for the bag of delicious greens, she unlocked the building's front door. It always stuck, so she had to knock it with her shoulder. Then she hurried up the two flights of stairs to their flat, made her way inside and finally caught her breath.

She found the biggest bowl she could. She dumped the leaves in, rinsed them quickly under cold water, found a fork and dug in.

* * *

Twenty minutes later, the bowl was empty, bits of green were stuck in her teeth, crumbs of soil clung to her lips, and she was still famished. Jessamine needed more. She stood up in the dark kitchen and went to the window.

Jessamine looked out onto the back of the block of flats, lit by floodlights to save the landlord insurance money, but with not a tiny corner of unpaved ground. A couple of dandelions had managed to grab a foothold along the fence on one side, but otherwise the area was bare, a lifeless slab of cement.

She could also see into next door's back garden. She could see a small and bent tree in the centre of the overgrown garden, undecorated and unkempt aside from a single ornamental scarecrow, scarier now no doubt, after surviving dozens of summer storms and hellish blizzards, than it had been when it was first stuffed and mounted.

Jessamine had seen these things before, standing at the kitchen's back window and looking out, letting the soothing steam from a cup of coffee waft up over her face on a winter morning. That was before she'd got pregnant, of course. She hadn't touched coffee in ages.

Tonight, she hardly noticed the tree and the scarecrow. Instead, her eyes slid over the unkempt garden and its beautiful yield: swaying dandelions, each boasting leaves grander and more delicious looking than any she'd plucked from her own garden.

She had to have them. She grabbed an empty paper bag, opened the kitchen window's screen, and stepped carefully over the windowsill and onto the fire escape. The neighbour had no floodlights. Aside from that, she was something of a mystery.

Jessamine stepped carefully down to the second-floor fire escape. The window on that level was dark as well; normal people slept at this hour, of course, no matter how hot it was. Jessamine's belly barely fit through the opening to the ladder that led to the ground. Still, she squeezed through. "I'm sorry, baby," she muttered as she went. "It'll be worth it."

At the bottom of the ladder, Jessamine let herself drop to the cement patio. She headed for the decrepit wooden fence that separated the gardens and got on her tiptoes.

The woman next door was a mystery, yes, but one about whom the neighbourhood loved to speculate. "She's the oldest woman in the street," they said.

"In the country," they argued.

"In the world!" they dared.

Unlikely, thought Jessamine as she went back behind her building and found a rubbish bin. She dragged it to the fence.

But that wasn't all they said. "She's still alive because of dark magic," they whispered.

"She's a witch," they said.

"She could kill you, you know," they threatened, "with a snap of her fingers."

Nonsense, Jessamine thought as she overturned the bin and carefully climbed on top. *There's no such thing as witches.*

Now she could see the whole of the next garden and the back door of the house. The lights inside were off. Surely even the oldest witch in creation would be asleep at this hour. Besides, it's not like Jessamine had any real crime in mind. She'd simply do some weeding. She was doing the old woman a favour.

Jessamine swung one leg over the fence. She groaned under the strain of pulling over the other leg and grabbed hold of the top of the fence to slowly let herself down. She dropped into a crouch again, a little less painfully this time, and immediately began picking up handfuls of dandelions and shoving them into her bag.

She was halfway across the small lawn, right at the foot of the scarecrow, on her hands and knees. Her bag was nearly full of dandelions, and so was her mouth. She smiled, the dark green chewed bits sticking out from her teeth, like she was some kind of madwoman. But she didn't care.

Behind her, something snapped, a twig or a light switch, maybe, and she froze. Jessamine slowly turned her head and found the house still dark and quiet, the back door closed up tight. Even the windows were closed. *The old witch must have air-conditioning,* Jessamine thought. Then, from the darkness, a small form leaped at her.

Jessamine shrieked and rolled gracelessly onto her back as a black cat, its hair matted and caked with mud, landed on her chest. It hissed at her, its rotten mouth open wide, centimetres from her face, and Jessamine shrieked again. The cat bounded away from her, leaped to the top of the fence, and cast her a wicked look before moving on to a different street.

Jessamine sat up and caught her breath. A light clicked on in the witch's house. Jessamine grabbed her bag of weeds and climbed to her feet. It wasn't easy. Even more troubling, though: she had no idea how she would get back over the fence to her own garden.

I have no choice, Jessamine thought, and she ran for the gate to the front lawn. She clenched her fists tightly around the rolled-down top of her paper bag. The gate's latch stuck a bit, so she stepped back and kicked it hard. The latch popped open and fell to the ground, and the gate swung wide.

The back door of the house creaked open. Light flooded the weedy garden.

Jessamine ran into the front garden and cut across her building's lawn towards the front door. Then it struck her: she had no keys.

They were upstairs on the kitchen table.

"Who is that?" creaked a voice from next door. "Who's been in my garden?"

Garden?! Jessamine thought. Her mind reeled. She pounded on the front door of her block of flats. "Please," she shouted. "Let me in!"

"I hear you," the old woman called to her with a voice dusty and old, but in a tone singsong and lovely. "You'll not get away, pretty pregnant neighbour."

Jessamine gasped. The woman knew who she was. *She* is *a witch,* Jessamine thought, the idea rushing through her body like ice water. She pounded harder on the door. "Anyone!" she shouted. "Please let me in."

"Jessa?" said a warm and gentle voice behind her.

She spun as she felt her husband's hand on her shoulder. "What's going on?" Bodhi asked.

Jessamine shook her head violently. "Just open the door," she said, practically sobbing. "We have to get inside right now."

"Why?" Bodhi said, but he pulled his keys from his pocket and opened the door. Jessamine hurried in and pulled the door closed behind them, making sure it was locked. Then she ran for the stairs.

"Jessa!" Bodhi called from behind her. But she didn't stop. She hadn't moved that fast in months. In seconds, she was at their front door, drumming her palms on her thighs, wishing her husband could keep up. When he unlocked the door, Jessamine shoved it open, pulled Bodhi inside and slammed it closed. She locked the bolt, put on the chain and crouched against the door.

"Shh," she hissed at Bodhi.

"I'll just turn on some lights," he said, but she grabbed his arm.

"Don't!" she snapped. "She's watching us."

"Who?!" Bodhi said.

Jessamine looked into her husband's face, filled with care and confusion, and she realized what she'd done. Her hand went to her mouth. "Oh, Bodhi," she said, falling against his chest. "I've been a madwoman."

"Tell me what happened," he said, and she did. By the time she was done, both of them were crying with laughter, sitting together on the floor in front of the door.

"Then ... then," Jessamine said, wiping the back of her hand across her eyes, "you showed up. 'What's going on?!'" She did her best deep-voice Bodhi impression.

"You should have seen you!" Bodhi said, smiling big. "You looked like–"

"A crazy person?" Jessamine said.

Bodhi nodded. "Exactly," he said. They smiled at each other. "We should try to sleep," Bodhi said. He stood up and offered his hands to his wife.

She groaned as she rose and said, "You know, I think I might sleep tonight. I feel … settled."

Together, they walked to the bedroom, Bodhi with his arm around his wife's waist, and Jessamine with her hands on her swelling belly.

* * *

For several nights, Jessamine and Bodhi slept well. He thought it was because of the cooler nights, as the temperature after midnight dropped below twenty-five degrees for the first time in weeks. Jessamine, though, thought it was because of the dandelion leaves.

"I was craving something, and I got it," she said at bedtime early the next week. "Now my body can finally and truly relax and shut down at bedtime."

Bodhi watched his wife roll to her side and hug a pillow. She had three pillows in the bed now. It took that many to hold her body just so. Lying down comfortably wasn't easy for a woman who was pregnant. Only when he knew she was asleep – her breathing slow, a snore like a babbling brook rising up from her open mouth – did Bodhi shut his eyes and let sleep take him as well.

Hours later, he woke with a start. It was still dark. The clock shined red numerals at him. It wasn't yet four in the morning. Something had woken him, though. Bodhi reached across the bed and found the sheets empty and cold.

"Jessa?" he said quietly. There was no reply. He sat up and found the switch for the lamp, but as he touched it, something crashed in the kitchen. He left the lamp off and got up.

As quietly as he could, Bodhi moved down the short, narrow hall. A light was on in the kitchen – the one over the hob. There came another crash of a bowl or plate falling and smashing against the worktop.

Bodhi jumped around the corner, into the kitchen and found his wife. She was up on the worktop, on her knees, digging madly through the cupboard, tossing things to the floor as she rummaged. A mess of flour, rice, bruised apples, smashed plates and glasses, and other kitchen items littered the worktop and floor.

"Jessa!" Bodhi shouted over the noise. She didn't reply. She didn't even pause in her madness. It was as if she was sleepwalking. He went to her and grabbed her arm. "Please stop!"

His touch seemed to snap her out of her trance, at least partially. She twisted her body to look at him. "I'm hungry."

"I see that," Bodhi said. "Let me help you down."

She did get down, but standing there, with her hands on his upper arms, her fingers digging into him like talons, the madness didn't drain from her face.

"What are you hungry for?" Bodhi said, though he suspected he knew the answer.

She leaned close to him, so her lips were almost against his. "Dandelions," she said, her voice deep and breathy. The word made Bodhi shiver.

"You're serious," Bodhi said. She nodded vigorously. Bodhi took a deep breath. He pushed her hair, wild and yellow, back from her forehead, like he was soothing a child. "Let's go back to bed," he said. "In the morning, maybe you'll feel more like yourself."

She knocked his hand away, though. "I am myself," she snapped. "And I want dandelions."

"Honey–" he began, but she cut him off.

"The witch's dandelions," she added. "Only those. Now."

Bodhi could hardly believe this woman was his wife, a good-humoured woman without a drop of violence in her heart. Now, standing here with her, he thought she might hit him.

"Don't you remember, Jessa?" Bodhi said. He used his gentlest voice. "Last time ... the old woman next door? She scared you really badly."

"It doesn't matter," she said, shaking her head. Her wild yellow hair fell around her face. "Are you too afraid?"

Bodhi thought of that night, his wife's panicked face as she pounded on their building's front door.

"Then I'll go myself," Jessamine said, pulling away from him.

"No!" he said, grabbing her wrist. "If you feel that strongly about it, I'll go for you. Of course I'll go."

Jessamine sat down at the table and crossed her arms. She stared at her husband with wild, wide eyes. "Well? What are you waiting for?"

"I'll have to get dressed first," Bodhi said, and he went to the bedroom.

* * *

"I can't believe I'm doing this," Bodhi muttered to himself. He didn't go down the fire escape like his wife had, and he didn't hop over the fence. With a canvas tote bag over his shoulder, he took his keys, went out the front door and stepped through the gate. Its latch was still broken.

Then he dropped to his knees, sighed deeply and began plucking dandelion leaves. He'd been at it not more than a couple of minutes when he spotted the cat on the fence watching him.

"Good morning," Bodhi said, still plucking leaves nearby the scarecrow's feet. "Do you belong to the mistress of the house?"

The cat prowled back and forth along the top of the fence, then leaped to the scarecrow's stiff shoulder to watch Bodhi more closely.

"I hope you don't mind," Bodhi said, putting his attention back on the dandelions. "Just taking a few of these weeds off your paws, and then I'll be on my way."

"I do mind, actually," replied a thin and raspy voice.

Bodhi looked up, convinced for a moment that this matted stray cat had spoken to him. When he realized the truth, though, his skin went cold. He looked straight up into the wide and living eyes of the scarecrow. It cackled down at him, and Bodhi fell backwards from his crouched position. He stumbled as he tried to get up and run.

"Run if you like," the scarecrow taunted him from behind. "I know very well where to find you."

Bodhi, up on one knee and about to speed towards the gate, stopped himself. He caught his breath. Surely the scarecrow hadn't spoken. It was impossible. Bodhi had gone mad. Whatever wicked virus had infected his wife's pregnant brain had his under its spell as well.

He almost laughed. Then he shook his head and turned around. The scarecrow, though, hadn't finished with him yet. It dropped down from its post. At first its footing was wobbly, like it might fall right to the ground in a heap of old clothes and straw. Quickly, though, it found its composure.

Bodhi saw, then, that this was no scarecrow at all. What he had first thought was a floppy bunch of rags packed with hay and held up with sticks, he now saw had a real nose, sharp and pinched. He saw it had real eyes, narrow and bloodshot, with centres that were almost yellow. It had hair, too, long and silver, tumbling from its head.

He also saw that it had hands, with crooked, knotty fingers. He knew this because one grabbed his wrist. This was no scarecrow.

This was the old witch herself.

"Retribution," she said, in the same raspy voice the scarecrow had used.

Not the scarecrow, Bodhi told himself. *It was the woman the whole time.*

"R-r-retribution?" he stammered.

"Payment," the witch said. She let go of his wrist. "You and your wife have taken bushels of my dandelion leaves."

She got up on her toes and leaned close to him, so close he could smell food on her breath, and added, "You owe me."

"For weeds?" Bodhi said.

"*Stolen* weeds," she said.

"I can pay you," Bodhi said.

The witch stepped back and looked him up and down. "That watch," she said, pointing one spindly finger at his wrist.

Bodhi pulled off the watch. It wasn't much to look at, but it had been his father's. "It's not worth much," he said.

The woman shook her head, dismissing the idea. She tapped one long black fingernail against her front tooth and squinted at Bodhi.

"Perhaps you'd like to think about this," Bodhi said, forcing a smile. He was desperate to appear calm. He wasn't calm, though. "I'll come back when it's more convenient." He backed away as he spoke, feeling behind him for the gate. To his surprise, though, he never found it. He only found tall weeds and the bark of narrow young trees.

The witch laughed. "Look around you," she said. "You'll not leave here until we've settled on a price."

Around him, the garden had changed. This was no longer a tiny, overgrown garden, hidden behind a pair of buildings. It was a thick forest, and the moon hung low and fat in the sky.

"Where am I?" Bodhi said. His voice shook.

"You're safe," she said, "for now. I'll release you when we've settled on a price."

"Please," Bodhi said. "My wife will be worried. I've been gone too long. She just wanted to eat some dandelion leaves." He laughed lightly. "You know how women are sometimes. They have these cravings."

The witch's face seemed to light up as Bodhi spoke. "She is with child," the witch said.

Bodhi nodded.

"Then the child," the old woman said. "She shall be the payment." She turned away from him, waving her hand. The garden shimmered, returning to its normal form.

"Wait," Bodhi said. He grabbed her wrist. She spun and stared at his hand, and pain like fire shot up Bodhi's arm until he let her go.

"We've settled on a price," she said. "Take your weeds – all you like – and go home."

"Not that," Bodhi said, unwilling to leave. "Anything but that." But the old woman was already heading back inside.

"Please!" Bodhi called after her as the door closed behind her. From the top of the fence, the black cat hissed at him. Bodhi, his shoulders sagging and his heart heavy, dragged his sack of weeds through the open gate and back to his flat.

* * *

"I don't know what you're so worried about," Jessamine said. She sat at the kitchen table, madly stabbing at the dandelion leaves with her fork and shoving them into her mouth. She hadn't bothered with a bowl this time. She'd simply dumped the sack onto the table and started eating.

Bodhi paced behind her chair. He could hardly believe what his wife was saying. Had she really lost her mind?

"It's not like she's just going to stroll in here and take our baby," Jessamine said through a mouthful of leaves. Dark green bits sprayed across the table. She didn't seem to notice.

"You didn't see her," Bodhi said. "Not like I did." His heart still raced. "She really is a witch … or something." He dropped into the chair beside his wife. "We have to run."

"Run?" she said, her eyes on her wild salad, her arm still working, moving the fork back and forth between her mouth and the pile.

"Away," Bodhi said. He took her hand, but she only pulled it away to continue eating. "We're leaving this place. Leaving this city."

"Oh, please," she said. "And where would we go?"

"Anywhere," Bodhi said, sighing. He stood up. "I'm going to pack. Only the essentials."

Jessamine grabbed his arm. "Stop," she said. "There's no hurry. I'm not due till Christmas."

Bodhi sat again, reluctantly. He sighed again.

Jessamine ate for a few more minutes, then leaned back with her hands on her belly. "Thank you," she said. "That was wonderful."

"You feel better?" Bodhi said.

Jessamine nodded, a big smile on her round and red-cheeked face, and stood up. "We should get some sleep," she said.

Bodhi nodded slowly. He was so tired. He could hardly keep his head up and eyes open. "There was something else," he said. His mind was unclear, like a fog had blown in and settled in his brain. "Something important."

"How important could it be at five in the morning?" his wife said. "Let's get to bed."

Bodhi stood and took his wife's hand. "I'm sure it was something urgent," he said, his voice quiet and weak. "I was going to do something. We were arguing about it. I think."

Jessamine squeezed his hand. "When we wake up," she said. "When we wake up."

* * *

The autumn was mild and lovely. Jessamine's health was good, and the baby, according to the doctor, was developing perfectly.

Bodhi was given a promotion at his day job, so he was able to quit his night job.

One morning in late November, Jessamine stood at the kitchen window, looking out over the cement behind the building and the wild garden next door. Three men worked to clear out the brush and weeds and ragged-looking little trees.

She called Bodhi to the window to look.

"Perhaps she moved," Bodhi said. "And perhaps the new owners are finally going to do something with that miserable garden."

Jessamine frowned. She didn't think that was right, but she wasn't sure why.

"I won't miss her," Bodhi said, stepping away from the window and placing his coffee cup in the sink. "She always gave me the creeps."

Jessamine frowned again. There was something about that old woman … but she couldn't quite put her finger on what it was. Come to think of it, she couldn't even bring a picture of the woman's face into her mind. She wondered, just for a moment, if she'd ever even met the woman.

She felt a kiss on her cheek and then heard the front door slam. It was the only way it closed. A moment later, she gritted her teeth, dropped her mug of hot chocolate and held on to the windowsill as if for dear life.

The baby was coming.

* * *

The labour was long. Bodhi stayed at Jessamine's side the whole time. Nearly twenty hours later, a baby girl was born. She had her father's pale blue eyes. She had her mother's little pursed lips, and she had a full head of bright yellow hair. The nurses had washed her and capped her head with a little pink and blue hat. Jessamine pulled it off, and the little girl's hair fluffed up like dandelion petals.

Then they remembered.

As Jessamine, her hair matted to her forehead, held her new girl against her, and as Bodhi knelt beside their bed, his eyes red, it all flooded back. It was as if someone had lifted the heavy curtains in a dark room, letting sunlight pour in.

Bodhi jumped to his feet. "We have to go," he said. "We have to run, right now."

"Swaddle her," Jessamine said, handing the brand-new baby to Bodhi. "I have to get dressed."

Bodhi nodded and wrapped the sleeping child in a thin hospital blanket. Holding her against his chest, he stuck his head out the room door. His skin went cold before he spotted her: the witch, standing at the nurses' desk only a few metres away, holding a bouquet of balloons.

Bodhi darted back into the room. "She's here," he hissed. He pressed the baby into his wife's arms, her coat only half on. He grabbed their small rucksack and Jessamine's big handbag, and then caught his wife by the elbow and pulled her out of the room.

The emergency exit to the stairs was nearby. Bodhi, with one hand still on his wife's elbow, slammed through the door. Alarms shrieked. A red light flashed in the hall. Nurses jumped up from their desks.

The new family of three rushed down the concrete stairs, their steps echoing through the stairwell, along with the steps of nurses following. At the bottom, Bodhi slammed his shoulder into the heavy exit door, sending another wave of sirens and red lights into a frenzy.

It had begun to snow in the night, and now it came with high winds and blinding whiteness. Jessamine wrapped her winter coat around her baby and followed Bodhi into the blizzard. He reached the car first, the old grey hatchback Bodhi had been driving since he was a teenager. Both of them wondered if it would start as he climbed in and cranked it once, twice, three times. Nothing.

Jessamine strapped the baby into the car seat and stayed in the back as her husband cursed to himself and thumped the steering wheel. "Come on! Start!" he shouted, and he brought down his fist on the dashboard. The car coughed and then roared to life.

The tyres screeched on the dry concrete. Jessamine leaned forward as Bodhi manoeuvred the little car towards the exit. "Turn on the heat?" she asked.

He didn't respond. He gripped the wheel with both hands so his knuckles were white. The car launched at the gate, down and waiting for payment, but Bodhi didn't stop. Jessamine curled her arms over the baby and shrieked as they ploughed right through the gate and into the blizzard. Bodhi found the motorway, took the first entrance he could and sped west.

* * *

"We have to stop," Jessamine said. She had to scream over the baby's crying. "She's hungry. She's wet."

"Not yet," Bodhi said. He kept his eyes on the road and his cramped hands on the wheel.

The snow had stopped an hour before. The little car zoomed down a desolate country road, flat and straight as far as the eye could see. On either side of the road sat snow-covered farmland, divided by strips of evergreen trees, tall and spindly.

"Please, Bodhi," Jessamine said. "There's no one fol-lowing us. Pull over. I'll feed her and change her and we'll keep going."

He looked in the rearview mirror at the barren road behind them, and he might have stopped for his wife and daughter. But at that moment, lightning cracked against the road in front of them, sending chunks of blacktop in every direction and leaving a crater behind. From the smoky hole in the road, a huge globe of light began to rise. It hovered towards the car.

Bodhi slammed on the brakes. The wheels screeched, and Bodhi lost control of the car. It rolled off the road and landed on its side. Bodhi's head spun. He struggled to open his eyes, but finally saw his wife in the backseat. Her eyes were closed. Her hair was matted against a bloody spot on her forehead. The baby screamed, her little eyes and fists squeezed tight against the noise of the howling winds and booming thunder.

Bodhi whispered, "The witch." He reached for his seat belt. But he could hardly move. Through the windshield, he watched the globe of light burst. A woman hovered before him. Today she was not the same bent old woman. She wore a blindingly white dress that hung past her feet instead of patched together black and brown rags. But he knew: it was the witch.

"No," he tried to scream, but he could hardly make a sound. The witch moved around the car, opened the door, and grabbed the baby.

The last thing Bodhi saw before he fainted was the witch floating off into the nearby fields, the baby in her arms.

* * *

A fourteen-year-old girl stood at her bedroom window, looking out over wintery fields. That window was where she always stood to practise her violin.

"It sounds wonderful, Dandelion!" her mother cooed from the hall.

Dandelion smiled a little, as much as she could with the instrument against her chin and throat. It did sound wonderful. It hardly felt like practising anymore. She could barely remember when it wasn't fun, in fact.

Mother had told her stories, of course, about when Dandelion was a tiny child, with a child's violin, throwing tantrums on the living room floor, unwilling to practise even a second more. Mother was patient. Always patient. And now Dandelion's talent shined as brightly as her golden hair.

"Your hair is as bright as the petals of a dandelion," her mother always said. Every evening, they sat together in the dressing room, and Mother pulled a brush through her hair a hundred times.

It had never been cut, Mother said, and Dandelion believed it. Her hair was long enough to tangle on her bed's footboard as she slept.

When Dandelion was six years old, she had gone to her mother, who was busy boiling something in the kitchen, as usual, and asked her, "Where's my father?"

"You have no father," her mother told her.

Dandelion thought of the families she'd seen at the supermarket in town. She thought of the stories she read in the books that filled the shelves in her little bedroom at the back of the house. "Why not?" the girl asked.

"You're far too special for a father," her mother told her, setting down the stirring spoon and placing a hand on each of the girl's shoulders. "I raised you, instead, from the earth. I planted a seed in the garden next to this house, and you grew up from the ground like a flower."

"Oh," Dandelion said, and she thought about her name and her hair that grew wild and yellow, and she smiled. She was a fairy tale.

"Now go and practise your violin," her mother said, taking up the spoon again. "You know I love to hear you play."

At fourteen, though, Dandelion had begun to feel that something was strange about her. She saw others her age, on the rare occasion that she went to Main Street on the weekends. A boy with hair like rough-hewn hay worked at the supermarket. He said hello to her once, and Dandelion scurried off, feeling her face go hot and red.

There was another boy she knew. He brought the newspaper. One morning, Dandelion was in the garden pulling weeds – all but the dandelions, of course – when she heard the paper *thwack* against the front door. She brushed the dirt from her knees and pulled off her gloves, and then hurried to fetch the paper for her mother.

To Dandelion's surprise, the delivery boy was still there, leaning on the corner of the house, his arms and ankles crossed, watching her with wide eyes the colour of chocolate.

"Morning," he said.

"Good morning," Dandelion said, and she pulled her eyes away from his to look at the path she stood on instead.

"Look, if your mother's home," the boy said, standing up straight and moving towards her, "she owes for the last three months of delivery."

Dandelion looked up. The boy held out an envelope. He shook it once, like she ought to take it from him. "It's the bill," he said.

She bit her lip and snatched the envelope from him. Then she turned on her heel and ran for the side door.

"Mother!" she said, running into the kitchen, where her mother was at the hob, her eyes on a recipe book. "The newspaper boy gave me this."

Mother glared at Dandelion over the top of her reading glasses and put out her hand for the envelope. She tore it open with a fingernail, scanned its message, and then tore it up and dropped the shreds into the pan on the hob. She went back to her book.

"Where did you get that?" she said.

"The paper boy," Dandelion said. "H-he handed it to me." She remembered his rich brown eyes. She remembered his black hair, which fell at an angle across his forehead, like someone had cut his hair with hedge trimmers while falling off a ladder. Dandelion giggled.

Her mother faced her and pulled off her glasses. "Did he do something funny?" she asked. Her voice was rigid and deep.

"No," Dandelion said. She crossed her fingers behind her back. She always did when Mother was angry with her, even if she didn't know why she was angry.

"You giggled," Mother said. "A most unpleasant sound."

"Sorry," Dandelion said. "I'll get back to weeding."

"A moment!" Mother said as Dandelion turned. "I'll be cancelling the paper at once."

"Why?" Dandelion asked, keeping her voice calm and gentle. But her heart sank.

She hadn't realized it, but she hoped to see that boy again. In some part of her brain and her heart, she even planned to be in the front garden tomorrow morning to greet him.

Mother looked down at her. She cocked her head and gave Dandelion a cold stare with one eye. "First, there was the boy at the supermarket," Mother said.

Dandelion flinched.

"You thought I didn't notice how he made your cheeks flush?" Mother went on. "You think I missed the look in your eyes?"

Dandelion crossed all her fingers.

"And now the paper boy has caught your eye," Mother said. "Giggling. At your age."

"I'm sorry, Mother," Dandelion said.

"Sorry?" She turned off the hob and closed her recipe book. "You're fourteen."

What did that have to do with anything?

"Yes, Mother," Dandelion said.

"Well," Mother said like the word was a breath of clean air after years underground. "Nothing to be done about it. I have a plan."

"A plan?" Dandelion said.

Mother smiled at her. She seemed her normal stature again, with her eyes just at the level of Dandelion's. She patted the girl's head, smoothed some wisps of golden hair that had escaped from the girl's complicated plaits and bun. "I'd better get to work," Mother said.

That was ten days ago. Since then, Mother had been keeping quite busy – not in the house as she usually was, but off in the woods, where Dandelion was forbidden to go.

Whatever plan Mother was hatching, she was hatching it out there somewhere, and Dandelion was worried.

* * *

The witch stood by the river. It rushed through the strip of woods – a two-hour walk from the back door of her house. She could hear it from her kitchen. It spoke to her.

Sometimes it said things idly, like: "The fallen oak near the Harrison farm on the A61 has finally been overtaken by fly amanita mushrooms. Go harvest them."

Sometimes it said things far heavier. It told her things like: "Mr Cole, at the bank, is struggling for breath right now. He's having a heart attack. He's dying."

This afternoon, as she'd walked from the house to the river, it spoke to her the whole time. "She'll betray you," it said, its voice bubbling and bright. "She'll throw herself at any boy who comes along."

The witch muttered a curse at the river and plodded along.

"Unless you lock her away," the river said, its voice now rushing and violent.

The witch smiled now, standing at the river, and held her staff over her head in both hands. She shouted in a language barely spoken in a thousand years. The earth around her rumbled. The river tossed and laughed with glee. Then the witch smiled and walked back to the house.

"Come with me," she said, standing at Dandelion's bedroom door. "Bring the violin."

"Where?" Dandelion said, already standing up and packing the instrument. She didn't disobey her mother.

The witch moved to Dandelion's dressing table and collected her hairbrushes. She shoved them into a bag and hurried to the back door.

"Mother?" Dandelion called behind her, but the witch didn't answer, didn't look back, didn't even slow down.

She heard the girl hurrying to keep up, her timid footsteps on the path behind her. The girl was always so timid. It sickened the witch, but she wouldn't have it any other way.

When the girl was beside her and keeping step, the witch said to her, "I told you, didn't I, that I had a plan?"

"Oh," the girl said. "I hoped you'd forgotten."

"Forgotten?" the witch snapped.

The girl was as big a fool as her mother and father had been, thinking she could commit any act she wanted, no matter how senseless, and go unpunished.

"I was stupid to think so," the girl said. "Obviously."

The witch nodded and hurried her pace. "We should hurry," she said. "It'll be dark soon."

Now the river screamed at her. It shouted maddening lies about the girl. It shrieked warnings to the witch. The witch growled at the river.

"Lies," she whispered to herself. "You're trying to protect her."

The girl coughed.

"The river is a greater romantic than I imagined," the witch said, laughing. Neither she nor the girl spoke again till they reached the woods that lined the river. It was quiet now, calm and bubbly, moving along like an old man on a summer night's stroll.

"That's better," the witch mumbled. She let herself smile and turned to the girl – her daughter. "I'm so pleased you're here, Dandelion."

The girl lifted her chin. She even seemed ready to smile. The girl hardly ever smiled anymore. Lately she was always red-faced or flustered, or stomping through the hall or the garden, frustrated or stricken or wallowing.

"I need you here with me to finish the enchantment, you see," the witch said. She took her girl by the shoulders and led her to a flat rock on the river's edge. "Sit."

The girl did so, carefully gathering her dress. She only wore dresses, unless she was working in the garden. She laid the violin across her knees and looked up at the witch – at her mother.

Once again, the witch held her staff in both hands over her head. She turned her back on the girl and spoke to the sun, now close to the western horizon. She dug deep inside her to find the right words to complete the spell she'd worked on for so many days.

My child will be safe now, she thought as she spoke the ancient words. *And the world will be safe from her.*

The world itself must have agreed with her, because as the witch spoke, the earth at Dandelion's feet cracked and seethed. It shot up two roots, which grabbed Dandelion's ankles and wrists, holding her in place on the rock. In a big circle around her, more rocks pushed through the soil, shook loose of dirt, and rose up around her, encircling her and lifting her up into the sky.

The girl screamed. The witch couldn't hear her over the violent din of her enchantment, but she could see her gaping mouth and her eyes wide with fear. Soon she'd cry, too, but it was all for the best.

Everything the witch did, everything she'd done for the last fourteen years, had always been for the best. Would the girl have preferred living in a stinking old block of flats in a disgusting city with horrible, thieving parents and going hungry as often as not? And by now she would have fallen in and out of love dozens of times.

She'd end up just like her mother, the witch told herself as she watched the tower of earth and stone rise up from the woods.

The spell was complete.

"Mother!" Dandelion called, and the witch looked up at her. The girl stood at the tower's window, her hands on the stone sill. Her face was dirty and bruised, with a fresh cut on one cheek. "What have you done?"

"My plan, daughter," the witch said. "You'll be safe there."

"From what?" the girl shrieked down at her. Her voice, shrill and panicked, sent an electric shiver up and down the witch's spine.

The witch shut her eyes and clenched her jaw against her senses. *Weak, timid and afraid,* the witch thought. *A few years in my tower will surely fix that.*

"Please!" the girl shouted down to her as the witch turned to walk away. "You can't leave me here!"

"You'll be safe there," the witch said. "Safe forever. You have your violin!"

The witch walked on, and she was halfway back to the house when she finally heard the sorrowful strains of the girl's violin.

* * *

Arthur Oak was fourteen, and he didn't care.

"Heading down to hunt for frogs again?" his big brother teased him as they finished their breakfast of microwave sausage patties and hard-boiled eggs. It was all the older boy knew how to cook.

"Don't worry about it," Arthur said. He popped his egg in his mouth as he pulled on his trainers. "I'll be back in time for the bus."

"You'd better be," his brother called after him. Arthur pushed through the back door. "If I have to explain why you missed the bus, I'll kick your bum into the middle of next week!"

The door slammed behind Arthur, and in a few moments he was clear across their back field. The Oaks' property ended at the low stone wall, but Arthur didn't care. He hopped over it. No one owned the land that ran for about a mile on either side of the river. At least, no one Arthur knew about.

He'd been coming down here, sometimes in the morning, sometimes after school, sometimes all day on a weekend, since he was four years old. He'd find frogs, build forts, try to catch a fish, go for a swim – anything he wanted.

Arthur's brother had stopped joining him on these explorations years ago. He said boys in secondary school shouldn't be playing with toads. They should be learning to drive and getting girlfriends and playing guitars. But Arthur didn't care.

He jogged the whole way to the river. Before he reached the narrow band of woods that protected his stretch of the river from eyes up on the road, he spotted it: a stone tower rising up just past the treetops on the far side.

"Huh," he said. "That's new."

But it wasn't new, not really. As he got closer, he could tell that the stones, green with moss and with no rough edges, had been there for centuries. Millennia, even. This tower was older than any building around here for miles.

"Why haven't I ever seen it before?" he said. He pushed through the woods on his side of the river and stopped right at the water's edge.

The river frothed against the rocks, spraying his bare legs even though the wind was calm.

Arthur stood at the edge, enjoying the feel of the spray on his legs. It was a hot morning, though already September. He looked up at the tower and wished he could get across the river to take a closer look. Arthur swore the river sometimes spoke to him, but today he heard something else. A new sound. A sound that didn't belong in the woods or on the river.

It was simple music. A violin, he thought, or one of those other things some members of the school orchestra played that looked like violins of different sizes. It was very beautiful.

Arthur took off his shoes and socks and stepped into the river. For some people, the river wasn't safe. The river would grab hold of a body and pull it along, tumbling and tossing it with the foam, into rocks and around bends till the river spat the body out ten miles closer to the city – if the body was lucky. Otherwise it might be dragged out to the sea.

Over the last ten years, Arthur and the river had learned to trust each other. He knew it wouldn't take him on a morning this peaceful.

A little closer to the tower, Arthur squinted up through the trees and spotted a window, but the inside was too dark to make anything out.

"But it's a person," he whispered. "There's someone up there playing music."

He put his hands around his mouth and called up, "Hello!" He waited an answer, for the music to stop. Nothing. He tried again. Nothing happened.

"Whoever it is can't hear me," he said quietly, shaking his head. "I have to get closer."

But just then, he realized he had to get back. "The bus!" he said. He hurried to pull on his shoes and socks. If he ran as hard as he could, he'd still catch the bus. Hopefully.

* * *

"What happened to you?" asked Jasper Steel when Arthur dropped into the seat next to him.

"What do you mean?" Arthur pulled up his shirt to wipe the sweat from his face.

"Are you kidding?" Jasper said. "You look like you just ran over here from all the way across town."

"I was down at the river," Arthur said.

"Of course," Jasper said. "What else is new."

Arthur shook his head. "Today was different," he whispered, almost to himself. "There was ... forget it."

"What?" said Jasper.

Should he tell him about it? Arthur wasn't so sure. The river had always been his, and now it had shown its greatest mystery of all: an ancient tower, haunting music.

Arthur turned and looked out of the bus window as it rumbled down the road. "Never mind," he said. "Just another frog. A big one."

The other boy laughed. "You never change, do you, Arthur?" he said.

"I guess not," Arthur said. But he had the distinct feeling he just had.

* * *

Dandelion sat in her tower room with her violin on her lap.

It wasn't a bad room. In fact, it was exactly like her bedroom at the house, except it was at the top of an enchanted tower instead of at the back of a little country cottage.

Somehow, her mother had created this tower out of stones and the ground, filling the room with a bed and chair and dressing table just like the ones Dandelion had always had.

For the first few nights, Dandelion didn't do much besides cry and play her violin. She was lonely, confused and angry. Before long, she was hungry, too. That's when Mother came.

"My dear daughter Dandelion," her mother called from below. "Let your hair down to me, so I can climb up."

Dandelion almost laughed. Using her hair as a rope to climb? It was ridiculous. She went to the window, her arms crossed, and let all of her anger seep into her words. "You must be kidding," she said.

"The plait will hold," her mother called. "Wrap it around the bedpost for extra support."

Dandelion sucked her cheek and stared down at her mother's big, silver eyes. Always a different colour, those eyes. Dandelion's were always blue – pale and flat, as interesting as a big, cloudless sky. But not Mother's.

She's not normal, Dandelion thought as she sighed and went to the bed.

She wound the plait around a bedpost, as her mother had suggested, and went back to the window. "Now what?" she shouted.

"Now throw down the end," her mother said. "I'll climb up to you." She held up a small basket. "I have your lunch here."

"What is it?" Dandelion called down from the window.

"Your favourites," Mother said, pulling back the cloth from the top of the basket. "Chicken salad sandwiches and watermelon slices."

"No chocolate?" Dandelion said. She risked a smile, and her mother smiled back.

"Perhaps," she said, and her teeth and eyes twinkled. She pulled her free hand from behind her back and held up a big chocolate bar, the kind with toffee – the best kind.

Dandelion whispered an excited "Yes!" as she tossed her hair out of the window. It fell just long enough so that her mother could grab hold of the end.

Mother climbed up with the basket hanging from her elbow. The climb looked much easier to Dandelion than she thought it would be.

Of course, Dandelion thought. *Everything is easy for Mother.*

She took her mother's arm and helped her climb in.

"We'll eat," Mother said, straightening her dress, "and then we'll play." She shot her daughter a stern glance. "You have been practising, haven't you?"

Dandelion dropped onto the bed and threw up her hands. "What else is there to do?"

Mother smiled at her, as if Dandelion's complaint was a minor issue, not as if being locked in an enchanted tower by a mother who was possibly a madwoman was actually anything to be upset about.

Mother laid a picnic blanket on the tower chamber floor and Dandelion joined her, sighing. Then she put out the bowl of watermelon slices – they looked like little smiling upside down Vs – and the chicken salad sandwiches.

"You have your books," Mother said. She sat down on the blanket and placed a hand on Dandelion's cheek. "You have me."

"Not for the last three days," Dandelion said in a serious tone.

Mother stood up. "Really, darling," she said. "It's not as if you've never been on your own before. I've been busy. You must learn to keep yourself busy, too."

* * *

After they ate, Mother put the dishes away. "Now," she said, "let's play something."

"What should we play?" Dandelion said.

In response, Mother went to the window and looked out for a moment. Then she turned back to face the room and began to sing.

Dandelion recognized it at once ... one of Mother's favourites. She never understood the words; most of Mother's songs were in a language Dandelion didn't understand.

Dandelion put her violin under her chin and began to play along. It was an easy piece for her, though her mother's part was erratic, with octave jumps and long holds of very high notes.

Dandelion kept her eyes on her mother at the window. The sunlight streaming in gave the older woman a golden aura. When the song was over, Mother clapped gently, smiling at her daughter.

"Can't I come home?" Dandelion said.

Her mother frowned. "My dearest girl," she said, "this is your home."

* * *

Arthur visited the tower every day. When he had the time, he'd run down before the school bus came.

By the end of the first month of school, Arthur had found a way to cross the river, but it was too far upstream for rushed mornings. There was a little bridge, probably made two hundred years ago by some farmer who used to own the land all over this area. Somehow it still stood.

It was after school each day that he took the extra-long walk along the riverbank and crossed to the other side, then hiked back downstream to find the tower. He circled the tower, thinking he'd find a door – probably a locked door – and instead found nothing.

"Hello!" Arthur called up, his hands around his mouth. Surely the violinist would hear him from this close.

But no reply came. The violin kept playing, and when it stopped to rest, Arthur shouted again, but only silence greeted him.

"A ladder," he said. "I'll have to get a ladder." But how he'd haul a ladder down here from his house all by himself, he had no idea.

* * *

Arthur never told anyone about the tower or the music. He never asked anyone to help him bring a ladder there. How could he explain? He'd have to tell them *everything*. But more than that, he'd have to share his tower.

So he simply visited every day, often before school, and always after school. He'd cross the river and sit on a big rock at the tower's base. He'd watch the river and listen to the music.

One morning, a couple of older boys on the bus spotted Arthur running up the hill to the bus stop. "Where you been, Art?" they said, knowing how much he hated that nickname.

Arthur tried to ignore them and make his way past them to find a seat. But the boys blocked the aisle. "We know where you were," they said. "You were down by the weird old tower, weren't you?"

Arthur froze. Did other people know about the tower? Were other people visiting it, listening to the music, wondering who lived inside?

He'd never seen anyone else there, and he was there almost any time he didn't have to be in school or at the dinner table or doing his homework.

"What do you know about it?" Arthur asked, narrowing his eyes at the boys.

They laughed. "Plenty," they said. "We know all about the girl who lives up there."

A girl?

"And we know she's crazy," they said, "just like her mum – the old witch."

A witch?

"And if you keep going down to the tower," they said, leaning close to him and sneering like hyenas, "you'll go crazy, too." They stood back, crossing their arms, and added, "As if you're not already. Art."

Arthur snarled and lunged at them, flailing and grabbing. He knocked them to the ground, having surprised them so well. But a moment later, they had him in their seat on his back.

They punched his arms and legs and chest until the bus driver slammed on the brakes and broke up the fight. Arthur found a seat right behind the driver. When he got to school, he was sent to the head teacher's office. Arthur had never even met the head teacher before. He'd only seen him walking the halls, slowly and menacing, towering over everyone else.

"Detention," the head teacher said. "All week. Beginning today."

Arthur did his time. He finished his homework in detention, but his mind was elsewhere. It was on the tower.

He wondered if those older boys on the bus had any idea what they were talking about. He wondered if there really was a girl up there. He wondered about the witch, too. He'd never seen a witch around, but he didn't get into town much lately.

Arthur took the late bus home. He dragged himself inside just in time for dinner.

By the time Arthur had done the dishes and shown his mother his homework, it was getting dark. He grabbed a torch, said that he was going for a walk and headed for the tower.

He'd never been down there so late. The night sky was clear and cold and filled with stars. The river was fast and shining, frothy at its edges, so the icy mist caught Arthur's face as he crossed the bridge to the tower's side.

The violin music was clear and fast as the river. It even shined. Arthur found his rock in the darkness and sat down. It was cold, but he didn't mind. "The music will warm me up," he told himself. And he listened.

After a moment, though, the violin wasn't alone. A voice joined in. It sang a melody so haunting and so foreign that it made Arthur's skin tingle. At first, he almost enjoyed it. Though he didn't understand the meaning of the words, he thought he understood their feelings. They struck him in the chest, and he clutched his hands together. Soon he was crying.

But before long, the voice became something too powerful, too strange, too frightening to listen to. Arthur became angry, afraid and breathless, and he had to get away.

He sped away from the tower, ran for the bridge and didn't stop running until he was inside his bedroom with the door locked behind him.

He decided he'd never go to the tower again.

But after a few days, it became clear the decision wasn't really his to make at all.

When he slept, Arthur's dreams filled with beautiful, strange images. Not pictures, exactly. They were just colours, icy ones and bright ones and sunny ones. If he had to try to identify what he saw, he might have said, "It's a perfect winter morning reflecting off the surface of a lazy, swollen river." But it wasn't just what he saw that haunted him. Had he only dreamed of those images, he might have been able to go on ignoring them, and the tower, for the rest of his life. No, he also *heard* something when he slept. He heard that violin.

Arthur couldn't remember the voice at all – the one that made his skin crawl and shiver and had sent him running back over the bridge and over the fields and into his bed. But the sound of the violin refused to leave his brain.

When he slept, it was the soundtrack to his beautiful dreams. When he was awake, he thought he heard it from around every corner. It was the song that seemed to leak from other people's headphones. It was the song that escaped through the open windows of passing cars on the road.

After three nights and three days of this, Arthur had to go back.

Arthur didn't even go into his house after the bus dropped him off that Wednesday afternoon. He dropped his rucksack in the porch and ran down the field to the bridge.

"I hope she's playing," he said to himself as he ran, hardly realizing that some small part of him did believe those boys from the bus. He was halfway over the bridge when he heard the violin, playing a happy and complex piece, as if in a duet with the rushing river beneath him.

He found his rock and was about to sit down to listen when he saw a woman approaching the tower from the far side. Quickly, he ducked into a thick patch of briar, wincing at the scrapes and catches of the thorny bushes.

The woman stopped at the base of the tower and looked up. She was very tall, with silver hair reaching past her waist. The way the witch moved, it almost seemed like she was floating just above the ground, rather than walking or standing.

"Dandelion!" the woman called out, looking up at the tower window. "Let down your hair to me!"

Arthur watched the window. The music stopped, and a girl appeared there. She had eyes as big and blue as the winter afternoon sky. Her hair was yellow and bright. She wore a simple green dress, as if she'd dressed to look as much like a flower as she could.

Arthur gasped out loud as the girl unravelled her yellow hair and let it down like a rope to the woman at the bottom.

If not for the river's rushing white noise, he'd have given himself away. As it was, he thought he saw the woman flinch, and he dropped deeper into the bushes and held his breath.

He sat there, listening to them play again. And again, the woman's voice, terrifying and exotic, sent shivers up and down his body. This time Arthur stayed strong, though. He sat on the cold ground with his arms around his pulled-up knees. He kept his eyes closed tight and his teeth clenched.

Arthur couldn't guess how long the piece went on. It could have been a few moments. It could have been an hour. When the violin and the singing stopped, he shook as if waking from a dream. A moment later, he heard voices.

"I don't want to stay up here!" said one voice, the younger voice.

That's Dandelion, Arthur thought.

"That decision is not yours to make!" the woman blasted back. "If you continue to argue with me about this, perhaps we should stop these visits for good."

"No!" Dandelion said, her voice now timid.

The woman laughed. "I thought your strong front was a lie," she said. "I'll be back tomorrow. I'll put the leftovers here for your breakfast."

Arthur poked his head out of the briar patch to watch the woman leave. This time she simply stepped off the windowsill and floated gently to the ground.

"She *is* a witch," Arthur whispered.

Dandelion ran to the window. "Please," she called after the woman. "Don't leave me here, Mother! Winter is coming," Dandelion said, nearly in tears. "I won't survive."

"You'll be fine," the witch called back in a singsong voice. "You'll be safe forever."

Arthur jumped up from the briar patch and ran for his house. He didn't know how yet, and he didn't know when, but he'd save that girl from the tower. He had to.

* * *

It was very late that same night, and the witch stood in her kitchen and stared into a simmering potion pot on the hob. She didn't sleep. She watched all day and all night.

The witch frowned. Didn't Dandelion see? The tower was for her own good, not for the witch's. The witch wished more than anything else that Dandelion could stay in the house with her, but a girl her age needed to be protected. And the world needed to be protected from her.

As the witch watched the pot, seeing all things at once, she became aware of the boy.

"I've seen this boy," she said aloud. "He lives on the hill beyond the river. He takes the bus with two dozen other dirty, foul little beasts."

"I know where you're going, boy!" the witch snarled at the pot.

She blasted from the kitchen and out the back door and flew towards the tower, just above the ground. As she streaked across the snow, she opened her mouth and let loose a wild, deafening shriek.

Fair warning, young man, she thought. *Leave my daughter alone.*

The witch zoomed across the snow-covered fields. In moments, the river was in sight, and beside it, standing tall and stark, was her daughter's tower.

Daughter, the witch thought darkly. *She's never truly been my daughter at all.*

The girl's golden hair hung from the window. The witch soared directly inside. "Where is he?" she roared at the girl.

Dandelion sat on the edge of her bed. "Wh-wh-who?" she stammered.

The witch sneered at the girl. "Don't try to deceive me," she said.

She sniffed the air. The boy hadn't been in the room; that much was certain. She hurried back to the window and peered into the darkness across the river. A lone black figure hurried up the white-covered slope.

"There he is," she said, letting a sinister smile crawl across her face. "I'll deal with him later." She spun on the girl. "But *you* will be dealt with right this moment."

"Please, Mother," Dandelion pleaded. "I haven't done anything."

The witch grabbed the girl by the wrist and pulled her to the window. "You let your hair down to that boy!" she snapped.

Dandelion pulled her arm, trying to get away.

The witch nearly laughed. "Where would you run to, girl," she said, "even if you were strong enough to escape my grip?"

The girl cried and stopped pulling, letting the witch lead her to the window.

"What will you do with me?" Dandelion said, sniffling.

"I will put you out," the witch said. "You've disappointed me, but it was my own foolishness. I should have known that raising a girl who wouldn't give in to these desires would be impossible in this world."

"Put me out?" Dandelion said. "Where?"

"In exile," the witch said. "You'll probably survive somehow, but you'll never find your way out of the woods. Before that, though, there is one thing I must do."

The witch pulled a pair of scissors from her sleeve.

* * *

Arthur stayed away that morning. For the first time in months, he was already waiting outside when the school bus rolled up to his stop. That sound – the witch rushing towards him … he couldn't get it out of his head.

"I never should have gone back to the tower," he muttered to himself.

He'd run away, leaving the girl alone to face that horrible woman. It haunted his memory all day. He couldn't focus on his lessons. Every sound he heard seemed drowned out by that terrible shriek.

"I have to go back again," he whispered to himself on the bus as it drove back towards his house.

From the peak of the hill a quarter mile up the road, he thought he could see the tower. He had to be wrong about that, though. He'd never noticed it from this point before.

Arthur hurried off the bus, dropped his rucksack next to the house, and ran down the hill, his feet sinking into the fresh snow. He slipped and slid and almost fell over and over, but he didn't stop. The bridge was icy with spray from the wild river. Arthur had never seen it so angry. "It's angry at me," he told himself.

He ran to the tower and was about to call up to the window when he stopped. The girl's hair still hung down.

"I've come back!" he said as he put his hands on the hair. He glanced up the hill, in the direction the witch had come from the night before.

He heard nothing. He saw nothing. Could it be safe?

Arthur climbed. It was harder work than the witch had made it seem. He went hand over hand, unable to use his feet to help him, as they slipped from the frozen tower whenever he tried.

When he reached the window, Arthur was breathless and his hands ached. His palms stung from the cold. But he made it. He climbed headfirst through the window and tumbled onto the stone floor.

"Dandelion?" he said, peering into the dark room. A figure sat on the bed, a violin in her lap.

"I've come back," Arthur said, getting to his feet. "To rescue you." He hurried to the girl and knelt at her feet.

He wished she'd respond. He wished she'd play the violin for him. But she stayed perfectly still. She only said, "Light." Candles erupted around him, circling the room in bright light.

Arthur jumped to his feet, and the figure on the bed lifted the violin and swung it at him. It struck his head, knocking him to the ground.

He looked up, dazed, as the figure stood. It wasn't Dandelion at all. It was her mother … the witch.

"I knew you'd come back," she growled at him. "Boys like you always do."

Boys like me? Arthur thought, pressing his palm against his head. It throbbed with pain.

"But I've protected her," the witch said, "and she's far from here. Far from you. Far from everyone."

"Where?" Arthur said, barely a whisper.

The witch grabbed him by the collar of his parka. "You'll never know!" she said, dragging him to the window. "You'll never see her again!" She lifted him to the window-sill. "You like to hide in briar patches?" she said. "You like to see what you're not supposed to see?"

How could she know? Arthur thought. The witch shoved him out.

"Briars!" she shouted from above as he fell. "Briars!" And from the snowy ground beneath him, bare winter briar patches, woody and covered in thorns, rose up to grab him, not to spare him from the fall, but to claw at his coat and his face. The thorns cut his parka to shreds as he tumbled. They scratched his eyes till he couldn't see.

Arthur slammed into the snow-covered icy ground and blacked out.

* * *

Dandelion lived in the woods, far to the north. Her mother, the witch, left her there. "The wolves will probably eat you," the witch had said. "But if you're skinny from starvation, perhaps they won't bother with you."

She was starving. It had been weeks, and Dandelion had been eating snow and the bark of trees. When spring came, dandelions came with it, and the girl gathered their leaves and ate them, laughing as she did.

"Ironic, I guess," she told herself, "that I can only eat the plant I'm named after." But she thought the leaves were delicious, and she was surprised to find they filled her up, as if she'd eaten a huge meal.

She felt so good, in fact, that she wished for the first time since her exile began that she had her violin. She felt like playing. She felt like dancing. So she sang. She didn't sing the words or melodies of her mother, though. She sang her own song. She couldn't think of the words to sing, though, so she sang a song without words.

It was while Dandelion was singing, collecting dandelion leaves as she went, that she came upon a cottage, hidden in the dense woods. She went inside. The table and bedposts were covered with dust. The hearth was cold and crumbling, unused for many years.

Dandelion moved in.

Her first night in the cottage, she had a strange dream. She was lying in her bed, staring at the door of her new home, when a figure, so bright and so green that she could hardly look at it, glided in.

"Who are you?" Dandelion asked, sitting up.

"I am a wood sprite," it said, "and these are my woods."

"Should I leave?" Dandelion asked.

The sprite laughed, and its laugh sounded like the river beside the tower on a calm autumn day. "You are always welcome here," she said. "I have come to tell you that the witch who drove you here is not your mother."

Dandelion's head swam, and for a moment she thought she might wake from the dream. But in her heart she knew it was true.

The sprite kissed Dandelion on the forehead, and then retreated from the cottage, giggling like water.

* * *

Arthur, blind and cold, never found his way home again.

He wandered the wrong way for two days and two nights. When he got to a town, he hoped it was the one from which he came – but instead he was very far from it.

"Please," Arthur said, grabbing strangers by their wrists as they passed him on the quiet streets. "My name is Arthur Oak. Don't you know me? Or my mother or brother?" But the strangers gasped at his face and torn clothes.

After he'd lived on the streets of that town for many weeks, and the weather began to warm, one kind man brought him to the police station. There, he cleaned up and was given food and clothing.

"We'll find your family," an officer said, patting the boy's cold hands.

"Thank you," Arthur said. But inside he was sad. Though he wanted to find his family, he mostly wanted to find Dandelion. He wanted to hear her play. In a world without sight, it was the only pleasure he could imagine.

Activity surrounded him in the station. Phones rang. Reporters arrived to speak to the boy who'd wandered in the winter for so long. Arthur hardly noticed it.

But one thing ... one distant, faint sound broke through the din. Arthur stood up and felt his way to the door.

A reporter put a hand on his shoulder to stop him. "Where are you going?" she asked. Arthur could sense a microphone in front of his face.

"Don't you hear that?" Arthur said, smiling. He hadn't smiled in so long. He pushed past her, into the street, and the sound grew louder.

"It's music," he said, and he followed it.

Before long, he smelled pine trees and the decay of a forest floor. He stopped a moment.

"You shouldn't go in there," a cameraman called after him. The rest of the crowd behind him murmured in agreement.

Arthur didn't care, though, and by now, so close to the source of the song, he was beaming. He entered the woods, and the reporters didn't follow.

He walked for an hour, the music growing louder the whole time, the air growing warmer, and his heart growing larger. Finally the sound was just in front of him. He smelled a fire burning in the fireplace and soup cooking.

He cautiously moved closer and felt his way to the door of a small cottage.

Arthur knocked and the music stopped. He heard steps on the soft floor inside.

The door creaked open. A girl gasped.

"It's you, isn't it?" the girl said.

Arthur nodded.

"What has she done to you?" Dandelion asked, taking his hand and leading him inside.

"It doesn't matter," he said. "Please keep singing."

Dandelion led him to the fire. "Sit next to me," she said. "I don't know your name."

"I'm Arthur Oak," he said.

"Sit next to me, Arthur Oak," Dandelion said, so he did. Dandelion put an arm around Arthur's shoulders and he leaned against her, shivering, as she sang.

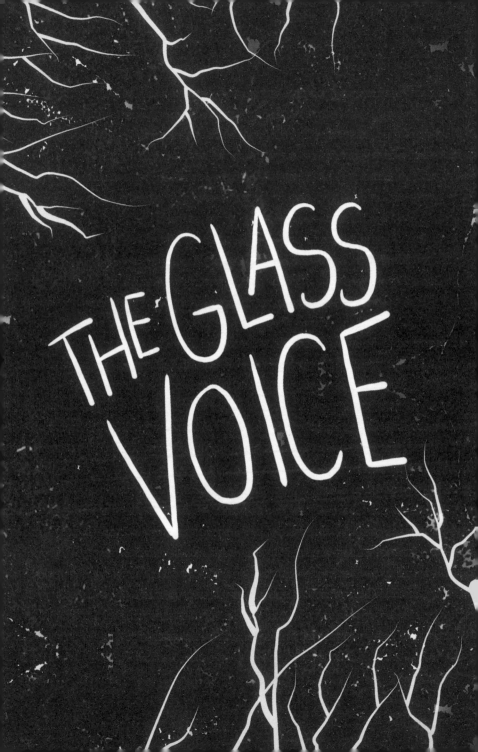

Chantella Verre sat in the dressing room in the church and sniffled. She ran her fingers over the green velvety fabric of the couch.

"No more crying," she mumbled. She lifted her chin and found her reflection in the mirror on the dressing table.

"Ugh, I look awful," she said to herself. Her eyes were red and swollen. Make-up ran down her cheeks. She stepped into the bathroom, blew her nose and wiped the smeared make-up from her face.

Then she heard a knock on the door. "You in there, Chantella?" her dad said. He stuck his head in as she came out of the bathroom.

"Hi, Dad," she said, doing her best to cover up the crying in her voice and the runny in her nose. She sat on the couch again and tried to smile for him – he *had* just got married after all – but it turned into a sobbing hiccup.

Her dad sighed and walked into the room. He squatted in front of his daughter – *of course he wouldn't sit down next to me*, Chantella thought – and put a hand on her knee.

"You're upset," he said, barely glancing her way. He never looked her in the eyes anymore.

"I miss Mum," she said. "I'm sorry."

Her dad sighed again. "I miss her, too," he said. "And when I look at you, I miss her doubly."

She took her dad's hand. He flinched a little as their hands touched. "You're her all over again," her dad said, his voice and eyes soft and caring. They almost never were nowadays. He looked at Chantella and pushed a chestnut lock of hair behind her ear. But Chantella knew he wasn't seeing his daughter. He was seeing his late wife.

She coughed, and her dad's trance ended. He cleared his throat and stood up. "That's over now," he said, tugging at the lapels of his tuxedo. "Now we have Mara and the twins. A new family. It'll be a fresh start."

But I don't want a fresh start, Chantella thought as he left, closing the door behind him.

Chantella followed him out a moment later, but rather than heading to the front of the church to throw rice and cheer with the rest of the guests, she went out of the side door into a small, serene graveyard.

From there, Chantella could hear the cheers as her dad and new stepmother hurried out of the ornate doors and down the steps to their waiting limousine. She could picture them both smiling and running, rice raining down on them.

She stepped gently past graves, old and new, and stopped at one of the newest. It shined. Its letters were still sharp and crisp: *Cordelia Verre, beloved wife and mother. She is singing in heaven.*

Chantella was tired of crying. Her mother had died a bit less than a year earlier, and she had been crying ever since. But today was the worst day in a long time. Standing at her mother's grave, listening to her family and friends applauding in front of the church, she thought she might cry again. But instead, she sang. *"You are my sunshine, my only sunshine."*

Her mother used to sing it to her at bedtime and bath time. When Chantella felt she was too old to be sung to like a baby, she asked her mum to stop. She was probably twelve then – just three years ago. Now she wished she'd never asked her mum to stop singing.

Chantella sang the whole song right there in the grave-yard, and when she was done, she was still crying. "My sunshine is gone," Chantella whispered to the stone, placing her hand on its cold, hard face. "I miss you, Mummy."

"She's gone completely insane," said a voice from behind her. It was Mara's son, Colin. And that surely meant Colin's twin, Colleen, was there as well.

"Talking to dead people," Colleen said, nearly cackling. "Twisted."

"Go away," Chantella said. It took all her effort to hold back more tears.

"Happily," Colin said. He leaned towards her, though, and added in a whisper, "We'll see you in the limo, sis."

With that, her new stepsiblings departed, laughing as they went. Now that she was alone with her mother, Chantella let the tears flow again.

But she couldn't linger in the cemetery much longer. From the corner, she could see her dad's long silver limo as it pulled away from the kerb. Behind it flew a ghastly banner: *Just Married*. And with that, her father's limousine was gone – headed to the reception.

Still at the kerb was a black limo, its back door wide open so the twins could take their places. The driver was waiting for her to climb into the back with those miserable twins. If she didn't get there soon, she could only imagine what lie the twins might tell him so they could leave without Chantella.

She pushed through the creaky iron gate of the cemetery and headed for the front of the church. *I hope we don't get stuck in traffic,* Chantella thought as she headed towards the limo. She was sure she could only stand the twins in doses of five minutes or less.

For once, Chantella was glad her father's work schedule was so hectic. He wasn't going to take a honeymoon with Mara, which meant she wouldn't be stuck at home alone with the twins. She sighed as the crowd of well-wishers began to thin, heading for their cars, and she quickened her pace to reach the limo before the twins could convince the driver to leave her behind.

Before she reached the door, though, she felt a hand touch her shoulder. Chantella was too upset to be friendly. It was no doubt one of her dad's friends or business partners, ready to offer hearty congratulations. She closed her eyes and took a deep breath to brace herself. Then she put on her best fake smile, opened her eyes and turned around.

"Hello, little wonder," said the woman in front of her. She was around Chantella's height, and about ten years older, with startlingly red hair worn high on her head. Suddenly, Chantella's fake smile turned real ... an ear-to-ear, shining grin.

"Verna!" she shouted with glee. She threw her arms around the woman's neck.

"My!" Verna exclaimed, her voice a pleasing mix of surprise and joy. "I never expected anyone to be so happy to see me!"

Chantella released the woman – her former nanny, whom she hadn't seen in five years, the last time Mum had gone on international tour.

"I'm sorry," Chantella said, smiling now, in spite of the tears still on her cheeks. "I didn't know Dad had invited you!"

"He didn't," Verna said. Then she leaned closer and whispered, "The truth is, dear, I'm not here for your father."

"No?" Chantella said.

Verna shook her head. "I'm here for you."

"Oh, then you shouldn't have come," Chantella said. "I hate this. I wish it wasn't happening."

"But that's why I came," Verna said. "To see how you were doing."

Chantella had always liked her nanny. She had spent nearly every afternoon with the young woman – a university student then – and occasionally stretches of days when her mother was on tour and her father was busy or out of town on a business trip.

Verna was a wonderful role model for Chantella. They had roamed the little city on the river together, sometimes on busy streets, in and out of sweet shops, ice cream shops, bookshops and museums, sometimes on the banks of the big river, their trousers rolled up to their knees, their shoes and socks safe and dry on the footpath, while they splashed ankle-deep in the ice-cold, crystal-clear shallows.

Chantella had loved her nanny then, and seeing her now, on this horrible afternoon, she realized she loved her still. But – and it troubled Chantella to think it – there had always been something a little off about the young woman. She sensed it even now. It was a glimmer in Verna's eyes – a greyish blue: pale and not quite human. It was a lilt in her voice, like she'd come from a land far away – a place not on maps.

Verna took Chantella's hand. "You should hurry now," she whispered. "Those two stinkers won't wait much longer."

Chantella sighed. "Perhaps I'll just go to the reception with you," she said. "I'd prefer it to going with them, and it will give us a chance to catch up."

"No," Verna said. "I'm not going to the reception. I merely stopped by to check up on my favourite former charge. But I will drop by soon, and we can catch up then. If that's all right with you...?"

"I'd love it," Chantella said. She hugged Verna again. "I should hurry. Thank you, V!"

With that, she turned and hurried towards the idling limousine. As she reached the car, the limo driver hopped out and opened the door for her.

"Finally," said Colleen, as Chantella slid across the seat. The twins sat across from her, their arms crossed and their faces grim and angry.

Colin leaned forward and banged on the divider the moment the driver was back behind the wheel. "Let's go!" he snapped. The limo pulled away from the kerb.

Chantella looked out of the window as they slid past the length of the church. Verna still stood there, and though the limousine windows were darkly tinted, she seemed to hold Chantella's eyes as the car passed.

* * *

Chantella kept to herself during the reception. She was envious of how well the twins were handling their mother's second wedding. "Don't they miss their father?" she muttered, her elbow on the table and her chin on her fist.

She watched them dance, saw them sneak extra desserts and spotted them teasing a distant cousin for not being married.

The new family went home to the Verre estate late that night. It was an old and impressive home that sat on top of a wooded hill. It had a remarkable view from up there – you could look down on the river on one side and over the city on the other.

Mara and the twins would be moving their things in the next day, and Chantella dreaded it. The new Verre family entered the house and almost immediately they all kicked off their shoes, fell onto couches and easy chairs, and sighed, happy to be home.

All except Chantella. Over the last year, she'd often thought that the big house, with only two occupants (who were both often very sad) was a lonely place. At one point, she might have thought a pair of siblings would be a welcome addition. Then she met Colleen and Colin and their dreadful mother. A big, empty house for just Chantella and her dad seemed like heaven now.

"We'll each have our own room," Colleen said as she fluffed up some pillows on the couch and grabbed a blanket to cover her legs.

Chantella sat on the end of the couch as she listed the house's bedrooms in her mind: there was her father's huge master suite, there was her own bedroom down the hall from it, and there was the spare bedroom – the one Mum had used as her music room – at the far end of the hall. There were rooms that Chantella's dad used as libraries, offices and game rooms, but she knew he wouldn't give those up.

That's only three bedrooms, Chantella thought, *and I'm certainly not giving up mine.*

"You certainly will," Mara announced, responding to Colleen. "I won't have my children sharing a room in a house so tremendous."

Chantella was about to protest when Mara continued. "Naturally Chantella will be happy to give up her room for one of her new siblings," she said.

"Where am I supposed to sleep?" Chantella asked the group, sitting up in shock. "That's been my bedroom since – well, since forever!"

"Now, Chantella," her father said. His voice was tired – tired of sadness, tired of grieving and tired of Chantella's complaining.

"You get the best room of all, dear," Mara said, standing up. She walked across the living room and dropped onto the couch beside Chantella. She even put an arm around her. "You'll have all the privacy you can dream of – your own bathroom and even a sitting area."

Chantella's face turned white. "The maid's quarters?" she said. She launched herself off the couch and stomped across the living room and then turned around to face her stepmother. "You're putting me in the maid's quarters?"

Mara put her hand to her chest, aghast. "Why, Chantella," she said, "you act as if we've banished you to the unfinished part of the basement or the garage!"

"Really, sweetie," her dad said. "It's the biggest room in the house, aside from the master suite. You'll have your own apartment."

Chantella opened her mouth to speak, but she could think of nothing to say. The truth was, the maid's quarters *were* spacious and private. *And I won't be anywhere near my new siblings or the bedroom that Dad will now share with Mara instead of Mum,* Chantella thought. *And it will be perfect for practising singing.*

"Fine," Chantella said, instead of protesting further. "I'll go get some of my stuff."

"Oh, it's already taken care of, dear," Mara said. "I took the liberty of asking a few of the men from your father's warehouse to come and move some of your things during the wedding."

"You *what?*" Chantella said. "You moved my stuff already?"

Mara leaned back and crossed her legs. "You'll be quite comfortable," she said, and she busied herself examining the state of her manicure.

Chantella glared at Mara, and then flashed an angry glance at her father. He only held her eyes for a moment before looking down at the carpet.

As Chantella marched out of the living room, Colleen and Colin cackled behind her. She waited until she was down the hall and out of their sight before she wiped a tear from her cheek.

* * *

That first night in her new "apartment" was long. Every creak of the floor was new. The maid's quarters were next to the kitchen, and the refrigerator's constant whir and occasional clicks and thuds haunted her, making her toss and turn for half the night.

It was nearly three in the morning when Chantella finally threw off her blanket and found the plastic tub that held her CD collection. Most of them had been her mum's. Since her mother died, however, Chantella had added quite a few finds of her own.

One in particular, though, was the object of Chantella's hunt through the bin, and she found it near the bottom. Its case featured a photo of the most beautiful woman Chantella had ever known: her mother. Chantella pulled the disc out and put it on.

Then she lay on her bed again and eventually drifted off to sleep, her mother's soothing voice serenading her with haunting, jazzy notes that drowned out the odd creaks and the hum of the refrigerator.

* * *

Chantella was the first one to wake up. She hadn't slept very well, even with the company of her mother's voice. It was barely six o'clock when she found her robe and dragged herself to the kitchen.

"I can't believe it's Monday," she mumbled as she filled the teapot with water and put it on the hob to boil. It had been an exhausting weekend. Chantella could hardly believe she had to be at school in less than two hours.

The house seemed quiet. Chantella didn't hear any footsteps as she cracked two eggs and beat them with a whisk. No shower ran upstairs as she put two slices of wholewheat toast into the toaster and poured herself a mug of tea. No voices drifted down from the second floor as she poured the beaten eggs into a pan and pushed them over high heat until they scrambled.

But as Chantella moved the eggs from the pan to a plate, two pairs of footsteps thundered down the back stairway. Before she knew it, the twins were charging into the kitchen, giggling. Colin snatched the plate of eggs and the fork from the counter. Colleen grabbed the slices of toast just as they popped up.

"Thanks a lot, Chantella," Colin said. He and Colleen each took a stool at the kitchen island and began to dig into Chantella's eggs and toast.

"That wasn't for–" Chantella began to protest. But Mara cut her off as she click-clacked into the kitchen.

"Ah!" she said. "Is my lovely stepdaughter fixing breakfast for her family this morning?" She sat beside her children and grinned at Chantella. "Just egg whites for me, please. And certainly no toast." She laughed as she reached for Chantella's mug of tea.

Chantella clenched her jaw and rinsed out the frying pan. "Is Dad coming down?" she asked. She brought the pan back to the hob and pulled the eggs from the fridge again.

Mara sighed grandly and said, "I'm sure my husband would rather stay upstairs. He'll come down after you've eaten and showered and left for school."

"Why?" Chantella said. She had a guess, but she couldn't bear to think it.

Mara had no such difficulty. "Oh, darling," she said, her voice thick with false sympathy, "you of all people know how hard the poor man has had it. He adored your mother

– though I hardly know why. And she left him so utterly destroyed, as I'm sure you understand."

Chantella did understand – far too well.

"Poor thing," Mara went on. She sipped her tea. "He looks at you and sees her. No wonder he doesn't want to spend any time with you."

Chantella pushed the egg whites around the pan as she tightened her jaw, holding back tears. Although it hurt to hear, she wouldn't give them the satisfaction of seeing her upset. When the eggs were done, she put them on a plate and passed them across the island to Mara. Then she left the kitchen and headed for her new bathroom.

Chantella stood in the shower and tried to sing, but at the first line, she croaked and sobbed instead.

* * *

Chantella had a hard time concentrating at school that day. She had given up trying to pay attention during third-period chemistry, the formulas on the whiteboard just swimming in front of her. Mara's comments from that morning still stung, but Chantella knew that her wicked stepmum was lying. *Dad was probably showering, shaving and dressing for work. Nothing unusual about that,* she thought.

Chantella managed to smile as she walked into the canteen for lunch. She looked forward to seeing her friends and complaining about her awful new stepsiblings.

Janis and Jaenelle – the Js – were at their usual table. But before she reached them, two more people sat down with their backs to her. *It couldn't be them,* Chantella thought. But then they turned in their chairs and flashed open-mouthed smiles her way. *The twins.* Still, Chantella sat down in her usual spot.

"Hi, sis," Colleen said, then turned her attention back to the Js. "We're so thrilled to meet our new dear sister's *dearest* friends."

Colin cooed, "She's so *dear* to us. Why, do you know what she did this morning?" He cast a long, loving look at Chantella. She could tell that the Js weren't aware of Colin's sarcasm.

"She made breakfast!" Colleen said. "For me, Colin *and* Mum. Isn't that wonderful?"

Colin put his hands on Chantella's. "What a great welcome to our new home," he said. "Can you believe we were nervous about moving in?"

Colleen nodded. "We certainly were. And this delightful girl cooked eggs and toast for the whole family."

"Well," said Colin, "not the *whole* family. Dad didn't come downstairs till we'd left."

Chantella turned her face to the window. She looked out over the school grounds, unable to watch her awful stepsiblings any longer. The Js couldn't pull themselves away. They leaned on the table, their lunches untouched, hanging on the twins' every word.

"Did you know she even gave up her bedroom?" Colleen said. "Just for me!"

"She sleeps in the maid's room now," Colin said, taking a bite of his pasta salad.

Colleen shifted suddenly to face her brother and gasped. "You know *what?*" she said, her smile wide and devious. "She sleeps in the maid's room, and she served us all breakfast this morning. She practically *is* the maid!"

The twins laughed so hard they buckled over in their seats, holding their stomachs. Even the Js twittered like birds. Unable to take it anymore, Chantella pushed her tray aside, got up and left the cafeteria.

* * *

The school week was long and torturous. Chantella had managed to sneak out of the house on two mornings without serving anyone breakfast, but the other days were the same as Monday. On Friday morning, after she'd made scrambled eggs for her stepfamily, Chantella grabbed her books and headed for the front door.

At the last moment, though, she ran upstairs as quietly as she could manage and knocked urgently on the door to the master suite.

"Dad?" she said in a frantic whisper. She hadn't seen her father all week. "It's Chantella. Can I come in?"

He didn't reply. Perhaps he was in the shower. But Chantella would never know, because at that moment, a long-fingered hand – more like a claw – gripped her shoulder. Chantella spun, facing her stepmum.

"How could you be so cruel?" the woman said as she leaned close to Chantella's startled face. Mara's long hair – a startling white-blond – hung in front of her shoulders. "You know how much it hurts him to see you," Mara went on, "yet you keep trying to stick your detestable face in front of him."

"I–" Chantella said. "I don't mean to–"

"Get downstairs," Mara said, clasping her hands in front of her and straightening her spine. She cast her gaze past Chantella, as if she was a duchess dismissing some lowly servant. "*My* children have already left for school. If you hurry, perhaps you won't be late."

* * *

The school day dragged. Lessons seemed never-ending. Chantella couldn't focus on anything. In maths, the numbers blurred together on the whiteboard. In English, words seemed to have no meaning at all.

Even lunch passed slowly. Chantella ate lunch at the end of a long table with people she didn't know. She refused to share the Js with the twins, and the Js, for whatever reason, seemed to like the twins. In fact, the Js hadn't even spoken to Chantella since her stepsiblings had befriended them.

When Chantella got home that afternoon, she found Mara sitting on the small couch in the maid's quarters. "Chantella," the woman said in her icy tone. "Sit with me a moment."

Chantella obeyed.

"I heard from your Deputy Head, Ms Paulsen, this afternoon," Mara said. She placed a hand on Chantella's knee. Chantella flinched at the touch.

"What for?" Chantella had never been in trouble in school before. Her grades had always been very good, too.

"It seems," Mara went on, "that you've been distracted this week. You missed some homework."

"Oh," Chantella said. It was true. But with everything going on recently, surely it was forgivable just this once.

"You failed a maths test this morning. Were you aware of that?" Mara asked.

"I kind of had the feeling I didn't do well," Chantella said. "It's been a hard week."

"Well," Mara said, standing up and facing Chantella, her chin low and her manner condescending. "It ends now. As of this moment, you will focus on only two things: your schoolwork and your housework."

"Housework?" Chantella said.

"I've drawn up a list," the woman said, pulling it from behind her back and presenting it to Chantella. She went to the door and called out, "Colin! Come here, please!" as Chantella read the list of new duties: vacuuming, cooking, mopping, washing windows, cleaning toilets, doing laundry. The list went on and on.

"I don't understand," Chantella said. "This is a list of every chore in the house! Don't Colleen and Colin have to do any chores?"

"*My* children are not distracted in school," Mara said. "I haven't received a call from Ms Paulsen about *my* children."

Colin stuck his head in the room. "You called, Mum?" he said.

"Chantella has been having some trouble focusing on her work. We're going to help her," Mara said.

Colin examined Chantella the way a hyena might examine a wounded antelope. "How?"

Mara went to Chantella's desk, closed her laptop and handed it to Colin. "This will stay in the living room from now on," she said. "That way," she added, looking at Chantella, "we'll always know what you're up to when you're supposed to be working."

Chantella swallowed hard. Her laptop held dozens of MP3s and videos of her mother. She couldn't bear to see Mara and Colin handling it.

Colin slipped the laptop under his arm. "What else?" he said.

Mara stepped up to the plastic bin under the window. "This," she said, looking down at it. "When Chantella proves that she can focus on her studying, then we can consider letting her have music on while she does."

Colin hoisted the bin onto his hip and headed for the door.

"Wait!" Chantella said, grabbing Colin's arm. "That has all my mum's music in it! Let me keep those CDs at least."

Mara scoffed. "Hardly," she said. "Those CDs *especially* have to go. I can think of no greater distraction – not only to you, but to the entire family – than your mother's warbling."

"Warbling?" Chantella yelled. "Warbling?!"

Mara clucked her tongue. "My, she's having a fit!" she said. She pulled Chantella's hand off Colin's arm – Mara was surprisingly strong – and the boy left the room.

"It's not fair!" Chantella shrieked.

"Fair," Mara said. Her tone made the word sound absurd. "The sooner you accept just how *unfair* things are about to get around here, the happier you'll be."

* * *

That night, after eating the supper Chantella had cooked, Mara stood up from the table full of dirty dishes.

"When you've finished cleaning up this mess," she said to Chantella as she patted the corners of her mouth with a napkin, "you will vacuum the media room."

"Quickly!" Colleen added. "My favourite programme is on soon and I will not have you drowning it out with that awful vacuum cleaner."

Chantella clenched her jaw and stacked dirty plates as her stepfamily left the dining room. Her dad hadn't been to dinner, of course. She wasn't even sure he was home.

Does he know what Mara has been up to? she wondered. *Does he know I've been made a servant in my own house?*

Chantella filled the dishwasher, switched it on and hurried to the media room with the vacuum. Colin and Colleen were already there, a bag of popcorn open on the couch between them, its oily contents spilling freely as they grabbed handful after handful.

"Finally," Colleen said. "You better hurry."

Chantella clicked on the vacuum and pushed it across the huge carpeted floor. "I don't see why you couldn't do this yourselves," she mumbled, "instead of stuffing your faces with popcorn."

Somehow Colin heard her over the roar of the vacuum. "Because our mother – who loves us dearly and enjoys spending time with us – is *alive*."

With that, he tossed a handful of popcorn, scattering the white and yellow puffs across the part of the carpet Chantella had already vacuumed. She rushed to finish the chore, with tears threatening to stream down her face.

Just as Colleen's programme had come on, and Chantella was wrapping up the vacuum's cord, Mara found her.

"After you've put that away," Mara said, "you can polish the wood furniture in the formal living room."

"What?" Chantella said. "I thought I was done for the night. It's late. I have homework."

"It's Friday," Mara said. "You have the whole weekend for schoolwork. Do as you're told."

As Mara walked away, she said, "I don't believe the furniture in the living room has ever been polished. What a miserable house your mother kept."

* * *

Chantella finished her chores late. After the living room furniture, there was the bathroom to scrub, the dishwasher to empty and a load of laundry to start and finish. She crawled into bed with the rest of the house asleep.

"That witch didn't get everything," she whispered. She reached under her bed and pulled out a thick, old book: a collection of fairy tales.

She put it on her lap and quickly flipped through the pages till they stopped on their own. There, sandwiched between the pages, was a photograph of a beautiful young woman with chestnut curls and loving eyes. Chantella pulled the photo out, pressed it to her chest, and curled up in bed as she sang herself to sleep.

Chantella dreamed of her mother that night, just as she'd hoped she would. They sang together, and then her mother took Chantella's hands in her own and said, "He loves you. He'll remember. You might have to help him."

* * *

The weeks marched slowly on, and as time passed, Chantella felt more like a maid and less and less like her father's daughter.

The twins had started coming home from their shopping trips or to the city with "gifts" for Chantella.

"I bought you the sweetest outfit today!" Colleen would say, holding up a heavy tan apron to her stepsister's chest.

"I found you a *darling* accessory!" Colin would say, pulling a feather duster from his shopping bag.

Mara would join in when she was feeling particularly cruel. "This will make your job a lot easier," she would say, laying a toothbrush on Chantella's desk. "Cleaning between the bathroom tiles will be a breeze now."

It was a rainy Saturday in October. The twins and Mara had gone out – to lunch, to the cinema, on a shopping spree; it could have been any of those things. Chantella, alone at home, had been assigned to clean the master suite.

Chantella sat on the edge of her father's bed and stared at herself in the mirror on the dresser. Her hair was pulled back, and her eyes were tired and dark. A smudge of dust ran across her cheek. She reached up to wipe the smear away, saw the state of her hands, and thought better of it.

I haven't been in here since before the wedding, she thought. *I haven't seen Dad since that night.* Chantella sighed, grabbed her bucket that was filled with tins of polish, rags and dusters, and headed for the suite's double doors, thinking a shower would feel very nice. If she hurried, maybe she'd have time to watch a little television before the stepfamily got home.

But as she reached the doors, they opened. Standing in the doorway was her father.

"Dad!" she said, ready to drop her bucket and throw her arms around him.

Her dad blinked at her and smiled – a smile like he might flash at a familiar face at one of his business gatherings.

"Chantella," he said. "I didn't think you'd be in here."

"Oh, I'm just finishing," Chantella said. She sighed loudly and was about to launch into a rant describing all the mistreatment she had suffered at the hands of her stepfamily, but her father rushed past her, loosening his tie.

"What a day," he said. "Nice to come home to a clean bedroom, though." He flashed a smile at his daughter. "You know," he went on, pulling off his tie and tossing it onto the bed, "I don't think that master bathroom has been cleaned in a while."

"Um…" Chantella said. "Dad?"

He must not have heard her, though, or else he chose to ignore her.

"Have Mara and the twins gone out?" he asked.

"Yeah," Chantella said. "They went to see a film or shopping or something."

"Good," he said. "They could use the time to kick back a little. Speaking of kicking back, I'm going to watch some TV and catch up on a few programmes. I'll leave you to the bathroom."

With that, he left his daughter standing in his bedroom, bucket of cleaning supplies in hand, and headed downstairs.

"Then it's true," Chantella whispered, shocked. "I'm really the maid."

* * *

One cold day in early December, as the joyful chaos of Christmas and New Year's Eve approached, Chantella was enjoying a handful of free minutes in her bedroom. She had a book of music on her lap – a yellowing little paperback her mother had loved to sing songs from – and was settling in to learn a new song before she fell asleep. As she studied the first song, she heard Mara in the kitchen. "I don't know if Chantella can handle it on her own," her stepmother said.

Chantella closed the book and moved quietly towards the door.

"I have three cousins coming here for Christmas," Mara said, "and then another three for New Year."

"Where will they all sleep?" Chantella's dad asked. Chantella could tell from his distant voice that he was probably sifting through mail or checking email on his phone while Mara babbled on.

"We'll find a place for everyone in a house this size," Mara said impatiently. "The point is, with Chantella's schoolwork and housework, I fear she won't have time to prepare the kind of meals I feel we ought to serve for the holidays."

"Hmm," her dad said.

"Therefore," Mara went on, "I think the best thing for our family would be to pull Chantella out of school, at least until spring."

"Whatever you think, dear," he said.

She can't be serious! Chantella fumed. *Is he even listening?*

Chantella tore out of her room and into the kitchen. Mara stared her down.

"Anything wrong, girl?" she said.

"Yes!" Chantella snapped. "Dad," she went on, craning her neck to look past Mara where her father was standing with his back to them, "are you really going to let her do this?"

"Hmm?" her father said, not even looking up from his phone. "Whatever you two think is fine with me." Then he left the kitchen.

"There," Mara said, putting her hand on her hip and flashing her pointy teeth at Chantella. "That takes care of that."

"You can't just pull me out of school," Chantella protested. "I'm fifteen. It's illegal."

"Oh, nonsense," Mara said, waving her off. "I'll tell them we're home-schooling. Whatever it takes."

"That is insane!" Chantella said.

"You just worry about learning how to make the perfect Christmas dinner," Mara said. "I expect a delicious turkey with all the trimmings. You've got a lot of practising to do, I should think. Have you ever cooked a bird?" Mara didn't wait for a reply. "I'm going upstairs. Mr Verre doesn't like to be alone for too long. Please turn off the light when you're done straightening up."

Chantella stood in the kitchen, listening to her stepmother's feet on the stairs. Chantella had cried too much. She'd protested too much. She'd cared too much. There was a time – it seemed like forever ago – that her father cared too. That he cried with her. That he screamed at the heavens with her. But he'd changed now, and it seemed he didn't even recognize her.

Chantella couldn't care anymore.

* * *

The holidays were a whirl of hard work and hurt feelings. Chantella collected coats. She served drinks and passed trays of crackers with cheese, tiny sausages on toothpicks and asparagus spears wrapped in prosciutto. She ladled out soup, served casseroles and stuffed a turkey for Christmas Day. On New Year's Eve, she filled champagne flutes and swept up broken glass numerous times.

No one thanked Chantella. No one hung her stocking over the fireplace. No one wished her Merry Christmas.

A red envelope did appeared on her bed, though. She tore it open and found a photo of Colleen, Colin, Mara and her dad standing on the lawn in front of the big snow-covered fir tree, in their most Christmassy sweaters, each with steaming mugs in their hands and smiles on their faces. Beneath the photo it read: *Merry Christmas from the Verres!*

Chantella tore it up and fell onto her bed in tears.

* * *

By the middle of January, Chantella began to realize her stepmother's cruelty was not going to cease with the end of holiday preparations. It seemed Mara would do whatever it took to keep Chantella in her new position as permanent, live-in housekeeper.

She's never going to let me go back to school, Chantella thought as she cleaned the bay windows in the parlour and watched Mara's luxury SUV pull into the circular driveway. Chantella watched Mara and the twins climb out of the car. It had snowed a little that morning, so a fine dusting still lay on the path from the driveway to the front door.

Mara burst in and snapped, "Chantella!" Then she added more quietly, "Where is that girl?"

Chantella sighed and put down her rags and the bottle of window cleaner. She walked quickly from the parlour to the front door where Mara stood, her arms weighed down by shopping bags. The door was open behind her, and Chantella could see Colleen and Colin on the sloping front garden, quickly gathering snowballs to toss playfully at one another. Their rucksacks lay in the driveway, thrown carelessly aside.

"There you are," Mara said, scowling. She didn't even fake a smile. She never did anymore – even when Chantella's dad was around. "What have you been doing, exactly? I'm sure just sitting around while the house falls apart around you."

Chantella didn't bother to argue. It wouldn't change anything. Besides, Mara barely stopped for a breath. She certainly wasn't expecting an answer to her question.

"You haven't touched the driveway or the paths, and the snow stopped hours ago," Mara said as she kicked off her heels and stalked past Chantella. "Get your shovel and clear the driveway and the paths – and be quick about it. I want supper on the table at six o'clock, sharp!"

Chantella rolled her eyes – she allowed herself that at least – and collected Mara's shoes, scarf and coat, which Mara had left lying on the floor. She took them to the cupboard, put on her heavy coat, grabbed the shovel and headed outside. As she walked down the steps to the driveway, an icy snowball struck her in the face. Colleen and Colin, predictably, cackled like crows.

"Sorry, Chanty," said Colleen, though she wasn't.

The twins grabbed their rucksacks and laughed their way past Chantella, into the house, locking the door behind them.

Chantella had a spare key in her coat pocket, but the twins didn't know that.

They're horrible, Chantella thought. *This whole family is horrible.*

She glared towards the door, and in doing so, noticed a fluttering piece of paper in the porch.

"Must have fallen from Colin's rucksack," Chantella mumbled as she picked it up.

Next Teen Star is coming to Riverview High School! Are you the next big thing? Come to the auditions this Saturday and show us your stuff!

Chantella held the paper against her chest. "This could be my chance," she whispered as she shoved the paper into her coat pocket. In a daze of daydreams, she took up the shovel to start the dreary work of clearing the path and driveway.

"I know I'm not as good as Mum was," she muttered, pushing the shovel across the light covering of snow. "But I do have some of her talent, I think."

Chantella passed the time shovelling snow in the dying afternoon light of January, singing to herself.

You are my sunshine, my only sunshine...

* * *

The grandfather clock in the hall sounded at nine o'clock as Chantella finished cleaning up after dinner. She leaned on the worktop and blew her hair out of her eyes.

"The pans have been scrubbed, the dishwasher is running, the table's wiped off and polished, the dining room floor has been swept, and the worktops are wiped down and disinfected," she mumbled.

Add that to all the other cleaning and shovelling she'd done, not to mention making and serving the supper, and Chantella was exhausted.

As usual, she thought.

She pulled off her apron and headed for her room to practise a little singing before bed.

On the way, though, she heard the most unusual sound coming down the hall.

"Is that Colleen?" she wondered aloud.

There was no one else it could be, but while Colleen often talked quite loudly – and laughed and cackled and shrieked and demanded and snarled and snapped and belittled and swore – she certainly never sang.

Chantella quietly moved down the hall towards the living room. She stopped, just out of sight, and held her breath. It was definitely Colleen singing, and a moment later Colin joined her. *They're singing a duet! Or trying to, at least.* Chantella thought, amused and very confused.

They kept cutting off each other's parts and messing up the words. Their voices weren't terrible, though. Better than Chantella would have guessed from listening to their unbearable speaking voices.

When they finished the song, the twins immediately began snapping at one another.

"You stepped on my cue!"

"You missed the harmony in the first reprise!"

"You blew the key change in the middle eight!"

"You sing like a dying cat!"

At that point, it must have turned into a physical fight, because Mara – who had apparently been observing – finally spoke up.

"Enough, enough!" she shouted. "You were both atrocious. If you're to have any chance of passing the audition on Saturday and getting on that programme – and winning the grand prize money and recording contract and tour – you'd better worry more about how to get better instead of which of you is worse."

They began shrieking at each other again, and Chantella took advantage of the loud distraction to hurry to her room so she could practise as well.

* * *

On Saturday morning, Chantella searched the house for her father, practising her audition song as she looked for him and straightened up. Perhaps he wasn't the father he should have been, or the father he once was, but he was more her parent than Mara was.

"If I could just find him," she told herself, "he'd let me go to the audition."

It may have been true; it may not have been true. It didn't matter. Chantella searched high and low all over the Verre mansion and never found him.

"Please," Chantella finally said when she came across Mara sitting in the parlour. "Let me come to the audition today."

"You?" Mara said, a look of disgust and disbelief on her face.

Chantella nodded firmly.

Mara sighed. "Very well," she said. "If you've finished your chores for the morning, you may come to support your brother and sister. It might do them good to have someone rooting for them."

Chantella felt her face redden. "No, Mara," she said. "That's not what I mean. I want to sing. I want to audition."

Mara shot to her feet as if a pin had just burst up from the cushion of her seat and poked her in the bum. "Audition?!" she snapped. "I have never heard such arrogance in my life!"

The twins, alerted by their mother's shouting, ran into the parlour.

"This uppity child," Mara told them, "seems to think *she* carries some kind of vocal talent within that plain face of hers."

The twins laughed cruelly.

"Do you think, girl," Mara went on, glaring at Chantella, "that because *some* people thought your mother had a smidgen of musical skill, that they'll think *you* contain something special?"

Chantella didn't respond. She didn't shake her head, and she didn't scream in Mara's face, though she wanted to. Instead, she just stared at her feet.

"Mum," Colleen said, running to Mara's side and grabbing her arm pleadingly. "Let her come. Let her sing. She'll embarrass herself!"

Colin cheered for the idea, but Mara didn't even smile. Chantella could read her face: Mara knew very well that Chantella's mother could sing beautifully, and she worried that Chantella could sing, too. *She's worried I'll be competition for her horrible twins,* Chantella thought. She wanted to grin, but held back.

"Very well," Mara said, her voice now calm, but cold. "You may come to the audition … if you finish all your chores."

"I have, Mara," Chantella said. "I finished all my Saturday chores this morning."

"Today," Mara said, pacing in front of Chantella, "is a *special* Saturday. Since both of the twins will be busy today, they won't have time to focus on their homework."

Chantella held her breath.

"Finish their homework," her stepmother said. "If you're done by noon – when we're leaving – you may join us."

Chantella could hardly breathe, but she didn't protest. She didn't shriek at them. She just stomped one foot and huffed out of the room.

"I'll bring you my maths and history handouts!" Colleen called after her.

Chantella ran to her room and slammed the door behind her. She fell face-first onto her bed and wailed.

"I can't take it anymore!" Chantella cried into her pillow to muffle the sound. "It's too unfair. Too impossible. How can I possibly go on like this any longer?"

"Perhaps you can go a teensy bit longer," said a familiar voice from behind her.

Chantella turned around. There, seated and smiling, with her legs crossed at the ankles and her hands folded in her lap, was Chantella's former nanny – and the former resident of this very room.

"Verna!" Chantella shouted. "What are you doing here?" She leaped from the bed and hugged her tightly.

"Shh!" Verna said with a little laugh. "I don't want your mother and siblings to know I'm here."

"They aren't my mother and my siblings," Chantella said, releasing her former nanny. "How did you get in here?"

Verna opened her hands to reveal a set of keys. "I've held on to these," she admitted. "I suppose I shouldn't have. But when I saw you at the wedding, I was glad I did."

Chantella nodded. "And I'm glad you did," she said. "I'm having the worst time, and I've had no one to talk to."

But now she did. Chantella let it all out – everything that had happened since she last saw Verna at the wedding. When she finished the whole horrible story, Verna's jaw hung open in shock.

"We must do something to fix this," Verna said. "But for the moment, let's just get you to that audition."

"How?" Chantella said. "Mara won't let me go unless I do her bratty children's homework."

"Then we will do their homework," Verna said matter-of-factly.

Suddenly, they heard a knock. "Our homework for you!" Colin called through the closed door. "And you better hurry! We're dying to see you screw up that audition!"

He and Colleen laughed as they retreated down the stairs. Verna stood up, opened the door, collected the books and notebooks, and brought them inside. She flipped through the assignments, nodding and clucking her teeth.

"I think," she said, "if we split this work, we'll finish in no time."

* * *

"Hurry, now!" Verna said. It was 11.55, and the twins' homework was done. While Verna touched up the last few maths problems, Chantella had practically thrown herself into her blue dress and white flats – the only outfit she owned that seemed nice enough for an audition for *Next Teen Star*.

Verna pressed the twins' books into Chantella's arms and practically shoved her out of the room. "She'll leave without you if you don't hurry!" Verna said.

"I'm going, I'm going!" Chantella said, smiling as she hurried down the hall. "Mara! Mara! I've finished the work!"

She ran to the front door, where Mara and the twins, with their coats and scarves on and looks of anxious excitement on their faces, were about to leave for the audition.

Mara glanced over Chantella's shoulder at the grandfather clock. "You almost didn't make it in time," she said, faking a smile – as if she'd wanted Chantella to join them.

Chantella passed the stack of textbooks and notebooks to the twins. Colin flipped through some pages, examining the work. He shrugged and said, "Looks like she actually did it all."

Colleen perused her stack as well. But then she said, "Wait a second. Where's the essay on fairy tales?"

Chantella's heart pounded hard against her ribs and then seemed to stop. "Essay?" she said. "You didn't say anything about an essay on fairy tales."

"Oh, didn't I?" Colleen said, dropping the stack of homework onto a table in the hall. "Must have slipped my mind."

Mara looked delighted. She laughed and patted her daughter on the head as the three left the front door standing open, letting a cold breeze waft into the house as they went outside and climbed into the SUV.

Chantella barely dragged herself back to her room. She should have been furious. She should have been stomping through the house like a goddess of rage and destruction, tearing Mara's art from the walls, smashing mirrors, and gashing cushions and upholstery.

But she was too exhausted. Instead of rage, she felt sorrow and exhaustion. Chantella collapsed on her bed. She might have fallen asleep if Verna hadn't come into the room a moment later.

"What are you doing here?" Verna asked, sitting beside Chantella on the bed. She felt her nanny's comforting hand on her back. "Shouldn't you be halfway there by now?"

Chantella rolled onto her back and held up the crumpled paper. "We didn't do it all," she said. "There was one more assignment: an essay on fairy tales. Colleen tricked us."

"Well, fairy tales will be easy," she said. "I happen to know quite a bit about them. I can write this."

Chantella shrugged. "What's the point?" she said. "I'd have to leave right now to make it to the auditions on time."

"And leave right now you shall," Verna said. "I'll drive you."

Chantella sat up. "They'll want to know if I've finished the essay," she said.

"Then you'll tell them you have," Verna said. "You'll tell them it's typed up neatly and that you've put it on Colleen's desk. They'll find it there when you get back."

Chantella had her doubts about this plan, but it was worth a try. She got up from the bed and checked herself in the mirror.

"Oh, I've ruined my makeup," she said. "And my dress is a wrinkled mess!"

Verna shook her head. "You can't go like that," she said. She thought for a moment, humming, and then snapped her fingers. "You fix your make-up – I have the perfect idea for a dress. I'll be right back."

Chantella went to her bathroom to freshen up. She heard Verna's fast footsteps on the stairs. When she'd finished, she heard Verna's footsteps rushing back downstairs.

"I found it!" she called. "I found it!"

Her nanny hurried into Chantella's room, holding a tall, black garment bag.

"What is that?" Chantella said as Verna laid it on the bed.

"I wasn't sure it would still be here," Verna said, smiling. "I thought for sure Mara would have found it and destroyed it. But it was just where she'd left it."

"She?" Chantella said. She had an idea she knew who Verna meant, but it was too good to believe.

Verna unzipped the bag and pulled out a dress. It was shimmering white silk, long and strapless, with a black ribbon around the waist. Chantella recognized it at once.

"Mum," she said in a hushed whisper.

She hurried to pull her secret stash of photos from under her bed and found it right away: her mum, only a few years older than Chantella, wearing the same dress on stage.

"It's the first night Dad met Mum," Chantella said, staring at the photo. "He took this photo that night, and he introduced himself after the concert. He says he couldn't help himself."

Verna nodded and smiled. "I've heard that story," she said. "Your mum told it to me a hundred times."

Chantella wiped a tear from her cheek.

"Put it on," Verna said. "Quickly."

Chantella did so and stood in front of the mirror, smiling at her reflection. "It's perfect."

"Good," Verna said. "But we don't have time to gape at you, even if you do look as beautiful as your mother. We have to get going."

Chantella stepped into her shoes and hurried with Verna to the front door. As they were gathering their coats, just about to leave the house, the door flew open, letting in an icy January wind and blowing snow. And suddenly, there was Chantella's red-faced father, bundled up in layers. He stopped inside the doorway, standing there on the doormat, staring at Chantella. It seemed like he barely noticed their former nanny.

"Dad," Chantella said.

"What is this?" he said after a moment. "Where are you going? Why are you wearing that dress?"

"Don't be angry," Chantella said. She stepped towards him and held one of his frigid hands. "Verna knew where to find it, and it's absolutely perfect."

Her father could only nod.

"I feel as if I haven't seen you in a very long time," he said.

"You haven't," Chantella said.

He shook his head. "That's not what I mean…" It seemed like he couldn't find the words he wanted.

Chantella didn't let him finish. She didn't need to. She wrapped her arms around his waist, and he held her against him.

"I've been a horrible father," he finally said, with his face pressed to the top of her head.

"Yes, you have," said Verna as she put a coat over Chantella's shoulders. "But now we really must go if your daughter is to make it to the audition on time."

"The audition," her dad said, lifting his head. "Yes, the twins mentioned something about that." He looked at Chantella again. "That's why you're wearing your mum's dress. It's perfect on you."

"Then you don't mind if I go?" she asked.

"Don't mind?" her dad said. "Honey, of course! You *must* audition. In fact, for the last few days, as I've listened to the twins talk about it constantly – I don't think I like them at all, by the way. They're always talking, aren't they? I had the most frustrating feeling of trying to work something out, but I couldn't work out what."

"Like you'd been under a spell?" Verna said mysteriously.

Chantella's father's face lit up, as if he was seeing her for the first time. "Verna!" he said. "That's it exactly! And now I see what it was that troubled me – the wrong children were auditioning."

"In fact, Chantella was doing their homework for them," Verna added with a little venom in her voice. "Not to mention acting as their maid."

Her dad gave Chantella a sharp look. "Is this true?" he said.

Chantella nodded. She told him about Mara's cruelty and described what she and Verna had been up to that morning, completing the twins' homework assignments so she could get to the audition.

"Enough, enough!" Verna pleaded. "You'll start crying again and ruin your make-up – again! We really must go." She nudged Chantella out the door.

"Just a minute," her dad said. "We'll take my car."

The three hurried out to Mr Verre's car.

"And believe me," he said as they hopped in the car, "Mara has a lot to answer for."

* * *

Chantella's dad's SUV screeched up to the kerb in front of Riverview High School.

"You'd better hurry," he said to his daughter. "If that flyer is right, they're closing the sign-up sheet in just a few minutes."

"Thanks, Dad," Chantella said. She leaned over and kissed his cheek as Verna jumped from the backseat, threw open Chantella's door and grabbed her hand.

"Good luck!" her dad called. "I'll find a place to park!"

Chantella let Verna lead her, running through the empty corridors of the school. She could hear music coming down the hall.

"The auditions are starting!" Verna said, tugging at Chantella's wrist. "Come on!"

They reached the hall. In front of the closed double doors was a long table strewn with clipboards and pens. There, organizing the papers and clipboards into piles, stood a young man in a bright blue suit.

"Are we too late?" Verna said, but the man wasn't looking at her. He was looking at Chantella.

"My goodness," he said, awestruck. "You're the spitting image of the great singer Cordelia Verre. Her voice was as pure and clear as glass."

Chantella felt herself blushing. "I'm her–" she began, but Verna cut her off.

"Can she still sign up?" Verna said.

"Oh," the young man replied. "To audition? Of course. Do you have background music?"

Chantella pushed her CD across the table, and the man handed her a clipboard.

"Thanks," Chantella said as she filled in the sign-up sheet.

When Chantella finished filling it out, she and Verna hurried to the "green room", which was really just a pair of science classrooms adjacent to the hall.

Inside, they found chaos. Dozens of teenagers sat and stood and leaped and danced and sang all over the room.

Standing face-to-face by the windows, with Mara behind them, were the twins. They spotted Chantella right away. Colleen tapped her mother's elbow and nodded at Chantella. Mara curled her lip and stalked through the crowd towards Chantella.

"Uh-oh," Chantella said. "Here she comes. And if you're here with me, you're obviously not working on that essay for Colleen. Mara is going to kill me."

"Working on it?" Verna said. She opened her bag and pulled out a thick, stapled booklet labelled *On Fairy Tales, by Colleen Verre.*

"I did it in the car on the way here," Verna said. She handed Chantella the essay.

Chantella faced Verna in surprise. "In the car?" she said. "But it's typed. How did you–?"

"What are you doing here?" Mara snapped at Chantella. "I made it very clear that you were not to come down here unless you'd finished your work."

Chantella held up the essay. "Done," she said, pressing it into Mara's hands. "Excuse me," she said as she stepped around Mara and walked away. Verna hurried to keep up.

"That was amazing," Verna said.

"I'm shaking like a leaf," Chantella said.

"You did great," Verna said.

At that moment, the door at the back of the room opened, and the young man in blue stuck his head inside. "Colleen and Colin, twins duet!" he shouted. "You're up!"

Chantella and Verna stood near the doors to listen to the twins' performance.

"They're not that bad, actually," Chantella said.

"They *do* have nice voices," Verna admitted. "Especially Colleen."

"Still," Chantella said, "they don't exactly work well together."

They couldn't see the stage. They could only hear the vocals. But the way the twins kept singing over each other, and with the commotion from the audience, it seemed like...

"I think she pushed him!" Verna whispered excitedly. "Is that possible?"

Chantella covered her mouth to stifle a laugh as the song finished. A moment later, Mara stormed into the green room, the look on her face revealing everything.

The twins hadn't done well.

* * *

They were well into the fourth hour of auditions when Chantella's name was finally called.

"You're up," the man in the blue suit said as he walked towards her. He smiled.

Chantella squeezed Verna's hand and followed the young man out to the stage.

"What's your name?" called a voice from the front of the dark hall – it must have been one of the judges.

Chantella shielded her eyes and squinted against the spotlight, trying to see them. "Chantella Verre." The microphone squealed, and she stepped back a little. "Sorry."

"Whenever you're ready," one of the judges said, and Chantella's background track began.

She listened to the familiar strains of piano, the whispering of snare drums and a double bass that sounded like gentle ocean waves.

And she began to sing.

The crowd – small though it was – went wild. Chantella beamed and bowed. The house lights came up, and she spotted her father, near the front and on his feet. He whistled and clapped and cheered.

"Thank you," said a judge, and Chantella hurried off the stage.

The young man in the blue suit took her hand. "You were amazing," he said to her. "It was like watching Cordelia." He sniffed and wiped a tear from his eye. "Your last name is Verre? You must be her daughter."

Chantella nodded. "I am," she said, and she found she was crying, too.

"You'll definitely win," he whispered.

Her father waited for her in the green room – along with Verna, Mara and the twins.

"My little girl!" her dad exclaimed, throwing his arms around her. "You were amazing."

Chantella could have stayed in that hug forever. But they weren't alone. They were surrounded by a pair of horrid twins and their wicked mother.

"Stop this ridiculousness at once!" Mara snapped, trying to pull her husband away from Chantella. "This girl *deliberately* disobeyed me by coming here."

Chantella's dad turned and faced Mara. "You," he said. "You've been a beast. So have your disgusting, bratty children."

Mara gasped. "How dare you!" she said. "You are my husband, and I will *not* have my husband speak to me like this."

"You certainly won't," her dad went on, matching her rage, and shouting just as loud. "The way you've treated my daughter over the past few months has been too awful."

Several performers, two of the judges, and the young man in the blue suit turned to watch the spectacle.

"Ha!" Mara said, stomping her foot. "As if you cared. You treated her as badly as any of us."

"Dad," Chantella said. She tugged at her father's sleeve. "Please stop shouting. Everyone's watching."

He ignored her. It reminded her of the recent months since the wedding, when he ignored her all the time, and it stung. Her eyes filled with tears.

"That's over as of today," her dad said to Mara. "And so is this marriage. I want you out."

Mara gasped. "I'll sue!" she shouted. "I'll take you for everything you're worth!"

Chantella was thrilled to witness the marriage crumbling right before her eyes. But she couldn't take the shouting anymore. Especially with all these people watching. With tears streaming down her face, she ran from the green room.

"Chantella!" Verna called after her. "Wait!"

"Sweetheart!" her dad called.

"Please!" shouted a third voice. "Don't leave!"

But Chantella didn't care. The day had been too much: too much emotion, too much work, too much remembering her mum and dad and how their family had once been. She burst through the doors of Riverview High School and hugged herself tight. The snow blew through the parking lot, blinding her, so she huddled against the side of the building and sobbed.

* * *

"I'm sorry about that scene," Chantella's dad said after driving in silence for several minutes.

Chantella sat in the back of the SUV with Verna, who had showed up outside just a moment after Chantella realized how stupid she'd been to run out into the cold January afternoon in a strapless dress without a coat.

"You didn't need to run off like that, though," her dad went on.

The SUV rushed along the winding streets up the hillside towards the Verre mansion. As they pulled into the driveway, Chantella saw Mara's SUV already parked there, and she groaned.

Verna patted her arm. "It's almost over," she said. "The story has just one more chapter."

The car stopped, and Chantella's father hurried to open the door for her. She took his hand and held it as they walked inside and settled into the kitchen, trying to avoid Mara.

"I'm going to change into something more comfortable," Chantella said, feeling exhausted.

Chantella hoped Verna was right. She hoped the story was almost over. It hadn't been a very good story, but an end would at least be an end.

* * *

Chantella showered and pulled on the jeans and T-shirt she always wore to do housework. They weren't glamorous, like her mother's dress. They weren't impressive, like the satin shoes she should never have worn in the snow. But they *were* very comfortable.

Chantella sat down with a sigh. She might have laid on the bed … slept until the divorce was final and the horrible stepfamily had moved out. But then she heard the deep tones of the doorbell.

"Someone else will get it," she muttered. After all, with her dad back in his right mind and Mara and the twins on their way out, Chantella wasn't the maid anymore.

But the excited shouts and hurrying feet made her curious. With a groan, Chantella got up from the bed and dragged herself out of the maid's quarters and into the living area.

"Please, sit here," Colleen shouted to the guest, excited and overly courteous.

Chantella couldn't see who it was, though, with the soon-to-divorce Verres hovering around him.

"Can I get you something hot to drink?" Colin said. "You must be freezing after your journey."

"Yes!" Mara said. "Get him some tea."

"Enough!" the man said, leaping from the chair. "I don't want to sit. I don't want any tea. I'm just looking for a singer at this address!"

Chantella gasped. It was the man who was working at the *Next Teen Star* audition! His suit was as blue and startling as she remembered.

"It seems someone found my clipboard and tore the papers to pieces," the man began. "And we're having a difficult time figuring out which singer goes with which number and which address. All we know is that she was the daughter of the great singer Cordelia Verre, and her voice was as pure and clear as glass – like her mother's."

"We auditioned!" Colleen said, stepping up to the man, flashing a smile and batting her eyelashes.

The young man peered at her. He pulled a pair of glasses from his jacket pocket, put them on, and peered at her again.

"Hmm," he said. "You look familiar. But ... I don't know."

"*She's* the girl you're looking for," Mara said, hurrying forward and squeezing Colleen's shoulder. "Voice like an angel!"

She smiled and whispered in Colleen's ear, "Sing for him, my darling."

Colleen's eyes went wide with fear, but she recovered quickly, cleared her throat and began to sing. She only sang her parts, though. Duets sound awfully funny with just one person.

"Wait a minute," the man said. Colleen stopped. "Do you have a partner for this song?" He scanned the room.

For the briefest moment, the man's eyes fell upon Chantella. He paused. Chantella lifted her chin and smiled, but in her housework clothes, she was unrecognizable to him.

"My brother!" Colleen said, grabbing her twin by the wrist. "He's my partner."

The twins nodded at each other, counted to four, and began to sing together.

"Stop, stop!" the man in blue shouted. "I recognize you both! I recognize your song!"

Colleen and Colin stopped, somehow still grinning and hopeful.

"He recognizes us," Colin said, stars in his eyes.

"We'll be famous!" Colleen swooned, her hands clasped to her heart.

"I recognize you because your act was so remarkably painful to watch," the man said. "You step on each other's cues. You constantly try to outdo each other. You sound more like a *duel* than a duet!"

Exasperated, he reached into his pocket and pulled out a torn and crumpled sheet of paper. He squinted at the ink on it and said, "Does anyone else live here? Another teenage singer who auditioned today?"

"No one!" Mara shouted, stepping in front of Chantella. "My twins, whom you've so rudely insulted this afternoon, are the only ones!"

Just then, Verna and Chantella's father, who had heard the commotion from the kitchen, hurried into the living room.

"Hmm," the man said again, trying to peek past Mara, "who is that, then?" He peered towards Chantella.

"That's my daughter," Chantella's dad said. "She aud–"

"She's just the maid!" Mara said, cutting him off.

"Nonsense!" Verna said, nudging Mara aside. "She's not the maid. This is more her house than it is theirs." She waved dismissively towards the twins.

"Maid or not," the man in blue said, "makes no difference to me. If she can sing, I want to hear it."

"Waste of time!" Mara shouted as Chantella stepped forward. "And who are *you* anyway?" she growled to Verna.

"A family friend," Verna said simply.

"What should we do?" Colleen whispered to Colin, but he just shrugged.

Then Chantella took a deep breath and stepped forward. Her heart pounded. Her skin tingled. Then she clasped her fingers together and began to sing.

The man's stern mouth turned into a gentle smile. His eyes, which before were almost disdainful, softened.

Chantella sang an entire song for him, feeling less nervous and more confident as she went. When she finished the refrain, the man clapped his hands.

"Beautiful," he said. "Your voice is every bit the voice of your mother's. I'd know it anywhere – even if I didn't recognize you when you weren't wearing that beautiful dress."

"Thank you," Chantella said.

The man picked up his coat and got ready to leave. "I suppose it goes without saying," he said. "You've won this audition. You're going to be a star!" Chantella couldn't speak. She smiled and hugged him.

"We'll be in touch soon," he said. "My name is Brendan Charmant, and I'm the producer of *Next Teen Star*. Contact me if you need anything at all," he said as he left. Chantella waved from the doorway as his sleek black car pulled out of the driveway.

Mara faced Chantella, her father and Verna with an evil look on her face. "This changes nothing," she said. "I'll take you for everything you're worth. The house. The cars. I'll get you for alimony till the day you die!"

"Alimony?" Verna said. "You've been married less than six months!"

Chantella's dad stood up straight, a peaceful and triumphant look on his face. "You know what, Mara?" he said. "You want the house? The cars? Take 'em."

"Dad!" Chantella said, horrified.

"My girl and I," her dad said, taking Chantella's hands in his, "are going to London, and we're not looking back."

"You mean it?" Chantella said. She could hardly believe it.

Her dad nodded. "It's what I should have done for your mother years ago, but I was obsessed with my business and money instead."

Chantella hugged him. "Can we bring Verna with us?" she asked.

Her dad shrugged. "I suppose," he said.

They both looked around the living room, but the nanny was gone.

* * *

Chantella and her father rented a flat in the centre of London. Because her father didn't put up any fight about money or property, the divorce was final quickly.

Chantella came in second in the national *Next Teen Star* competition. She lost in the very final round to an opera singer from Alaska. He was an impressive musician, Chantella had to admit.

And the "Girl with the Glass Voice", as Chantella came to be known on the show, was a huge hit with the audience. Her performance in the *Next Teen Star* finale, though it didn't win, got over a million views online in just two weeks.

The producer of the programme, Brendan Charmant, had so much faith in her talent that he left his job at *Next Teen Star* to become her manager, booking performances and meet-and-greets for her all around the country and preparing to sign a contract with a top record company for her first album.

If you watched the video of Chantella's final performance very carefully – which Chantella often did – you could see a young woman in the front row of the audience. She was wearing a bright-green dress and a matching hat with a green feather in it, and she was the first person on her feet when Chantella finished her performance.

Chantella watched the video over and over just to see that woman: Verna, her former nanny, whom Chantella hadn't been able to track down since moving to London.

Maybe one day, when Chantella needed her more than anything, Verna would pop in again like a fairy godmother and grant her all her wishes.

But for now, living happily in the capital with her dad, Chantella felt like all her wishes had come true.

With Brendan teaching her the ropes of the singing business, Chantella quickly became popular throughout the country. Brendan booked her on a national tour that began immediately after her work for *Next Teen Star* wrapped up. Chantella's show in her home town is already sold out.

THE GLASS VOICE

I'm in the basement again. It's dark down here, and it smells like mildew and fabric softener. Light flickers at me from the huge flat screen mounted on the far wall. It faces my couch. Well, I call it a couch. It might as well be a bed. I sleep down here. I eat down here. I play video games down here. I–

"Carlo!" It's my mother. I don't bother responding. "You've been down there all summer!" she says. "Are you coming upstairs ever again?"

"Not if I can help it," I mutter to myself. Maybe she'll just assume I'm sleeping with the television on. Her high heels clomp down the bare wood stairs. I quickly roll to my side and close my eyes to fake sleep.

"I know you're awake," she says. "I heard the channels changing."

"Fine," I say. "What do you want?"

"I'm going out now," she says. I open one eye first, then the other. She's in a fancy black suit, with her dark hair blown out in ridiculous waves. She's wearing loads of make-up, too.

"Have fun," I say.

She puts a hand on her hip and sighs at me. "What will you do for dinner?" she asks. I lift the remote and switch from some action film with a man in a suit to an action film with a guy in a tank top. I shrug.

"I'll ask Santino to make something for you," she says. Santino's our chef. He lives somewhere in the south wing, I think.

"I can make something myself," I say. It's true. I can. I am an expert at preparing all types of cereal.

"Then I'll give Santino the night off," she replies.

"Whatever," I say, and I push the volume button up with my thumb. "Bye!"

The next thing I hear is the front door slamming.

"Great," I say to myself after the house is quiet. "Now I'm hungry." I swear I wouldn't have even thought of food if Mum hadn't mentioned supper.

I push myself up off the couch and manage to get upstairs. The orangey light in the kitchen means it's after seven. It also means it's late August. It also means school starts next week. I'm not ready for that.

I pour myself a bowl of something colourful and sweet with a little plastic toy inside the box. Then I lean on the kitchen worktop to eat.

"Ah!" says Santino as he steps into the kitchen. "I would have made you something."

"It's all right," I say.

"This sugary rubbish," he says, "is *not* all right. I could have made that pasta from last week you liked so much."

My eyebrows shoot up. I love his food. I just don't like the idea of being waited on, like Mum and I are some kind of royalty. We're not. We're two fools living in a ridiculous mansion that neither of us paid for. We're just lucky because Dad was very, very rich.

Was.

Santino obviously sees my interest in his pasta, because he gives me a big grin. Even though he's already hung up his apron, he grabs a pan from the cupboard.

"Penne with vodka sauce," he says. "Fresh peas. A little cream."

"You don't have to do this, Santino," I say, but I'm already ditching my cereal. "You're off the clock."

"Please, please," he says. "I'm happy to. What am I going to do tonight anyway? Fall asleep in front of the TV? What fun is that?"

Well, it's not that *bad,* I think.

"You know I'm happy to make a good supper for you and Mrs Mostro," he says, "any time."

"Thanks, Santino," I say.

"Now get out of here," he says, turning his back to me and strapping the apron on again. I'm about to head right back downstairs when the doorbell rings. It makes me jump.

I turn and watch Santino chopping pancetta. "Well?" I say. He's not the butler; he's the chef. Still, when he's around, he usually answers the door. And with our housekeeper Catalina off on holiday, I really expect him to step up. But no.

"Ah-ah!" Santino says, not even bothering to turn from the chopping board to look at me. "I'm off the clock."

I laugh, but he's not kidding. "You expect *me* to open the door?" I say. Santino pretends he can't hear, continuing to chop and whistle to himself. So I shove through the swinging kitchen door into the big entrance hall. Lightning cracks outside – I didn't even know it had started raining.

When I open the door, a man rushes right past me, his coat pulled up over his head.

"Whoa!" I say, flinching at the spray as he shakes off.

"I'm terribly sorry to bother you at this hour," he shouts over the thunder. "Car trouble."

Santino comes through the swinging door, wiping his hands on a tea towel.

"Sir," the stranger says, moving to shake Santino's hand. "I'm so sorry for bursting in. If I could just use your phone, I'm happy to wait outside."

He thinks Santino is my dad. It reminds me of what I've tried to forget. My dad is dead.

"I'll show you the way to the phone," I say, stepping between them. "Mr...?"

"Forgive me. I'm Jack Beaumont," he says. He stands up straight for the first time since he burst in. He has a greying blond moustache. He pulls off his hat to reveal a head of thinning hair, the same shade as his moustache.

"I'm Carlo," I say. "This is my house. And this" – I thumb at Santino – "is our chef." I pause, thinking for a minute.

"Don't you have a mobile?" I ask.

"Ah," he says, looking away from me. "The battery died. Very annoying." He forces a smile and a shrug. For some reason, I think he's lying.

"Follow me," I say. I lead Mr Beaumont through the kitchen, through the back door to the courtyard, and out to my mother's greenhouse. We have other phones, but the greenhouse is the only room enclosed in windows. That means I can keep an eye on him from the kitchen.

"Right here," I say, gesturing to Mum's wicker patio set, with a phone on the side table. "I'll let you have some privacy."

He thanks me and sits down. I pull up my hood and dart across the courtyard to the kitchen. I sit on the stool by the window to watch Mr Beaumont. He has the phone cradled under his ear, and he's wandering through Mum's prize-winning indoor garden. Now and then he stops to read a label or take a leaf between his thumb and forefinger, like he's testing the quality of a piece of fabric.

"I shouldn't have let him in," I say to Santino.

He sighs. "Maybe," he says. "But this is some storm."

* * *

I can't imagine what's keeping Dad, I think as I sit in my bedroom. Well, sort of my bedroom. It was Dad's office until my room upstairs sprung a leak in the ceiling. Now I sleep in Dad's office.

Not that he needs it. His business went belly-up two years ago when one of his planes crashed in the middle of the Pacific Ocean. It was carrying most of the company's merchandise. When it was lost, Dad was responsible. He went bankrupt. Since then, we've lived modestly. This once-magnificent house on one of the most beautiful streets in the city is crumbling.

But tonight I feel hopeful. Dad had an important meeting out by the ocean, near the big homes and the cute villages with fudge shops.

The phone rings and I dive to grab it. "Dad?"

"Hello, Belle," he says. I can hear the disappointment in his voice.

"What happened?" I say. I hate the sound of my own voice, full of disapproval. I imagine that I sound like a scolding mother. But my mum died when I was young. I don't even remember the sound of her voice.

"Just a little mishap with the car," he says. "Belle, the ocean here under the moonlight is positively breathtaking."

"Where are you?" I ask.

"Just waiting for the tow truck," Dad says. He takes a loud, long breath through his nose, like he's smelling something.

"Where are you waiting?" I ask.

"The most amazing house," Dad says. "It's the sort of house you'd love, on a hill overlooking the ocean. I can hear the waves crashing from here."

"Whose house is it?" I ask.

"I didn't get the last name," Dad says. He seems distracted. He sniffs again and sighs.

"Dad," I say. "What do you keep sniffing?"

"Flowers," he says. "I'm in a greenhouse."

At the very word, I feel like I'm there too, surrounded by winding paths through the ornate glass wing of the estate, each path greener and more floral than the last. There are even butterflies, and it's warm and smells sweet inside. I'm jealous, and Dad knows it.

"I'm sorry, sweetheart," he says. "I wish you could see this place. The roses" – he actually gasps – "the flowers are so big and fragrant. It's intoxicating."

"Red ones?" I ask.

"Red ones," he says. Then he adds in a whisper. "Perhaps … perhaps you *can* see one."

"Dad," I say. I know what he's thinking. "Don't."

"Oh, you worry too much," he says. "They won't miss one little bud."

But I know my dad, and he won't pick some little bud. He'll pick the biggest, most beautiful flower in the greenhouse. "Dad, please don't," I say. "What if you get caught?"

Dad laughs. "By who?" he says. "The cook or the teenager? Trust me, Belle. It'll be fine."

* * *

"I'll kill him," I growl, marching towards the kitchen door to the courtyard.

"Carlo," Santino says, grabbing my elbow. "Try to stay calm. I'll speak to him."

I pull my arm away and throw open the door, stomping outside. It's still storming, and rain blows into the kitchen.

White light cracks across the sky. Thunder booms – the perfect soundtrack for my rage. Then lightning cracks again, this time right overhead, as I enter the greenhouse.

"How dare you!" I roar.

Mr Beaumont jumps at the sound, dropping the phone and the rose he's stolen from my mother's prize-winning crop. His jaw drops too, and he throws up his hands. I grab him by the lapel of his jacket and lift him 15 centimetres off the ground, so we're eye to eye. "P-p-please," he stammers, his voice high and thin, like a frightened child's. "I meant no harm."

I give him a shake. "Those are my mother's prize-winning roses," I snarl. "They're worth a fortune – in money and time and pride."

"I didn't know," he says. "I thought– I thought my daughter might like one."

I give him another shake. "You should have asked," I say. Then I toss him to the rubber mat on the ground.

He looks up at me, covering his face with his arms. "Please," he says. "I just took it for my daughter. I'm very sorry. She just loves flowers so much and I can't afford to…"

He's petrified. Terrified. Of *me*.

I haven't always been an angry, violent boy. I don't know what comes over me sometimes. I become a monster. I take a few deep breaths to clear my head.

"I'm calling the police," I say, and I move to pick up the phone from the ground. I can hear a girl's voice on the other end of the line. Mr Beaumont grabs my wrist.

"Please," he says. "Don't call the police. I couldn't live with the shame. And my poor daughter…"

I grab the phone, but instead of hanging up and calling the police, I put it to my ear. There's someone shouting. "Stop," I say into the phone. The line goes silent, aside from some nervous breathing. "How old are you?"

"Um," says the girl. I assume it's Mr Beaumont's daughter. "Fifteen."

I hang up. "You can go," I say. "I won't call the police. You can keep that flower."

Mr Beaumont slowly stands up. "Thank you," he says. "You've been so generous, I–"

"I wasn't done," I say. I grab him under the arm and lead him back into the house. "Our housekeeper has another week of holiday left," I say as we reach the front door. "And the house is in a dreadful state."

Mr Beaumont's head swivels as he looks around. "It looks okay to me," he says.

I ignore him. "Your daughter will make up for it," I say. "Send her here tomorrow. She will clean the house for the rest of the week, and the rose will be paid for."

"A week of labour for a single flower?" he says, shocked.

"Would you rather I call the police?" I say.

He stands up straighter. "No," he says.

Now *I* am shocked. Will Mr Beaumont agree to this absurd plan? I only meant to humiliate him.

"If that is what it will take to renew my family's honour, then so be it," he says proudly.

"Fine," I say, and I open the front door for him. Orange and yellow lights flash across the front of the house.

"A tow truck has arrived for me," Mr Beaumont says. "Thank you for your hospitality." He bows to me as he departs. "My daughter will be at your door first thing tomorrow morning."

"See that she is," I say, closing the door behind him. I watch from the front window as he climbs into the tow truck's cab.

I don't believe for a moment that the old loser's daughter will actually show up. But it was fun to make him squirm a little.

* * *

Dad still isn't home, and I'm tired of waiting. Shouldn't *he* be the one worrying and waiting up for me?

I pull my phone from my pocket. It doesn't work as a phone though. Some expenses just had to be cut, and that included mobile phones. But the phone's clock works, and sometimes I use the Wi-Fi from the café across the street.

It's ten o'clock when I hear keys jingle outside the front door. I pull it open before Dad can get it unlocked. "Finally!" I snap. He jumps. "Do you know how worried I've been?"

Instead of apologizing and offering an explanation for disappearing from our phone call, Dad holds out a single long-stemmed rose. "For my Belle," he says, smiling.

I wish I could explain what comes over me when Dad gives me a rose. All the anger that's been bubbling up inside me, pacing in the front hall for the last hour and a half, fizzles away. I take the rose and put it to my lips so I can feel the softness of its petals and let its perfect fragrance fill my nose.

"It's beautiful," I say.

"My dear, what an evening I've had," Dad says. There's laughter in his voice.

"I don't understand why you're in such a good mood," I say. "Your meeting went terribly. You wrecked the car. And who knows what happened in that house!"

In an instant, Dad is bent over laughing, slapping his legs. His face is bright red.

"Tell me what's so funny!" I demand.

So he does. He tells me about the crash – how he'd had his eyes on the ocean under the sunset and didn't see the curve in the road. He tells me about the mansion on the hill above the beach. He tells me about the awful young man – dark hair, dark eyes, dark mood.

"He was a beast," Dad says as I follow him into the living room. He sits in his old recliner. "Ill-tempered. Violent. Just extremely irritable."

"Sounds like a monster," I say, sitting on the arm of the chair.

Dad puts an arm around me. "I haven't told you the best part. He caught me helping myself to that one rose – not even that special, really. I've seen hundreds like it."

I nod, but it's not true. The rose Dad brought home tonight is extraordinary. I've never seen a rose so red, with petals so fine.

"He fell into a mad rage!" Dad says. "I thought he might tear me to pieces with his bare hands!"

I gasp, on cue. "But then he seemed to calm down," Dad goes on, "and he made the most amusing suggestion. He'd let me go unharmed, and he'd even let me bring that ordinary rose home to you, on one condition. That *you*," he says, taking my chin in his hand, "go and work for him as a *maid!*"

He stares up at me, his mouth open in an amused grin, as if expecting me to laugh right along with him. Instead, I slide off the arm of the chair and put my hands on my hips. "Are you kidding?" I say. "The nerve..."

"I know!" Dad says. He gets up and walks to the bookshelf at the far wall. That's where he keeps his fancy whisky – the only trace of his wealth that remains. "Astounding," he says as he pours his drink. "Well, it was that or – get this – he'd call the police. All for a lousy rose!"

"He *didn't!*" I say, leaning forward. "He called the police?"

Dad cocks his left eyebrow in that funny way he has. It must've been charming when he was a young man.

"Of course not," he says. "I told him you'd be happy to come and clean, and then I hopped into the tow truck." He sips his drink. I stare at him. "What?" he says.

"You told him I'd..." I say, not able to believe it.

"Oh, Belle," he says, "I certainly never meant for you to actually go there to clean." He takes another sip. "The idea," he says. "My Belle Beaumont should clean that showy mansion for a loud, pushy son of social climbers? I think not."

"Then you lied," I say, my voice quiet.

"Hmm?" he says, looking at me through the bottom of his tumbler.

"You lied," I repeat.

"I suppose I did," Dad says, shrugging. "What would you have me do now? Call the police? Turn myself in for stealing a rose?"

"That won't be necessary," I say. "I intend to keep the promise you made."

"What?" Dad says. "You can't be serious."

"I'd better get to bed so I can catch the early train to the beach," I say, heading upstairs.

He laughs. "But dear, you don't know the address."

* * *

In the morning, I'm up with the sun. I hear Dad's loud snores as I creep past his room. I hurry down the steps, find his coat, and dig in the pockets. It's as I guessed: the tow truck receipt is there, folded and wrinkled but very much legible.

Now I have the address. By the time Dad wakes up, I'll be at the mansion on the hill above the ocean.

* * *

I'm dreaming. It's thundering in the dream, and there are voices – Mum and Dad. Mum is shouting. "Dad is back!" I scream at her. Back from the dead, I mean. "Don't shout at him!"

Then there's another voice – a voice I don't know. A girl's voice. It wakes me, and I sit up on the couch in the dark basement to find my blanket and pillows on the floor – and shouting coming down through the ceiling. I can hear Santino and Mum.

And then there's the girl's voice – quiet, almost timid. I can't make out what she's saying. Especially with Santino and Mum yelling over her.

"It's too early!" Mum shouts.

Mum usually speaks in a shout. Sometimes an excited shout, sometimes an angry shout, sometimes a shout of sorrow, but almost always a shout. "My head is pounding. My feet are throbbing. Explain yourself."

The girl replies, but it's a murmur. Santino's gentle, deep voice interjects now and then: "It's true," he says. "Ah," he adds. "Of course, of course," he agrees.

"I don't know anyone called Beaumont," Mum says. I sit up a little straighter.

Beaumont. It begins to come back to me – what happened last night.

"Carlo," Santino says. His voice is comforting. "He knows what this is about."

I sure do, I think as I pull on yesterday's jeans. Barefoot and wrinkled from sleep, I make my way upstairs to the entrance hall, pushing my way through the swinging door and running a hand through my greasy, floppy mess of hair.

"*There* you are," says Mum when she spots me, and the swinging door hits me in the back when it closes.

Mum's in her dark green terrycloth robe and slippers. She's got one hand on her hip and another on her head. She had a late night, apparently. Santino is in his chef's whites, a towel on his shoulder and an omelette pan in his hand.

And between them, with hair the colour of maple leaves in October and eyes as grey as the sky over the ocean during a storm, is the most beautiful girl I've ever seen.

* * *

I've been standing in the entrance hall of this house for the last three minutes being yelled at by a woman who'd fit right in on a reality show about rich housewives. And there's a chef who pops in once in a while with a know-it-all remark.

Now this boy is staring at me from the doorway. He's my age, but he looks like he hasn't seen the sun in years. His hair is wild and greasy. His clothes are stained and wrinkled.

The kitchen door swings closed behind him and knocks him in the back. I giggle. I can't help it.

"*There* you are," the woman says to him. He's her son, I assume. "Do you know what this girl wants?"

"I'll handle it," the boy says. His voice is quiet and gruff.

"Good," the woman says, walking away. "I'm going back to bed."

"Ah, well," says the chef. "Carlo, this is–"

"Just go and make me breakfast, Santino," says the boy – Carlo, apparently.

"Of course," Santino says. He smiles at me and slips past Carlo into the kitchen.

"I didn't think you'd actually show up," Carlo says, crossing his arms.

"My dad didn't want me to come," I say. I'm trying to appear confident and calm, but I didn't think this through. Am I really going to spend the last few days of my summer holiday cleaning the huge home of a very rude family?

"But I believe in keeping promises," I continue. "Even to a beast like you."

"A beast?" he says.

"You'd have to be a monster," I say, "to force a girl to be a servant because of a single silly rose."

He narrows his eyes and stares at me a moment too long. "What's your name?"

"Belle," I say.

He grunts and turns his back on me. "Cleaning stuff is in this cupboard," he says, banging his fist on the cupboard door. "You can start in the dining room. It's always dusty."

He puts a hand on the kitchen door to leave and then stops, looking at me over his shoulder. "Stay out of the greenhouse," he says. He pushes the door open and calls back, "And the basement!"

* * *

"This is insane," I mumble. I'm pacing in the basement, and upstairs is a girl. A girl my age. A beautiful girl my age.

"Can that really be her name?" I say to myself, falling backwards onto the couch. I pick up the remote and click on the TV. "Belle – like a fairy-tale princess? It's too much."

I can't believe how quickly I'm falling for this girl. There was this feeling I had in my chest when I saw her face – kind of like someone had taken my heart and squeezed it. It's all I've felt besides sadness or anger for the last five months.

"I have to see her again," I whisper. Rather than run up from the basement to find her in the dining room, I simply switch inputs on the TV to access the house's closed-circuit security system.

Cameras. They're all over the house. We never use them, really. Now and then I'll check them to make sure the kitchen is empty before I sneak up there for a midnight snack. But otherwise, they're strictly for security. If some-one were to break in, we'd have full-colour photos of the criminal.

I click to the dining room camera, and there she is. She has a rag in one hand and a bottle of polish in the other. She sprays the table and wipes it down.

Eventually she leaves the dining room. I have to click through the cameras to find her. When I do, she's in the living room, pushing the vacuum across the carpeted floor.

I've been wasting my time staring at the surveillance channels for far too long when I realize I'm hungry again. It must be almost lunchtime. I'm thinking of sticking my head into the kitchen when Belle disappears from the living room.

I click through all the channels – kitchen, dining room, upstairs, greenhouse, Mum's workout room, rear grounds – and find no sign of her.

I'm hungry anyway. I might as well go up and ask Santino to make lunch. Maybe I'll catch a glimpse of Belle while I'm up there. I click the TV off and head upstairs.

I'm almost to the top of the basement steps when the door flies open, sending me sprawling back down the wooden stairs, and onto the carpeted basement floor.

* * *

"Oh!" I say. I reach for him – much too late. Then my hands go to my mouth as he tumbles down the steps onto the basement floor. "I'm so sorry!"

"What are you doing?!" he snarls up at me. "I told you to stay out of the basement!"

"I'm really sorry," I say. He's not hurt – just embarrassed. He should be, too. Not because he fell, but because the basement is a dank and disgusting place, smelling of old laundry and tomato sauce. And I get the feeling he spends all of his time down here.

"Did you finish cleaning the living room?" he snaps as he gets to his feet.

"Living room?" I say, because he asked me to clean the dining room, not the living room. I did some cleaning in the living room, too, but how would he know that?

"I mean the dining room," he says, looking away from me. "Did you or not?"

"Yes," I say, "but I came to tell you that I'm leaving now."

"Already?" he says. I can't tell if he's angry that I haven't done more work or just disappointed that I'm leaving.

"Yes," I say. "I have a job at the hospital in the after noons. The trip back to the city is very long on buses and trains and all that."

"Oh," he says. "Fine, then." He starts up the stairs towards me and puts a hand on the door, as if to slam it in my face.

"I'll be back tomorrow morning," I say. And it's true. I'll keep my dad's promise, even if it's insane. Dad needs to know what it means to be honest in business, and I need to show him.

"You better," Carlo growls. "And the day after that, too, and after that – till our housekeeper Catalina is back."

"I will," I say, and I quickly step back as Carlo slams the basement door, barely missing my toes.

"What a nerve," I mutter to myself as I turn away from the basement door, and there's Santino, watching me. Watching us. He looks away quickly.

"It's fine, Santino," I say. "You have a right to keep your ears and eyes unplugged while you're in your own kitchen."

I lean on the marble island and stare at the Mediterranean tile floor, which I'll probably have to clean in the morning. I hope Santino isn't a messy cook.

"He's been through a lot lately," Santino whispers. "Try not to hold it against him."

"He makes it very difficult," I say, sighing.

Santino suddenly brightens. "Here," he says, and he grabs a paper-wrapped parcel, holding it out to me. "Lunch."

"Oh, I shouldn't," I say. "I really have to get going. The bus will be by in a few minutes."

"I made it to take away," Santino says.

Whatever he's been cooking in here all morning smells amazing. If this is even a tiny sampling of that, it'll be the best lunch I've had in ages. "Thank you," I say. "It's very nice of you." He waves me off, like I shouldn't mention it.

"I really should go now," I say, heading out of the kitchen. "I'll see you tomorrow."

"Tomorrow!" he calls after me.

* * *

I cannot believe that chef of ours. He's just given her lunch! I hear her footsteps hurrying through the house. I hear the front door close when she leaves. An instant later, the basement door creaks, and a sliver of light from the kitchen pokes into my sanctuary.

"What do you want?" I snap. I don't know if it's Mum or Santino, but it makes no difference.

"Hello, *luce del sole*," Santino says. It means "sunshine" in Italian. He's hilarious. He's carrying a tray, which means it's lunchtime.

"I don't want it," I say, turning the TV on.

"Who says this is for you?" Santino cracks. "Maybe I'm planning to eat my lunch down here in front of the TV. Ever think of that?"

See? He's hilarious.

He puts the tray down on the small table next to the couch. "Look. Eat something. You seem extra grumpy today."

I turn up the volume.

"Is it because of the girl?" Santino shouts over the blaring TV. So I turn it up even louder. He grabs the remote from me and turns it off.

"She's very nice," Santino says. "And very pretty."

"Go back upstairs," I say.

Santino sighs. "You know," he says, "she could be the one."

"The one?" I repeat because I don't know what he's talking about.

"The one to break the curse," Santino says. "The curse of the boy who has locked himself away in the basement of misery and despair for these last five months."

"Go upstairs," I repeat.

"I'm just saying…"

So now I roar at him: "Go upstairs!"

He finally retreats, his palms turned up and a fake apologetic grin on his face.

* * *

When I get home after eight o'clock, my back and feet are sore, and my hands are callused and cramped. I open the front door and see Dad pacing across the living room floor. He looks worried.

"Finally!" he shouts, his face turning red.

So maybe he wasn't worried … just mad.

"Do you know the state I've been in all day?" he shouts.

I slide past him and hobble over to the beat-up couch in the living room, falling onto it with a sigh.

"I was worried sick," he says.

I manage to lift my eyes to glare at him. "Why?" I say.

"Who knew what might have happened to you!" he says.

"You knew where I was," I reply with my last ounce of strength.

"I certainly did," he says. "Which is the other thing. You disobeyed me."

"Mmhmm," I mumble. "And you lied."

"To a stranger!" he says. "To save my reputation."

"Ha!" I say, lifting my head to face him. "I saved your reputation by keeping your stupid promise!"

Dad snorts and sits heavily in his recliner, and I drop my head back again. I can feel him glaring at me from all the way across the living room.

"Well, you won't go back again," Dad says. "You've made your point. Now stop this foolishness. A girl your age, working as a maid *and* a hospital orderly. It's inappropriate."

"So is lying," I say, "and making promises you have no intention of keeping."

"Enough!" he snaps. "No more, is that clear?"

"It's clear," I say, "but now *I've* made a promise – to go back until their housekeeper returns – and I intend to keep it."

"You're crazy," Dad says.

I take a deep breath and push myself up into a seated position. "The boy who lives there," I say. "Carlo. He's something, isn't he?"

"I had the pleasure," Dad says sarcastically.

"He really is awful, huh?" I say, remembering the tone in the boy's voice and the anger on his face. But I also remember what Santino said, and I remember Carlo's tone when I told him I had to leave and he said, "Already?"

"He probably just needs a friend," I say. I don't even mean to say it aloud. I'm not even sure I believe it. Dad sure doesn't. He laughs – a short, dismissive laugh.

"Well, it's true," I say. "I mean, locked away in that house, in the dark basement, with only his crazy mother and their chef for company. Of course he's miserable."

"Maybe he does need a friend," Dad says. "But it doesn't need to be you."

"I think I can get through to him," I say.

Dad groans. "I had a very long day," he says. "I'm going to bed." He kisses my forehead. "I suppose you'll be gone before I'm awake?"

"Unless you're up before five," I say, blowing him a kiss.

* * *

I'm on the balcony this morning, looking down at the driveway. When the doorbell rings, I step back against the wall. I hear Santino hurry for the door. "Just a second," he calls. Then he pulls open the door. "Ciao, Bella!" he says.

"Good morning, Santino," Belle says as she steps inside.

There's that feeling in my chest again, only this time, the hand that takes my heart and squeezes it holds on just a little longer, and my breath is gone for just a little longer. When I can breathe again, I gasp and cough.

Santino and Belle both look up and find me on the balcony, looking down at them.

"Start in the library today," I roar down. "It'll probably take all morning. It's covered in dust."

"Some people," Belle says, holding my gaze with her stony-grey eyes, "open with things like 'hello' or 'good morning'."

I throw my hands onto the railing and shout down at her, "Library!" Then I turn my back on them and open my bedroom door.

I've hardly been in here all summer. In fact, as I sit on the edge of the bed and stare at the desk across the room, I realize I haven't been in here at all in five months.

My action figures are still there on my desk, lined up in a neat row. There are books there, too – stories of monsters, knights, dragons, elves, trolls and kings. I used to love reading books. Last winter, when Dad was already ill – though we didn't know it yet – he and I spent the cold months passing our favourite books back and forth. Now I can hardly look at them.

There's a photo in a plain red frame on the desk. I'd forgotten about that photo. It's Mum, smiling and happy, and me, about nine or ten years old. And with his arm around me, there's Dad. He looks exhausted and happy. It was the last day of our Caribbean holiday on Dad's weekender yacht. He was both captain and crew.

I actually smile for an instant, remembering the holiday and remembering Dad. But the tiny spotlight of happiness isn't strong enough to push out the anger and the sadness. I lift the picture over my head and slam it against the desktop. The glass shatters into a hundred pieces.

* * *

I jump at the sound coming from upstairs. Santino flinches a little, but he hardly seems to notice.

"He's been so unhappy," Santino says. He's leading me through the house to the library. As we're walking down a long hallway, decorated with paintings and photographs from all over the world, Santino stops.

"His father passed away," he says quietly.

"Oh, I'm sorry," I say, and I truly am. I should have guessed something traumatic happened to him.

"Carlo is a sensitive boy," Santino says as he starts walking down the hall again.

I follow along, all the while thinking, *Carlo? Sensitive?*

"To tell you the truth," Santino says as we reach a pair of closed doors at the end of the hall, "I was surprised he asked you to clean the library."

Santino pulls a key from his pocket, unlocks the doors, then pushes them open. "Because no one ever comes in here," he says. "It was Mr Mostro's private sanctuary."

"Wow," I say walking into the room. It's huge, and there are bookshelves everywhere. "I guess Carlo's dad was a big reader."

Santino closes his eyes and nods. "The biggest. Carlo, too." My eyes widen. "I know it's hard to believe these days," Santino continues, laughing, "but he and his father were cut from the same cloth."

"He couldn't possibly have read all these books," I say, turning around the massive room. I love books. I used to buy books all the time, but I haven't since Dad's business failed. Now I go to the library when I can.

"He may have missed a few," Santino says, "but you'd be surprised." He shows me around, explaining, "These are biographies. Here are mysteries – Mr Mostro's favourites. Here are the fantasy and science fiction stories – Carlo's favourites. World history. Philosophy. Theology. Mythology. It goes on and on."

"It's an amazing collection," I say. "I could spend all morning here, reading instead of cleaning." I add, "I mean, I wouldn't, of course. I'm here to work, like I promised."

Santino chuckles. "Don't be silly," he says. "We all know this arrangement Carlo and your father made is … well, it's crazy."

"A bit," I say. "But I'll keep my promise."

Santino shrugs as he heads out of the room. "Suit yourself," he says. "I'll be heading back to the kitchen. I wonder what lunch I should pack for you today…"

With a smile on my face, I pull the duster from my bucket and start in on the shelves of leather-bound books, reading their spines, some printed in fine gold lettering. There are stories in Italian and English and Latin and Greek and languages I can't identify. There are tales of dragons and spaceships and colonies on Saturn's moons. There are thick volumes of poetry and ancient myths and histories of ancient people who sailed the world's oceans.

It's too much to bear, smelling their paper and glue and bindings, dusting the shelves and the spines, but unable to pull one out to pore over its pages. I think I might burst.

* * *

I'm back in the basement, where I can wallow in darkness and think about exactly nothing: not about Dad and our perfect life before he became ill, not about Belle and her perfect face.

I slouch on the comfy basement couch and stare at the huge screen across the room, shooting my way through the hordes of zombies.

It's got to be almost noon when I hear Santino's knock on the basement door. He doesn't wait for my reply, though. He just throws the door wide open, flooding my basement with light.

"Close the door!" I shout.

"Oh, please forgive the interruption," Santino says. He's being sarcastic, of course. "Belle will be leaving in a few minutes. I thought you might like to come upstairs and do something civil for a change, like say goodbye."

"Nah," I say. "Is that all?" I glance at Santino as he rolls his eyes and departs.

The moment the door closes, I switch to the surveillance video and find Belle in the library. But she's not cleaning at all. Instead, she's perched on the edge of one of the red leather chairs near the fireplace, one of Dad's books open on her knees and a stack of books – perhaps ones she's already paged through – on the floor beside her.

I jump up from the couch, roaring as I run upstairs and through the kitchen.

"What's happened?" Santino says, but I ignore him and head for the rear hall. As I bang open the library doors, she jumps up from the chair.

"What do you think you're doing?!" I growl as I cross the library's huge floor. I stop in front of her, grab the book she is looking through, and slam it down on the pile beside her, sending the tower of books to the floor.

"I'm sorry," she says quietly.

"You're just like your dad," I say. I can feel my face getting hot. "You come into our house, into the spaces that are most precious to my family!" I shout. "You put your filthy hands on the things that matter most to us." She cowers as I scream, but I can't stop yelling. I don't even *want* to stop yelling. "Like you're entitled to everything we have," I say. "But you're not! You couldn't possibly understand what it's like to be us! Because you're nothing! You're worthless!"

And Belle slaps my face. Hard.

★ ★ ★

"Ow." Carlo stares at me, holding his hand on his cheek.

"Oh my goodness," I say, putting a hand to my mouth. "I'm sorry." He turns away from me, so I take his wrist. "Let me see," I say. "I'm so sorry."

"It's fine," Carlo whispers, pulling his arm away from me.

Santino clears his throat in the doorway. He's been watching us the entire time. "Don't be sorry," he says. "He had it coming."

• 236 •

I shoot Santino a glare, hoping he'll take the hint to leave. He does, but not before he holds up a paper bag and places it on the table by the door. My lunch, to take away.

I put a hand on Carlo's back, and he flinches, but he doesn't pull away. "I'm sorry I hit you," I say. "I have to go now. I'll be back in the morning." I head for the door and grab the paper bag. I look back at Carlo.

"No," he says. "You don't have to come back."

I should be happy. I should simply thank him and never come back.

"No," I say instead. "I'll be back in the morning."

* * *

That night, I dream I'm in a French garden, lost in a maze of rose bushes, stone benches and fountains. I'm not afraid, though. I'm aware that someone is chasing me. But it's for fun, and I'm laughing. He's laughing, too.

I round a corner in the maze and shriek with laughter as I run smack into him. He laughs too and picks me up in a hug. He has the brightest eyes, full of joy and love – love for me. I know his eyes.

Then the world around us goes black, and I'm alone, still in the garden maze. I'm not laughing anymore. Instead, I'm breathless with fear, afraid to run and afraid to stand still.

I hear my pursuer making his way through the shrubs – he isn't laughing now. He breathes and snarls like a monster, and I cower into the darkest corner I can find, hoping the sun will come out. When I catch a glimpse of the beast as he rounds the corner, I sit up in bed with a start, scared out of the dream.

* * *

I'm awake before Santino this morning. I'm spreading peanut butter on toast when Santino comes into the kitchen wearing his chef's outfit.

"This is a nice surprise," Santino says. He heads towards the coffee pot. "You're up awfully early – or have you not gone to bed yet? I can never tell the difference."

"Ha ha," I say.

Santino fills the pot with water. "So why are you up then?" he asks. "Just keeping me company?"

"I'm too angry to sleep," I say.

It's not really true, though – that I'm angry. I mean, it should be true. She actually slapped me across the face.

"Can you believe she hit me?" I say.

"Yes," he says, and at that moment, the doorbell rings.

"I'll get it," I say to Santino, doing my best to make my voice sound strained and angry. But I feel excited.

I run to the entrance hall, open the door, take a step outside and say, "Good morning."

Belle is shocked for a moment. "Hello."

"I shouldn't have yelled at you," I say.

"No," she says. She starts to make her way inside. "That wasn't nice."

"But you shouldn't have hit me," I add quickly, making her stop again to look at me.

"Fair enough." She puts out her hand.

"Okay," I say, and we shake hands. She smiles at me, but then I remember that I probably still have peanut butter on my fingers from that toast I was eating, and I pull my hand away quickly.

It's too late. She definitely has some peanut butter on her hand, but she's too polite to say anything about it.

I can feel my face turning red as I wipe my hand on my jeans and head towards the kitchen. "You can clean the rooms upstairs today," I shout to her over my shoulder as I flee. "Start with the bathrooms!"

Then, without stopping to rinse my plate or say anything to a very surprised Santino, I hurry down the basement steps, into my den of solitude.

* * *

I'm watching her on the closed-circuit TV as she cleans the rooms upstairs. She's been in my bedroom – my real bedroom – for a few minutes, poking around.

But I won't yell at her this time. I'm not even sure I care.

And now she's standing in front of my desk, holding the cracked picture frame with the picture of my family ... from when we were a real family.

And she's crying. She's crying for me.

I don't know why she cares. I've been horrible to her. I've been horrible to her father. I've even been horrible to Santino.

I'm crying now, too. I shake it off and wipe my sleeve across my face. Then I hurry upstairs to the library. The pile of books is still on the floor from yesterday. I grab the one on top – the one Belle had been reading – and I sit down with it at the table.

* * *

Maybe it's because I'm finding that I care about him, that I want him to be happier, that I feel like I can help him be happier. Maybe it's just curiosity. Whatever it is, it makes me wonder about him. With a glance over my shoulder to make sure no one is watching, I slip into Carlo's bedroom and close the door behind me.

It could be any boy's room – well, any boy with a collection of action figures, a view of the ocean, a walk-in wardrobe and a queen-size bed. It's decorated with posters and bookcases and some photographs.

I walk towards the desk beside the big window that looks out over the ocean. My foot crunches on something, making me flinch. It's a piece of glass – the desk and floor nearby are littered with glass. I've found the only thing in the room in the slightest disarray – a broken picture frame and the photo it held.

There's a woman – Carlo's mother. I hardly recognize her. There's Carlo, an adorable young boy, with a smile bigger than all the outdoors. And there's a man who must be Carlo's dad.

My mother is dead, but I never knew her. It hasn't been easy – growing up without a mother. Still, I can't imagine pain like that.

I think of Carlo, so deep in darkness, living his life without joy, and my eyes fill with tears. I'm not just crying for him, though. I'm crying for myself and for Dad. I'm crying for Carlo's mother. I'm even crying for Santino. I let myself sob, just for a moment, and then wipe my eyes with the back of my hand. I know better than to dawdle here when I'm supposed to be cleaning.

* * *

It turns out there are four bathrooms on the second floor. I don't think any of them are in very heavy use, though, aside from the one in Mrs Mostro's master suite.

I spend most of the morning cleaning it, wondering if Carlo's mum is home somewhere in this huge house, or if she's gone out for the morning, or if she simply never came home at all last night.

Around noon, I walk down the main staircase and find Carlo at the bottom, apparently waiting for me. "Um," I say, stopping halfway, "am I in trouble again?" I smile at him so he knows I'm joking.

He's still in the rumpled jeans and hoodie. I wonder if he's washed the peanut butter off his hands. His handshake earlier was sticky, but I know he meant well. He's holding a paper bag and a gift-wrapped package.

"Are you leaving now?" he asks. His voice sounds gruff, but it has the tiniest smidge of friendliness.

"Yes," I say as I finish the trip downstairs. "Bus to catch." I stop in front of him, by the front door. "What's this?" I say, nodding at the packages.

"Lunch," he says, stiffly holding up the paper bag.

"Thank you," I say. "Thank Santino for me, too, please."

He nods, staring at me.

"And that?" I ask, gesturing towards his other hand.

"Oh." He holds the package up. "It's for you."

I take the package, wrapped in shiny silver paper with a forest-green ribbon.

"Thank you," I say, and I smile at him. I begin to peel away the wrapping, but he takes my hand to stop me.

"Not yet," he says. "Wait until you leave."

"Okay," I say, pleased that his hand is no longer sticky. "Why do I get a present?"

He grunts and shrugs. "Will you be back tomorrow?"

"Of course," I say.

Carlo reaches past me and opens the door. "Goodbye," he says.

* * *

I reach the bus stop with a few moments to spare and tear off a corner of the silver paper. It's a book – the book I'd been reading yesterday when he found me in the library.

"One of his dad's," I whisper.

* * *

I stand in the front hall, watching through the open door as she walks down the driveway to the main road and the bus stop.

Her hair, in the bright afternoon sunlight and blowing in the strong ocean breeze, is shining and waving like a sunset reflected on the water.

I hear the kitchen door swing open before Santino speaks. "That was a very nice thing you did," he says.

"I don't know what you're talking about," I answer.

"Of course you don't," Santino says. "But if you keep this up, that girl might actually stop slapping you."

The kitchen door swings again as Santino retreats to the kitchen. As Belle disappears around the curve at the bottom of the hill, I finally close the front door. I realize my cheeks hurt, just a tiny bit, because I've been smiling since she left.

* * *

"Chicken Marsala!" Santino announces as he comes down the basement steps with dinner.

"Thanks," I say, sitting up on the couch. He puts the tray on the little table in front of me.

"And now," Santino says, "I say good night. I'm going out for the evening."

"Out?" I say. "Where?"

He raises his eyebrows. "Can't I have a private life?" he says. "Or are you the only one who's allowed to catch a lady's eye around here?"

"Oh, come on," I say. "Get out of here."

"Mark my words," he says. "Belle cares for you." I secretly hope it's true.

Santino leaves, and I dig right in to my dinner, but my mind is spinning. *Can Belle possibly care about me?*

I'm not charming, or funny, or even clean. Let's face it, I haven't showered, brushed my hair or changed my clothes in … well, too long. I've been a monster to her.

* * *

I don't know if I've ever felt this tired. When I get home from the hospital, planning to treat myself to a short, hot bath before turning in for the night, I put the book from Carlo on the table by the door.

Then I hear voices. I peek into the living room, and I'm surprised – and not happy – to find that Dad has company. It's company Dad hasn't had in a very long time.

"Hello, Belle," says his guest. I know him at once. He's young and good-looking, but he's the kind of man who knows how good-looking he is. Totally annoying.

"Hello, Francis," I say. I force a smile.

"Sit down, darling," Dad says, patting the sofa beside him.

I reluctantly sit down. Francis was Dad's assistant until the business went belly-up. I haven't seen him or heard his name since, so something serious must be happening.

"What are you doing here, Francis?" I ask. I'm tired and in no mood for entertaining.

Francis laughs, like my rudeness is adorable. "How have you been, Belle?" he asks, crossing his legs. He picks up the glass from the table beside him – whisky from Dad's last bottle.

I shrug. "I'm tired," I say. "I should really get to bed. Tomorrow's another long day."

"About that," Francis says. He takes a sip. "I'm here to help."

"What?" I say, glancing at Dad.

"I called Francis last night," Dad admits. "I told him what happened. He's studying law now, so he can help."

I roll my eyes. "We don't need help," I say.

"On the contrary," Francis says in his most arrogant tone. "I've been in touch with your father's lawyer. She's already on her way to the Mostro household."

"What?" I say, leaning forward. "Why?"

"Did you think forcing a girl of fifteen to work tirelessly for the theft of a single rose was legal?" Francis says, smiling like a cat. "But not to worry. We'll put a stop to it." He stands and so does Dad. "The car's out front," Francis says.

"Where are you going?" I say, getting up and grabbing Dad's arm. "To Carlo's house?"

"Please," Dad says quietly, taking my shoulders in his hands. "Don't make this more difficult than it needs to be."

"It doesn't need to *be* at all," I say. "Just stay out of it!" I add, glaring at Francis over Dad's shoulder. He doesn't even look back at me.

"We should hurry," Francis says.

"Of course," says Dad. "You wait at home, Belle. You're exhausted anyway. Get some sleep."

The two of them shuffle out the door.

I rush to my bedroom and grab the phone. I dial the Mostros' number – it was printed on that tow truck receipt along with the address. But the operator comes on. Our phone's been disconnected except for emergencies. Dad hasn't paid the bill in months.

"Great," I say to myself, tossing the phone to the floor and heading back to the living room. Short of catching the train to the beach and then two buses that, for all I know, don't run this late, I'm stuck.

I see the book from Carlo still sitting on the table by the door, so I bring it into the living room and sit in Dad's chair. It smells like Dad – it always does – but now it also smells strongly of Francis and that awful cologne he wears.

I flip open the cover. For the first time, I notice the writing there, the scrawl of a teenage boy.

Belle,

Having you at the house the past few days
has been great. You've been like a beautiful sunrise after
a long, dark night. I'm sorry I've been such a beast.

I hope we can stay in touch once you're gone.

– Carlo

At the bottom, he left his email address.

I hurry across the street to the café, connect to their Wi-Fi, and type in Carlo's email address on my video chat. It rings and rings, but no one picks up.

* * *

Santino's been gone for an hour or so, and the dinner he made was pretty delicious. Since then, I've watched about half of some animated film I've seen before. I'm just about to doze off, thinking about Belle, when the doorbell rings.

"Mum!" I shout, as if she'd hear me in this huge house. She might not even be home. With a groan, I get up from the couch and hurry to the door. The doorbell rings again.

"I'm coming, relax!" I bark. I pull open the door. In shoves Mr Beaumont. "What are you doing here?" I say, but before he answers, another man grabs me by the collar of my sweatshirt and slams me up to the door. My head bangs hard against it.

"Hey!" I shout. "Get off me!"

"You're in a lot of trouble," the man says. He has a wicked glare, and he's taller than me. Just then, a woman wearing a suit and carrying a briefcase walks up behind him.

"Belle has been so depressed," Mr Beaumont says. "Having to come here every morning. She says you're a monster. Shouting at her. Threatening her with violence."

"I never–" I start to say, but the other guy throttles me again, slamming my head against the door. "Ow!"

The woman with the briefcase pops it open and pulls out an envelope of legal papers. "This outlines the Beaumonts' case against the Mostros," she says, holding it out. The tough guy grabs it and shoves it against my chest.

"The Department of Labour will be in touch," she adds. "Let him go, Francis."

Francis lets me go. Right onto the ground. The two men step over me, and the three of them leave. I don't even get up. Why bother?

I can't believe I imagined that Belle would like me. I'm mortified that I gave her that book. Has she read that sappy message I wrote in the front? I hope not. I can't believe I thought she and I were getting along. And now she's sent these three after me, like a horde of villagers carrying torches and pitchforks to a monster's castle on the hill.

* * *

My spirit is bruised. My ego is bruised. I'm pretty sure my neck is bruised, too. But I'm not in the basement. I'm in my bedroom – my *real* bedroom.

Belle propped the family photo against a couple of action figures on my desk. She must have done it after crying over how pathetic my life is.

Staring at the picture, I realize it's not just my father I miss. It's also my mum. I miss the mum I had back then – before Dad got sick and before she started going to these all-night parties to try to forget her sadness. I miss myself, too. I miss enjoying life and enjoying books. I miss jumping in the ocean before breakfast and splashing around. I didn't do that once this summer.

I'm staring out of the window now. The moon is high and full, reflecting in the wild ocean waves. My laptop starts beeping. An incoming video call. I don't recognize the username, but I answer it. And there she is – Belle. I quickly end the call and snap my laptop shut. It beeps again a moment later, but I don't care.

I hope I never see her again.

* * *

I catch the last train to the beach. All I can do is hope that the buses are still running this late.

When I arrive at the station, I run to the bus schedule posted on the wall. It's faded and hard to read.

For a few seconds, I convince myself the last bus is at two a.m., but I know I'm kidding myself. It says midnight – there's no doubt. The last bus is already gone.

"Ciao, Bella!" shouts a familiar voice from a blue car. "What are you doing here?"

"Santino!" I shout, running to the kerb. "Am I glad to see you. Can you give me a lift to the house?"

"I'm headed there!" he says. "Get in."

I climb in, and he pulls away from the kerb. "What are you doing here?" he says.

"I have to see Carlo," I say. "Don't make me explain."

Santino coughs. "You don't have to explain," he admits. "He called me, interrupted my date night. He told me everything."

I stare at my hands. "Then you must think I'm horrible."

"If you came out here to see Carlo," Santino says as we turn into the driveway of the mansion, "then you can't be as horrible as he believes."

Santino lets me in the front door before parking the car. "He's in the basement," he says, pushing the door open.

"Thank you, Santino," I say before running into the house, through the kitchen and knocking on the basement door.

"Carlo!" I shout. I try the door – it's locked. "Carlo, it's Belle. Please let me in!"

No reply. Maybe he's not even down there.

Santino comes in through the back door. "Won't he let you in?" he says.

I shake my head. "It's locked. Maybe he's asleep."

Santino pounds on the door with his fist. "Carlo," he says, like an angry father. "Open this door at once." He turns to me. "It doesn't have a lock. I don't know why it won't open."

Santino tries again. "I'll break this door, Carlo," he shouts. But still no response.

"Look out, Belle," Santino says. He steps back from the door and charges. The door flies open, and a chair that had been jamming the door closed falls down the stairs.

I hurry down the steps and find Carlo sitting on the floor, hugging his knees and shaking with sobs. I drop down beside him while Santino waits at the top of the stairs.

With my arm around his shoulder, I say, "Carlo, please don't cry. I never said any of the horrible things they told you. I didn't want them to come here tonight."

My cheeks are wet, and I realize I'm crying, too.

"Please, Carlo," I say. "I like coming here. Even if I didn't have to clean, I'd come out here anyway. I'd come to see Santino, and– and to spend time with you."

I lay my head on his shoulder and listen to his sobs. "I'm sorry, Carlo," I say. "I'm sorry they treated you like this. I care about you," I say. "I understand you."

* * *

"What?" I ask in shock. Belle shrugs. The tiniest smile appears on her lips.

"I guess I said I care about you," she says.

"But *why?*" I say. "I've been awful."

"Not too awful," she says. "I think you're very thoughtful when you want to be."

"I'm not beautiful," I say, "like you are."

She blushes a bit. "But you are," she says. "You have beautiful eyes, and I like your wild hair." She pushes it back from my eyes. "But more than that, you have beauty inside. I can see it, even if you can't right now." I guess Santino was right. Belle was going to break the curse.

* * *

When I wake up the next morning in my real bedroom, the first thing I see is the ocean. Then I see the photo. Instead of making me cry, it makes me smile.

I miss Dad. I always will. But I still have Mum, and I can help her remember that she still has me. I get up and find clean clothes. I shower and brush my hair back from my forehead.

Santino grins when I walk into the kitchen. "What?" I say with a smile. But I know what he's staring at: me, out of my basement and out of my misery.

Then Belle comes into the kitchen. Her hair is in a ponytail, and her face is flush with sleep.

"Good morning," I say. I almost run to her.

She takes my hand and says, "You look nice. You even smell nice." She gives me a quick hug.

"Come on, come on," Santino says, clapping twice. "We need to get moving."

We run out to the car, and a few minutes later, we pull up to the Beaumonts' house. Mr Beaumont sees Belle first, and the relief on his face is obvious. An instant later, he sees me behind her, and his face turns red with rage.

"Dad," she says sternly, "you have to stop the legal action against Carlo's family."

"I can't do that," Mr Beaumont says. "The law is complicated, darling."

Belle takes a deep breath and says, clear as a bell and twice as loud, "I like him."

"What?" Mr Beaumont says. He's looking right at her, stunned. I can't help smiling.

"I like him," she says, reaching for my hand.

"And what do you have to say?" he asks me.

"I like her, too," I say. She grins at me. "Isn't it obvious?" I say, smiling back at her.

He looks up at us and sighs. Belle looks at him and says, "Is it so terrible, Dad?"

Mr Beaumont watches us holding hands in front of him, both of us looking happier than we have in a long, long time. "All right," he says. "I'll call off the attack lawyers."

Belle drops my hand and throws her arms around her father. "Thank you!" she says.

"I owe you an apology," I continue. Mr Beaumont looks at me. "And quite a lot more than that," I go on. "I mistreated you. I was violent."

It's like I was a different person, I think. *No, not even a person. An animal. A beast.*

"And for the last few days," I go on, "your daughter, who deserves so much better, cleaned my house." I look at Belle and add, "I shouted at her. I owe you both. And I intend to pay it back in full and with interest. A lot of interest."

"How will you do that?" he asks.

"I'll speak to my mum," I say. "Once I tell her that Belle – the girl I care about – is in need, I know she'll be happy to help."

Mr Beaumont is hesitant. "Charity?" he says. "I don't know ... I don't like the idea of accepting charity."

"Then think of it as payment to Belle for her hard work," I say. He's still unsure. "I also physically attacked you. So you could even think of it as an out-of-court settlement."

Mr Beaumont laughs. "If that's the best you can do," he jokes, "then thank you. I'm sorry I misjudged you."

"You didn't," I admit. "I was a beast. But thanks to Belle, I'm not a beast anymore."

I put my arm around her. "You're beautiful," I say to her, looking into her storm-coloured eyes.

She smiles and says, "So are you."

It's December at the Lakeview Sunrise Group Home for Boys and Girls. From the caged window next to our dormitory bunk bed, we can see the concrete courtyard covered with fresh snow. But no one is thinking about Christmas or presents, sledging or huge turkeys in the oven. No one is even thinking about gathering mounds of snow into snowmen, and no one is thinking about igloos and forts.

Not here anyway.

Lakeview Sunrise Group Home for Boys and Girls is really just a long and lovely way of saying "orphanage". And this orphanage is as filthy and overcrowded as anything Little Orphan Annie or Oliver Twist ever knew.

It's nowhere near any lake or stream, unless you count the puddle of sewage overflow that visits the corner of Jacobs Street and Carroll Avenue each spring. And you couldn't spot a sunrise from here unless you were standing on top of the boarded-up Lang Department Store two streets away. It's the only way you can see over the other run-down grey and brown buildings.

We should know. We live here.

We are Hansen and Gracie. We are twins. And we hate it here.

We haven't been here forever. That is, we've had other homes before. We don't remember being born, obviously, because no one does.

We do remember several foster homes ... here in the city, out in the country. But they blur together, so sometimes Gracie believes the family with the big yellow dog was the one who had tuna casserole every Friday, when in fact, Hansen insists, the big yellow dog was in the house with two dads. Gracie says none of the homes had two mums, and that's where we couldn't agree.

It was all so long ago. We've been in the orphanage – no matter what it reads on the sign outside, we usually call it the orphanage – for almost ten years.

Here's the thing about being raised by the state: if foster home after foster home says there's something strange about you, eventually the state stops trying to find you a home. They stop trying to find you a family.

And they put you in a place like this.

It's on this early, cold winter morning that Gracie, always the one of us most likely to get in trouble, is sneaking around the kitchen, sticking her nose into cupboards and cabinets. She's looking for the food the grown-ups save for themselves.

She does this now and then, though all she's ever managed to find worth snatching was a single banana. It was the best banana we ever tasted, of course. But still. With the trouble Gracie would get into if she were ever caught, Hansen isn't a huge fan of these expeditions.

"I can't find anything," Gracie whispers into the silent, pre-dawn kitchen, frustrated. She knows there has to be good, fresh bread somewhere in here.

"Then get back here," Hansen murmurs into his pillow.

We're far apart – Hansen up in the dormitory and Gracie deep inside the pantry among sacks of buggy flour, dusty tins of sweetcorn and carrots and evaporated milk, and boxes upon boxes of powdered potatoes.

But we can still hear each other. We can always hear each other.

For a long time, we didn't know it was a weird thing. But we eventually realized that not all brothers and sisters were like us. Not even most twins were like us. It turned out it was not only a weird thing, it was *the* weird thing. That's why we could never stay long in a foster home.

All our foster parents were too weirded out to let us stay more than a month or two. They didn't know why we always answered questions the same way. They didn't understand how we were able to tell them what the other was doing, seeing, hearing and even thinking at that exact moment. Once they found out about our connection, they threw us out.

But we can't be thrown out of the Lakeview Sunrise Group Home for Boys and Girls. The orphanage is the last refuge for troublemakers and freaks.

That's why we belong here.

"I'll be back in a second," Gracie whispers. "I just heard something in the corridor. I think it's Ms Young."

Ms Young is the woman who runs this place. She's not as miserable as you might guess. She's nice enough when she's in a good mood, and we think she probably got into the business of running an orphanage for the right reasons. But it's a miserable job, and things never seem to go as well as grown-ups think they will. Even grown-ups who have the best intentions.

"Oscar is with her," Gracie adds, and Hansen – who could just make out the voices as well, hearing them through Gracie's ears – shivers.

Oscar, as far as we can tell, is some kind of building maintenance man. Or he's supposed to be. But he really only fixes drips and creaks when he gets around to it. He prefers to spend his time trailing behind Ms Young, offering advice she doesn't ask for. Unfortunately, Ms Young is often too meek to ignore his advice, and his advice … well, that's what makes the orphanage such an especially unpleasant place.

"Make him sleep next to the boiler for seven nights," Oscar might say when a boy hasn't finished his supper, and Ms Young will click her tongue and agree, sending the boy to the basement.

"Put her in the courtyard for some quiet time," he might whisper in Ms Young's ear if a girl's language is foul when she's doing her chores. And off the girl goes, though both grown-ups know very well that the courtyard is infested with rats the size of terriers.

This morning, Gracie huddles deeper into the shelves of food, where she'll never be spotted. She pulls in her knees and holds her breath.

"Get back here," Hansen says, his voice full of worry.

Gracie shakes her head. "I wanna hear what they're talking about," she says. "Besides, they're still in the hall. How would I ever get back?"

Hansen clenches his jaw and grumbles.

"Hush," Gracie says. "I want to listen."

So Hansen hushes, and he strains to hear the conversation, too.

"It's the way they look at everyone," says Ms Young. "Like they're, I don't know…"

Oscar finishes for her, his voice a cruel and raspy whisper, "Like they're watching us on TV."

We can hear the solemn agreement in Ms Young's voice when she replies, "Yes. Like we're not real. Like we exist only for their morbid amusement."

"It's time to get rid of them, then," Oscar says. His voice is brave now, louder than it should be – not that he knows we are listening to him.

"What does he mean?" Hansen says, and Gracie shushes him again.

The woman clicks her tongue. Her feet shuffle on the old wood floors.

"I've tried," Ms Young says. "I've really tried. The two have been in and out of foster homes since their parents passed away."

"Then another won't hurt," Oscar says.

Ms Young moves into the kitchen. Her clunky footsteps and her ice-cold voice echo off the tile floor and walls.

"I'm afraid it's not that simple," she says. "Some of these children I could place in foster homes, in theory. But these two ... it's impossible."

"I suppose so," Oscar says, as if he might drop the matter. But then he says, "There might be another way."

Ms Young stops and leans on the counter. Gracie can see her now, just barely, from her hiding spot in the pantry. "What are you getting at?"

"Have they ever run away?" Oscar says. We can almost see him sneering now, showing off his hyena grin of brownish-yellow, broken teeth.

"Of course," Ms Young says. "Dozens of times. They're infamous."

"Then they'll run away again, won't they?" he says.

"Who knows," says Ms Young, her voice slow and sad.

"You misunderstand, ma'am," says Oscar. Gracie sees his feet, in well-worn work boots, move closer to Ms Young's at the worktop. He continues, "So I'll be blunt. Tell them they've been adopted or that some family is interested in adopting them. Some family miles away from here, mind you."

He carefully paces his words as he speaks, like he fancies himself some sort of criminal mastermind.

"I'll drive them out to meet the fantasy family, but I'll take them to the middle of nowhere, perhaps to a forest,"

Oscar continues, his voice sounding more and more excited, "or a city they've never seen before. I'll leave them, then, on the side of the road like unwanted puppies."

"That's awful!" Ms Young says. But a moment later, her voice softer now, she adds, "When can we do it?"

* * *

"They can't get away with this," Hansen says when Gracie appears a few minutes later at their bunk bed in the dormitory.

"Of course they can. They get away with everything," Gracie says, sighing. She climbs into the top bunk and stares at the ceiling. Just centimetres from her face, nails poke through the bare wood beams holding up the rickety roof.

"But don't worry," Gracie continues, a mischievous smile forming on her cheeks. "I have a plan."

"Tell me," Hansen whispers, poking his head out from his bed to look up at his sister on the bunk above him.

Her hand sticks out from the top bunk and opens, dropping something. Hansen quickly catches what falls.

"A phone," Hansen says, turning it over in his hands. "Where did you get it?"

"Stole it from Oscar. He left it on kitchen worktop," Gracie says.

"Who are we going to call? The police?" Hansen asks.

"Nah," Gracie says. She rolls onto her side. "The nasty woman is just going to tell the police we ran away. Why bother?"

"Then who?" Hansen says.

"No one," she says. "The phone has GPS. They'll leave us, and we'll use the GPS to get back. Easy."

"Ha!" Hansen says. He pokes at the phone's touch screen, looking at all the maps and apps. "Good one, sis."

"Thank you," Gracie says. She smiles.

The sun is up now, barely over the horizon, hidden behind blocks and blocks of flats and office buildings. Hansen takes a deep breath and puts his head on his pillow. "Any second now…" he whispers.

Gracie nods.

The dormitory door slams open.

"Rise and shine, children!" Ms Young's voice wobbles through the huge, sparsely furnished room. The lights flicker on and shine too bright. Beds creak as boys and girls sit up and rub their eyes or roll over, desperately clinging to the dreams they'd been having. The dreams were, no doubt, more pleasant than the reality to which they've just awoken.

"All of you, get down to breakfast," says Ms Young, and before the commotion of children yapping and dressing and dragging their feet across the cold wood floors can begin, she adds in a piercing voice: "Except the twins! You two – get your coats."

All eyes slide in our direction. We keep our faces like stone.

Gracie drops down from the top bunk. Hansen stands and passes Gracie her coat. Hand in hand, we walk towards the door and the flickering light from the hall seeping into our dark dormitory on this gloomy, grey morning.

"Oscar!" Ms Young calls down the lighted hall when we reach her.

He comes jogging towards us a few moments later, wearing his green work jumpsuit and shaking his head.

"I've lost my phone," Oscar says, panting. "I can't understand it."

"I'm sure it'll turn up," says Ms Young, her smile straining against her cheeks like knives in a plastic shopping bag. She turns back to face us. "Hansen. Gracie," she says, bending her back and rounding her shoulders as she always does when she talks to children. "I have some very exciting news for you."

We hardly listen. We know all about the fantasy family and the little drive Oscar will take us on this morning. When she's done, Gracie says, "Should we pack?"

"Oh, no," Ms Young says. She even puts a hand on Gracie's shoulder. She sounds too delighted. "You'll just be meeting the couple today. You won't be moving in with them yet!" She forces a twinkle of a laugh.

"That's right," says Oscar. "Just a little get-together this morning." Oscar has the most ridiculous southern twang, but only sometimes.

He does it to seem friendly, Gracie thinks as loud as she can. *I hate him.*

Hansen glances at Gracie and nods the tiniest bit.

And with a hand of Oscar's on each of our shoulders, his stout figure between us, we walk down the hall under the long fluorescent lights. At the end of the hall, he pushes open the metal door for us and leads the way down the stairs to the big front doors, which are always locked.

Oscar pulls the long chain of keys from the little retractor on his belt. He hunches over the bunch as if our knowing which key opens this door would be a huge tragedy. He selects one and opens the door, letting in the blowing snow and frigid air.

We move closer together, Hansen and Gracie, and Gracie puts her arm around Hansen's waist.

Oscar hardly pauses in the doorway. He stomps down the icy, snow-coated steps and towards his car – a huge blue two-door vehicle. The passenger-side door squeaks and whines in an awful way as Oscar pulls it open. He pushes the passenger's seat forward, and we climb into the huge backseat.

As Oscar walks around the front of the car, Gracie pokes the stolen phone, switches on the GPS to make sure it's working, and then shuts the display again before Oscar climbs into the driver's seat with a grunt.

"And here we go," he says, grinning at us in the rearview mirror, as if a flash of those crooked brown teeth would make us feel excited, or even comfortable.

Gracie shivers. *Hate*, she thinks.

Hansen puts his hand on hers on the vinyl seat between us. The huge car rumbles through the slick city streets towards the motorway.

We don't resist when Oscar pulls us out of the backseat, nowhere near any house, nowhere near any neighbourhood or city or town.

We get out and don't cry and don't yell as he climbs back into the driver's seat of the huge blue car. We stand in silence and watch as the car chugs down the lonely, snow-covered road out of these woods, towards the city and the Lakeview Sunrise Group Home for Boys and Girls.

When he's out of sight, Gracie pulls the phone from her jacket pocket and wakes it up. The little thinking wheel spins, the map zooms in and we start to walk.

We don't give up easily. We don't tire quickly. We've known hunger and we've known long walks with nothing to keep going for, but we've still gone on.

We find the Lakeview Sunrise Group Home for Boys and Girls late the next night. The snow has stopped falling, but it covers the ground, almost glowing under the moon-light.

Before we climb the front steps and ring the bell, not even sure they'll let us in, Gracie pulls the phone from her pocket. With the tiniest sliver of battery life left, she makes a phone call.

"Please send a police car to the orphanage," she tells the operator.

The operator asks, "The Lakeview Sunrise Group Home?"

"Of course," Gracie says. "Two children have been mistreated."

Hansen nods and crosses his arms.

"Who is this?" the police want to know, but Gracie ends the call and drops the phone onto the pavement. She lifts her heavy winter boot and brings it down hard, once, twice, three times, till the phone's glass screen is a cracked mess and the circuits and wires are spilling out, destroyed.

She looks at Hansen, and Hansen climbs the steps and presses his finger against the doorbell. He holds it there so the buzzing tone (so rarely rung, but so annoying to Ms Young when it is) drones on and on.

Before long, Oscar's heavy, plodding footsteps echo from behind the front doors. His keys jangle. The doors open. His jaw drops when he sees us.

"We found your phone," Hansen says.

Gracie laughs. We push past the man and into the orphanage.

* * *

It's a couple of hours later, and we're in our beds, lying awake and still seething, when the doorbell rings again. We smile as we hear Ms Young's tired feet drag down the hall. Soon Oscar's clomping boots join her.

"Let's go and see who it is," Gracie whispers as she drops down from the top bunk.

Hansen sighs, but he follows.

We stalk across the dormitory floor in our bare feet and pyjamas, and then down the hall to the top of the drafty stairs. The steps are ice cold and covered in wintery grit, but we go down and wait around the corner as Oscar opens the front door.

"Is there something we can help you with, officers?" he says.

We exchange a look, our eyes bright with anticipation. We're thrilled. We dart out from the corner and the shadows and towards the front door, despite the chilly gusts pushing past the police officers and into the home.

The one in uniform is young, and he has a friendly, open face. He spots us and lightly elbows the woman beside him. She's not in a police uniform, and we think for a moment that she's with child protective services. Maybe she's even here to do a full inspection and then shut this place down forever.

She produces a badge, though, and suddenly she's nothing so wonderful. She's another police officer. She explains they got a call from Oscar's phone number. Four sets of grown-up eyes turn to look at us.

Hansen swallows hard and takes a step back.

Gracie thinks, as loud as she can: *hate.*

"We called," Gracie says. "That man left us in the middle of a field to die." She points to Oscar. "We had to walk back. It took almost two days."

The uniformed officer's eyebrows go up in surprise. The woman beside him twists her mouth and narrows her eyes. She looks at Oscar.

"These are the two children who ran away," he says.

The woman nods slowly and pulls a pad of paper and a pencil from her coat pocket. "Hansen and Grace," she says, looking them up and down.

"We didn't run away," Gracie says, stepping closer to the grown-ups by the door.

Stop, Hansen thinks. *We should go back to bed. Right now.*

No, Gracie thinks, twisting to face Hansen. She pushes the word at him.

"They wanted us to die," Gracie says. "They left us in the middle of nowhere. They should go to prison."

Oscar clicks his tongue and shakes his head, looking down at the floor. *What a shame*, he seems to say. *The girl is so sad and angry that she's invented such an obvious lie.*

Ms Young steps closer to Gracie and bends in front of her, the same way she had when she told us about our fantasy family out in the suburbs, desperate for twins just like us.

"We're not angry with you," Ms Young says sweetly. "But calling the police was going too far."

Gracie clenches her teeth, and we're not sure that she won't pull back a fist and use it on Ms Young's chin.

But Ms Young stands up straight and faces the police officers again.

"I'm very sorry you had to come out at this hour," she says. "The girl stole Oscar's phone the other day. She must have called the station on that. We just found it smashed up outside the home."

"We have to check these things out," says the woman officer. "You understand." She glances at us and frowns.

"Of course, of course," Oscar says, shuffling the police officers out of the door and back into the cold middle of the night. He and Ms Young look pleasant standing in the doorway, each with a hand on one of our shoulders, their grips a bit too strong.

"No harm done!" Oscar shouts after them.

The officers wave goodbye from the driveway. The door to the orphanage closes with a heavy thud and click.

Ms Young and Oscar both turn slowly to face us again. She stands up as straight as a flagpole, with her chin high and her eyes cast down on us. He hunches, his hands open and out to us, like he might grab us each by the throat and toss us out into the snow.

But he won't – not right away.

"It was the phone, wasn't it?" he says. He takes a slow, heavy step towards us. "That's how you got back." He takes another step.

"Take it easy, Oscar," Ms Young says. "This is why we took precautions."

Oscar stands up straight – or as straight as he can – and bites his lip.

We want to go back to bed now.

Hansen shuffles backwards till his back hits the railing of the stairwell. Gracie catches Hansen's wrist and pulls him closer to her.

"If we hadn't reported you two as runaways immediately," Ms Young hisses at us, "those officers would have had to investigate fully."

"We're going to bed," Gracie says.

"By all means," Ms Young says, her voice dripping with hate.

We hurry up the stairs towards the flickering light of the hall and run through the dormitory to our bunk bed by the cold window. Half of the children are sitting up, wide awake in the dark, waiting to hear the news. "What's happening?" they ask us. "Where were you?" some want to know.

"Why'd you run away?" asks the littlest one, a five-year-old boy they brought here just a few days ago. He's still too stupid to see the truth about this place.

We don't answer any of them. We almost never do.

We get back into bed, and somehow we fall asleep. We dream about a house. It's far away from here, set on top of a soft green slope. It's a white house with storm-grey shutters, or it's a pale blue house with red shutters, or it's a butter-yellow house with black shutters, and it's encircled by a wood fence.

An apple tree crouches in the front garden, and it dangles little sweet apples, coloured red and green. We pick as many as we can carry in our upturned T-shirt fronts. And when we're done, our mother opens the front door and calls us inside.

But we wake up, and it's only Ms Young standing over us.

She takes us from our beds. Oscar is there. They take us by our collars and drag us from the room before the lights click on, before the other children can even open their eyes and sit up. Not that that would have helped.

They don't pretend this morning. There are no stories about a couple who'd like to meet us. No lies about the perfect little house in the suburbs. There's no breakfast, no packing of clothes, and there are certainly no goodbyes.

There's only the backseat of Oscar's giant, smelly car. The doors slamming. The motor coughing and chugging. We're on the motorway again, and this time he takes us farther. We don't recognize the road signs. The farmhouses and the silos are unfamiliar after living in the city.

We shouldn't have smashed the phone. We shouldn't have called the police. We shouldn't have argued with them. We should have been sweeter children.

Gracie keeps looking out of the window, reading signs, looking for landmarks, tracking the sun on the horizon. *It's no good*, Hansen thinks. *We won't get back twice. He'll make sure of that.* Gracie wipes the back of her hand across her eyes. Hansen puts a hand on her back.

"Why don't you just kill us?" Hansen snarls towards the front seat.

Oscar chuckles. "I'm not an animal," he replies.

* * *

He leaves us deep inside the woods this time. A place we've never seen.

We stand at the side of the road and watch the huge blue car shake and rocket away, coughing out grey and black smoke as it drives down the dirty country road, covered in road salt and snow-filled potholes.

There are no billboards or road signs. No telephone poles or farmhouses. All we can see is this road, this forest and, once in a while, a logging truck passing by.

We hope his car breaks down. We hope he ends up stranded in these woods, too.

"Which way?" Hansen asks. Gracie takes Hansen's hand. We start to walk.

We keep to the road and follow it as it goes on and on. When the sun sets, it sets behind us, and we're pretty sure we've been walking in the wrong direction.

"I don't care," says Gracie. "I don't want to go back."

"I don't either," says Hansen.

Ahead of us, far on the horizon, city lights twinkle as the sun sets.

"It's a different city," Gracie says. There's almost hope in her voice. We walk through the night.

Soon, a sliver of light emerges from the horizon, and the road we're on is well paved and marked with a bright yellow line down the middle.

There's a petrol station on the corner up ahead. There's a tiny old restaurant. There are homes now … on this road and on smaller roads that shoot off of it like baby branches on a sapling tree.

Around us, the world is changing from a forbidding forest to a plain country lane.

Eventually it changes again, from a small farming town to a lively and bright suburb, and our road – the one we've been walking on forever it seems – has become a tree-lined boulevard. There are pavements, shovelled and clear of snow.

It's mid-morning now, and the locals are out. They're hurrying between the post office and the hardware shop. They're shuffling between the coffee shop and their nice-looking cars, which are lined up neatly along the kerb.

They're juggling toddlers and shopping and peppermint hot chocolates with whipped cream. Some of them look at us, but they don't really see us. Some of them see us, and they quickly look away, turning back to their shopping or their coffee flasks. Some of them see us, and they stare.

Everyone wonders why we're here – we can tell. They wonder what happened to us.

They'll take us back, Gracie thinks. *I don't want to go back.*

Hansen takes her hand. He leads us off the main boulevard, under elm trees that hang over snow-blanketed, narrow streets, past driveways and front gardens strewn with snowmen, Christmas displays, and red and blue and pink and green sledges.

This is a place we'd like to live.

We almost expect the house we dreamed about, with its wooden fence and perfect apple tree, to appear each time we turn a corner. But we don't say it out loud.

Before too long, we've walked the entire width of this little suburb, and we still haven't found our dream house. In front of us is a road that leads into the city. The city sits on the horizon to the east, grey and smoggy and gloomy.

But we know it's not the city we came from, at least.

"What should we do?" Gracie says. She wishes as hard as she can, because she wants to find that house – the house with the big, friendly apple tree.

She wants to find that house and knock on its door and go inside and stay there forever, picking apples, baking delicious desserts and sleeping in warm, comfortable beds.

She wants it to be our home.

"It was a dream," Hansen says gently.

And Hansen leads us to the city, because in the city we can survive.

* * *

The city feels colder than the suburb did. We arrive tired, our clothes torn and wet, icy at the hems that hang past our feet, picking up mud and snow as we trudge along. We're hungry. We both know it. But Gracie says it out loud, and it becomes that much more real.

It's night again, and we can't remember the last time we ate. It was back at the orphanage, of course. And that was days ago now. Our stomachs rumble as we walk.

Gracie is crying again. She wipes the back of her hand under her nose and sniffs hard.

Dirty snowbanks are piled high on the sides of the city streets. But there's a courthouse, a town hall and even a sports stadium nearby. And in the centre of this new city, the night bustles and gives us hope.

Restaurants and cafés and bars, with grown-ups pouring out of open doorways, send heat from inside out into the street.

Everyone here seems rich, cheerful and loud. Everyone is eating and drinking and celebrating.

"I'll get us some food," Hansen says as they pass by a restaurant. He steps away from Gracie.

Hansen slips into the crowd of people outside the restaurant. The air around us smells like French fries and hot sauce and pickles. He pushes through them. The workers hardly notice he's there, it's so busy. They don't notice when he finds a table whose diners are up and mingling on the dance floor.

Hansen grabs two burgers from the table, wraps them in napkins and jams them into the pockets of his coat, looking around carefully to make sure no one can see him. Gracie smiles and pulls in her lips. "Get the fries," she whispers.

Hansen snatches the French fries off the table and stuffs them under his armpit inside his coat. He's pushing his way through the crowd again and towards Gracie when a shout rises up behind him. "Hey!"

Someone must have seen him snatch the fries.

We gasp. We hold our breath.

Hansen keeps moving. A pair of hands grabs his shoulders, so he pulls away, leaving his coat and our dinner behind. *Run,* he screams in our minds. Gracie steps slowly away from the crowd as the people grow enraged.

Hands claw at Hansen, but he pushes through them. His clothes tear. His skin, still raw from a day and a half of walking in the frigid cold, burns and stings with pain as their fingernails scratch violently at his arms. Some people even try to trip him, sticking their feet in front of his as he tries to escape.

The crowd swells through the doorway, catching Hansen in the middle of the group like he's a fallen surfer caught in a huge wave. Then, not knowing what else to do, Gracie balls her hands into fists and shrieks.

Everything stops.

The crowd loosens its grip on Hansen and everyone turns their attention to Gracie. All the crowd's shouts and curses of angry rage die out, so we can only hear the music from within the restaurant.

Hansen moves towards his sister. The crowd, as if under Gracie's spell, lets him. He takes Gracie's hand. We run from the restaurant, past a dozen more just like it, and we keep running for streets and streets.

Soon the streets are cobblestone and the buildings are quiet and dark, stout warehouses and factories set against the unfriendly, charcoal-coloured sky. Only one faint light shines in this part of the city: a blue globe on a steel post to mark the entrance to the local police station.

"They can help us," Hansen says.

We're so hungry. We're cold and tired. It would be so easy to go inside. To give them our names. To sit down. To ask for a doughnut and two cups of hot chocolate. They would help us.

Even if they believed we were runaways. They'd help us.

We walk between parked police cars and motorcycles and stop at outside the station. We can see the officers inside, laughing and playing cards, doing paperwork and drinking coffee.

"If we go in," Gracie says, giving Hansen's hand an extra squeeze, "they'll take us right back to the orphanage."

Hansen takes a deep breath.

"I don't want to go back," Gracie says, facing her brother.

"We'll starve," he says. We're so hungry. Hansen's coat is gone. We'll freeze. Hansen sighs. "But we can't go back to the orphanage."

So we turn our backs on the police station and walk.

We walk until the sun is coming up in front of us. There's a wide river on the city's east side, so we walk along the river road until we reach a high, lighted bridge, alive and shaking with early-morning commuter trains and road traffic. We hold onto the railings of the pedestrian path as we cross, wary of the shaking steel that is holding us up.

"It's supposed to shake," Hansen says, and we believe it, but it doesn't help to know.

On the far side of the bridge, the city is gone, and there are trees and small homes and petrol stations and a post office, just like there had been in the suburb before the city. The road bends around and becomes a main road. We can't walk safely there, so we take a turn after the post office and find ourselves on a narrow street, with cars parked all along one side. There are little white homes with dark blue shutters and fences of wrought iron and white-painted wood.

We stop at the far end of the block, where the street becomes a wide cul-de-sac on a gentle slope. At the top of the slope sits a house that we both recognize at once. The sight of it makes us catch our breath and grab one another's hand.

The house is pale blue-grey, with bright white shutters and a door so boldly red against the snowy landscape that it makes our eyes water. A gate sits open in the centre of the wooden fence that encloses the front garden, which is covered in untrodden snow. There's the friendly-looking apple tree reaching towards the sun in the clear sky, waving its supple branches back and forth in the winter wind.

"It can't be real," Hansen says, his voice cautious. But it's right there in front of us, just like we dreamed it.

"It is," Gracie says, facing her brother and taking his hands. "We should go in. We should ring the bell!"

Hansen shakes his head. We're anxious. We're afraid. But we feel excited. We feel jubilant.

"Something doesn't seem right here," Hansen says slowly, looking at the house suspiciously. "Dreams don't come true like this, Gracie."

"Not ever?" she says, her eyes pleading and her lips blue with cold.

We don't have to decide. We don't have to argue. Because just then, the front door of our dream house swings open and a woman appears in the doorway. She isn't our mother. But she's smiling, and her face is open and kind, and she says, "Good morning, children. Please, come in out of the cold."

So we do.

And there's soup for us, and there's ice cream afterwards, and she washes our clothes and mends our trousers. The woman even has a new coat for Hansen. She lets us each take a bath in water so warm it makes our toes tingle. When it's dark and we're warm and full from eating, she puts us to bed, too. We sleep in beds so fluffy and warm that we feel we could sleep for days, waking only to eat hot soup and smell fresh apple pie baking in the oven.

We thank her as we drift away. Since we know we're in our dream house, tonight we sleep, for the first time we can remember, with no dreams at all.

* * *

When we wake up, the floor is cold and the beds are gone, and Hansen is in a cage and Gracie's ankles and wrists are shackled with metal rings and rope.

The woman is with us, directly across the low-ceilinged, cement-floor room. There are no windows and it is damp and cold. She says, "Good morning, darlings. Did you sleep well?" Then she laughs an evil laugh as she climbs the steps out of the basement.

It's not our dream house after all. It's our nightmare.

We knew dreams didn't come true. Hansen had even said it out loud. But we came inside anyway. When we saw her in the open doorway, we didn't care. When she put her arms around us, smelling of apples and honey and lavender, nothing could have stopped us from going with her.

And now we're paying for our foolishness. For being willing to believe. For being babies.

Hansen sits on the floor of his cage, hugging his knees tight to his chest. His cheeks have been dry for a long time now. The sobbing and screaming have done nothing more than leave his throat sore and dry and his dirty cheeks streaked where tears spilled from his eyes.

Gracie leans against the bars outside the cage. She had cried along with him. We wonder why. *Why is Hansen in the cage, but Gracie outside? Why is Gracie in leg irons, her hands tied in ropes?*

But we don't need to wonder for long. Once we are silent, the woman floats back downstairs.

"You've calmed down," she says as she walks across the cement floor. "Perhaps now we can speak."

We have nothing to say to her, we think. *Don't say anything to her.*

"You're both so hungry and so skinny," the woman says. She shakes her head, like it's a great shame that we've been through so much, like she cares about us. "I can't have two skinny weaklings, not for my needs."

It turns out the woman does care – kind of.

"Gracie, darling," she says, and she runs a hand over Gracie's head, pushing her hair back and tucking it behind her ear. We shiver at the touch. *We hate her.*

"You will be my helper," she says, folding her hands together and smiling down at Gracie. "You will clean, and you will wash, and you will learn to cook."

Don't answer her, we think.

"You," she says, turning to the cage.

Hansen shrinks like a pet gerbil, pushing his back against the farthest corner. She only smiles at him, lets out a little giggle, like he really is a pet gerbil.

"I have something much more important in mind for you."

Don't answer her! we think, but Gracie's eyes are watering again, and she can't resist.

"Why don't you let him out?" she says. "He can help me clean."

The woman frowns at her, the sort of frown that has a smile inside it. "No, no," she says. She waves the idea away. "That would never do."

You shouldn't have answered her, Hansen thinks.

"We work better as a team," Gracie says.

Stop, Hansen thinks.

"I'm afraid," the woman says, "I've seen too many boys attempt housework and fail miserably. No, no. They make much better meat than maid."

"You're lying," Hansen says, glaring at her. "You're just trying to scare us."

But the woman doesn't seem to hear him. Her eyes and mind are far away. "The last time I had a brother and sister down here," she says, pacing slowly in front of his cage, a delighted and wicked smile forming on her lips, "she created the most perfect Béarnaise sauce. She had no idea that a few hours later I'd pour it over her brother's glistening golden-brown carcass."

She's a monster, we think. *We have to get away.* But we can't.

The woman claps twice and brings her heels together as she faces Gracie. "My dear," she says, "let's get you started out front."

"Someone will see me," Gracie says. "They'll see me wearing these *things*," she says, shaking her shackles and ropes at the evil woman, "and they'll set me free. They'll call the police, you know."

"And you'll end up right back where you started," the woman says.

We almost gasp. *How does she know?* we think.

"I know a couple of runaways when I see them," the woman goes on. "Besides, what kind of miserable witch do you take me for? With the charms I've placed on this house, any passers-by – not that we'll have any on a frigid morning like this – would wave good morning and wish you the best of the season."

Impossible, we think. But she continues, "They wouldn't see your ropes. They wouldn't see your leg irons. They wouldn't even see the state of your clothes or the knots in your hair or the bruise on your cheek. My spells can't be broken until I reverse them."

Gracie reaches for her cheek before she remembers the ropes. She awkwardly strokes under her eye and feels pain. She can't remember when she got the bruise. *The witch must have given it to me,* she thinks.

"And don't think about running off, either," the witch says as she heads for the stairs. "As long as I'm alive, this house and garden are a fortress as far as you two are concerned."

Then we'll kill her, we think. *Somehow, we'll kill her.*

* * *

For the next several days, we are strong.

Gracie works hard. She cries, but she is fed well and she manages to sleep a few hours. Hansen, still in his cage, refuses to eat more than a few bites of bread or a spoonful of rice.

The witch fumes at him, pushing bowls of ice cream into his cage. Hansen lets them melt into soup and pushes the bowls back, still full, the spoons untouched.

She brings him plates of cupcakes iced in every colour of the rainbow. Hansen turns them upside down on the plates, showing off the brown-stained paper cups. Cupcakes don't look delicious from the bottom. He smears the different colours of icing together into a colour no one would want to eat.

"You can't hold out forever," the witch says, crouching beside the cage and sneering at him, her eyes glinting.

But Hansen is sure he can. We're both sure.

And every time Hansen stomps a bacon sandwich till it's flat and dirty and marked with the pattern from the sole of his shoe, or dumps a plate of chips on the floor and paints the cage bars with ketchup, or just sits back and watches a bowl of macaroni and cheese grow cold and congealed, the fork nearly standing upright, Gracie smiles.

She might be bent in the kitchen, scrubbing the floor. She might be in the back bedrooms, polishing the old wood furniture. She might be pushing a shovel up and down the bumpy driveway, covered with new snowfall for the fourth time this week.

But she smiles, because she knows we're beating the witch.

* * *

It is our seventh morning in the house. Gracie is sent to the attic with a broom.

"It's full of dust," the witch says, ushering her up the narrow, steep staircase hidden in the cupboard in the back bedroom. She closes the cupboard door and heads for the basement.

She's coming, Gracie thinks. *She's bringing breakfast.*

Hansen looks up. His head aches. His body is covered in welts and bruises from living and sleeping and ranting in his cage. He's hungry. He's so hungry.

Gracie feels Hansen's hunger, too. She clutches her belly as she works. She eats simple meals – lumpy oatmeal, heels of stale, hard bread, scraps of dry meat.

Hansen enjoys the tastes whenever Gracie eats, but it just makes him more hungry. Gracie wants to cry whenever she has a meal. She knows Hansen can taste the miserable stuff. But no matter how much Gracie eats, Hansen will still be hungry afterwards.

"Rise and shine, my little roast of lamb," the witch says in a menacing tone. She walks slowly. This morning, she carries a plate of toast. Just toast. It's not even buttered. She places it beside the cage and steps back.

There's a chair not far from the cage where she sits to watch Hansen eat – or, more likely, to watch him not eat.

"If you don't eat," the witch says, crossing her arms and legs and smiling at him, "you'll starve."

He looks up at her, his hunger and exhaustion making his vision blurry and bright. He thinks again about how beautiful she is, how beautiful she smelled when she embraced them in a hug. He even remembers how much he loved her – really loved her – when she first opened the front door to them that happy morning just one week ago.

"More to the point," she adds, her voice playful and sharp, *"I'll starve."*

We hate her.

"I don't care," Hansen says. "I'll waste away if I have to."

"You'd leave your poor sister all alone?" the witch says. Hansen swallows.

Don't answer, Gracie thinks.

"She's been eating quite well, you know," the witch says as she stands. "She's working hard and no doubt her knees are bruised and sore and her hands are callused and cramped. But she eats three meals a day. She often has seconds."

"It won't work," Hansen says. Gracie smiles for him. "You can't make me any more hungry than I am."

His throat is dry and his voice is tired, but he goes on. "You can't make me jealous, because Gracie is my whole world, and I couldn't be jealous of her if she was taking bubble baths every day and eating all the food I've turned down."

"What makes you think she isn't?" the witch says, leaning forward.

Don't answer, Gracie thinks. *She doesn't know about us – not really. She doesn't know we're connected.*

Hansen crosses his arms and bites his lower lip. He looks at the wall. The witch comes up next to the cage, right next to Hansen, and before he can skitter away, she takes hold of his wrist through the metal bars.

"It doesn't matter," she hisses in his ear. "I've decided to let you rot, to let you die here in your own filth. I'll be happy to never come down to this basement again."

"You'll have nothing to eat," Hansen says, and his voice and throat are so dry it sounds as if he's already begun to decompose.

"Do you think only boys are made of meat?" the witch says.

Hansen's skin tingles and goes cold. Two storeys up, in a low-ceilinged dark room, with a rag in her hand, Gracie shivers.

And we think: *hate*.

* * *

At noon the same day, Gracie descends the attic stairs. Her legs are sore and the stairs are steep and her irons are heavy, so it's slowgoing. She coughs and sneezes, too. The attic was indeed a plague of dust, and as she worked, much of it found her nose and throat and lungs.

But Gracie would like to stay in the attic forever, because she knows what the witch has planned for her now.

The witch is waiting for her, sitting on the edge of the loveseat, the one with the wooden legs that Gracie had polished for an hour only a few mornings ago. She's smiling a tiny, cruel sort of smile.

"All done?" the witch says.

Gracie doesn't answer her. She just stands there, her wrists bound together in front of her, a few dirty brown rags dangling from one hand that is just as dirty.

"Go to the kitchen, then," the witch says. She keeps her eyes cast downwards as she brushes lint from her lap. "I'm having trouble with the oven."

Gracie shuffles past the witch, her irons clanking and the wet rags in her hand slapping against her thigh. The witch grabs her wrist to stop her.

"Take the long matches out from the cupboard," the witch says, and her voice doesn't tinkle like it sometimes does. Instead it crackles like a fire. It doesn't bubble like a cool stream. It sizzles like a juicy slice of meat dropped into a hot frying pan.

The witch lets go of Gracie's wrist and stands up. She follows Gracie down the main staircase and into the kitchen. The witch leans on the worktop as Gracie pulls the box of long matches from the cupboard, eyeing her carefully.

"Do you know how to light it?" the witch says, a little too eagerly. "Do you know where the pilot light is?"

Gracie pulls a single long match from the box and closes the box again.

The witch tugs on the heavy oven door. It creaks and groans as it falls open.

"It's in the back of the oven," the witch says. "You'll have to lean all the way in."

This is it, we think.

Don't lean in, Hansen thinks. *She's lying. The pilot is lit.*

Gracie strikes the match against the box and reaches her rope-bound arms along the wall of the oven, straining and stretching to get her hands into the depths of the huge contraption while staying steady on her feet.

"No," the witch snarls. "You'll never reach it like that. Climb inside."

Gracie grunts and stretches farther. "I can reach it," she says.

"Just climb in!"

Gracie sighs and stands. "I don't know what you mean," she says. "And I can't find the pilot light anyway."

"It's right there!" the witch snaps. "You have to climb in."

"Show me," Gracie says.

Hansen laughs.

Shh, Gracie says, barely able to hold in her own laughter.

The witch narrows her eyes at Gracie.

We hate her.

The witch brings up her fist, tight and hot, and it begins to glow.

It's evil magic, we think.

She shines her magic light towards the back of the dark oven.

"I can't see it," Gracie says. "It's in the back?"

The witch ducks her head and leans into the oven, reaching her glowing hand towards the far corner. "It's right there," she says, frustrated.

"Oh," Gracie says. She quietly moves around behind the witch.

Do it, thinks Hansen. *Do it now.*

Gracie leans down. She takes a step back and charges, shoulder down, into the witch's backside. The witch loses her footing and falls face-first into the oven.

"What are you doing?!" she shrieks. Her voice is now a fiery rage that seems to tear at her throat as she pushes it through, and it echoes off the oven's steel walls.

We're laughing now, both of us. We're laughing loudly and madly.

Gracie reaches her bound hands to the door and shoves it up, sending the witch deeper into the huge oven. She slams the door closed and throws the lock.

How hot does it go? Hansen thinks.

Gracie scans the control panel and turns the oven knob as high as it will go – 300 degrees Celsius. Then she sees the "grill" setting, and turns the knob there.

She grins then, and Hansen grins in his cage in the basement, and she turns the knob to "clean".

The witch bangs on the walls of the oven as it begins to heat up. "Let me out of here!" she screams.

It's her truest voice, her most vile voice. It's the voice of a demon. It's the voice of the devil himself.

The witch slams her body into the oven's door. Her voice is more like a growl now, like the violent rage of a wild animal, of a monster. The oven shakes. The kitchen shakes. The witch is trying to break through the oven door.

Don't let her out! Hansen screams through our minds.

Gracie pushes her body against the door. With all her strength she holds the door closed, the witch's screams piercing Gracie's ears till they've nearly deafened her.

She can feel the heat pressing through the door, and the witch's screams grow still louder. The kitchen is filling with smoke and the acrid smell of the burning witch.

"Is it almost done?!" Gracie screams over the din.

"Yes!" Hansen screams back from his cage in the basement. He's on his feet now, his hands gripping the bars of his cage in anticipation. "Hold on a little longer!"

The screams begin to waver and dry, like they're turning to dust, turning to ash. They soften. They begin to plead. They are no longer screams.

Instead, Gracie hears the woman's false voice – the one she used to welcome Hansen and Gracie into her house, with apple on her breath and love in her arms. Gacie begins to cry. She pulls her shoulder back from the door and puts her hand on the lock.

Stop! Hansen thinks. *She's a witch.*

Gracie shakes away the thoughts.

"We hate her!" Hansen screams from the basement. It doesn't matter who hears him now. "We'll kill her!"

Gracie pulls her hand from the lock like it's a rattle-snake, and as the begging from inside the oven dies out, she runs from the kitchen to the basement steps.

There's only silence now. Silence and thick grey smoke and the nauseating smell of burnt witch.

"Hansen!" Gracie shouts, her voice a strange mix of gleeful and grotesque as she goes down the steps as awkward as ever, her ankle irons clanking between her feet, almost making her fall.

Grasping the banister with her bound hands is nearly impossible, but she moves faster than she has in a week.

"She's gone," Hansen says. He's on his feet at the front of the cage. He's holding the bars and he's actually smiling. His cheeks are even sore. We both feel it, and it makes us smile even more.

"Let me out," he says, but at the bottom of the steps, Gracie stops suddenly, remembering something. She starts to speak, but she doesn't have to.

"She had the keys," Hansen says, his smile dropping away.

Gracie almost panics. *Can we live our lives here, with Hansen in a cage and with Gracie bound in irons?*

"No," she says. "I'll find them."

She turns and clang-clangs her way up the stairs. She stands in front of the oven, still hot, and takes a deep breath. "Okay," she says. "She's dead."

Gracie pulls open the oven's lock and the appliance groans and clunks. She opens the oven door, half expecting the woman – her face mutilated from the heat – to reach for her and pull her inside. Instead she finds a pile of ashes on the floor of the oven and, in the center of the oven, a ring of keys.

She grabs a rag from the counter, because the keys are still too hot to touch, and wraps it around the ash-covered key ring. Then she hurries back downstairs, almost falling as she goes.

Unlocking the cage with the keys wrapped in the rag is difficult, but Gracie finally throws open the cage's big barred door.

"Now me," she says.

Hansen is weak. He manages to pick up the keys wrapped in the rag, but he can't turn the lock in his sister's ankle irons. Gracie puts her hands on Hansen's and we turn the key together. The irons fall away, clanking on the basement's cement floor.

Hansen is strong enough to undo the ropes. With us both free, he feels strong enough for anything. But for now, we are happy to throw our arms around each other.

* * *

She's dead, and her charms are wearing off. It doesn't happen all at once, though, like we thought it would. Instead, little bits of the enchantment change or disappear completely, one at a time.

First it's the house. What once appeared to be a beautifully decorated bungalow begins to crumble. Inside, the wallpaper is peeling where it had been pristine only hours ago. The antique furniture Gracie polished tirelessly for hours is only a heap of broken junk now. Out the front, the apple tree is a gnarled and ghastly thing. Its branches are bare and ragged, looking more like the deformed limbs of a mythical beast than a friendly fruit tree.

We rest. We eat. We sleep.

But the only bed in the house is the witch's, which we now realize is not a beautiful four-poster with a thick and fluffy mattress and downy comforters as it had appeared when the charms still held. Now we see that it's an iron basin filled with mud and blood.

She was a beast, we think.

But we wouldn't sleep in her bed even if it were the most comfortable bed in the world. Not for anything. So we sleep on the floor, but not in the basement. We'll never go back to the basement.

We have to keep an eye on the front of the house as well. With the witch's charms gone, the neighbours have begun to notice the house. It's crumbling, after all. And it's finally beginning to look like the haunted house it's always been.

The neighbours don't stop by ... not yet. But soon, we know, they'll get curious. First the children will start to throw rocks at the windows. Then the grown-ups will silently wonder what happened to the woman who had lived here. One brave adult might come and knock on the door. Eventually, someone will call the council. And they'll come and condemn the building, maybe even knock it down. We'll end up back at the home.

So we work. We clean everywhere and repair everything that's broken. Gracie is good at this by now, and Hansen is better at housework than the witch predicted.

Gracie is hunting for the source of an odour in the front cupboard while Hansen is fixing the big window in the living room. Gracie finds a tiny door at the back of the cupboard, hidden by years of debris and dust. We force it open, Hansen wielding his screwdriver like a crowbar.

We gasp together. We've found the witch's treasure!

Jewels, Gracie thinks.

Gold, Hansen thinks.

And cash, too. She was a modern witch. We find bundled notes and chequebooks and even a couple of credit cards.

We can survive here, we think, and we run to the computer in the witch's office. Thankfully, the computer is not disguised as an enchanted cauldron anymore. It's a real PC with an Internet connection.

Before long, we've made adoption papers and printed them out, complete with forged seals and signatures.

"Did she have a name?" Gracie says as we stare at the blank line, where the name of the adopting parent should be entered.

We don't know. So we give her one, and we finally have a last name: Appletree.

* * *

We spend most of our time alone now, in the witch's house. The neighbours don't stop by often, but when they do, we say, "Our mother is out. Can we help you?" or "Mum's napping. Can you come by another time?"

We enrol at the local secondary school, too. It's easy. We fill out all the forms and submit them online. We forge anything requiring signatures or doctor's notes. By the time the spring term starts – just days after we burned the witch to death – we have decent clothes, school supplies and a place in Year 10.

We are nervous at first. We lie in our beds the night before our first day. We're sharing a room in the back of the house, with two small beds pushed against opposite walls.

"I'm scared," Hansen says.

"It's what we've always dreamed of," Gracie says. "A perfect little house in a perfect little town. Going to school with other children our age. We'll be safe and we'll be happy."

Hansen says, "Okay," but he still isn't sure. Neither of us is sure.

* * *

We're in our first class on our first day. Our teacher is a grim man, middle-aged and tired-looking. He speaks to us and the rest of the pupils in clipped, angry sentences. When the bell rings to start the day and the term and the rest of our educational lives, he calls over the conversations and greetings of the returning pupils.

"We have to welcome a couple of new pupils to our class today," he says, and he motions for us to stand, so we do. "You're twins, aren't you?"

We glance at each other.

"Where did you move from?" he says.

Don't answer, Hansen thinks.

But the teacher is looking at us, and his phony smile is growing stiffer and sterner.

"Did you hear me?" the teacher says.

Hansen coughs into his hand.

"When you're asked a question in my class," he says, his smile now totally gone and his face growing red, "I expect you to answer. Right away and truthfully."

The class starts to giggle and the teacher shakes his head at us, disappointed and horrible.

We hate them, we think. *We hate all of them.*

Mum sighed. "No," she admitted. "Jack, I'm sorry, but you're going to have give up this paper route. You're not making enough money doing that job."

"Huh?" Jack said. "Give up the paper route?" He pulled the orange juice from the fridge and poured himself a glass. "Mum, I know it's not much money, but it's better than nothing."

He downed the juice quickly. "Oh, hey, I almost forgot," he said. He dug into the pocket of his faded, too-tight, too-short jeans and pulled out a crumpled-up pair of notes.

"Payday today," he said. He dropped the money on the worktop. "Cha-ching!" he added, trying to make his mum laugh.

Mum smiled at him and pushed back his hair.

"Well done, Jack," she said, looking down at the money. Then she sighed. "But honey, it's just not much."

"I know," Jack said, suddenly feeling hurt. "At least it's something, though."

"We'd make more by selling that bike of yours," she said.

Jack's jaw dropped. "Sell my bike? No way. You can't mean that," he said. "How will I get to school?"

"You can walk to school," Mum said. "Marie walks, doesn't she?"

Jack groaned. Marie, in Year 8, lived up in Flat 5B. Yeah, she walked to school. But it was a really long walk, and Marie always looked tired, and she never had good grades.

"It takes ages, though," Jack said. "I wouldn't have time to do anything. Like homework."

"I'm sorry, dear," Mum said. "But I don't know what else we can do." She checked her watch. "I have to get to work," she added. "I can't be late."

She put her empty coffee cup in the sink and grabbed her bag. "After school today, please start looking for a buyer for the bike," she said. "I'm sure one of those bike shops in town would be happy to give you ... oh, say fifty pounds for it?"

"Ha!" Jack said. "Fifty quid?"

The bike was worth a lot more than fifty pounds. He'd won it in a raffle held by the newspaper. He'd only bought one ticket, but it was the one that counted.

"It would really help us out," Mum said from the front door. "Now you get off to school, okay?"

The door slammed and Jack rested his head on the worktop. It was cold and smelled like a wet, dirty rag.

"Whatever," he muttered.

Mum shouted from the corridor through the closed door: "Things will get better soon! You'll see!"

Jack groaned. "Yeah, right."

* * *

Jack didn't bother going home after school. Instead, he went into town on his bike, straight to his favourite bike shop, Slim's.

"Why the long face, killer?" Slim said when Jack pushed his bike through the shop's front door. "Bike trouble?"

Slim was a big man – fat, despite the nickname. He was always sweaty, from being in the shop's back room doing repairs. His hands were thick and covered with grease more often than not. Slim wiped off a wrench – looked like a fifteen millimetre – and slipped it into the back pocket of his overalls.

"The worst kind of bike trouble," Jack said. He leaned his bike against the shop's counter. "Mum's making me sell it."

Slim's eyes went wide. "What?" he said. "That's horrible. I'm sickened."

"Me too," Jack said. "But I guess we need the money worse than I need a bike – or a paper route."

Slim shook his head slowly and clucked his tongue. "So, what are you going to do?" he asked.

"That's why I'm here," Jack said. "Wanna buy it?"

Slim's face fell. "I can't help you, killer," he said. "I don't buy used bikes."

"Aw," Jack said. "Why not?"

Slim picked up a black binder from the counter. He flipped through the pages and then turned it to face Jack. "How do we know it's not stolen?" Slim said, pointing at the open page. It was a list of bikes, by colour and size and style and brand, that had been reported missing.

"Come on," Jack said, grinning. "Seriously? It's me! You've repaired this bike for me a dozen times."

"But the police don't know that," Slim said. He stepped back from the counter. "It's the same at every shop, all over town. Ask anyone you like."

"So you won't buy any used bikes?" Jack asked. "That's that?"

Slim shook his head. "It's way too much of a risk for me," he said. "One stolen bike sold, and I could lose my whole business." He looked at Jack's bike and smiled. "Sure wish I could," he added. "Your bike is a great one."

"I know," Jack said sadly.

Slim disappeared into the back room. "Sorry, killer!" he called out.

"It's okay," Jack mumbled.

He rolled his bike back outside. There were a few other bike shops nearby. He realized it would be a long afternoon.

* * *

By five o'clock, Jack had been in every bike shop in town. As it turned out, Slim was right. No one would buy a used bike because used bikes were often stolen bikes.

Jack rolled his bike outside. He thought if he couldn't sell it, at least he'd get to keep it. That thought cheered him up, and he hopped onto his bike to ride home.

He'd just started through the alley behind the only sky-scraper in town when someone called out to him.

"Hey, you!" a dry and raspy voice said. "That's a great bike. Is it for sale?"

Jack squeezed the brake lever hard. His rear wheel came around, squealing, and he skidded to a stop. He looked around frantically, but there was no one around.

"I'm right here," said the voice. And right in front of Jack – how could he have missed him? – was an old and bent man dressed in clothes so dirty and ragged that it was impossible to say where the coat ended and the trousers began. In fact, Jack thought as he got a closer look, he couldn't be sure this man wasn't dressed in something like an old canvas robe or gown – something a wizard would wear in a children's fairy tale.

"You want to buy my bike?" Jack said as he hopped down from the seat. As he got closer, he gagged a little.

The man smelled. He smelled of the street and of sweat and of smoke and oil and petrol, like most people who live on the street. But this man had another scent, too – spicy, earthy and foreign.

The old man nodded several times, very slowly. His grin was wise, wide and toothy, and his teeth were bright and sharp.

"Because you don't look like a big cyclist," Jack said.

The man ignored the comments and started digging through his pockets, taking out random items. He pulled out scraps of paper, some metal toys, a banana, two apples, a cooked chicken leg ... but no money.

"My mum wants me to get at least three hundred pounds for this," Jack said. He was sure this weird old guy wouldn't find that in those ragged pockets.

"You want money, eh?" the man said. He was short, Jack realized, and the man looked up at him with the expectant and mischievous smile of an ill-behaved toddler. "I can give you money."

"Great!" said Jack.

"I can make you rich beyond your wildest dreams!" the man went on.

"Wait, what?" Jack said. This guy seemed crazier by the second. And those teeth were kind of scary, like bared fangs on a rabid dog. Jack started to back away. "Listen, never mind," he said. "I think I'll keep the bike."

"Wait!" the man snapped, and he snatched for Jack's wrist. His hand was quick – so quick that Jack hardly saw it move. It was more like a blur, and then it was around Jack's wrist, hard – painful.

"Let me go," Jack said. He tugged and tugged, but the little man's grip was a vise.

It was just a moment – just the briefest instant – but the man sneered wickedly, his face darkening and his eyes flashing red. Then, as if it had never happened, the man released Jack's wrist and put up his hands.

A grin spread across his face like wings. "I mean no harm," he said. "Simply, do not run off just yet."

"Okay," Jack said, rubbing his wrist. "Ow."

The man bowed, and, staying stooped over, clasped his hands together as if to beg. "You think me crazy?"

Jack shrugged. "No…" he said. His voice was tentative and shaky.

"You do," the man said, nodding quickly. "Oh, you do. I've seen it so many times. But look!"

He reached into his pocket again. This time he didn't search wildly or pull out loads of junk and rubbish. He knew just what he was grabbing.

"Magic," the man said, and now his voice was deep and rich. He held up a tiny bag made of shining, golden fabric.

The bag was cinched at the very top with a narrow cord of black thread.

Jack took the bag. He opened the top and turned it out into his hand. From the bag tumbled a half dozen brown and pale grey...

"Beans," Jack said. "They're beans."

The man's grin grew wider still. His eyes were shining and bright as he looked up at Jack.

"They can be yours," the old man whispered, as if someone would desperately want a handful of beans, "along with all the magic they possess. All you have to do is give me the bike."

Jack almost laughed. "Come on," he said. "What do you think this is? A fairy tale?" And he looked directly into the man's shining eyes, and the man reached out again – more gently this time, almost carefully – and took Jack's wrist in his hand.

"The magic is real," he said, and now his smile vanished. His voice became quiet and heavy, like it came not from his body, but from somewhere deep in the Earth itself. "It only remains to be seen whether you will take the chance and grab it."

Jack's mouth opened – he meant to speak. He meant to say no, or to laugh, or to pull his hand away and ride home as fast as his legs would take him. But instead he said, "Riches?"

The man nodded. His grin, with its rabid-dog teeth, returned.

"Riches," he repeated. "Beyond your wildest dreams."

And then it was done. Jack's hand closed around the beans, and the man led the bike away.

* * *

"What?" Jack's mum shouted. "Beans?"

"Mum," Jack said. He looked at the beans on the little table in their makeshift dining room. "They're magic."

He could hardly bring himself to believe it anymore. Why had he been so stupid?

Mum put a hand on her hip and stared at her son.

"I'm sorry," he said, letting his chin fall to his chest. "I think he hypnotized me or something."

She took a deep breath and sighed. "Just take them back," she said. "Find this magician, give him his stupid beans and get your bike back. It's worth more than beans, I'm sure."

"I can't do that," Jack protested. "We traded fair and square." Besides, Jack thought without even meaning to, they might be magic.

"You just said he hypnotized you," his mum replied. "That doesn't sound very fair to me."

Jack groaned and rolled his eyes. "That's not the point," he said, even though it was the point. Why couldn't he shake the feeling that he had to keep those beans?

"Go," she said as she pulled him up by the elbow.

"Right now?" he said.

"Were you planning to wait till this man was a hundred miles away?" Mum asked.

She opened the front door, practically shoved her son down the hall and slammed the door.

* * *

To Jack's surprise, when he went back to the alley behind the skyscraper, the wizened old weirdo was still there. He was sitting on the ground, leaning against a big, blue recycling tub.

"Hey!" Jack said as he jogged over. "Am I glad I found you. Listen, my mum is pretty upset with me."

"Is she?" the man said.

"Yeah," Jack said. "And to be honest, I don't know what I was thinking giving you my bike for a bunch of silly beans." He dug into his pocket and pulled out the beans. "So here they are," he said, holding out his hand.

Jack stared down at the beans. He couldn't take his eyes off them. *Stop it*, he ordered himself. *They're just beans.* He blinked hard and shook his head to clear it. "You can have them back and I'll take the bike back."

The man laughed. "I'm afraid I can't do that," he said.

"Why not?" Jack said. "Come on. Here's the beans."

"It would be impossible," the man said.

"Why?" Jack asked.

"I already ate your bike," the man said. He climbed to his feet, groaning the whole way up from the dirty ground.

"Ate it?" Jack said. "You are crazy, aren't you?"

The man cackled and coughed. He put up one finger, as if telling Jack to wait, and then disappeared around the far side of the recycling tub.

"Good," Jack said to himself. He shook the beans in his loose fist, thinking the man would be back at any moment with his bike. "He sure has a weird sense of humour, though."

After nearly a minute, the man still hadn't reappeared. "Hey," Jack called, peeking around the recycling tub. "What are you up to?"

But the man was gone.

Jack looked down at the beans in his hand. "Well," he muttered, "Mum's going to kill me."

With that, he headed out of the alley. He found that the beans grew warm as he walked. Soon, they were uncomfortably hot in the palm of his hand.

"Ow," he muttered, and without thinking, he tossed the beans over a brick wall.

* * *

Mum was furious when Jack showed up at home with no bike and no beans. He tried over and over to explain that he was sorry, and that this man was definitely crazy. He admitted time and again that it was his fault, but Mum just wasn't satisfied.

The next day was Saturday, and in the morning – before seven o'clock – his mum woke him up. "Get dressed," she said.

"What? No school today. No more paper route," Jack protested.

"Time to find a better job," Mum said.

"Now?" Jack said. "No one's even open yet."

"Cafés are open," Mum said. "And they need dishwashers."

Jack sat up on the sofa – it doubled as his bed these days, since he and Mum had moved into the tiny flat. He rubbed his face to help himself wake up.

"Okay," he muttered. "I'm awake."

* * *

The streets of Jack's little city were empty. Mum was right – the cafés were all open, and so were the bakery and the coffee shop. But they all had dishwashers already. They let him fill out an application, but it was pretty obvious to Jack that he'd never hear back from them.

By eleven, he'd written his name and address and relevant experience (that is, none) on about ten different forms. And he was hungry. He was about to head home when he spotted – like a bright-red streak of lightning – his bike.

"Hey!" he shouted, and he took off running. "Stop!"

It was the little odd man, zooming around town. As he zipped and flew down the empty streets, he laughed and hollered: "Can't catch me, Magic Jack! Can't catch me!"

"Come back, you crazy old–" Jack shouted. He tore down streets and alleys. Every time he turned a corner, the bike zipped by and was out of sight.

Finally Jack was back at the alley behind the skyscraper. But the bike, it seemed, had vanished for good. Jack didn't see it – or the crazy old man – anywhere. And after running for so long and so fast, Jack was exhausted. He sat down against a fence and wiped the sweat from his forehead and the back of his neck.

"That's funny," he said to himself, staring at the thick-trunked, bright-green tree across the alley from where he sat. "I don't remember that tree being there yesterday."

He shaded his eyes and squinted up at the tree, higher and higher. It twisted and turned as it climbed, so high that he couldn't see the top of it. It seemed to be as tall as the skyscraper it grew behind – maybe even taller. And all the way up, it was green and smooth, with lots of vines and big, broad leaves growing out of it, instead of rough and brown and covered with bark, like a tree should be.

Jack climbed to his feet and walked across the alley. "I don't think this is a tree," he mumbled. Closer to the tree, he saw that the vines, which climbed all around the big plant and the fence and even onto the skyscraper itself, bore little pea pods. Jack pulled one off and tore it open.

Bright-green beans tumbled to the pavement. Jack smiled. These were his beans. This was his beanstalk.

Magic, he thought.

Then he started climbing.

He seemed to climb for hours, but it was never difficult. It was warm, and a cooling breeze pushed him from behind, as if to help him climb.

As he went, he sometimes picked a pod of beans – he ate a handful, and shoved some in his pockets. After all, they were really magic, weren't they?

Now and then, Jack could see into the skyscraper beside the huge beanstalk. Most of the floors were offices, with men and women hunched over desks, or walking sternly down lushly carpeted corridors, all well dressed in dark suits and all serious-looking, with set jaws and no smiles.

None of the people glanced out of the huge windows. No one seemed to notice the sinewy, bright-green stalk that had sprung up overnight beside the tower. None of the people – so distracted and busy and committed to their tasks – saw the boy climbing, just a metre from their desks.

On other floors were flats, most with drawn blinds and lights off, their residents no doubt at work – maybe at the offices right there in the same skyscraper.

That would be something, Jack thought as he climbed. *To live and work right there in the same building.* He wondered if there was a school inside this skyscraper too, and hairstylists and restaurants and supermarkets. Maybe these people simply never went outside.

And it was then, when he'd almost forgotten he'd been climbing, that Jack reached the top of the beanstalk.

The narrowing plant startled him from his thoughts and he looked down. The world spun around him. The wind picked up, and he hugged the stalk for dear life. Dark clouds moved in from the southwest. The air was cold and seemed to sing with electricity. It would storm any second, Jack knew.

"What am I doing?" he shouted to himself against the sound of the approaching storm. It was as if all the magic of the beanstalk and his long and easy climb suddenly fell away. He realized at once that he was in great danger, three hundred metres above the streets of his little city.

Jack searched desperately. Below him, about six metres down, jutting out from the top floor of the huge building, was a covered balcony. As lightning cracked across the darkening sky, Jack knew he had no choice but to climb down to that balcony to find cover.

The stalk was slippery now. He clawed at its sides to hold on. The skinny vines that tangled up and around the stalk clung to his legs, as if trying to stop him or trying to trip him.

Jack tugged free of the vines and, half sliding and half climbing, made it to the balcony.

He jumped from the stalk and landed in a crumpled heap on the balcony floor. At the same instant, the sky opened with rain – a torrential downpour. Jack hurried farther under the balcony's roof. He huddled against the big glass doors that led into the flat beyond.

When lightning cracked again, Jack turned, desperate for a safe, dry place. The glass door was open, just a little bit. It slid easily all the way open and Jack, still crawling, hurried inside. He closed the door behind him, silencing the storm.

Jack leaned against the inside of the glass door and stared at the room he'd found himself in.

It was like nothing he'd ever seen, outside of films and TV programmes. The furniture was covered in soft-looking, dark leather. Framed paintings hung from the walls. A big wooden desk boasted small sculptures and golden trinkets. Hanging on the wall facing the desk was a huge flatscreen TV.

"Wow," Jack said. "Whoever lives here must be the richest person in town."

And the riches were his for the taking.

Jack shook the thought away. He wasn't a thief, after all. He was a hardworking boy with a paper route and good grades. He hoped to move out of his neighbourhood, but for now, just because he lived among so many thieves didn't mean he had to be one himself.

But this is magic, Jack thought.

Here, in the safety of the flat, the storm that had sent him fleeing inside seemed many kilometres away. From where he sat, he could see fancy crystal pieces, expensive electronics, jewellery and even an egg made of pure gold.

Any one of those things would pay his mum's debts, and probably keep them above water for months.

Those things could change their lives.

"This is the magic," Jack whispered into the dark flat. "This is it. Not the beans. The beanstalk was just the way up here, really. But the crazy old man was right. I found riches beyond my wildest dreams."

Jack got to his feet and moved towards the big wooden desk. "Besides," he said, "these people are so rich, they wouldn't even notice if something was missing."

He was about to grab the golden egg from its resting place when he spotted a box. It was smaller than a loaf of bread, trimmed in leather and mother of pearl.

Jack flipped up the top and caught his breath. Inside were dozens of shining gold coins.

"Real treasure," he said in a quiet, worshipful voice.

Then he reached in, grabbed handfuls, and shoved the coins into his pockets.

As he reached for the golden egg again, something thumped in the hall. Footsteps grew louder and faster.

Someone was coming.

With his pockets heavy and jingling, Jack ran for the sliding door. He threw it open and, not bothering to close it behind him, was across the balcony in two long strides. He leaped over the railing and grabbed hold of the beanstalk.

As he slid and twisted among the vines and bean pods on the giant stalk, Jack squinted through the rain and gloom at the glass door. He could just make out a figure – a huge figure – stomping through the room.

The huge man stood in the middle of the room, sniffing the air, as if he might pick up the scent of a thief from the broken-down block of flats at the top of Farmhand Street. But through the rain and dark, he couldn't see Jack outside; Jack could tell.

But he might at any moment, Jack thought, so Jack climbed and slid down as fast as he could.

* * *

Jack slammed into the flat, the smile on his face as big as the whole outdoors. He ran into the kitchen, shoved past his mum and turned his pockets out onto the worktop.

"Ta-da!" he said.

Mum's jaw fell open. Her face went white and she brought her hand to her mouth.

"Wh–" she started. "Wha–"

Jack laughed and threw his arms around her. He held her by the shoulders, grinning. "We're set, Mum," he said. "No more debt. No more dumpy flat."

"Where did you get these?" Mum asked. She wriggled from his hug and ran her fingers over and through the piles of gold.

"I found them," Jack said, but his mum could hardly hear him – she was barely listening. Instead she sorted through the piles of coins, trying to guess the value of this treasure.

Without another word, Mum grabbed a plastic bag from under the kitchen sink. She slid the coins into the bag and grabbed her coat. She shoved the bag into her coat's big pocket.

"Let's go," she said.

"Go?" Jack said, hurrying to keep up as his mum slipped out the front door. "Where?"

Mum was already a flight down the steps.

"Don't you plan to lock the door?" Jack shouted.

"Why?" she called up to him. "To protect our worthless junk? We have riches, right here in my pocket!"

Smiling, Jack jumped down the steps, two at a time.

* * *

On the north edge of town was a small, curious shop. Hardly anyone went in, but everyone who passed it wondered about it: what could there be in there? How does the crazy shopkeeper stay open, if no one ever buys anything?

The window display was so cluttered that one couldn't see into the shop, but one could see a collection of the oddest things imaginable: copper-headed horse dolls, antique cuckoo clocks, thick books bound in leather and edged in gold, and all manner of contraptions that no one other than the shopkeeper herself could identify.

But such a lot of clutter was intimidating to most of the people in and around town. So no one ever went in – and most of the townspeople assumed that's how the shopkeeper liked it: quiet, dusty, cluttered and empty of strangers.

When Jack and his mum pushed through the heavy front door – its glass opaque with years of grime – and set the bell to jingling, the shopkeeper behind the counter at the back of the shop nearly fell off her stool.

"What do you want?" the shopkeeper said. She found her glasses on top of a pile of junk on the high counter in front of her and slipped them over her hooked nose. On her stool, she looked rather like a ragged and tired old vulture. "The shop is closed!" she said.

"The sign says you're open," Jack pointed out. "Besides, the door was unlocked."

"Ah, well…" the woman said. She pulled off her glasses and rubbed her eyes. "Very well. Don't touch anything."

"We're not here to shop," Jack's mum said. She stepped forward and dropped the plastic bag on the counter. At the jangly sound of the coins, the shopkeeper's eyes went wide, as did her grin.

"Selling?" she said. "Very good. Very good."

Eagerly, she opened the bag and reached in. She pulled out handful after handful of gold coins until the bag was empty and the coins were in neat piles in front of her.

"A nice collection," she whispered. "A very nice collection."

Then she looked up at Jack. "In my experience, a person doesn't come across such a collection by accident," she said, peering at him.

"What's that supposed to mean?" Jack asked, frowning.

The old woman looked at him with her eyes narrow. "I think you know," she whispered.

Her gaze seemed to burn – was it more magic?

Or was it guilt?

Nonsense, Jack told himself. *We need this money. I don't feel guilty at all.*

In a flash, the shopkeeper's face went bright again. She grinned and said, "It's a fine collection. I can pay you well – if you wish to part with it."

"Of course we do," Jack's mum said, smiling gently at the shopkeeper. "That's why we're here."

"Very well," the shopkeeper said, and she hopped down from her stool.

To Jack's surprise, off the stool she was shorter than he was – only a metre tall. She hobbled into a back room and came back with a chequebook as big as she was. Then she climbed back up onto the stool, pulled out a cheque, and, with her big feather pen, hunched over the chequebook and filled it out in big flamboyant writing. "There you are," the woman said. "Take it or leave it."

"How much?" Jack said, trying to get a look over his mum's shoulder. But she folded it and tucked it away.

"Thank you," Mum said. She stayed composed, but Jack could tell that inside she was ecstatic.

"Have a good day," the shopkeeper said as she came down from her stool. She hurried around the counter and pushed them towards the door. "We're closing right now. Goodbye."

In a moment, Jack and his mum were on the street outside. The door slammed behind them, and bolt after bolt slid home.

"She's weird," Jack said.

"Jack," his mum said, reaching into her bag. "My dear, sweet son. Look at this."

She held out the cheque.

"It can't be right," Jack said. "It can't be."

It was more money than Jack had ever seen in his life.

"Our problems are solved, Jack," Mum said. "We're out of the woods."

* * *

The cheque changed their lives. Mum paid all their overdue bills. She caught up on their rent. The cheque was so large, in fact, that Mum was able to pay off the remainder of their lease on the flat and buy them a small house in a nicer part of town. She resigned from two of her jobs.

Everything was great. But Jack still wasn't happy. He wanted his bike back. It was a long shot, but it was summer now and Jack didn't have anywhere he needed to be. So one morning, after his mum headed to work, Jack got dressed and started walking.

Their new house, which was light blue with white trim, sat on a beautiful green lawn, with shrubs and a single fat-trunked ancient apple tree in the middle of the back garden. It sat among hundreds of other houses, some light blue like Jack's, others white or pale grey or canary yellow or soft green.

The neighbourhood squatted around the lake on the east side of the city, as far from Farmhand Street as a person could get. The walk to the skyscraper in town would take an hour or more. Jack didn't mind. He knew he probably wouldn't find the old man who bought his bike. But if he did, maybe the man would sell it back.

After all, Jack definitely had enough money to buy it.

And if the man wasn't there – well, Jack had a few other ideas about what he might do with his morning. Maybe he'd go back up to the palace in the sky.

Nah, Jack thought as he walked towards the town centre, thinking of the beanstalk to the clouds. *It's probably been cut down by now.*

But it hadn't been. Several streets from the skyscraper, Jack spotted it. The passers-by – and there were many – ignored it.

Maybe that's part of its magic, Jack thought. *Maybe only I notice it, because I know to look for it. Because it's mine.*

Jack moved through the sea of weekday people – some were shoppers, some were workers, some seemed to have nowhere in particular to be. Not one of them seemed to notice the beanstalk that climbed over three hundred metres into the sky.

Jack slipped into the alley behind the skyscraper and there, at the base of his giant plant, was the odd old man – the man who traded him the magic beans.

And he was sitting on top of Jack's old bike.

"Jack's back!" the old man said. He cackled, and one of his eyes twitched and winked madly.

"I want my bike back," Jack said. He dug into his pocket and pulled out a thick wad of cash. "I can pay you way more than it's worth."

That just seemed to make the old man laugh even more. He nearly fell off the bike. "This bike," he said, crying with laughter, "is not for sale."

So suddenly that Jack flinched, the man stopped laughing and his face became quite serious.

"Why don't you climb again?" the man whispered. "Climb again and steal some more, Jack the Thief."

Jack shoved his money back in his pocket – worried, just for an instant, that someone might see it.

"It's not stealing," he said. "It's magic."

The man laughed and laughed. He rode off, still laughing, and called over his shoulder as he rode away: "Yes, it's magic, Magic Jack. It's magic!" His laughter echoed through the alley as he vanished. Jack was left alone.

"Forget that weird old man," Jack said to himself. "I will climb again. I'll find enough riches up there to buy a hundred bikes – the best bikes in the world, too!"

And so climb he did.

No storms came. No wind threatened to pull Jack from the beanstalk and send him tumbling to the ground and his demise. This time it was easy. He climbed all the way up to the top.

Then he hopped down lightly from the giant plant, onto the safety of the terrace, and once again the sliding door was ajar. Jack slipped inside. The big living room's lights were off, and the next door, which led to the rest of the palatial flat, stood open. The hall lights, too, were off.

No one home? Jack thought. *It can't hurt to have a look around – see what else this millionaire might have.*

Jack sniffed the air. Something smelled great – the scent of freshly baked desserts wafted into the living room. Jack couldn't help but follow the smell. Maybe the millionaire had left something delicious sitting out. Or his housekeeper had.

Jack tiptoed down the hall. Every door he passed stood open, just a little bit, and every light in every room was off. He made his way to the kitchen and gently pushed open the swinging door.

"Whoa," he said. Even though they had moved – even with his new house, with their new kitchen and his own bedroom and the family room in the basement – Jack was blown away by this flat's kitchen.

The worktops were huge and high and made of slabs of black stone. The refrigerator and oven gleamed as if they were covered in gold. Huge windows on the far wall let in the bright noon sunlight.

Jack squinted against the light and spotted a plate of doughnuts on the big island in the middle of the kitchen.

"Ah!" he said, and he grabbed two at once. "I knew I smelled something." In seconds, his mouth was full and his face was powdered with icing sugar.

He stood in the middle of the huge kitchen, licking the sugar from his fingertips. They were the best doughnuts he'd ever had. In fact, he might have forgotten why he was in this magical, millionaire kitchen. He might have found a bag, filled it with the rest of the doughnuts, and left.

But then something clucked.

Jack stopped, frozen, with one finger in his mouth.

It clucked again.

"Hello?" he said, though he was certain he'd heard a chicken, and a chicken probably wouldn't respond to "hello".

Cluck!

Jack spun and found the source of the cluck: a cupboard with a big door with a wire screen in the middle – like an old-fashioned pie cabinet. But this cabinet definitely didn't contain pies.

Jack moved carefully across the kitchen as he finished licking the sugar from his fingers. He bent down. The cabinet was near the tiled floor, under the heavy slab worktops. Jack peered through the screen. It was dark in there. He could just make out a vague, white shape.

Cluck! Cluckcluckcluck!

Jack yelped and jumped back. Inside the closed cabinet, the chicken flapped and clucked madly.

"Shh!" Jack said, hurrying back to the screen. "Good chicken."

But the chicken wouldn't be calmed. It clucked and squawked and flapped and hopped around.

"Please!" Jack said. "Be quiet!" He tried the cabinet door, but it wouldn't budge. *I have to let it out,* he thought. *It's probably scared to death.*

Jack pulled open the kitchen drawers. He found towels and cling film and wooden spoons. There seemed to be a hundred drawers, but finally he found something that might work. He pulled out a big ladle – made of heavy metal – and ran back to the cabinet. The chicken was insane by this point, flapping its wings and clucking its head off.

Jack wedged the big spoon's handle into the cabinet door. He pulled and tugged, and the door cracked open, just a tiny bit – but it was enough to jam in the whole spoon and really give it a tug.

With a great snap, the door flew off. It fell to the tile floor, clattering loudly. The chicken followed the door, clucking and flapping its wings, bouncing around the kitchen.

It snapped its beak at Jack. It hopped onto the worktop, sending the doughnuts and their plate crashing to the floor. The plate shattered into a hundred pieces.

"Shush!" Jack said. He chased the chicken around the kitchen. He dived for it, his arms out in a hug, and he missed. He tried again and again.

Finally he got close – he came away with two handfuls of soft white feathers that the chicken had shed – but he dived straight into the empty chicken cabinet.

With his head inside, he could see the chicken's nest and the eggs inside it. They were sort of yellow, he realized, not like any chicken eggs he'd ever seen.

He grabbed one as he struggled to back up out of the cabinet – and nearly dropped it right away.

It wasn't warm, like a fresh egg ought to be. It was cold – and heavy.

Jack pulled himself out of the cabinet and, on his knees, grabbed an egg in each hand. They were both very cold and very heavy. He stood up, holding the two eggs, and, as he watched the chicken pecking around the kitchen, he realized something.

The golden egg in the living room – that was no jeweller's creation. It came from this nest. That chicken laid eggs made of pure gold.

"No wonder this person is so rich," Jack said. "He has a constant supply of gold."

If Jack had a chicken like this one, he'd have as many bikes as he wanted. His mum would have a kitchen like this one. She could resign from her job. They could travel the world. He wouldn't need school, or university – he wouldn't need anything, ever! His grin grew to a huge smile.

"Come here, cute little magic chicken," Jack said.

He moved slowly towards the chicken. It was much calmer now. Jack stayed low to the ground. As he crawled towards the bird, he scooped up a chunk of the fallen doughnuts. He held it out to the bird. Surely even a chicken would love a sugary treat.

It worked. The chicken, hesitant at first, strutted towards Jack. It pecked at the crumbs in his hand. It hurt a bit; the little beak was sharp. But Jack knew it would be worth the pain.

As the chicken snapped up bit after bit of doughnut, Jack suddenly threw his arms around the fat bird's body. He quickly clamped one hand over its beak, stood up and ran from the kitchen.

Halfway down the hall, Jack skidded to a stop. At the far end of the hall, the front door was opening.

For a second, Jack stood there, frozen, staring at the wide-open front door and the giant man it framed. He had to stoop to fit through the door. His shoulders barely squeezed through. If this giant got his hands on Jack, it would be the end of him.

"You!" shouted the man in the doorway. He sniffed, and he sniffed again. He squinted and twisted his mouth, as if thinking and struggling to recall something. Then his eyes went wide and he bellowed, balling his hands into huge fists: "You stole my coins!"

Jack, barely able to breathe, found the open door to the living room. He hurried through and leaped over the couch. Behind him, the giant stomped down the hall. But big as he was, he wasn't fast, and Jack was on the terrace before the giant was in the room.

"See ya!" Jack said. He cradled the chicken under one arm like a football and leaped to the beanstalk.

"You can't escape!" the huge man called after him, his voice booming like thunder.

But Jack did escape. He slid and climbed quickly down the beanstalk, its top hidden in the clouds, and the huge man at the top never knew where Jack had disappeared to.

* * *

"A chicken?" Jack's mum said. "Jack, what do we want with a chicken?"

Jack dug in his pockets. He pulled out two, three, four eggs and put them on the table. They rolled and wobbled.

"What is this, Jack?" his mum asked. She picked one up.

"It's gold," Jack said.

"Gold," she whispered. She smiled. She picked up the other eggs and said louder: "Gold." She looked at Jack. Their eyes met, and they both smiled happily.

Then, in a flash, the smile was gone. Mum held up the egg and snapped at Jack, "Where did you get this ... thing?" She pointed at the hen under his arm. "Tell me the truth, Jack. Right now."

And finally, after so many months of wealth, and the newfound everlasting riches that could come from the hen, Jack told his mum everything.

He told her about the weird old man. He told her how the beans had sprouted and grown into a ladder that reached up to the sky. And he told her about the palatial flat at the top of the skyscraper.

After Jack's tale, Mum sat down in a dining room chair. She didn't say anything. Jack waited, but for minutes, she didn't speak. She stared at her reflection in the golden egg in her hand, and then she stared at another of the eggs that sat on the dining table in front of her.

"Mum," Jack said, sitting down next to her. "I can see you're upset. You think I'm a thief. But it's not like that. It's magic. Don't you see? The magic got us all this stuff. You've worked so hard, and now you won't have to anymore."

"No," Mum said. She shook her head. "You stole this stuff. We stole this stuff!"

She put down the egg and stood up. "Show me," she said. "Show me the beanstalk."

* * *

They took Mum's car into town. They parked in front of the skyscraper. Even though they were rich, they didn't have any change for the meter. *Too bad the parking meter doesn't take golden eggs,* Jack thought.

"Don't worry, Mum," Jack said, hurrying her along. "We can afford a parking ticket."

Mum sighed, but she followed him down the alley without paying for their parking spot.

At the base of the big plant, Jack stopped and put his hands on his hips and smiled.

Mum's face went white. "This is it?" she asked. "And it goes all the way to the top? You're sure?"

Jack nodded.

"I know who lives there," Mum said.

Jack gasped. "You do?" he asked. "Who lives there?"

"That's the penthouse flat of Don Briareus," Mum said, her voice hushed and afraid.

"Who's that?" Jack asked.

"He's the most powerful man in town – one of the richest and most powerful men in the world," Mum explained. She took a deep breath. "Jack, that man owns half of the city. He owns the block of flats where we used to live – and most of the rest of Farmhand Street, probably."

"But Mum," Jack said. "He's rich because of that silly chicken. He's rich from magic too!"

"No," Mum said. "We can't let this continue. We have to give everything back. The house. The coins. The gold eggs. Everything. He'll find us. He'll make us pay."

"He doesn't sound very nice," Jack said, looking at his feet.

"Nice isn't the issue," Mum said, and she grabbed Jack by the hand. "Come on. We're going upstairs."

"What?!" Jack said. "No, Mum. We can't do that."

But his mum dragged him around to the front of the building, right into the lobby and up to the security desk.

"We've been expecting you," the guard said as he stood up. He leaned both hands on his desk. His mouth twisted into a satisfied and unpleasant smile. "You can go right up."

"Thank you," Jack's mum said. "But first–" She reached into her purse and pulled out a five-pound note. "Do you have change for the parking meter?"

* * *

On the hundredth storey of the building, Jack and his mum stepped out of the leather-lined, golden lift. The floor was covered with a thick, lush, red carpet.

"Wow," Mum whispered.

A single huge white door stood before them. On it, rather than a number, was a name in shining gold letters: BRIAREUS.

"I suppose we should knock?" Mum said. She stepped forward and raised her first, but before she could strike, the door swung open.

The hall was completely unfamiliar to Jack. All the lights were on, and it made the long hall seem welcoming – inviting, even. Jack and his mum moved slowly down the hall. It had been years since Jack held his mum's hand, but now he did.

All the doors along the hall were closed tight – except one. They stopped in front of the open door, about halfway down the hall, and looked in.

There, sitting on a big leather couch, was Mr Briareus. When he saw them, he smiled and stood up.

Though Jack had seen him before – had fled from him – as Mr Briareus stood to his full height, Jack and his mother both gasped at the enormity of the man.

"Welcome to my home," he said. "Please, come into my office and take a seat." He waved at two chairs facing the big couch.

"Thank you," Mum said. "We're so sorry about all this."

Mr Briareus nodded and ushered them to the chairs.

Jack's mum did her best to smile, but she was still afraid
– Jack could tell. Who wouldn't be afraid of this man? He
was powerful not just financially and politically, but physically. If he wanted, Jack realized, Mr Briareus could crush
the two of them in one hand.

Jack refused to smile, but he sat down in the chair next
to his mum's and crossed his arms.

"Do you have something to say to me, little man?" said
Mr Briareus through his toothy smile.

"No," Jack snapped back.

"Jack!" his mum whispered harshly. "Apologize. Confess!"

But Jack didn't answer. He didn't apologize or confess.
He didn't nod or shake his head. He just grunted once and
refolded his arms across his chest.

The big man laughed. "It doesn't matter, miss," he said.
"You and I – and your boy – all know what he did. And we
all know exactly how much he's stolen from me."

Mum shifted in her seat. "Oh, dear," she muttered.

"You're right to be nervous," Mr Briareus said, giving a
short, angry laugh.

He strode across the hardwood office floor, stepped
around to the far side of his desk, and sat down in his big
desk chair. With his back to the window, a shadow fell
across Mr Briareus's face so that Jack couldn't see it. But
Jack was sure the giant's smile was gone.

"Today," the man said, "I am your arresting police officer. I am your judge, your jury and your prosecutor. And
today, I find you both guilty of theft."

He leaned forward and pushed a button on the desk. Before Jack or his mum could move, straps shot up from the floor and the arms of their chairs.

They were trapped.

"And," Mr Briareus said, "I sentence you to life imprisonment."

The giant dragged Mum's chair out of the room as she struggled against her bonds.

"I'll be back to deal with you in a moment," Briareus said.

"Help me, Jack!" Mum cried.

But Jack couldn't budge from his chair, no matter how hard he struggled.

"Mum!" he shouted as Briareus pulled her through the office door. "Let her go! She didn't do anything!"

But his shouting was in vain. The office door slammed behind them. Jack heard a key in the door, and the click of a lock.

"Mum!" he shouted once more, but no one answered.

Desperately, Jack looked around the room for anything that might help him escape from this chair and this room before Briareus got back.

He shuffled his chair, and it scraped loudly. He smiled a little, thinking of the nasty scuff marks it would leave on the perfect wood floors. At home, his mum would ground him for that. Quickly, Jack scraped and hopped his chair towards the low cabinet along one wall. Jack pulled open every door and scanned every shelf.

There were books and little sculptures and an antique harp and other useless junk. None of it would help Jack escape.

Jack paused a moment and strained to hear even the slightest sound in the hall. Silence. Wherever that giant had taken his mum, it was taking a while to get back.

He slid his chair towards the big desk, then shimmied so one arm was against the front of the desk, and he grabbed the drawer.

Locked.

But on top of the desk, right in the middle, was a letter opener – it looked like a plain, symmetrical knife. *It might work, if I could reach it,* Jack thought. But he couldn't reach it. He had to knock it to within reach.

With a great grunt of effort, Jack slammed his chair into the desk, giving it a good shake. The letter opener hopped a few centimetres. He slammed into the desk again, and the opener moved some more. He was making a huge racket, but it was working. He had to keep trying.

One more great thump, and the desk scraped loudly on the floor. The letter opener leaped into the air and skidded across the big desktop, all the way to the edge. It teetered, and then it fell with a clang.

Jack hurried, scraping and hopping madly. Then he took a deep breath, closed his eyes and pushed himself over.

He landed with a heavy thud, his head knocking on the wood, ringing like a coconut. But he could reach. He grabbed the letter opener and began scraping its sharp edge against the bonds on his wrist. It was hard work, but soon he heard the bonds ripping and pulling away. His hand was free.

Getting the other three bonds was much easier, and soon, with the letter opener in hand, Jack was free.

He ran for the door, but stopped. Someone was singing. Right there in the office, he heard music and singing – it was the most beautiful thing he'd ever heard.

He looked around for a radio. But all he could see was a harp.

It was golden, and its frame was shaped like a woman in a dress. The woman's arms were plucking the strings as she sang.

"Amazing," Jack whispered, and the harp stopped playing.

"Don't stop!" he said quickly, because it was the most beautiful music he'd ever heard, and she was the most beautiful woman he'd ever seen. "Please, keep playing."

She smiled at him. He stood right beside her now.

"I am only supposed to play for the master," she said in a voice that sounded like crystal, and Jack thought for a moment that he would cry, because he'd never hear that song again.

"You sang for me just now," he said.

"I shouldn't have," the harp said. "The master would be angry."

And then Jack did cry. He didn't want to. But he cried, more than he had in years and years. He could think of nothing other than the harp's song, because the harp, of course, was magic, too.

"You should not stay here," she said.

"Why?" Jack said through his tears. "Where else would I ever want to be?" He could not imagine being away from this harp. Even if she wouldn't play, he'd rather be close to her, just in case she decided to play again one day.

"You must help your mother," she said. Her voice was not only beautiful, it was sad, a sadness so deep and profound that Jack could hardly listen to her without crying again.

But the word "mother" seemed to snap something in his mind. He remembered where he was and what he was doing – and what he had to do: find his mother and get her out of this mad giant's flat.

"You're right," he said. "But what about you?"

"Me?" the harp said.

"You're a prisoner here too, aren't you?" Jack said.

"Something like that," the harp said. "Will you help me to leave too?"

"I will," Jack said, and he grabbed the harp. "But you have to help me first."

* * *

Jack popped the office door open with his letter opener. He stuck his head into the hall and spotted Briareus leaving the living room and locking the door behind him.

"Here he comes," Jack whispered. "You know what to do?"

The harp smiled and nodded, and Jack put her down on the thick, red carpet, just outside the office door. Then he ducked back inside, leaving the door open the tiniest crack. He stood at the door and waited.

He didn't have to wait long.

"What are you doing out here?" the giant shouted. His footsteps thundered down the hall as he ran towards the harp. "Did that little thief get away?"

But the harp didn't answer. Instead, she began to play. It was her finest song, and her voice was more pure and beautiful than even Mr Briareus had ever heard it before.

By the time he reached the harp, he was slow, calm and happy. He began weeping tears of joy that flowed down his cheeks and over his grin like a salty waterfall.

Jack risked a peek through the crack in the door. Briareus picked up the harp and held it against his chest. She looked tiny against his huge frame. The tears still streamed down his face, and he smiled with his eyes closed.

Now was Jack's chance. As quietly as he could, he slipped out of the office door and ran down the long hall, thanking his stars that the thick carpeting muted his footsteps.

At the living room door, he picked the lock and hurried inside. "Mum!" he said. She was still bound in her chair.

"Oh, Jack," she said. "Thank goodness. He's insane!"

"I know," Jack said, nodding. He bent down and started to cut the straps that held her to the chair.

"We have to hurry," he said. "We can climb down the beanstalk."

"What?" she said. She rubbed her wrists and stood up. "Why don't we go out the front?"

Jack pulled her into the hall. There was Mr Briareus, between them and the front door. They waited and watched until he went into the office.

"Go out on the terrace," Jack said. "I'll be right there."

"Where are you going?" Mum asked.

"I made a promise I have to keep," he said. "Just go."

Jack closed the living room door and ran back to the office. He stopped just outside the door and peeked inside. The harp spotted him. It was her cue to stop playing and singing. She stopped, and the silence in the office, after her magical song, filled Jack's chest with sorrow and pain. But he pushed through it. He had to, if they were to escape.

The giant, though, sat on the big leather couch with his head in his hands, and he sobbed. "Why won't you play?" he said through his hiccups and tears.

But the harp would not, and the giant just sobbed and sobbed. His great shoulders bucked and he hiccupped and coughed like a toddler having tantrum.

Jack tiptoed across the wood floor. He put his hands gently on the harp and turned to leave. Everything was working perfectly.

"Please…" the giant said.

Jack was almost out of the office.

The giant lifted his tear-stained face to plead once more.

"Play–" he started to say. Then he jumped to his feet. "You!"

Jack ran. He tore down the long hall, nearly past the closed living room door. He slammed into it shoulder first, not bothering with the doorknob. "Come on, Mum," he said without stopping. "We have to go now. Seriously, come on, hurry up."

With the harp against his chest and belly, he ran across the room, hurdled over a couch and launched himself off the terrace, right onto the beanstalk.

Mum stayed close behind. Soon they were both on their way down.

The magic was with them, and the climb was fast. But above them, Mr Briareus climbed too. The beanstalk swayed under the giant's weight.

"You won't escape, little thieves," he shouted down at them.

When Jack and his mum reached the safety of the pavement, he handed her the harp.

"Mum, this is Harp," he said. "She's … magic."

The harp smiled.

"I'll be right back," Jack said, and he ran to the front of the building.

Inside, the guard jumped to his feet. "How did you get down here?" he said.

But Jack ignored him. He ran to a glass door marked FIRE, and he closed his eyes and smashed the door with his elbow. Inside, he found an axe.

"Whew," he said to himself as he ran from the lobby. "If there'd just been a hose and no axe, I'd be in trouble."

He ran back to the beanstalk. "Step back, Mum," he said, and he swung the axe.

Thwack!

He swung it again.

Thwack!

He swung it again and again, sweat trickling down his face and back. One more big swing, and he was clean through the beanstalk.

Then he waited.

Like a great, ancient tree, the beanstalk leaned slowly, and then faster and faster and faster it toppled, bringing Mr Briareus down with it.

The beanstalk fell, and the giant landed on the pavement many streets away.

* * *

Months later, Jack cycled through his new neighbourhood. From the bag on his back came beautiful music, and though no one stopped him to ask what it was, all who heard it knew – way down deep – that it was magic.

He pulled his bike into the garage and leaned it against the wall. In the house, he found his mother sitting in the armchair in the living room, reading. He pulled Harp from his bag and put her on the table by the window, where she liked it best.

Mum looked up and smiled at both of them, and Harp began to sing.

Harp had told Jack everything – about Mr Briareus, and how he'd come to have his riches. (It was not by being nice, or by being savvy in business. He was a crook and a killer.) And Harp had explained more about the magic beans and the odd old man.

It had all been magic, Harp said, and Jack would never go hungry again.

Jack sat down on the couch and put his feet up. He closed his eyes and just listened.

A HOME IN THE SKY

For as long as he could remember, Brendan walked with a book. He used to wander Three Rivers with a book in front of his face. Somehow, he never crossed a street against the light. He never stepped in front of a moving bus or fell into one of the city's rivers.

He did, however, get lost. Often.

And that's what happened today, his third day in his new town. Brendan walked – deep in his book – up hills and down hills, and through parks and past rows of shops. He crossed the tracks and crossed them again. But he couldn't stop. He was so close to the end.

Within minutes, he'd read how the hero would save himself and then save the village and then defeat the evil king of the land beyond the mountain.

He reached the last page at the same moment he reached the top of the highest hill in Oldtown. He leaned against a knobby old elm tree and devoured the last chapter. He was really there – in the story, riding alongside the hero through the Haunting Woods and across the River of Fire, into the land beyond the mountain where the evil king ruled with a closed and iron fist.

After he – with the hero – had faced and defeated the evil king and his legion of troll warriors, Brendan closed the book and looked up. The elm tree he'd chosen sat on the long, sloping lawn of a huge stone house that was covered from foundation to eaves with crawling, thick ivy. It was enshrouded in a cloak of overgrown shrubs and weeds so thick that no one could have got in or out of that house.

Brendan slipped his book into his bag and stared up at the house. *Abandoned?* he wondered. *A hermit?* he imagined. *A witch?* he supposed.

The sun was setting, and an early-autumn wind blew in from the north. His mum wouldn't worry – Brendan was always so responsible and great at looking after himself – but he hurried home anyway, taken with a chill.

* * *

What happened at school that day was entirely out of character for Brendan: he spoke to other pupils. Since he and his mum had moved to this town, he'd been keeping himself to himself. But today he approached his classmates. He cleared his throat.

"Um," he said to a group sitting at the back of the room before the first lesson. "Do any of you know the big house up on the hill, right at the end of Willow Avenue?"

A boy in a hoodie looked up from the laughter and conversation, his jaw hanging open. "Yeah. Everyone knows that house. It's the biggest house in Oldtown."

"And the most famous," said the girl sitting nearest, a short girl with frizzy black hair.

"Everyone, he's new here," said another girl. She flashed Brendan a tight-lipped, pale smile. "That's the Sova House. It's haunted."

The boy in the hoodie guffawed. "What are you, five?" he said. "It's not haunted. A mad man lives there. I heard he murdered his whole family and still lives there with their corpses and dresses them up and has meals with them."

The black-haired girl shivered.

"That's ridiculous," said the pale-smiling girl.

The black-haired girl ran her hand over her forearm. "My dad says the owner probably lives in the city," she said. "That's why it's all overgrown like that."

Brendan listened, but he could tell none of them really knew. "Thanks," he said. Then he took his seat for class.

* * *

It was lucky, in a way – if you look back on it – that Brendan ate his lunch on the back lawn. And it was lucky that he sat at the picnic table farthest from the school where he thought no one would bother him.

And it was lucky that it turned out that the picnic table he chose was actually the favourite picnic table of a boy known as Chunk and three of his friends.

It was also lucky that Chunk picked Brendan up by the hem of his trousers and tossed him face-first from the picnic table.

It was lucky because Brendan went to the nurse, and there he got his scrapes cleaned up and bandaged.

Plus he met the school nurse.

"You're new around here," the nurse said. "When you're the nurse at this school, you get to know the picked-on children pretty quickly."

"Is it that obvious?" Brendan said. "How do you know I didn't just fall down?"

She gave him a sideways look. "It was Chunk, wasn't it?" she said.

Brendan's eyes went wide.

"It's easy," the nurse said. "The gravel I picked from your knee – it had some yellow paint in it. The only gravel like that is next to the car park, right near Chunk's favourite picnic table."

"Ah," Brendan said. "You know, they should really put information like that in the new-pupil handbook."

The nurse smiled. "You read it?" she said.

"I read everything," Brendan admitted.

She nodded at him. Then her look flashed, like she'd been inspired. "So," she said as she turned away from him and turned on the tap to wash her hands. "You're new, but have you seen the house up on Willow Avenue?"

Brendan could hardly believe it. "Yes!" he said. "I've been asking people about it. The Sova House, they called it. No one knows a thing, though."

"No?" the nurse said as she dried her hands. "They didn't tell you it's haunted? Or that the owner is a crazy murderer?"

"Oh, no," Brendan said. "They said all that. But it's not true."

"No, it's not," the nurse said. "But I can tell you its secret."

"Please," Brendan said, hopping down from the exam table.

The nurse tossed her paper towel into the bin. Then she closed the exam room door. The lights seemed to dim. Brendan leaned back against the table.

"It's sealed up," she said in a quiet, almost prayerful voice. "Just like it looks. The place hasn't been opened in years. It must be ten years by now."

Brendan held his breath.

"But they're still in there," she went on. "They'll never leave. They've been locked in there for years and years, dead to the town – dead to the world."

"How," Brendan said, and he found he was whispering. He cleared his throat. "How do you know?"

"I used to live there," she said. "I worked for them. But I couldn't take it anymore. I fled the house. It wasn't long before the ivy and briar and thorns and vines climbed across the walls and windows and the iron fence. I'm glad I left when I did, or I'd be sealed in there with them now."

"But it's a secret," Brendan guessed.

She nodded. "The gravest of secrets," she said.

"Then why are you telling me?" Brendan asked.

She opened the door, and daylight flooded the exam room. "You remind me of the girl," the nurse said.

"The girl?" Brendan said as he hefted his book bag. "There's a girl in there?"

The nurse smiled.

"Why do I remind you of her?" Brendan said.

She thought a moment, standing in the open doorway. "You both have a magic about you," she said. She looked him up and down, and then settled on the heavy book bag that hung from one of his hands.

"Maybe," she said, "it's the books."

* * *

After the last bell, Brendan couldn't board his bus for home. He couldn't even go home. He had to go back to the house. Now if only he could remember the route he took to get there.

Brendan stood on the pavement in front of the school as the dozen or so school buses revved their engines, puffed grey smoke and chugged away, taking pupils home.

When the smoke cleared, Brendan scanned the Oldtown streets. He had no idea which way to go.

"Willow Avenue…" he muttered to himself.

He could have asked someone, but all the children and bus drivers were gone, and all the teachers – even the few unlucky souls in charge of getting the pupils safely on their buses – were inside the school. They were in their offices, no doubt drinking coffee with each other and yapping about which pupils were failing history and which pupils were sinfully ugly and which pupils would probably never hold a job once they got out of this dump.

"But the nurse," Brendan said to himself, "said there's magic in me. In me and the girl and the house."

He opened his book bag and pulled out a thick paper-back – a sci-fi novel, the newest in a series he'd been reading since book one.

"The magic is in the books," he said. Then he started walking – and reading.

And it worked. When Brendan finished chapter five – with the settlers' small ship crash-landing on a planet that, it turned out, looked remarkably like their home planet, even though they'd been in space for five generations – he looked up.

And there it was: the Sova House.

It looked somehow more imposing today, maybe because today Brendan planned to approach it. And to get inside.

He put away his paperback and shouldered his book bag. He strode up to the iron gate. It was twice his height, and tangled with thick vines, covered in wide deep-green leaves and long, serrated thorns.

Brendan took a deep breath and carefully put both hands on an iron upright. He pricked his fingers once, twice, a third time – wincing each time. His fingers bled, but he didn't pull away. He held fast to the upright, and he pushed.

And the gate groaned, and the vines rattled and swung. But it moved. Slowly, the gate scraped across the paved driveway. It rang out like a siren, bellowing from the hill-top of Willow Avenue. Brendan imagined the people of Oldtown getting up from supper, switching off their TVs and video games, hurrying to the windows to gaze up at the Sova House – to see who dared to swing open the huge iron gates.

When it was open enough, he squeezed himself through, and the vines and thorns seemed to reach for his arms and legs. A tendril pulled at his wrist. A thorn scraped the length of his arm from his wrist to the end of his T-shirt's sleeve. A thin line of blood ran like a creek.

But Brendan pushed on. The path was not clear, even beyond the heavy gate. The vines and tendrils reached across the paved path – itself cracked and weedy, with tall and gnarly growth reaching and struggling for sunlight in the thickly shaded garden. Brendan hacked and pushed, but the vines seemed to fight back. They wrapped around his ankles and tore at his trousers. Thorns tore holes in his clothes. Vines whipped across his face.

Brendan stopped, right there on the driveway, halfway to the front door, and he looked down at himself. His clothes were ripped and dirty. He was bleeding in five places he could see straight away, and he could tell his face was bleeding too.

"This is crazy," he whispered – to himself and to the vines around his wrists and ankles. They loosened, just a little. "Even if that weird old nurse was telling the truth – and I doubt she was – am I about to knock on the door of this crazy house looking like this?"

The vines pulled away. The path behind him, back to the street and away from this house, cleared. Brendan took a last look at the house, at the shuttered windows hidden behind ivy and briar. "Besides, what if the nurse was telling the truth? What if the girl in there is really…"

Brendan ran from the house, suddenly afraid that someone might be watching him from one of those shuttered, overgrown windows. His book bag bounced heavily on his back as he descended Willow Avenue.

* * *

"I blew it," Brendan said as he slumped into the chair in the nurse's office.

The nurse got one look at him – head to toe covered in scrapes and messy bandages and welts and bruises – and gasped. "You certainly did," she said.

She nodded towards the exam room. "Get in there. I'll clean up these bandages. Who put these on?"

"I did," said Brendan as he hopped up onto the exam table. "Didn't I do a good job?"

He looked down at his arm: the bandages – he'd needed fourteen of them – were wrinkled and loose, hanging off in places and exposing the dried blood and dirty scrapes underneath.

"Do I need to answer that?" the nurse said, and in a flash, with no warning, she tore the dirty bandages from his skin.

"Ow!" Brendan snapped, jerking his arm away. "Let me know next time, okay?"

"Will there be a next time?" she asked, and her eyebrows danced.

"Maybe," he admitted. "I still want to get inside that house ... but I don't really know why."

The nurse patted his book bag, which lay beside him on the exam table. "It's the magic," she whispered. "I'd know it anywhere."

Brendan lifted his chin and whispered back, "I think I could have made it to the door. I was close."

"Yeah?" the nurse said. She swabbed his wounds with alcohol and he winced.

"Not that close," Brendan admitted. "It's the vines. I think they're alive."

"Well, yes. Vines usually are," the nurse said. She unwrapped some gauze and wrapped his arm.

"I mean alive like animals, not like normal plants," Brendan explained. "They grabbed me. They didn't want me to go to the house."

"No, I expect they didn't," the nurse said as she taped up the fresh bandage. She stepped back to consider the cuts and scrapes on his cheeks. "Her father is as magical as she is. Get up from there and wash your face. Use the soap next to the sink here."

Brendan hopped down and went to the sink and turned on the tap. He pumped the orange soap three times and lathered up his face. "What exactly is going on up there?"

"He was obsessed," the nurse said. "I think he spent a bit too much time in his books, but who knows. Careful there. You're splashing everywhere."

"Sorry," said Brendan. He finished rinsing his face and fumbled for the paper towels. The nurse handed him a couple. "Go on."

"The girl was adventurous," the nurse said. "She liked to read, but she also liked to live. She was the type of five-year-old to climb the biggest tree, to explore the darkest and deepest caves, and to plod through the soggiest marshes."

Brendan pictured this girl – dirty and strong, with crooked, short hair the colour of wet clay – stomping around the reedy shore of a lake, sliding down a gravel path into the depths of the earth, and running through a dark wood and waving a stick over her head like a sword.

"I remember the day well," the nurse said. She settled into the chair next to the desk and stared at the wall behind Brendan. "She'd been out, as usual, playing in the woods behind the house. They run all the way down the other side of the hill, right to the river and the caves and the marshes. It was heaven for her."

"Sounds nice," Brendan said.

"She was careless," the nurse went on. "She was always so careless. She never cared about what she was doing, or if it was raining, or if the ground was slippery or the rocks were loose. And that day – it wasn't even breakfast yet – it had been raining. It only cleared up for a moment and she was out the door and into the wild.

"She must have slipped," the nurse said, her face pale and faraway. "I can't think how else it could have happened." She stared beyond Brendan, and her eyes shone.

"What happened?" Brendan said.

The nurse seemed to wake up, considering the boy for the first time. With a sigh, she stood up and leaned towards him. She swabbed his cheek and his cuts stung, but this time he didn't flinch.

"The poor thing took a tumble," she said. "She broke her neck, her leg, her arm. The doctor said she was lucky not to be paralysed. As it is, she could hardly walk – the last time I saw her."

"Is she, like, in a wheelchair?" Brendan said.

The nurse nodded. "Usually," the nurse said. "She was learning to use crutches when I left. But I doubt she ever uses them."

"Why?"

"Like I said, her father was obsessed with protecting her after that," the nurse said. She pressed a strip of gauze against his cheek and taped it down. "He sealed up the house. Threw out the TVs, the phones, the computers – he even burned all the books. Then he sacked the staff – that is, me – and planted briars and vines and thorn bushes. If you ask me, he cast a spell on the place."

Brendan thought she was probably right.

"No one has contact with the outside world," the nurse said, as if to sum up. "Not Mr Sova or Ms Sova or little Talia."

Brendan whispered the name back to her: "Talia."

"It's pretty, isn't it?" the nurse said. She shrugged one shoulder. "My idea."

She stood back. "You're all set," she said. "Next time, wear long sleeves and a beekeeper mask or something."

Brendan picked up his book bag.

"They must be half insane by now," the nurse muttered. "Locked up all these years. She's your age by now, I suppose, and probably a zombie. Might as well have been sleeping for ten years."

* * *

Brendan skipped the rest of the day. He hurried home – no reading, no meandering, no getting lost. At home, he went straight to the garage.

They'd just moved in. His mum hadn't had the chance or the desire to investigate the junk the previous owners had accumulated and deposited to collect rust and dust.

But Brendan had popped his head in once or twice, and he'd spotted something hanging from some nails on the far wall. He climbed through the rubble and the wreckage, over piles of junk and hidden treasures, and he ignored it all. He kept his eyes on the dull grey blade, high on the plain garage wall.

On his toes, standing on a dry and cracked old tyre, he could just reach it. He wrapped his hand around the hilt of the machete and pulled it from the wall.

* * *

Brendan marched up Willow Avenue. He found it this time not with magic, but with an online map. Now, with the rusty old machete looped across his back through the straps of his book bag, he climbed Oldtown's highest street.

The Sova House stood at the hill's peak, and the sun was setting behind it, casting it in an orange and pink aura. Beams of white and dusty light shone between the vines.

The iron gate still stood open, and Brendan slipped through and drew his machete. He hacked and he tore and he sliced at the vines. They fought back – he thought they might – grabbing at his wrists and tearing his clothes. But Brendan gritted his teeth. He chopped with all his strength, remembering the fantasy heroes of his thick paperbacks and heavy hardcover tomes.

The vines couldn't fight back fast enough or strong enough. The boy's machete spun and whirled and slashed like a combine, cutting down the overgrowth and clearing the paved path to the front door. When Brendan reached it, he looked back at the open gate, and the path was littered with scraps and twigs and leaves and torn vines.

His brow dripped with sweat, and his shirtsleeves – he'd worn a heavy work shirt today, remembering the cuts of the previous afternoon – were torn right up to his shoulders. The thorny vines had put up a better fight than he thought. Fresh scratches, like random lines of red ink, dashed up and down his arms. His face, too, stung with the perfect little wounds, as precise and narrow as a surgeon's incision.

Brendan took a deep breath and a long look at the Sova House's huge front door. In its day, it would have been a sight: thick, huge and made of ornate, dark-coloured wood. In its centre was a diamond-shaped stained-glass window, depicting a child in bed, surrounded by figures. Her parents were easy to pick out, kneeling together beside the bed. There were other people as well, though, and they made Brendan shiver.

They stood together at the foot of the bed, all of them tall and slim and dressed in long, almost translucent robes, and each wore an ornament as a headpiece. One was a star, one was a moon, one was the sun and one was a skull. Aside from the odd crowns, though, the four looked identical.

Brendan stared at the image, lit from within, until the characters seemed to swim in his vision. They began to move. The parents at the bedside hiccupped with woe. The figures at the foot leaned together, as if they were speaking – consulting.

As Brendan stared, their voices grew from the whisper of wind in the vines all around him to hushed tones, and then to intelligible voices.

"She will die," said the figure who wore a skull. Her voice – it sounded like a woman, but Brendan couldn't be sure – was gravelly and thin. It was like the air rushing out of a closed tomb, opened after thousands of years.

"No," said the others – the sun and the star and the moon. Their voices together rang in a three-part harmony. Together they sounded like crystal, if crystal could talk – or sing. "She will sleep."

The skull nodded slowly and dropped to her knees. The others followed, but they kept their heads high, and the girl on the bed rolled over and pulled up her knees.

Then it was over. It was as if a film had ended and the TV screen went blank. Brendan's face was only centimetres from the stained-glass window now, and the picture it held was as static and drab as any other. He shook his head, as if that would restore his sanity, and found the doorbell. When he pressed it firmly, it crumbled under his finger.

"Hello!" he shouted through the door. He pounded on the heavy wood, and the sound echoed down the hill, all through Oldtown, but the door remained closed. No footsteps sounded inside.

"Is anyone there?" he called, pounding again. Still there was no response.

Brendan stepped back to get a better look at the house. Aside from the light on in the entrance hall behind the heavy door, a dim light flickered in a window on the first floor. Brendan tightened his grip on the machete, and – with a deep breath and returning determination – set his sights on that window.

Vines gripped his wrists. They strangled him and tore at him. They ripped his clothes and scratched his face.

He fell once, and the vines came up from the earth and held him. He swung his machete – his sword. Vines split and released him, and others came up to hold him down.

With all his strength, he got to his feet, tearing vines and briars at their roots. His shoes were gone – lost in the mud and detritus of the wild garden. He reached the window, and he peered in, and she was there.

The flickering light came from a lamp – an old one, burning some horrid and smelly oil, so it cast a lurid and sickly light over the girl's face. And the girl: she sat there, hunched and tired, her eyes half closed and her mouth half open. She had a plain face, with a sharp nose, made sharper in the low flickering light. Her hair was short and jagged, like she'd cut it herself, and, though it was tinted green through the window, Brendan could tell it was the colour of wet clay.

He knocked on the glass. She didn't flinch. He knocked louder, and she only stared.

"The nurse was right," he muttered. "She's a zombie."

Brendan raised his machete.

Smash!

The butt of the machete sent the hundred-year-old pane of glass shattering into the little lamp-lit room. The girl jumped, finally lifted – just the tiniest bit – from her stupor.

Brendan knocked away the shards still in the window frame and climbed inside. He dropped his heavy book bag and knelt beside the girl. She gaped at him, and he smiled up at her. Her eyes, now wide open, were a startling pale blue. The contrast with the deep orange of her hair seemed magical.

"Are you all right?" he asked her, but she didn't reply.

She saw him – he could tell she saw him. But it was like he was barely there, like she was seeing him through a fog or a dream.

"The magic," he whispered, and he opened his book bag and dumped it out on the floor. He grabbed a book at random and held it out to her. She glanced at it, like one might glance at a familiar stranger in a crowd. And Brendan began to read.

He read her the story of an assistant pig keeper, destined to be a hero and king.

He told her of travellers to Mars, and the eerie surprises they found there.

He read to her the love story of a girl and a boy who would live forever.

He didn't know what stories she loved, back when she was allowed to read them, so he chose book after book, and he told her the magic inside.

She smiled just a little at each telling, until finally she was kneeling on the floor with him, pawing through the pile and savouring the stories she found inside.

"You're awake now," Brendan said, and she took his hand in hers and thanked him.

"But you have to go," she said. "You have to go right now."

Brendan stood up and pulled her to her feet. "Why?" he said. "I came to find you. To meet you. The nurse at school – she said we–"

The girl cut him off, shaking her head and urging him back towards the window. "My father," she said. "He'd never allow this. He'll be furious."

But the overhead light flicked on, casting its pallid glare over the dust and dank in the room. Her face was so pale, so ill, though life began to shine. Brendan pulled his eyes from her face, though, and found the door. There, with his hand still on the light switch and a beard as long as his arms, stood Mr Sova.

"I always knew you'd come," Mr Sova snarled. He dragged Brendan by his tattered collar, and his book bag with the other hand, along the worn and dusty carpet of the house's main hall. With his shoulder, Mr Sova smashed into the parlour – a huge room with a high ceiling and gigantic fireplace, which swelled with a raging blaze.

"Please," Brendan said, his voice straining and ragged. "I mean no harm!"

"Father," the girl said, grabbing at the man's arm, pleading and tearful. "Let him go. He only wanted to help me!"

"Help you?!" Mr Sova shouted, his face red and his eyes dark and swollen. "You so quickly trust the intentions of a stranger? One who would smash his way into our home?"

He laughed and shook his head as he dropped the boy into a chair and the book bag in a heap beside the fire. "Sit there, boy," he snarled, "and watch."

He reached down and picked up a book – the biggest one he could find. It was heavy and thick and bound in cloth, tattered at the corners. It was well read and well loved. Mr Sova read the cover. "Witchcraft," he said in a deep and sombre voice. "That's the story here."

He tossed it into the blaze, which coughed and heaved, like a hungry wolf on a too-large bite of deer. Mr Sova reached for another book. The girl ran at him.

"No, Father!" she demanded. But he merely held her back with one hand and used the free one to grab one, two, three slim paperbacks. He looked at one cover and said, "Rebelliousness," and tossed it into the fireplace.

He looked at the second: "Unrealistic romance," he said, "and suicide." He threw it into the fire.

He looked at the third: "Nonsensical fantasy," he said. That book, too, fell to the hungry tongues of the fire.

He turned to his daughter – down on one knee, tears on her cheeks – and he looked at her with a caring eye. "Talia," he said. "I'll not lose you again – not to this boy, not to the lies in these books, not to the horrors of the world outside our safe walls."

"Safe as houses," said a woman's voice.

Brendan looked up. Standing in the broken parlour doorway was a woman, tall but bent, with long hair – dark at its tips but white at its roots that was plaited but falling still to her narrow hips. She looked tired and sad, with the same circles under her eyes that her daughter and husband also had.

"Isn't that what you said, dear?" Ms Sova said, for who else could it be? She moved into the room and put a gentle hand on her daughter's shoulders. The girl got to her feet.

"I stand by it," Mr Sova said. He kicked the pile of books. A slim hardcover fell from the heap. Ms Sova picked it up.

"Ah," she said, looking at the cover. "This was one of my favourites when I was in school." She moved towards her daughter and held the book out to her. "We read it together, your father and I. Remember that, dear?"

Mr Sova nodded and smirked.

"Look at her," Ms Sova said as she took her daughter's face in her hands. "She's so pale and weak. We've nearly destroyed her."

"Nonsense!" Mr Sova said. "She's alive, isn't she?"

Brendan pulled himself out of the chair, though it hurt every part of him to do so. He hadn't realized how taxing the evening had been, but the cuts and bruises – not to mention the way Mr Sova had handled him – had left Brendan feeling utterly beaten.

"Is she?" he said, and his voice was as battered as his body. "She sits like a zombie in front of an ancient box all day, every day, doing what?"

"Learning," Mr Sova roared. "She's learning important things. Heaven knows what they teach in those schools these days, with these books." He kicked the pile once more.

"Don't you see, dear," said his wife. She faced him now and kept one arm around her daughter's sagging shoulders. "This is what we've been waiting for."

"I don't know what you're talking about," he said, turning his back on her.

Ms Sova helped her daughter sit down. Brendan hurried to the girl's side and sat with her.

"You've forgotten," Ms Sova said. "I have too – from time to time – but this boy has awakened me. You and I have become something unhuman as well, dear. We've been cut off from the world, just as Talia has."

Mr Sova dropped himself into one of the high-back chairs that flanked the fireplace. He leaned his head on his hand and his elbow on the arm of the chair.

"The spell," Ms Sova said. She sat on her husband's knee. "This boy is the one we've been waiting for – only we gave up, and we forgot to wait. We forgot to know him."

Mr Sova looked at his wife and his glare softened. He glanced at Brendan, tattered and beaten, sitting next to his daughter on the settee. "Him?" he said. "Look at him. He barely made it through."

"Dear," said his wife, but he went on.

"Why, a delivery man at the wrong address got as far as the front door not last week," Mr Sova said.

"That was four years ago, dear," said Ms Sova.

He coughed. "Was it?" he said, and his eyes darted in his head and his mouth twisted like he was trying to remember the taste of some out-of-season fruit. He stood up in front of Brendan. "But him? I mean, really. Look at him!"

His wife stepped up behind him. She shook her head and said, "Look at her."

Brendan watched a smile come to life on the man's face, behind that Rip Van Winkle beard. It was slow to wake up, just like Talia had been from her stupor in the pallid light of the lamp. But Brendan could see where the smile was coming from. He turned to Talia beside him on the little dusty couch, and her face glowed. Yes, from the swelling flames of the hearth, but also from her eyes and the apples of her cheeks. She was grinning, with one hand on Brendan's hand between them on the couch and her eyes on the paperback in her other hand. Quietly, while her parents and Brendan clashed, she'd pulled it from the pile and begun to read.

"She's alive again," Ms Sova said. "Really and truly. She walked on her own. She smiles now, and we have this boy to thank."

Mr Sova's grin, growing till then, collapsed to a frown.

"I suppose we do," he said. "That's what that old witch said, isn't it? That she'd sleep, stupefied – and we along with her – until love found her. She said until love slashed its way into our home and into her heart."

Ms Sova leaned on his shoulder and held his arm. She smiled and gazed at her daughter as Talia tightened her grip on Brendan's hand.

"I'm sorry," said Mr Sova. He looked at Brendan and said in a firm voice, "What's your name?"

"Shush!" Talia snapped, looking up from her book for an instant. "This is a really good part!"

* * *

That Saturday morning, Brendan was at the Sova House just as the family finished breakfast. Mr Sova and he, both dressed in heavy denim and long sleeves and thick leather gloves, armed with machetes – gleaming and sharp – and clippers, attacked the wild garden. They hacked it and cut it and shaped it.

At lunchtime, they sat on a bench – it had been lost under the growth all these years – and ate sandwiches and drank iced tea.

"You never told me," Mr Sova said, "but I think I've guessed."

"Told you what?" Brendan said. He had to squint and shade his eyes when he turned to look at Mr Sova – the sun behind and above the man was bright and big, as if finally able to attack the Sova House. With its shade hewn and gone, it would now attack without mercy, sweltering and blinding.

The man's face – just yesterday pale and tired, with a beard laughably long – was now clean shaven and red with sunburn. He smiled, the littlest bit, so heavy lines grew on his cheeks. "It was the old nurse, wasn't it?" he said. "She works at the school now, isn't that right?"

"I found your house by accident," Brendan said. "I get lost a lot. But yes. It was the nurse who told me who was inside. I think she must have known..." Mr Sova leaned forward, waiting for Brendan to finish.

"She knew about the spell," Brendan said, "and I think she knew I was the one to end it."

Talia's father leaned back on the bench and looked down Willow Avenue. "I'd say she knew about it," he said. "She placed the spell on our house."

Brendan opened his mouth to speak, but nothing came out. What could he say?

Then he remembered the stained-glass window, and the funny little movie he'd seen – or he thought he'd seen.

He had probably just imagined it, exhausted and bleeding, inhaling magical plant spores all afternoon.

Still … it had seemed so real.

"Did she…" he started. He faltered and coughed.

"Yes?" Mr Sova said, leaning forward.

"A crown," Brendan said. "Something like a crown – a wreath."

"That's right," said Mr Sova.

Brendan stood up, dazed. "Then it was real," he said.

Mr Sova looked up at him and nodded slowly. He dropped his head. "It was real."

"Then she would have died," Brendan said.

"But we made a deal," Mr Sova said. He looked past Brendan again, towards Oldtown's village square at the bottom of Willow Avenue, bustling on a sunny autumn Saturday. "She saved our daughter – spared her, really – and we agreed to her terms."

Brendan knelt in front of Mr Sova. The man seemed to be mourning his daughter all over again, as if she really had died that day, ten years ago.

"Spared her," Brendan said, and then he saw it clearly. "She lied to me."

"Lied?" Mr Sova said.

"She said Talia fell," Brendan said. "She said it was an accident. That she broke her neck, and her legs. I never imagined it was her fault."

"Ah," said Mr Sova, waggling a finger in the air and grinning, "fault is a difficult thing to place, as always."

"Then it was an accident?" Brendan asked.

Suddenly Mr Sova stood up from the bench and threw

back his shoulders. He nodded at the street, at a figure walking there – walking towards them.

"Ask her yourself," said Mr Sova, "for our old nurse walks this way."

Brendan looked down the hill and spotted that familiar figure – the nurse from school. But she was different today.

This wasn't the same as seeing a teacher at the supermarket or the local pizzeria, when their casual clothes and air made them seem foreign and weird.

This was something quite real.

She stood up straighter and walked with a posture unimaginable in the school's corridors. Her hair – usually tied up in a bun or back in a ponytail – flowed down from her head, no longer grey, but silver, shimmering in the high sun. And her clothes – these were not the typical jeans and jumper of a school nurse on her day off. Her gown shimmered like her hair, woven with silver and gold thread, and it hung about her like it was made of the icy wind on a February morning.

"What do you want?" Mr Sova said. Though his words were brave and stubborn, Brendan heard the tremble of fear in his voice.

The nurse must have heard it too, because she laughed out loud. In her voice, Brendan heard the crystal of the sun and the moon and the star, but he also heard the raspy threat of the skull.

"She's all of them," he whispered, almost to himself.

He felt Mr Sova's hand on his shoulder, just for instant, as if to say that Brendan was right, but also as a warning: *This nurse is dangerous.*

"I only come for my old position," the nurse said, "now that you're all awake."

Mr Sova let out a sorrowful sigh.

"And Talia?" the nurse said. She sat on the bench and smoothed the lap of her gown. "She is well?"

"Yes," said Talia's father in a deep, reluctant voice.

"Wonderful," said the nurse. She caught Brendan's eye and smiled. "Mr Sova is reluctant to have me back, I think."

Brendan didn't reply. He just stared at her face, and he imagined he could see all four of those figures within her.

She laughed her crystal laugh and patted her hands on her knees. "He remembers how close the girl came to death," she says, still smiling, "but he forgets it was I who pulled her back."

"It was you who sent her there!" Mr Sova said, and his body quivered and deflated.

She didn't look at him, despite his explosion. She kept her eyes on Brendan. "He sees things in black and white," she said, patting the bench beside her. "He always has."

Brendan sat next to her and sat at an angle to face her. "Who are you?" he asked.

She looked at him, sort of cockeyed, like a confused dog – like it was the most obvious thing in the world, and maybe Brendan had taken a knock on the head. "I'm your nurse," she said. "Don't you remember?"

"But that's not at all who you are," Brendan said quickly.

"And you," she said, "are not only the new boy in school."

Brendan thought he knew what she meant. He still felt dizzy and blinded, though, as the nurse stood up. "I'll go and check on Talia," she said.

"No," Mr Sova protested, grabbing her wrist.

The nurse looked down at his hand – in that instant, Brendan was sure he saw that skull on her forehead, just like he'd seen her in the stained-glass window – and Mr Sova released her. When she spoke, the crystal in her voice was gone, and only the smoky whisper remained: "You cannot hold me back. You cannot control me. You cannot stop me."

Then, with the same grace she carried as she walked up Willow Avenue, the nurse stepped around the bench and walked up the path, opened the door and went inside the Sova House.

* * *

Though Brendan spent much of his time at the Sova House after that day, and nearly all the rest of his time at school, he didn't see much of the nurse. She resigned from the school, and the new nurse – though competent in every way and very kind to Brendan when he'd show up with a bruised knee and scraped chin, evidence of another run-in with Chunk – she wasn't magical.

At the Sova House, the nurse stayed in her room on the third floor. She appeared now and then, passing through the second-floor hall or wandering the garden as dusk fell over the house.

In fact, except at those odd moments – when Brendan found he hardly recognized the old school nurse, instead seeing her like a dream, a spirit, a ghost from distant time – Brendan hardly thought about the nurse. He was in love, after all, with Talia, and she with him, and the two spent most of their time reading stories and telling stories to each other.

"We'll get married," Talia told him.

"Of course," Brendan told her.

And that day after school, the two walked with their hands clasped together – and each, with the other hand, held a book to read. Of course they got lost, as they often did, and they would continue to for their rest of their lives together.

* * *

They did get married, Brendan and Talia, and they did stay in the Sova House. The old nurse stayed there too, in her room up on the third floor, and after many years, Brendan and Talia forgot about her.

If someone had asked, "Didn't that nurse used to live up there?" they certainly would have remembered, if only for that instant. But they never thought of her, and when they glimpsed her only briefly, floating down a hall or through the manicured gardens, they only rubbed their eyes and poured a second cup of coffee.

They had three daughters, and they were named Roxanne, Dawn and Aurora, the youngest. Only Aurora, perhaps due to her youth, truly saw the old nurse. She watched her closely and caught her smiles and her glares, and she tried to touch the hem of her shimmering gown. She never quite could, though.

Aurora also spent a lot of time in the kitchen. Her parents were quite successful, and as is often the case with great success, they were also quite busy. Neither had much time – nor the desire – to cook, so they hired a cook.

"Brendan loves lamb," Talia said with a pad on one knee.

"I make a wonderful lamb," the cook said. She was heavy and dour, and her plump face was freckled and blotchy – whether from sun or allergies or nerves, no one could guess.

"And the girls will insist on goose," Talia went on.

"I make a beautiful goose," the cook said. She smiled with pride and closed her eyes. With a hum, she seemed to be imagining the flavours of her goose. "Beautiful."

Talia went on. "And I," she said, "could not go on if our cook didn't have a marvellous recipe for pork loin."

"Then you're in luck," the cook whispered. "Mine is the most marvellous you'll ever try."

Talia smiled and closed her pad. "You can begin at once?" she asked, and the cook nodded, and so she took the job.

Aurora and the cook became fast friends. The littlest Miren girl climbed the tallest kitchen stool and sat at the worktop, watching dough and sauce and cake and scones come together. "How many eggs?" she asked, or "How much flour?" or "Do you need the bicarbonate of soda?" So it was the cook, rather than her mother or father or sisters, whom Aurora first talked to about the wandering spirit of the nurse on the third floor.

The cook spat. "Haunted," she said, and she looked around the huge old kitchen as though it had been keeping something from her. "I shouldn't be surprised."

"I think it's a kind ghost," the little girl said, and she shifted on the stool to reach the biggest wooden spoon. "At least, it usually is. Sometimes it hisses at me."

"Hm," said the cook. She measured out flour, and then she dumped it into the largest copper bowl and added a pinch of salt and a tiny spoon of bicarbonate of soda and put it in front of the girl. "Stir."

"But usually she smiles," Aurora said, and she held the big spoon with both hands and messily stirred the bowl of dry ingredients. She flashed the cook a big, toothy grin as she worked.

The cook grunted and cracked an egg, then another, then another, into a second bowl. "I don't like it," she muttered, pulling a whisk from its hook. She began to beat the eggs, her arm thrashing so fast it grew blurry, and her face going puffier and redder. Aurora's stirring slowed as she watched the cook work.

"You should stay away from that spirit," the cook grunted, short of breath. She tossed the whisk into the sink and went to the refrigerator. When she came back with the milk, the girl was gone from the stool and the kitchen. A trail of flour footprints led to the door.

"You should really stay away," the cook muttered as she measured out the milk.

* * *

The Sova House wasn't built in one go. It was the oldest house in Oldtown, built by the first Sovas to settle at the top of that hill. Over the years and decades and generations, rooms had been added and expanded. Walls had been taken down and put back up. Doors had been covered and revealed.

Though her mother had slept through the years she should have been exploring the house, Aurora had no such curse. When it rained – and sometimes when it didn't – she took to finding old passages and hidden doors and rickety back stairways.

It was one day, an especially rainy and thundering summer afternoon, that Aurora lost track of time and steps. She climbed a spiralling staircase behind a little door in the wardrobe in Dawn's bedroom and found herself in a tiny, dark space. Only a sliver of light found its way inside, through a tiny crack near the floor.

Aurora was not the sort of girl to panic. She felt around the sliver of light and traced the outline of a tiny door – no bigger than a volume from her father's set of encyclopedias. There was no handle, though, and no doorknob. When she pushed it, she could tell it was blocked on the outside.

"It's probably a tremendous dresser," she whispered to the darkness, "or the back of a couch."

Aurora decided that the little door would prove a dead end. She was about to head back down the narrow spiral staircase when she heard a great screech on the other side of the door. The floor beneath her began to shake and vibrate. She held on to the railing at the top of the steps, closed her eyes tightly and shrieked.

"Oh, stop that noise at once," said a voice, and Aurora knew it at once, though she'd never heard it before.

The girl opened her eyes and found that the door was gone. In its place was a square of flickering light and a pair of bare feet caked with soil, with toenails painted silver and gold and glittering, watery green. The feet moved to the side and Aurora crawled and slithered through the tiny door. She barely fit.

"Before long, you'll be far too big for that way in," the spirit said as it walked across the room to the door. This was of course the nurse's chamber on the third floor, and Aurora's tiny room at the top of the spiral staircase was indeed hidden behind a settee. "Next time, use the door."

The nurse glowered at the girl as Aurora kept her eyes on the floor and walked quickly across the room. The door opened as Aurora reached and she stepped out onto the landing at the top of the central staircase. She faced the nurse. "I'm sorry," she said.

"For what, dear child?" the nurse said, smiling. Her voice was made of ringing bells and shattering glass and feet scraping across gravel.

Aurora stared at the nurse's face, and she couldn't be sure if she was seeing a woman, or a spirit or several of each.

Thunder boomed outside, and – Aurora counted – three seconds later, the room flashed brightly. "I didn't mean to bother you," the girl said. "I didn't know where that funny staircase would go."

"They always go up," the nurse said, "or down."

"Yes, ma'am," Aurora said. Still she stood in the open doorway and stared at the spirit's face.

"Was there something else, sunshine?" the nurse said.

"The cook thinks I should stay away from you," Aurora said.

"Does she?" the nurse said, and Aurora nodded. "Well, lots of people – especially grown-ups – are afraid of things they can't control."

"Like you?" Aurora said.

"Like me," the nurse said.

Aurora pulled her eyes from the spirit's face, with its shining eyes and gentle smile, and looked at the worn, wood floor.

"You may speak your mind," the nurse said. All roughness vanished from her voice, and Aurora hurried to speak.

"Who are you?" she said.

The nurse laughed, and it was like a concert of bells. "So few have asked me so directly," she said. "Your father did."

Aurora was stunned. Her father was a middle-aged man. He was more obsessed with his books and his business than with things like spirits and questions. Had he ever spoken to this striking figure?

"He was a boy then, of course," the nurse said. "I'll tell you most of what I told him: I am the sum of my parts."

Aurora didn't know what that meant, but she didn't feel confident any longer. She coughed into her fist. "I'll go downstairs now," she said.

"One more thing, sunshine," the nurse said as she retreated to the settee and sat down. "I'm quite hungry. It's been ages since I ate."

"I'll ask Cook to make you something," the girl said. She was excited for an excuse to run to the kitchen and tell the cook everything.

"Would you?" the nurse said. "Wonderful. It will give you a clearer idea of who I am." The nurse picked a book up from the side table and opened it to its middle. "If you please, sunshine, tell your cook that I'd like to have Roxanne for lunch."

"Roxanne?" Aurora repeated. "My sister?"

The nurse nodded, still smiling. Her eyes were black and shone like a polished stone. "With a sauce of butter and mustard."

Aurora stood there, staring from the landing, until the door closed.

She walked in a daze down two flights of stairs on the wide central staircase. She pushed the swinging door into the kitchen and found Cook, bent over and pulling a tray of scones from the oven.

"You're just in time, littlest," the cook said as she dropped the tray onto the centre island with a clatter and

clank. "We can have one each with cream in a few minutes."
She looked at Aurora and smiled, her brown teeth and
ruddy cheeks flaming.

"I've been upstairs," Aurora said, and she didn't smile,
and she did not seem to notice the tray of cranberry and
orange-zest scones on the island – her favourite flavour.
"With the spirit."

The cook gasped, and she clucked her tongue and
shook her head. "It can't end well," she said.

"She's hungry," Aurora said, "and you're the cook."

"Not for her," the cook spat. She pulled the second tray
of scones and dropped them onto a wire rack. The triangles
– speckled with red and orange – bounced and slid. One fell
to the floor, and the cook did not care. "She can have that
one," she muttered.

"She lives in this house," Aurora said, "so you have to
cook for her."

The cook snorted and went to the refrigerator. She
came back with a tub of cream and dropped it on the island
next to the cooling scones.

"She wants Roxanne for lunch," Aurora said.

The cook slammed her open hand on the island, sending another scone to the dirty kitchen floor. She stomped
on the fallen scone and coughed with anger. "How can you
say this to me?" she said to the girl. The cook's face grew
redder and redder – nearly crimson. "Your own sister!"

But Aurora hardly heard the cook. "With a butter and
mustard sauce," she finished.

The cook leaned heavily on one hand and tapped her chin with the other. "Go to the refrigerator, littlest," the cook said, "and fetch a goose."

"Didn't you hear me?" Aurora said. "She doesn't want goose."

"Do as I say," the cook said, "and when you've done that, run and find Roxanne and bring her here as well."

★ ★ ★

The cook worked for an hour on the spirit's lunch. The sauce was rich and spicy, and the meat was tender and full of flavour. She arranged the choicest cuts on a silver platter, with a jug of sauce and a dish of root vegetables and glazed carrots. She covered the platter and gave it to Aurora.

"Bring this up to the fiend," she told her, "and don't join her for lunch. Come back at once."

Aurora did as she was told, but she cried and cried as she walked, for she believed she carried her oldest sister.

When she reached the nurse's door, it stood open. In the centre of the room there was now a small table, set for two. The spirit sat at one seat.

"Hello, sunshine," the nurse said. "Put it here, please." She motioned to the centre of the table, and Aurora obeyed. She pulled the cover off to present the dinner.

"Ahh," said the spirit, clapping like a pleased child. She inhaled deeply with her eyes closed, savouring the food's scent.

Aurora was sickened, watching the woman so excited to devour the meal.

"Join me," the spirit said, but Aurora shook her head and hurried out of the room.

* * *

"You'll have to go and collect the dishes," the cook said when Aurora returned, out of breath and crying.

"I don't want to," Aurora said.

"I can't climb all those steps," the cook said. She collapsed into her chair near the window and took a deep breath of the air from her herb garden outside. "You're young and healthy and you'll collect the dishes."

Aurora stamped her foot, but she knew the cook was right. But rather than hurry up to the spirit's room, she went to Dawn's room. Dawn lay on her bed on her belly with a book open on the pillow.

"What do you want?" said the middle sister, looking up from her paperback. Aurora recognized it at once as one of Dad's old fantasy stories.

"Nothing," Aurora said. She sat down on the edge of the bed next to her sister. "I just wanted to say hi."

"Hi," Dawn said. "Now get out so I can finish reading."

Aurora got up from the bed, took a last look at Dawn and slipped into the closet. Her sister, engrossed in the fantasy story, didn't even notice.

Up the twirling staircase in the dark. Aurora thought about the shape of the stairs and the darkness in the stairwell and the musty smell and the age of the house. At the top she crawled to the crack of light near the floor and she listened.

She heard the spirit, chewing and slurping, loudly devouring. She heard the snapping of brittle, cooked bones. She smelled the spice of the mustard in the sauce, and the sickly sweet of the sugared carrots. Aurora pounded on the tiny door as she cried.

"You'll use the door," the spirit said after she'd pushed aside the settee again and let the girl into the room. "Next time, you'll use the door."

Aurora didn't reply. She didn't even look at her. She hurried to the table and, with her eyes closed tight, covered the platter and hurried from the room.

"I'll have dinner now," the spirit called after her, her voice as sparkling as ever. "Bring me Dawn."

Aurora hiccupped and coughed and nearly dropped the dishes, but she bit her bottom lip and tensed her shoulders. She could not let the spirit see her cry.

"Fetch a lamb," the cook said. "There's one in the freezer. Put it in the sink."

Aurora obeyed, and knew well enough to turn on the cold tap as well to help the lamb defrost. She stood at the sink, watching the slim stream of cold water run over the lamb in its vacuum-sealed plastic wrapping. "She said she wants Dawn for supper," Aurora said.

"Do as you're told," the cook snarled, banging roasting pans and metal spoons and sauce pots. "Now go and collect your sister and bring her here."

Aurora left the tap running, climbed down from her stool, and plodded across the kitchen and through the door.

She stopped for a moment at the window seat near the front door and looked out into the garden. The spirit was there, walking across the muddy ground, even though it was raining hard.

Thunder clapped while Aurora watched, and she counted: one, two – and the sky lit up white. The instant it did, the spirit flicked her eyes onto the girl and grinned, and Aurora gasped.

* * *

"Come to the kitchen," Aurora said, standing in Dawn's open doorway.

"Why?" said her sister without looking up from her book.

Aurora sniffled and shook her head.

"Ugh," Dawn said. She folded down the corner of her page and got up from the bed. "Fine."

Aurora led her sister down the main stairs and through the swinging door.

"It stinks in here," Dawn said. "What are you cooking?"

The cook's knife slammed onto the cutting board, crushing a head of garlic to a sticky and smelly paste.

* * *

"I have your supper," Aurora said. Trails of tears stained her cheeks, but she didn't cry as she stood in the open doorway of the spirit's room. The rain on the roof sounded like gentle applause.

"Finally," the ghostly woman said as she took a seat at the small table. "You'll join me this time."

Aurora put the platter in the centre of the table. She pulled off the lid, and the steam wafted up at her and stung her eyes till they ran.

"Wonderful!" the spirit said, her shining eyes wide with gluttony. For an instant, her smile fell and her eyes darkened, and she looked at Aurora. "We will devour her."

But Aurora didn't take her seat and she didn't reply. She merely hurried from the room, down the stairs, past Dawn's bedroom – where the door stood open and the light was still on – and to the kitchen.

"Is she satisfied?" the cook said, but Aurora ran at her and collapsed into her open arms. The cook held her in a hug as strong as the Sova House, and she ran a meaty hand over her hair to soothe her. "There, littlest. There, there. You'll collect the dishes before too long."

* * *

The spirit lay on the settee on her back, one hand in the air as if conducting an invisible orchestra. "The rain is like a song," she said, and her voice was soft and oily.

Aurora stood beside the little table. The platter was clean, with only smears of the butter and mustard sauce left. Every vegetable and every speck of meat was gone.

"You missed a wonderful meal," the spirit said, still conducting the rain.

Aurora piled the plates and forks and knife on the platter and covered it. She hefted it up and left the room.

"I'm not satisfied," the spirit called after her. "I'll need a little something before bedtime."

Aurora stopped.

"Just the littlest something," the spirit said, and Aurora dropped the platter. It clattered down the main stairs, plates shattering and the large silver dome lid ringing like an alarm bell.

* * *

The cook found the girl on the second-floor landing, lying on her side and clutching her belly. "She's still hungry," Aurora said, but her voice was rough and raw from crying.

The cook gathered her up and carried her downstairs, through the swinging door and into the kitchen. She sat her on her stool at the worktop.

"There's a pork loin in the basement freezer," the cook said. "I'll go and fetch it. You stay right there."

"But she doesn't want pork," Aurora stuttered through the hiccups of her sobbing.

"Do as you're told," the cook growled, and she disappeared down the rickety basement steps.

Aurora sat on her stool, and soon she stopped crying, and then she stopped sniffling, and then she stopped hiccupping. Then she heard whispering and hisses from the big pantry with the heavy wooden door.

The littlest Miren climbed down from her stool and went to the pantry. The handle – heavy and metal and tightly latched – was always tricky for her, so she put both hands on the thing and tugged with all her might and weight.

The latch popped, and the heavy door began to swing open.

"Who is it?" came a fearful whisper from within.

"It's that lousy cook," came a second whisper, "who locked us in here to rot."

"Like this head of lettuce," said the first, and then the whispers giggled.

"Roxanne?" Aurora said, peering into the dark pantry. "Dawn?"

"Let us out of here!" Dawn said, running for the door, but the cook's heavy hands fell on to Aurora's shoulders.

"And littlest makes three," the cook snarled. Aurora fell forward, knocking the middle sister back and into the darkness. Then the door slammed closed and the latch clicked.

"Aw, nuts," said Dawn. In the dark pantry, Aurora couldn't see her sisters, but she heard the middle girl kick something – probably one of cook's giant flour sacks. "Nice going, runt."

"Don't blame her," Roxanne said. Her voice was always so still and rich; it reminded Aurora of cold gravy. "She didn't know the cook was behind her."

"Yeah, yeah," said Dawn. She kicked the sack of flour again. Aurora could smell the dust of it in the heavy pantry air.

"Are you ghosts?" Aurora said quietly, as if the pantry was the church and her sisters its spirits.

"What is she talking about?" Dawn said.

"Beats me," Roxanne said. Aurora felt the air shift as her oldest sister moved towards her. "You all right, sunshine?"

Aurora shivered at the nickname. Though it was hers often enough among the three of them, lately she only heard it from the nurse in the attic. Aurora realized she was crying, and, shaking her head, she reached blindly for Roxanne's hand. She found her arm and pulled it around her.

"Whoa, what happened?" Dawn said, joining her sisters by the giant jar of olives near the door.

Dawn always started out so cold, but when she warmed up, she became loving and lovable, and that made Aurora sob even more. Her poor older sisters, still clueless about why they'd been locked in the pantry, had to wait and soothe her and coo in her ear until she was calm and collected enough to tell them everything.

But finally she did, and then the two older sisters cried too: they cried because they were afraid and relieved to be alive and so thankful for the cook and how she'd saved them.

"But won't we have to stay in here forever?" Roxanne said.

Aurora had to admit she didn't know. She hadn't been part of the cook's plan, and she couldn't guess what the spirit would do when she found out the girls still lived.

As she sat there, wrapped in her sisters' arms and love, she thought it over. Would the cook be able to climb the two flights to the spirit's room to deliver the pork loin that was meant to be Aurora?

Then there came a great crash from the other side of the pantry door.

"What trickery is this!" shrieked the spirit. The crystal in her voice shattered.

"Get back," the cook roared at the spirit. "You're not welcome in here."

The spirit laughed – the sound now was so chilling that Aurora shook in Roxanne's arms. "This house belongs more to me than to you, cook," the spirit said. "It belongs more to me than to the Sovas themselves."

"Lies," said the cook. "You are a wicked thing and every word you utter is a lie." She spat. "Out."

"I hear them whispering," the nurse said. "What did you feed me?" The cook didn't answer, but an instant later there was a great clatter and the rattle of pans being thrown and big metal spoons falling in piles to the tile floor.

The girls heard the cook grunting and howling in pain. Then everything was quiet.

"She's coming for us," Aurora whispered, and her sisters nodded. "We have to get out of here."

"How, runt?" Dawn said. "The door is locked from the outside."

"Come with me," Aurora said. "Hold my hand so we don't get lost." And she led her sisters deeper into the huge pantry, all the way to the back corner. There, she needed Roxanne's help to heave bags of flour out of the way, and then a big jar of tomato paste, and then a wooden crate lid leaning against the wall. It revealed a sliver of light, right in the corner.

"What is it?" Dawn said.

"It's a secret," Aurora said. "This house has a lot of secrets."

"It certainly does," Dawn muttered.

Aurora crouched down on her knees at the sliver of light and felt around with her fingers. She found a tiny latch.

The nurse's gentle footsteps echoed on the other side of the pantry door.

"She's coming," Roxanne whispered.

Aurora twisted the tiny latch.

The pantry door clicked and began to open.

Aurora stood up and kicked at the sliver of light, and the secret little door sprung open. "Hurry," Aurora said, and the three girls dropped to the floor and slithered out and closed the door behind them.

"Where are you?" the spirit sang in the pantry behind them. They heard tins and jars and boxes crash to the hard pantry floor as the nurse searched for them.

"Now what?" Roxanne hissed. "She'll work out we're not there pretty quickly."

But Aurora had thought of that, and she was already planning. The tiny door had let the girls out in the guest bathroom, right next to the sink. Aurora got up from the chilly tile floor and ran from the room. She heard her sisters behind her.

"What are you doing?" Dawn called after her, but Aurora didn't want to take the time to explain. She ran down the main hall, across the foyer and slammed into the kitchen.

"She'll hear you!" Roxanne said.

Aurora didn't care. She was counting on speed, and she

raced across the kitchen floor, hardly noticing the cook, sprawled out on the tile, groaning in pain. She was pleased that the big woman was alive, and Aurora was smiling as she ran at top speed into the pantry door. It slammed closed with a satisfying thwack. The latch clicked, locking the door.

"Let me out!" the nurse shouted, banging on the door with her fists. "Let me out this instant!"

The cook sat up, shaking her head to clear the knocks and bruises she'd suffered. Aurora put an arm around her big shoulders.

"I'm glad you're okay," she said.

The cook, gulping back tears, took the littlest Miren in her arms. "And I'm glad you are," she said.

The older girls stood nearby, shuffling their feet. They felt awkward, shy and confused.

"And you two, too," the cook said, "even if you don't think much of me."

"We do," Roxanne said, and she elbowed the middle girl.

"Yes," Dawn said, rubbing her side. "We do."

* * *

When Brendan Miren returned that night to the Sova House after an exhausting day of making books, his daughter Aurora ran to him straight away.

"Why aren't you in bed?" he said. "Isn't your mother home yet?"

She wasn't, and Aurora apologized for still being up. She took her father into the main floor guest bathroom.

She showed him the long crack that ran up the wall near the floor next to the sink.

"Hm," he said, rubbing his chin. "I'd better seal that up." And he did, with tape and filler and plaster. Then Aurora showed him some other cracks in some other walls, and with boards and nails and plaster, he sealed those as well.

The cook stopped using the pantry for storage, and she had to buy quite a lot of flour in the next couple of weeks, not to mention one goose, one pig and one lamb. But Mr and Mrs Miren didn't mind much, and no one noticed that the wandering figure – with soil on her feet and dressed head to toe in shimmering gowns – never appeared in their halls or garden again.

IN THE WORLD OF DREAMS, ANYTHING IS POSSIBLE.

You can soar through the sky on a dandelion seed, change into an animal, find a long-lost friend.

But anything is possible in nightmares, too. Your mother could be taken by witches. You could be hunted by a skull-shaped cloud. And the Plague Dreamer could release a tidal wave of black, buzzing pestilence, destroying both the dream world and ours.

If you hurry, there is still time to stop him. And you will not be alone on your journey. **The Fearless Travellers swore an oath to help anyone in need – and bring them home.**

Bee is an orphan, alone in a poor, crumbling kingdom. In desperation, she steals a bun from a bakery. But instead of punishment, she's offered a home. As she learns to bake, Bee discovers that she has a magical power and that even a small orphan girl with just a bit of magic can help save a kingdom.

AMELIE DAY LOVES TO BAKE

– cupcakes, biscuits, tarts and muffins – so she's thrilled when she's invited to compete in Britain's Best Teen Baker of the Year. But Amelie has Cystic Fibrosis and some days she can barely breathe. Determined not to let her condition or her mum stop her from taking part, Amelie musters all her flour power, but will it be enough to get her there?

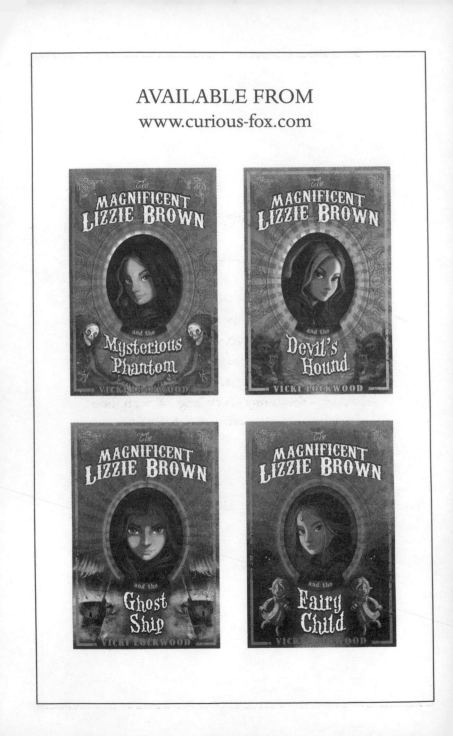

Lizzie Brown has escaped the slums of Victorian London and joined Fitzy's Travelling Circus. By accident, she discovers that she has an amazing ability: in a world of charlatans and tricksters, Lizzie may be the only truly clairvoyant palm reader in existence! Lizzie musters together her gang of circus children – the Penny Gaff Gang, all with their own amazing talents – to use her visions to solve mysteries.

For more exciting books from
brilliant authors, follow the fox!
www.curious-fox.com